IMPOSSIBLE GOLD

Ronald K. Myers

IMPOSSIBLE GOLD

DOUBLE DRAGON

PROLOGUE

Blondie stared straight ahead and focused his opal-green killer eyes on Myers Hill. Even though the 1948 Chevy pick-up truck was struggling under the weight of Al Capone's vault, he had to coax the six-cylinder motor to get up enough speed to get up the hill.

He gripped the black knob on the floor shift, shifted through all four gears, and jammed the accelerator down. With black, oily smoke pouring out its rusty tailpipe, the tailgate rattling, and a broken spring, causing the little green truck to tilt to one side, he charged the bottom of Myers Hill.

As a yellow splash of sunlight danced on his shoulder, a red flash of his girlfriend's polished red fingernails caught his eye. He jerked his head in her direction.

Carolyn raised her hands in protest. "I know you're trying to get away from a life of crime. But slow down!"

"We'll be all right."

Carolyn dropped her hands to her lap and raised her voice. "The tires are bald. They'll blow out."

Determined to make it up the hill, Blondie stared straight ahead. "I know that."

With a look of excruciating discomfort filling her lovely face, Carolyn balled her hand into a fist. Rearing back to strike Blondie's shoulder, she screamed, "Slow down!"

Blondie kept his foot flat to the floor. "The illegal gold we have in the back is our future. If we get stuck, they'll take it."

For a moment, Carolyn's cheeks grew tight with fury, but she slowly lowered her fist and jerked her silky black hair to the side. As it flowed over her red gingham shirt of her bra-less body, she forced a nod and tensed for a crash.

Halfway up the hill, the motor groaned and began to lose power. Blondie downshifted into third gear. After a few yards, the truck slowed.

Carolyn relaxed.

Blondie hit second gear. For a moment, the truck gained a little speed, but it was not enough. He double-clutched and jammed the transmission into low gear. Letting the engine run wide open, he jerked his foot off the clutch pedal. It popped up off the floor. The transmission whined and the engine bogged down. Smoke and the smell burning asbestos rolled out from under the floor. Just as it was about to stall, the engine surged with new energy. The truck increased speed.

Near the top of the hill, the engine slowed. Trying to encourage the truck to go faster, Blondie banged on the steering wheel. "Come on, you piece of junk."

With its overworked engine protesting in a steady moan, the truck crawled toward the top of the hill. It was going to make it. Blondie was finally going to be a rich man. The tension of a lifetime vanished. With a relieved grin, he looked over at Carolyn.

Her prominent cheekbones accented her lovely face and reminded him of a movie star. Soon, they would have a beautiful life together. He reached over and gently touched her on the shoulder. Tomorrow, we'll be married."

Carolyn reached over and placed a reassuring hand on his shoulder. "Yes, we will."

Before the truck got to the top of the hill — there! The black blur of a Cadillac lurched to the right. It swayed so far over, for a moment, it rode on two wheels. Then it leapt over the centerline and came right at the truck. Cutting the wheel to swerve away from the impending crash, Blondie hit the brakes. The bald tires locked up. The truck skidded toward the Cadillac.

Carolyn shrieked.

In the Cadillac, horror filled the man's face. He jerked the steering wheel. The speeding Cadillac flew off the road.

Just when Blondie felt he had avoided a crash, the vault in the back shifted toward the broken spring side of the truck. The sideways movement jerked him across the seat. He mashed Carolyn against the door. As he tried to get back behind the steering wheel, the bald tires let the truck slide off the road.

He managed to pull his body back behind the steering wheel, but it was too late. They were rapidly heading down the steep side of Myers Hill. He glanced off to the left. As if they were in a race to the river, the Cadillac sailed down the hill ahead of them. Grass and brush whipped at the front of the Cadillac, but the heavy front bumper cut and whapped it, sending it flying into the air.

Carolyn held her hands straight out and braced herself on the dashboard. The truck hit the grass.

The Cadillac shot into the water.

The speed of the truck increased. Grass and weeds flew up and plastered the windshield.

Carolyn screamed, "I can't see. Hit the brakes!"

Standing on the brake pedal with both feet, Blondie could not stop the truck. Rushing toward the water, it hit a boulder. Blondie flew up. His head clunked on the metal roof and sent a bright four-pointed star into his mind. He felt the truck lift off the side of the hill. As it sailed into the air, a tingling sensation rolled in his stomach. The truck whipped across the water with incredible speed but finally slowed and came to a stop. Just before he blacked out, an earsplitting squeal of steel being ripped apart burned into his brain.

Sometime later, Blondie opened his eyes. But it was as if he were looking through a curtain of mist. A yellowish-green ribbon of river water sprayed passed by the doorpost of the truck and brushed across his face. Struggling toward consciousness, he blinked the water from his eyes and peered out the opened window. A hundred yards downriver, the water kicked up, hissed into a spray, and burst into angry, raging rapids. Where jagged black chunks of rotten-teeth-like rocks hung from the shoreline, high waves of water exploded and swelled into pure white foam.

Directly over Blondie's head, streaks of lightning signaled the start of a downpour. In the center of the pale-green river, the arm of the man who had been in the Cadillac made one last dismal splash. When the fingertips of his hand slipped under the surface, a widening pool with a core of air bubbles followed them.

Blondie wanted to swim to the center of the river, dive down, and save the man before he was

8

carried to the rapids, but it wasn't a heroic gesture. Blondie wanted to see what the idiot that had forced him off the road looked like, but the murky water was up to Carolyn's knees. With rain slanting across the cracked and grass spattered windshield, he reached over to lift her from the seat. Her eyes were closed.

He shook her. "Carolyn, are you all right?"

Before she could answer, something under the truck clunked. A powerful jolt jerked him sideways. The truck tilted to one side and sank down. Twin torrents of mustard-colored water rushed down the riverbank and poured over the passenger side window, filling the cab of the truck and began covering Carolyn's head.

Blondie took a deep breath, bent over, and stuck his head into the rising water. Groping around, he found her arm and pulled. It didn't budge. He felt the right side of her body. One of her lovely legs and her frail arm were mashed between the firewall and the caved-in passenger door. He thrust his head up out of the murky water and looked at Carolyn's face. Her unblinking eyes bulged wide open. Her beautiful jaw hung open to her chest, and her wet hair was plastered against her head.

"Don't die now!" Blondie cried. "We've come too far to quit."

A jagged tail of lightening zigzagged through the treetops and sizzled across the roof of the truck. Chest-pounding thunder exploded and echoed down the valley. Water gushed out of the charcoal sky and pounded on the river so hard the water seemed to boil.

The bluish tint in Carolyn's oxygen-deprived face told Blondie the only girl he had ever trusted had met her Maker. Pain he had never felt before, filled his chest. Tears welled up, but he had no time to cry. The water was rising fast. To save himself, he had to get out of the truck, but he couldn't free his left leg. He was scared, but the essence of any good gangster was the ability to admit to himself that he was afraid and then have the discipline to channel it into something that would save his life. He tried to slow his racing heart and assess his options.

During the crash, Al Capone's gold vault, as big as a coffin, had crashed through the back window and grazed his left shoulder. Now the vault tilted at an odd angle. It felt as if its full weight of two thousand pounds was sitting on his left leg. Blondie pushed on the vault. It didn't move. He stretched his neck to the left to see if he could find a way to move the vault off his leg.

The end of the vault was wider than the back window. During impact, its weight had caused it to plow right through the metal surrounding the back window. Then with the power of a runaway freight train, it had zipped past his shoulder, hit the left side of the steering wheel, bent it down, and stopped at the bottom of the steering column. He could see that the vault was jammed as tight as if it had been pounded in with a gigantic hand. He would never be able to move it.

He reached down and grabbed his trapped leg. Pushing with his other foot, he pulled. His leg slipped out an inch but seized solid. The water was up to his chest. With the rain falling fast, in minutes, the water would be over his head. Hoping he could signal someone in a passing car, he craned his neck and searched the far away top of Myers Hill. But in the rain, cars going past up on the road would not see the tracks the Cadillac and Chevy had made when they had gone over the edge. People would drive on by without even a vestige of curiosity. The only way he could get out the death trap would be to cut his leg off.

He reached into his pocket for his knife. It wasn't there. As a goodwill gesture, he had left his suit coat at the old Peacock Alley Bar for Neal, the young man who had made things happen. In his haste to haul the valuable vault away, Blondie had forgotten about the encoded message that led to a box of money at the old Peacock Alley foundation. His knife and the message were in the suit pocket.

He needed something sharp. When the vault had gone through the back of the truck, it may have sheared off a piece of metal. If it had, he could use it to cut off his leg. He felt around on the seat. Nothing. He felt under his arm. His 38 Colt was still there. Seven bullets. Maybe he could shoot his leg off. The water had covered Carolyn's face and rose to a foot below his chin.

He screamed, "Finally I'm a rich man! Why does this have to happen now?"

Trying to gain a little more freedom, he wiggled his body. His leg stayed trapped. He pounded on the bent steering wheel and moaned.

Common sense should have told him not to trust an old gangster like Smeal. Mob guys were dangerous, and there was no telling what they would do. But if he had paid just a little attention to politics, he would have known President Franklin Roosevelt had imposed a ban on U.S. citizens buying, selling, or owning gold in 1933. To him it didn't make any sense to make gold illegal, but the government had done it. In January 1934, the price of gold had risen sixty-five percent. Making owning gold illegal and enforcing the law with a fine of ten thousand dollars, ten years in jail, or both, stopped hoarders from profiting after Congress devalued the dollar. Even at the frozen price of thirty-five dollars an ounce, Blondie figured the troy weight of the vault to be over two thousand pounds, and worth eight hundred forty thousand dollars.

No wonder Capone had devised encrypted letters and made special keys that had led Blondie and three young men to the notorious Jungle Inn Casino, where an unsuspecting victim, thinking he had found the vault and was going to take it, triggered a hidden shotgun that blew his chest wide open. Although the man had been killed, the wooden stock of the shotgun contained clues that led to the hidden mine, and the vault. Blondie wasn't going to sit back and let the wealth of the vault pass him by. He didn't know how, but he was determined to grab a share for himself.

Even though mob guys said Smeal didn't have enough sense to hold down a blow job, he had the connections to get the gold vault across the border. And to stay out of jail, it was always a must to do your business through front men.

Overhead a flurry of hail rattled on the roof. Blondie turned and looked out the open window of the truck. The river pitched magnificently and fired sheets of water into his face. With a vengeance, a chill wind scooped down into the river, sending another volley of spray. It drenched his face and blond hair.

The water level in the truck rose to just under his chin. Holding the Colt in his hand above the water, he checked the action. Would seven bullets be enough to shoot his leg off? Seven good shots might shatter the bone and he would be able to rip his leg free. So what if he would end up with only one leg. When he cashed in the vault, he could buy a new leg and much more. He placed the gun under the water and pointed it at his leg just below his knee.

"Wait!" he yelled.

When he had shot a man in the leg, as a warning, the bullet had hit an artery and the man had bled to death. He didn't want that to happen to him. He reached down, slipped off his belt, and clinched it around his thigh. He held the barrel of the Colt two feet away from his leg. At that distance he couldn't miss. He placed his finger on the trigger, but he didn't fire. He thought about Smeal.

Smeal had made it seem so right. He even had a code name for the vault: "Milk Horse." Blondie wished he had gotten the truck himself. If he had, it wouldn't have been overloaded, and he wouldn't have gotten a beat-up 1948 Chevy truck with a broken spring. For cryin' out loud, it was 1962. He would have stolen something new. He would have stolen something with good tires that wouldn't have slid off the road and sent him and the only girl he had ever loved, sliding down the steep embankment of Myers Hill and crashing into the river.

He grimaced and pulled the trigger on the Colt. It jumped in his hand. A dull plunk came from the water, but he didn't feel the bullet hit his leg. He took a deep breath and bent his head into the water. The water from the cloudburst had rushed down the riverbank and washed yellow mud into the river. He couldn't see. He reached down, and felt where the bullet should have gone into his leg. Nothing. He pulled his head up out of the water. Maybe it was a bad shell. He shot again. Still, nothing.

Then it dawned on him. The cold water had made his leg numb. Now the water was just below his nose. Tilting his head back, he gulped in deep breaths of air. Then he ducked down, bent over, and emptied the Colt into his leg. With all his might, he tried to pull his leg free. Pain shot through his entire body. Throwing his head upward, he gasped for air, but breathed in water.

Struggling to get his head higher, and between coughing out sprays of water from deep in his lungs, he gulped in a few good breaths of air. Then he yanked and twisted his trapped leg. He contorted with pain and belched water, but no matter how much he struggled and squirmed, his trapped leg would not separate. At the last moment he remembered that there were two bones in his bottom leg. He figured had only managed to shoot through one. Now the only way he could shoot his leg off would be to hold the barrel directly on his leg, but he had already spent the last five bullets.

He reached down and felt his leg. Where it should have been shredded from the bullets, it seemed unscathed. Too late, he realized the resistance of the water had slowed down and stopped the bullets. They hadn't even penetrated the cloth on his pants.

As he sat back and waited to drown, he wondered how Al Capone had died in the coalmine that had hid the vault, but he figured in a few minutes he would follow Al Capone's footsteps. He too would shake hands with the Devil.

Although Blondie had always broadcasted a tough guy image with no feelings, he didn't want to face death alone. Holding his breath, he reached over, grabbed Carolyn's limp hand, and pulled. Her lifeless body broke free. He pushed her out the window. With one eye barely above the surface of the water, he watched her beautiful head float face up. If he could free his leg, he could pull her to shore and maybe revive her, but the water went over his head.

He pulled on his leg. It moved about six inches. He stretched his neck and managed to lift his head above the water. There was still a chance. He let loose of Carolyn's hand. She drifted for a moment. Then the current swept her into rising mists of the raging rapids. The last thing he saw of her was a dim flash of her red polished fingernails just before they disappeared in the mad swirling water.

More than ever, Blondie wanted to save her. He pushed against the broken steering wheel and pulled. His leg moved. The rain slowed.

He gulped down one breath of air. Like the coup de grâce on a dying man, the wind moaned overhead, bringing a hideous squall that rushed down from the black sky and gushed into the window of the truck. The truck turned sideways and rolled over onto its roof.

While the rain washed away all traces of where the truck had gone off the road, Al Capone's gold vault, the truck, and Blondie sunk to the bottom of the Shenango River.

As gloom and the darkness of death surrounded him, Blondie wondered what would have happened if he had shared the vault with Freddy Crane, the muscular black-haired kid, Rafferty Allnut, the orange-headed wise guy with the wide-toothed smile, and Neal McCord. They weren't the usual fresh-faced kids whose youth made them loud and arrogant. They were quite inventive, and although they came from the wrong side of the tracks, they didn't let it slow them down. When Blondie thought about the third of the trio, Neal McCord, a little laugh escaped from his mouth and sent air bubbles to the surface. When Neal made love with a girl, it was said that they generated so much excitement that people ran for tornado cellars. But then, sadness filled Blondie's chest. He and Carolyn would never make people run for tornado cellars.

He was out of air.

were from Bomb Town would enhance his image and strike fear in his opponent. But Freddy didn't care what the announcer said. Hunger pains from not eating to make weight and little money for food made him want to get the fight over, collect the money, and eat.

The usual custom of both boxers coming to the center of the ring didn't happen. Elbowing the referee to the side, the announcer held the microphone and talked to the crowd.

"Gentleman, you know the rules. Let's have a nice clean fight."

While the microphone slowly followed the cord back up into the rafters of the dilapidated building, the announcer stepped through the three ropes of the boxing ring that had been set up on a hardwood gym floor.

The main lights came on.

Freddy looked toward his opponent's corner. Burke was sitting down. A white robe hung from what looked to be shoulders of stone. Even though the robe covered what seemed to be a potbelly, Burke looked as big as an old steel refrigerator. Freddy grabbed Terry's shoulder. "Are you nuts? He's not all fat." He stood up. "I'm getting out of here."

Terry pushed him back down. "You can take this guy."

"But I'm not in shape for six rounds."

"This guy ain't nothin'."

"Then why do they call him Bonebreaker?"

"That's just to scare people."

Freddy forced a smile. "He's doing a good job of it."

"Yeah, I know. That's why his opponent chickened out. This is the only match we could get."

Freddy looked across the ring. Burke sprang to his feet. His trainer helped him slip off his robe. The massive man stood six-foot-six, and he didn't have a potbelly. His tiny waist looked like Freddy could put his hands around it until his fingers touched. And it caused his shoulders and chest to look bigger. His big boxing-gloved fists looked like iron wrecking balls hanging down on long lethal arms, ready to break Freddy's little bones. With his arms raised, Burke danced in circles, accepting the cheers of the crowd. As Freddy watched in awe, Burke's leg muscles rippled like they would never tire.

The referee signaled Freddy to stand up. Like a trapped animal, Freddy squirmed on the tiny stool. Protesting to Terry, he stood up. Cheers from the crowd drowned out his protests. Terry bent down and took away the stool. Freddy glanced at Burke then at Terry.

Terry smiled. "What are you worried about? You'll be wearing headgear." Terry placed a leather boxing helmet onto Freddy's head and smudged Vaseline on his eyebrows. "This will keep you from getting cut."

The uncomfortable helmet constricted Freddy's sight. He wiggled it around on his head and turned to Terry.

"This thing's too big. Do I have to wear it?"

Terry nodded. "Even this dump has rules."

Freddy reached up and adjusted the oversized headgear. "But I'm no heavyweight."

"We didn't have a choice. I bet every cent we had."

Freddy's stomach churned. He didn't like the idea of not having any money for bus fare to get home. Miles of running to get in shape for the fight had worn holes in the bottoms of his only pair of shoes. If he lost, it would be a long seventy-five miles back home.

He looked to Terry. "You didn't bet all the money, did you?"

Terry nodded confidently. "It's a sure thing. I even borrowed a big chunk of dough from the loan sharks."

With his eyes narrowed, Burke stood in the center of the ring and fiercely stared at Freddy. As Freddy cringed under the threat, Terry handed him his mouthpiece. Freddy put it in and clinched down. Burke waved his gloved hand in a come here gesture.

The bleachers were filled to capacity, and many people were standing. The people cheered and called Freddy's name. If he backed out now, they would think he was a coward.

Terry stepped behind Freddy and massaged his shoulders. As Terry's fingers jerked on his neck, he hoped Terry would call off the match, and give the money back to the bone-breaking loan sharks. He tried to relax for a second, but the bell rang.

In a blazing fury, Burke jumped to his feet, ready for action.

Feeling as if he were walking into an execution chamber, Freddy stepped to the center of the ring.

Burke held out his gloved hand.

Freddy touched it.

The fight was on.

Knowing he wasn't in shape for six rounds, Freddy knew he would have to conserve energy. He danced around, but didn't throw a punch. Suddenly, the big canyon mouth of Burke's trainer roared, "Come on, Burke, One-two! One-two!"

Before Freddy could turn his head, Bam! Bam! Two, quick hard whaps landed on the top of his helmeted head. The helmet dropped over his eyes. He reached up with both gloved hands and pushed it up. Like double-barrel shotgun blasts, Bam! Bam! Two more punches shot straight into his face. The helmet went down over his eyes again. He pushed it up and was rewarded with another one-two punch. Moving away, he jerked the helmet up off his eyes and jammed it high up onto his forehead.

Terry yelled from the corner, "Get Inside!"

Freddy moved in. Burke's fists came at him like shots from exploding cannons. Freddy ducked. The flying fists sailed over his head. He jabbed back. His fist only flicked air. Burke was too far away. Bam! Bam! From out of nowhere, that one-two got Freddy again. Freddy turned and pushed up the helmet. Then he moved in close. Burke jumped back and moved from side to side. As if they were coming from somewhere outside the ring, punches from his long arms flew at Freddy. Punch after punch landed on his head. As bright fireworks danced on the backs of his eyelids, he covered up and stood his ground. He tried to jab, but hit nothing.

The bell rang.

Staggering to his corner, Freddy felt the leather athletic supporter, boxers were required to wear, droop down around his behind. Riffles of laughter trickled in from the stands. When he finally made it to the stool, he pulled up the supporter and sat down, Terry was there with Q-tips in his mouth. He held a water bottle in one hand and Vaseline in the other. Holding his mouthpiece in his hand, Freddy huffed for as much air as he could suck into his oxygen-deprived lungs. Feeling his chest rise and fall with each breath, he turned to Terry. "I can't make it."

Terry smeared more Vaseline of Freddy's eyebrows and handed him the water bottle. Freddy took a mouthful of water and spit it into a dented bucket. Terry put both hands on Freddy's shoulders and looked into his eyes. "We can't quit now. The crowd's cheering for you. When you win, we win a lot of money."

"When I win?" Freddy questioned and sucked in a deep breath of air. "I won't last another round."

The bell rang.

Terry jumped out of the way.

Freddy didn't get up. He sat on the stool and turned to Terry. "Throw in the towel. I quit."

Burke stood in the center of the ring and waved his arm in a come-here gesture.

Freddy stayed on the stool.

The crowd booed.

Terry jerked the stool out from under Freddy. He started to fall, caught his balance, and staggered to his feet. Terry patted him on the back and talked in his ear.

"Go out there and knock him out. The fight will be over."

Freddy wondered why he hadn't thought of knocking out his opponent before. If he knocked him out, it wouldn't matter if he couldn't last six rounds. The fight would be over. He would have enough money to have the electricity turned back on at his mother's house. All he had to do was knock the big lug out. He pulled on the heavy athletic supporter and shambled to the center of the ring.

Again, "One-two! One-two!" blared out from Burke's corner.

Even though Burke had an extremely long reach advantage, Freddy was sure he wasn't going to get caught with that one-two again. Bam! Bam! It got him anyway. Pain raced through his eyes and exploded in his brain. Blood ran from his nose. Fighting to gain back his equilibrium, he looked into Burke's face. Burke laughed as if he had already won the match. But when pain crawled into Freddy's chest, anger erupted.

"Get inside!" Terry yelled.

Freddy put his chin on his own chest. Walking slow and deliberate, he waded toward the long-armed skyscraping opponent. Burke's punches rocketed off the top of his head. He didn't care. He had to get close enough for his short arms to do some damage.

He jabbed.

Burke jumped to the right and mockingly smiled. Freddy stepped in and got inside. As fast as he could, he threw three good punches into Burke's stomach. Burke moaned and bent over. Freddy looked into Burke's face. His smile disappeared. He backed away and fired that one-two. This time it whizzed over Freddy's head.

Freddy stepped in and caught Burke in a clinch. Burke tried to wiggle out of it. Freddy caught him in a bear hug and lifted him off the canvas.

Someone in the crowd mocked the lift and jeered, "Eeww! Strong man!"

That felt like a slur against Freddy's fighting abilities and a personal attack at him. If this were a street fight, he would have hoisted the big bully onto his shoulder and flipped him right on his head. He'd be looking up. Freddy flexed his knees to lift and throw. Laughter erupted from the stands.

The referee tapped Freddy on the shoulder. "Break it up. Fix your supporter."

Freddy's supporter was drooping down again. He lowered Burke and pulled the supporter up almost to his chest.

The referee started them again.

Freddy bulled his way in and kept punching. That helmet went over his eyes again. Burke punched it up. Freddy kept punching. He pushed Burke against the ropes. The loose ropes sagged and wrapped around the sides of Burke's body. Now Burke couldn't jump back. Now he couldn't jump from side to side. Now he couldn't make Freddy miss.

Like a trapped wild animal, Burke punched back. Freddy bobbed and weaved in a steady rhythm. Burke's lethal punches fell out of sync with Freddy's rhythm. Over and over, Burke's punches zinged past Freddy's shoulders and swished past his head. When he realized all of Burke's punches had missed, Freddy punched back with newfound strength. Even though the laughter of the crowd changed to an oceanic roar, he could hear sounds of pain erupt from deep inside Burke's body.

Finally, the seemingly indestructible Burke stayed bent over. Now his head was within range. To set him up for a good hit, Freddy jabbed. Burke jerked to the right. Freddy let a powerful right-cross fly. It landed square on the side of Burke's face. He fell against the ropes. As his face turned purple with rage, his enormous weight caused the posts that held the ropes to sag to the floor. Suddenly, they were standing outside the ring, boxing on the hardwood gym floor.

Freddy dropped his arms and looked toward the ring. With a punch that seemed to come from outside the gym, Burke blasted him right in the nose. Freddy felt it snap. Spangles of tiny blue stars exploded in front of his eyes. He lifted his arms for defense. Burke cocked his arms for another punch. Freddy's legs didn't want to move.

From out of Burke's corner, came, "One, two! One two!"

In his mind, Freddy yelled at Burke, You're not going to blast me with that one-two again.

On the edge of losing consciousness, Freddy tried to take a step toward Burke, but his wobbly legs would not support him. Off balance, he fell forward. His head crashed into Burke's chest. It felt like a huge hard rock, but it stopped him from falling to the floor. He regained his footing, shook the cobwebs out, and waded into Burke. With every ounce of strength left in his body, he jackhammered Burke's stomach with punches.

Falling back, Burke let the one-two fly. Bam! Bam! He got Freddy again. Like fabulous silver fireworks, bright stars exploded before his eyes. Through a gray haze that was filled with spangling spiders, he followed Burke's body and fell forward. On the way down, he kept punching. Burke's head was a foot off the hardwood floor. Freddy's right cross came out of the universe and smashed into Burke's jaw. Burke's head clunked on the floor. His body collapsed. He was out cold.

The referee excitedly waved the fight over. In a blind rage, Freddy kept on punching. Trainers and the referee seemed to come from somewhere in the middle of all the cascading stars whirling around Freddy's head. As they pulled him off the fallen Burke, he looked back over his shoulder. The people in the bleachers looked like they were fighting each other. Terry ran to Freddy and lifted his arm in victory.

"You knocked him out," he said, with jubilation. "We won. They threw in the towel."

Freddy couldn't breathe through his nose. He spit out his mouthpiece, opened his bloody mouth, and sucked in deep drafts of air. His raised arms over his head felt like a heavy iron weight. He lowered them. Terry cut the ties to Freddy's boxing gloves and slipped them off. As he threw a robe around Freddy's shoulders, a flashbulb went off in front of them. A man with a crazed look on his face stormed out of the bleachers and rushed up to Freddy.

"What did you hit him when he was down for?"

A jovial, redheaded man walking past, said, "Anybody that can knock an ape like that out of the ring can't be all bad."

The man with the crazed look went after the red-haired man. The bleacher crowd, booed, and cheered at the same time. Terry jumped up and down next to Freddy.

"You won! We're rich! We're rich!"

The announcer stepped to the center of the ring. The crowd went silent.

The announcer talked into the microphone and pointed to Burke. "And the winner, by disqualification...Bonebreaker Burke."

The crowd roared in approval, but Freddy had lost the fight for hitting his opponent while he was down, and Terry had lost all their money. If they could get away from the loan sharks, it would be a long walk back to the place where kids with black and blue eyes lived on the wrong side of the tracks and jumped at their own shadows. It would be a long walk a back to the place he was trying to get away from. It would be a long walk back to Patagonia.

Chapter 2

Clutching gym bags that contained their meager belongings, Terry and Freddy snuck out of the back door of the locker room. As they stepped into the alleyway, Terry looked at Freddy. "We're good, so far."

Freddy breathed a sigh of relief, but it was shorted lived. Down the littered alley, a man wearing a three-piece suit, who appeared to be the boss, grabbed a man's shoulder next to him.

The man turned his pit-bull-like face in the boss man's direction. "What?"

The boss man pointed at Freddy and Terry. With menace radiating from their thug-like bodies, both men walked toward Freddy and Terry. Freddy wanted to cry. He had planned to box long enough to get enough money to help his mother, or do something to free himself from the lure of a bleak but prosperous future in one of the steel mills. Now there was a good chance the loan sharks were going to break his legs.

He shook Terry's shoulder. "They see us."

Terry looked toward the two men. They were coming right at them, walking at a brisk pace.

Terry glanced at Freddy. "I hope you're in shape for a good run."

Freddy and Terry sprinted down the alley, turned right at the sidewalk and ran down another alley. From out of a dark doorway, two more men stepped in front of them and blocked their getaway. Freddy turned to run back the way they had come. The boss man and the pit-bull-faced man stepped into the entrance to the alleyway. That way was blocked, too.

Freddy turned toward the men in front of him. One man had a scar across a jaw that had been broken and healed at a lopsided angle. The steel pipe, the man held in his right hand, had a jagged end that could rip the flesh off a man's body. The other man with a big nose and a downturned mouth seemed to have a permanent scowl on his face. He made a fist and pounded it into the palm of his hand. "You going somewhere, boys?"

Terry didn't answer.

The man with the scared jaw waved the pipe in a threatening circle. "Tell Ice Man what he wants to know."

"We're not going anywhere," Terry said, as if he weren't afraid, but the fear showed in his trembling voice. "We were just going to get the money we owe you."

Scar-jaw tapped Terry's gym bag with the jagged end of the pipe. "If you're coming back, why are you carrying this? We gave you lockers."

Terry didn't have a chance to answer. The pit-bull-faced man stepped behind Terry and answered for him. "Because they're trying get out of paying what they owe."

Freddy took an aggressive stance. "We'll pay. We don't take nothin' from nobody."

Terry looked right then left. There was no escape. Panic filled his face. He held up his hands in a stopping gesture. "We were going to pay, honest."

Smiling as if he were going to do something he would enjoy, the boss man folded his arms across his chest and motioned to the pit-bull-faced man. "Go watch for the cops."

The pit-bull-faced man trotted to the entrance to the alley and stopped. The boss man leaned back. "Go ahead, boys, do your job."

Ice Man nodded and reached for Terry's throat. As if he were boxing and blocking a punch, Terry batted Ice Man's hand away. Then in one motion, Terry crouched down and came up with an uppercut that caught Ice Man directly under the chin. Ice Man stumbled back, wobbled for a second, and fell face down onto the filthy ground.

Scar-jaw swung the ragged pipe. Its smooth side landed on the back of Terry's head. Bone cracked. Terry's knees buckled. He groaned, crumpled to the ground, and lay on his stomach, watching Ice Man.

Scar-jaw lifted the pipe to strike again. Freddy reached over and jerked the Scar-Jaw's arm. Scar Jaw lowered the pipe and turned toward Freddy. Freddy stepped back out of range of the pipe.

Keeping his arms crossed across this chest, the boss man bent over and yelled in Ice Man's ear, "Kick his guts out."

Scar-jaw encouragingly waved the pipe. "Yeah! Kick his guts out."

Ice Man jumped up and reared back to give Terry a hard kick to the ribs. But the moment his foot was raised, Terry sprang forward and crashed his shoulder into Ice Man's supporting leg. Ice Man's leg buckled backwards. To keep from falling, he dropped his raised leg to the ground. Terry grabbed it by the ankle, leaped up, and lifted it toward the sky. Ice Man's lone supporting leg

31

flew out from under him. His head and shoulders thumped on the black dirt-covered alley. As he struggled to get up, Terry smashed his fist into the side of his head. But when Terry loaded up for another swing, Scar-jaw wound up and swooshed the jagged end of the pipe at Freddy. Freddy ducked. With a sickening crack, the pipe hit the side of Terry's head. Like a miniature oil well, blood from his head, squirted three feet into the air, spattering all around them. Terry's knees collapsed. He crumpled to the ground. As he lay there, blood oozed from his lifeless mouth. His leg twitched for a second then went limp.

Freddy knew Terry was dead. He wished he would have reached up and stopped the pipe, but everything had happened too fast. He began to tremble, but such a reaction would not help him now. As the pipe wielding Scar-jaw hovered over him, Freddy managed to regain control. Ice Man staggered to his feet and stared at Terry's lifeless body.

The boss man jerked his fist at Scar-jaw. "You didn't have to kill him. Now we'll never get our money." He pointed to Freddy. "Now we have to keep *his* mouth shut."

Scar-jaw smacked the smooth side of the pipe into his opened hand. "No problem."

Like the one-two punch of the boxing match, Freddy saw the deadly pipe coming. He jerked to his left. The swishing pipe zinged past his head. He wrapped his arms around Scar-jaw's thighs. Using the power of his legs, Freddy crouched and stood up. For a moment he held Scar-jaw on his shoulder. This time, it wasn't a boxing match.

There was no referee to stop him. He threw Scar-jaw off his shoulder. With a painful thump, Scar-jaw hit the ground, headfirst. The pipe fell from his hand and clanked on the side of the dirty red brick building.

The boss man uncrossed his arms, waved them in the air, and yelled at Ice Man. "What am I paying you for? Get that little creep."

Ice Man reached for Freddy. Freddy jerked away from his grasp, and took off running. Ice Man ran after him, but after thirty yards, he stopped, bent over and huffed to catch his breath. When Freddy got to the end of the alley, the pit-bull-faced man stood in front of him. Freddy stopped and jerked to the right. The pit-bull-faced man took a step to stop him. Freddy jerked to go in the opposite direction. The pit-bull-faced man stepped in the other direction. Freddy didn't. He ran past the pit-bull-faced man.

A ways later, Freddy slowed to a fast trot but kept going until he was sure no one was following him.

After he was absolutely positive he had gotten away, running away bothered him. He had never been a coward. He had never run from a fight. He had always stuck up for members of the old Patagonia gang, and he had kept his mouth shut around cops. But if he had stayed and fought, he would be just like Terry. He would be dead.

Although they were illegal, he figured he would start carrying a switchblade in his back pocket. If he ever got jumped again, he would not hesitate to use it. He had been scared too much. If he had a knife, he could whip it out, hit the button, and a razor sharp six-inch blade would be ready to use. No one would ever to beat or kill one of his friends again.

Chapter 3

Years of living in Patagonia had taught Freddy how to shut off his emotions. If he wouldn't have, he would have gone crazy. He was usually pretty cool, but Terry's death was making him lose the will to live. For three days, it was as if he were living in a vacuum. He went through the motions of hiding, walking, hitchhiking, and not eating. Most of the time, he didn't hear what people were saying. The words came into his head, but his brain did not recognize them as speech. This made it even more difficult to hitchhike. When he finally made it back home, he figured it was time to return to the world of the living. Every time he left and came back, the sickening sulfurous stench, the place emitted, seemed to grow stronger. Under the tar-papered roofs of the dilapidated houses, yellow lights struggled to send warmth and joy, but they only managed to send a weak amber glow through dirty windows.

Before what Freddy called 'the wild Neal days" he believed there was no possibility that John Dillinger or Al Capone had ever walked through his dump town neighborhood. And he definitely doubted the exaggerated stories of Neal McCord's legendary exploits. Some people said he could actually walk on air.

Unlike others before him, Freddy longed to break the bonds of the mill town. He dreamed of rising above the squalor and breathing air that didn't have the thick iron stench of Patagonia.

Most people in his neighborhood worked in huge filth-covered, corrugated monstrosities, called steel mills. Here, men were killed or maimed every day. Freddy wasn't afraid of the physical dangers of the mills, and he wasn't sure he would die like his father had died, but he couldn't shake the industrial pall that hung over a valley he felt was filled with corruption and greed.

On his deathbed, wracked with pain, hacking and coughing from damaged lungs, and coming in and out of consciousness, Freddy's father had called him near and whispered in his ear, "Don't work in the mill. There're things there that caused my cancer."

Sitting at the kitchen table in his mother's house, Freddy looked down at the electric bill. It was way past due. The electricity had been turned off for days. Traces of fumes, from the kerosene lamp, filled the kitchen. Just before he had left for Cleveland, in the dim glow of a flickering candle, his mother had talked about eating dog food.

Now, he shamefully watched her. She had mixed flour with water, kneaded it into dough, and was frying it. Although a tear had formed in the corner of her eye, she turned toward Freddy and managed a smile. "Because your father was such a fine worker, the people at the mill said they will start you out lining brake shoes like your father did."

Freddy stood up and gently placed his hand on his mother's shoulder. "I know, Mom, but Dad said he got cancer from the mill."

Freddy's mother's eyes turned skeptical. She turned back to the frying pan. "Your father was delirious before he died. A little asbestos dust won't hurt anyone." She wiped her hands on her

36

apron and gave him a pleading look. "The men at the company said there was nothing in the mills that caused your father's cancer. And they should know. They're college graduates."

"But, Mom, even cranberries cause cancer." Freddy threw his hand into the air. "Nobody has cranberry sauce for Thanksgiving anymore."

His mother turned the dough in the skillet and waved the spatula at him. "That's not so. It was on the radio. On Thanksgiving Day Vice President Nixon ate four helpings of cranberry sauce, and Senator Kennedy drank two glasses of cranberry juice."

"Come on." Freddy let his hand fall to his side. "That was in 1959, years ago, and people still don't eat cranberries."

His mother turned and slyly looked into his eyes. "There are no cranberries in the mill, and with no education that's the only place you're going to find a decent job."

Freddy could feel her eyes staring at him waiting for an answer. It wasn't true, but the only thing he managed to blurt out was, "But I almost got rich boxing."

His mother slowly shook her head. "It doesn't matter how you make a living, but if you become rich and get around those uppity people, just remember, if you're a rotten person before you become rich, you'll still be one after you're rich."

Freddy held up his hands in defeat and sat down. "I know, I know, but I just don't want to get cancer."

Cancer wasn't the only reason Freddy didn't want to work in a steel mill, but when provoked, his mother could be upright, straight-faced, and Bible thumping. He didn't want her to turn that on him.

"Hey, Mom," he pleaded. "It's the sixties. Things are going to be different from now on."

"When my father was your age, he thought that, too. And things did change." She sighed and slumped her shoulders. "There was a depression."

Freddy didn't want her to get started on the horrors of the depression. She could go on for hours. Looking at the aging wallpaper he had had helped his father put on the walls, he nodded. "I know, Mom. Working in the mill gave you and Dad a better life than Grandma and Grandpa had, but there has to be something more exciting out there."

She held up one finger and looked to the ceiling. "Freddy, the Lord knows we don't think the same way. But you could try working in the mill. Then if you don't like it, you can quit."

Freddy didn't reply. Working in the mill would be a big problem. If he went to work there, he would become like all the other people who worked there and hated it. He would become a slave to the big money. It would keep him there forever. He didn't want to die working a dead-end steel mill job. He gave her a reassuring nod. "I'll have to think about it."

His mother let out a sigh of relief.

Freddy did, too. He had managed to delay going to work in the mill, again.

He pulled out a wooden chair and sat at the chipped Formica-topped table. His mother shoveled the fried dough out of the black cast-iron skillet, placed it on a plate, and set it in front of him. "Eat up, Freddy. When you work in a mill, it's like boxing. You've got to keep up your strength."

Freddy cringed at the thought of working in the mill, but he held in his feelings. "I'll be okay." He half smiled. "It's not good manners to eat before everyone is served." As if he were praying, he placed his elbows on the table and rested his head on his hands. "I'll wait for yours to get done."

His mother began frying another slab of dough. "You're such a fine young man, Freddy. Your father would be proud of you."

Freddy felt a slight blush creep over his face. "Yeah, I still miss him."

As the frying dough sizzled in the skillet, Freddy tried to see things his mother's way but he couldn't. Most of the mill workers he had known were hard working, beer-drinking weirdoes. Although they earned big money and seemed to be happy, they were only drinking and wishing their lives away.

Even if working in a steel mill was only a cancer scare, like the cranberries were turning out to be, there had to be something better than doing the same narrow-minded thing day after day. And there had to be something better than asking the same stupid question day after day. The same stupid question was even asked in Pidgin English. But no matter how it was said, just the thought of hearing, "What turn ya' workin'?" made his stomach churn.

When he finished breakfast, he stood up, walked to the wooden screen door, and went outside. Sitting on the side of the dirt road, he looked back at the front of his mother's broken-down house. Age and harsh winters had beaten the wood trim around the door and windows so bad that it would take five or six coats of paint to make them look decent. The screens in the windows had been patched so many times they resembled quilts.

A timid dog padded across a stretch of dried mud, spider-webbed with heat cracks, and sniffed at Freddy's feet. Freddy reached over and petted the dog on its head. Looking for something to eat, the dog sniffed Freddy's hands and looked up at him with sad begging eyes. Freddy showed the dog his empty hands. "I don't have anything."

The dog sniffed Freddy's empty hands one more time and ambled away. As Freddy adjusted the cardboard he had slipped into his shoes to cover the holes, he realized the path to a secure life others had taken was one he couldn't ignore any longer. He hated the thought of doing it, but he decided to lower his expectations, ignore his father's dying words, and get a job in a steel mill. He had to.

To brace himself for the eventuality, he took in a deep breath, but the smell of kerosene, in the kitchen, seemed to have followed him outside. It reminded him of his hunger. It reminded him of his mother's talk of eating dog food. It reminded him that the electricity would not be turned on until he paid the bill.

When he turned his foot sideways to adjust the cardboard covering the hole in his shoe, Neal McCord pulled up in a 1940 Hot Rod Ford and stopped. Leaning his head out the window, he looked down at Freddy. "Hey, man, if you had a set of wheels you wouldn't be wearing holes in your shoes."

Embarrassed, Freddy quickly turned his foot

down to hide the hole and stood up. Without saying a word, he turned his back to Neal and walked toward his mother's house. Keeping his head down, he stared straight ahead. His broken-down, one-speed bicycle that had seen better days leaned against the old red insulating material called Insul-brick that covered the house. It didn't look like bricks. Here and there, missing pieces revealed the dark ugly tarpaper underneath. To him it was slum-brick.

Neal jumped out of the Ford, ran up behind him, and grabbed his shoulder. "Come on, man, don't walk away. I was only kidding."

When Freddy was growing up, other kids had always made fun of his shoddy clothes. Even though Neal had dropped out of the boring high school, way before Freddy had, he had a reputation for being an all right guy, but only for people on the wrong side of the tracks. Being hard and tough, Neal was the type of guy who could take anything. But when he wasn't hard and tough, he could turn in an instant. Freddy was a good fighter and could play it cool, but he was sensitive. Being sensitive in Patagonia could get you hurt.

When people got jobs in the mill and started making money they changed. Freddy was afraid Neal was just leading him on for a bigger laugh at his expense. But Freddy didn't have to take the abuse anymore. He had lifted weights and his body had matured from the rigors of training for boxing. Now that he had strength way beyond the scum that had taunted him for years, fear and anger seemed to confuse him.

Although Neal had been arrested, was known to

get drunk, lie, cheat, and steal, he was intelligent and you had to respect him. But as the nervous and bitterness from Terry's death grew inside him, Freddy didn't care what Neal could do.

Turning around, Freddy reached up and knocked Neal's hand from his shoulder. Looking directly into Neal's suspicious looking eyes, he tensed and curled his right fist into a ball. He didn't know if he could beat him, but if Neal mocked him again, hate would pour into his right fist, and nothing could stop it. Neal would be in for one hell-of-a fight.

Neal stepped back. In a surrendering gesture, he held up his hands. "Don't get excited, man. I used to be just like you. But I got tired of being pushed around by big business and the government."

Sensing something in common, Freddy relaxed his fists and looked at the Ford. Its steel body boasted a coat of gray primer. Although not a finished paint job, the primer was the status symbol of a Hot Rod work in progress, always being made faster and better. Inside, the blue color of the rolled and pleated leather seats reflected upward, causing the white interior roof of the Ford to give off a royal blue glow. Screwed into the top of the floor shift, a clear plastic rectangular wedge from a beer tap handle encased the word "Koehler's" and the beer company's logo: a black eagle crest. Protruding out from under the back bumper, dual exhaust pipes with chrome tips bragged that the engine was a souped-up V-8.

Still wary of a trick, Freddy studied Neal's blue eyes. Although the suspicious look was gone, they didn't show the contempt he had learned to read in other people's eyes. Being known for flimflamming, Freddy wasn't sure what Neal was up to.

"You're a high school dropout like me," Freddy said. "How can you afford a car like that without working in the mill?"

Neal leaned back. With his palms up, he held his thumbs out to the sides. "Simple, I didn't sit alongside the road waiting for something to happen. I got up and made something happen."

Still not believing Neal could have bought a car like the Ford without working in a mill, Freddy stared at it. "I don't care what you say. I think you work in a mill."

Neal leaned forward. His manner took on a significant air. "I tried that." He frowned. "All those mills do is steal your future and pay you big money to be an idiot."

Freddy thought about the stories about how Neal had jumped people and bragged about muggings in New York. "Then how did you get the money for this car?"

Beaming with pride, Neal made fists, turned his thumbs up, and pointed to his own chest. "I did what they don't teach you in school. I went to work for myself."

Freddy figured Neal considered mugging people as working for himself. But he kept an open mind. "I never thought of it like that."

"It's not your fault," Neal said with enthusiasm. "Of all the silly classes you had to take in school, did any of them teach you anything about going into business for yourself?"

Freddy paused and thought about it. "I don't think so."

Neal nudged him with his elbow. "Can't you see?" he said with pleading concern. "Schools only teach kids how to work for somebody else. They make it so we can't win against the rich people."

Not winning against rich people made Freddy's ears perk up.

Neal continued. "You know the rich get all the breaks. And even if you beat them up and mug them, it doesn't change that fact."

Freddy nodded but he was still suspicious. "So... what kind of business do you have?"

Without the slightest bit of hesitation, Neal proudly announced, "I collect garbage."

Freddy burst into a laugh. Being a low-life garbage man was the last thing anyone would want to be. "You're kidding?"

A radiant smile beamed from Neal's face. "That's the beauty of it. People don't know how much money can be made from garbage."

Freddy was beginning to think there was something wrong with Neal. He wasn't going to tell him, but it came out anyway. "I think you're nuts."

"Of course everybody thinks I'm nuts." Neal arrogantly leaned his back against the Ford. "But that's good. It's just what I want people to think. It keeps them out of the business." As if he were considering something, Neal paused, looked away, and then looked back. "Do you want a job or not?"

Working on a garbage truck was worse than working in a steel mill. Freddy figured Neal had to be some kind of mental case. Not wanting to rile

44

him and maybe make him turn into some nut house thing, Freddy suppressed a laugh and started to walk away. But the cardboard came loose in one of his shoes. He tried to readjust it by scraping his foot on the side of the road. "I don't know," he said, trying to be polite. "Somebody might see me."

"So what? It's better than trying to hide a hole in your shoe."

Freddy felt like the old begging dog that had just walked away. Neal's words cut into his pride, and he sensed Neal was right. But he didn't want the stigma of being seen hauling garbage.

He figured if he told Neal he was going to box, Neal would forget about giving him a garbage job. He raised his fists and took a boxing stance. "I think I'll go back to boxing."

Neal leaned back and squinted at him with one eye. "You can, but doesn't that give you headaches?"

Neal was right. Every day, after Freddy had boxed, he had gotten a headache. "Yeah," he said and lied. "But I can stand the pain when I'm making money."

Neal shook his head. "I heard you've got a good right, but did Blinkey tell you that if you got your brains beat out, you'd be rich?"

"I don't know anybody called Blinkey." Freddy jabbed at an imaginary opponent.

"If you haven't heard of Blinkey, you weren't even close to being paid. Blinkey controls boxing in America. Nobody gets in without his say so."

Freddy stepped out of his boxing stance and lowered his hands. "So? I could still get in."

"So, hell! If they let you in, they'll just use you

for a punching bag for other fighters on their way up. If you want to be a bumbling idiot in an old folk's home sitting on a bed pan with snot running out of your nose, waiting for someone to come along and wipe your ass, then boxing's for you."

Terry, Freddy's trainer, had never mentioned Blinkey. Maybe Blinkey was behind Terry getting killed, or maybe they had just been in the wrong place at the wrong time. But even if he really wanted to box, the loan sharks would be waiting for him. They couldn't let an eyewitness to a murder live. They would shut his mouth permanently. His boxing days were over.

In the distance, a strong truck motor labored to climb the semi-steep street that ran past his mother's house. As the sound grew louder, a white truck with Shenango Valley Water Company painted on its door pulled off the road and stopped in front of Neal's Ford. A man in brown coveralls and a hard hat stepped out of the truck and looked at Freddy's mother's house. "Is this 87 Superior Street?"

Freddy stared at the man and answered. "Yes, it is."

"Sorry, buddy," the man said. "I have to turn your water off."

Freddy's heart sunk. Now, in addition to having no electric, his mother would have no water. He stepped up to the man. "Can't you wait a few days? I'm sure I can get enough money to pay the bill."

Shaking his head, the man reached into the back of the truck and slid out a long metal pole with a forked end. "We have sent notice after notice."

46

He threw the pipe onto the ground and took a wrench from the bed of the truck. "It's out of my hands now."

He stepped to the round iron plate that covered the water shut off valve, bent over, placed the wrench on the bolt, and turned it until the plate came off. Then he picked up the forked pipe, slid it down into the opening, and turned off the water. After he put the iron plate back on, he threw the wrench and the forked pipe into the bed of the truck and drove away.

Ashamed of having the water turned off, Freddy turned from Neal and started to walk back into the house.

Neal stood next to the Ford and laughed. Freddy eyes clouded. Tears began to well up, but were replaced with anger. Ready to fight, he turned back toward Neal. "What's so funny?"

Neal pointed to the metal cloths prop supporting a clothesline in the back yard. "You want me to turn the water back on?"

Freddy's anger waned. He didn't like the idea of stealing water, but with his mother talking about eating dog food, he didn't want her to go without water, too. He nodded. "I got to see you try."

Neal walked into the yard and stopped at the clothesline. He grabbed the cloths prop and came back. After he threw it next to the round iron plate, he took a wrench from under the seat of the Ford and took off the plate. Then he put the forked end of the clothes prop into the hole and turned the water back on.

Being afraid someone might see what Neal had done, Freddy quickly grabbed the clothes prop, ran into the yard, and put it back onto the clothesline. When he walked back to Neal, Neal opened the passenger side door to the Ford and gracefully bowed. "Hop in. I'll take you on a tour of the dump."

Still trying to decide if Neal had broken his chains and escaped from a nut house, Freddy hesitated. He surely didn't want to go to any stinking dump. But he had never sat in a leather seat, and he had always wanted to sit in a hot rod Ford. The soft interior of the car gave off a rich blue glow. It invited him, called him, actually caused him to daydream how it would be for the first time in his life to sit in luxury.

With the sun shining on his greased-back hair, giving it a raven sheen, Neal hooked his thumbs in the sides of his pockets and looked at the Ford. "Don't be timid. You won't be walking on holes anymore."

Freddy took a step toward the Ford and stopped. "I'm not sure."

Neal stepped away from the Ford and placed his arm on Freddy's shoulders. "Have you ever worked in a steel mill?"

"No, but I'm thinking about it."

Neal's face took on a hurt look. "Let me tell you about it." Freddy nodded. Neal spoke matter-of-factly, no compassion in his voice. "It's a rotten stinking hell hole. The thermometer gets over one hundred twenty degrees. It's like a pressure cooker. Sweat runs down the crack of your ass and soaks your socks. Everybody gets old fast. You walk into the place and you think you've stepped into an old gray history book picture. It's like you're in the eighteen hundreds, working in broken down factories, surrounded with skinny, sick kids. There's no color there. Every day you suck enough dust and dirt down your throat to fill a bucket. There's white-hot flying steel that'll take your eyes out in a second. There's poisons we've never heard of. It's a nightmare land where people wear dirty-white hats and tell you to do things that will get you killed. I've seen big black fifteen-pound rats" – he held his hands apart – "this long, run up men's backs and steal food right out of their hands." As if exhausted from just talking about the mill, he took a breath. "And when you leave the place, the smell follows you all the way home."

Freddy had been to the city dump. The smell there had been so bad, it actually did follow him all the way home. He wasn't sure he wanted the smells of a garbage truck following him home.

He looked to Neal, and asked in a whisper, "Doesn't the garbage dump smell bad, too?"

"I'm glad you brought that up." Neal said, and his smile displayed brilliant white teeth. "On the truck we're out in the open air. It's not like the steel mills where you stay inside and breathe the stink eight to sixteen hours at a stretch. When we go to the dump, we're in and out." He paused. "Hell, you could hold your breath the amount of time we'll be there."

Freddy's interest spiked. "It sounds pretty good, but I just don't know."

Then Neal attacked Freddy with a great, passionate soul that only a conman could have, saying, "If you go work in a mill, before you know it, you'll be too old to get out. You got to get out of this town's rut while you're young. And besides, what else have you got to do? Come on, man. Do it."

That day, Freddy rode in luxury.

In the weeks that followed, working with Neal, Freddy managed to make enough money to have his mother's electricity turned back on. After Neal turned the water back off, the water company turned it back on. It was a strange time. Sometimes it seemed as if Neal were half boy, half man. Although at times, he acted a little crazy, he wasn't mentally ill. For those who didn't know him, he could become a delusion, a phantom, or a mirage. It seemed as if he could be everywhere at the same time. With an incandescent personality, he rarely yawned or whined about everyday things. Shambling in Neal's shadow was like hanging onto the shirttail of a mad man racing on the edge of a cliff as if it were a four-lane highway, racing toward the exciting land of some magical city. Once caught up in Neal's freewheeling ways Freddy grew up fast. When Neal was around, sleeping or nodding off from boredom was never an option.

Chapter 4

Months after Freddy had started working on the garbage truck, he had gone along with one of Neal's schemes. They had discovered a gold vault worth enough money to last a lifetime. Even though a gangster called Blondie had tricked them out of the vault, the scheme hadn't been a total loss. Freddy had gotten enough money to fill his mother's cupboards with food and pay the bills. After that, he had splurged for a new pair of shoes and a few other things. But now, he stood just across the state line in the sparsely populated area of Hubbard, Ohio leaning against the fender of the dirty-white dump truck Neal and he used to haul garbage.

As he waited for Neal to collect money from a customer, the hot summer sun beat down on Freddy's tanned face. With paint fumes from the General American Railroad Tank Car factory filling the air, he fantasized how he was going to date Julie, the girl of his dreams.

"Julie," he said out loud.

The name rolled off his tongue and had a romantic ring to it. He could see her fluffing out her long golden hair and smiling brightly. Some things in this world go beyond class. Julie's social stratum of elegance, style, taste, and manner went beyond class. He could see her walking toward him with her long-legged sensual sway that hypnotized him every time he saw her. He hoped she would never see him picking up garbage.

Even though she was way out of his league, the money Neal and he would make with a new truck and a bigger contract would be more than enough to take her out in style. People usually go by looks. And when he drove the new truck he wouldn't be wearing dirty leather gloves and a long-sleeved, navy-blue work shirt. He would have clean hands. He would be wearing a new black T-shirt. He wouldn't be running into yards picking up fly-spotted garbage cans, hoisting them over his head, and dumping them into the back of the dump truck. He would be sitting in a brand new truck, waiting for his helper to hoist the garbage cans and dump them into the truck.

From behind him, a high revving motor roared. He snapped out of his daydream, spun around, and faced the threat. A Dodge with faded blue paint flew around the bend in the road and screeched to a stop. A portly man with a gray gangster-style hat turned down on one side shifted his eyes. Then he stuck his head out the window and yelled, "Did you punch my milk horse?"

As Freddy slipped off his gloves, he wondered if the man had escaped from an insane asylum. But when he got a look at the man, he couldn't help but stare. A sickening pale color of death covered the man's wax-like face. His thick lips gave off a weird feeling of uncaring meanness Freddy had never experienced before. An aura of a freshly exhumed corpse seemed to surround the man. Right away, Freddy didn't like the man.

As if it were a threat from a cadaver came back to life, the man repeated, "Did you punch my milk horse?"

Freddy had seen dirty-white milk trucks rattling wire cases of empty milk jugs down side streets and over rough roads, but he had never seen a milk horse. As a defensive show of strength against the man's spooky aura, he tensed his muscular body. "I haven't punched anything, mister." Keeping a wary eye on the man, Freddy rolled up his shirtsleeves. "Where have you been? They haven't used horses to pull milk wagons for years."

As if he were about to cause Freddy physical harm, the man cast an appraising stare toward him. If he wanted to, Freddy could reach into the Dodge and yank the old man out from behind the steering wheel. But the bizarre look in the man's eyes intensified, reminding Freddy of a dead animal's sightless gaze. There was nothing human there, nothing at all. The man radiated death, sort of like he was measuring a victim for a coffin. A creepy feeling crawled up Freddy's spine.

Slap! Freddy's heart jerked. With his right hand protecting his face, he spun around and faced where the sound had come from. Across the street, Neal walked away from a house counting money. Behind him a screen door had smacked shut.

Freddy's heart slowed.

Neal had just collected a garbage-hauling fee.

Neal was wearing his familiar black T-shirt with the sleeves rolled up. Walking toward Freddy, he reached up and ran his strong hand through his black, slicked-back hair. Although Neal and he didn't have new cars or tailor-made clothing, they had long hair. It was sort of a trademark, and they were proud of it. If they got caught doing some trivial thing that was considered illegal, the law would make them get a haircut. Freddy knew it was just the cop's way of trying to break them. Before he had started working on the truck, it hadn't mattered. The cops couldn't take anything away from him because he didn't have anything to take.

Neal stopped next to Freddy, and stared at the man in the Dodge. The man turned his head and looked straight ahead. Still looking straight ahead and not moving his head, the man stiffly reached over, put the Dodge in gear, and pulled away.

With its engine screaming, a 1958 blue Chevy, coming the other way, sped toward the Dodge. Just before a head-on collision, the Dodge stopped. The Chevy popped out from right in front of it and flew at Freddy and Neal. They leaped out of its speeding path. With tires screeching, the car swerved, just missing the garbage truck. A man with a taunting laugh and a crazed look on his scared face stuck the barrel of a sawed-off shotgun out the side window.

Boom! One shotgun blast peppered the front fender of the truck. With a steady stream of blue exhaust fumes blasting out of dual tailpipes, the Chevy sped away.

Freddy watched the Chevy fading down the road. Boom! The sawed off shotgun fired again, sending a load of buckshot toward him. But by the time the pellets reached him, because of the short sawed off barrel, the pellets had spread to the sides. Only a few bounced harmlessly off the pavement at his feet. Getting out of the way of another blast, he turned and covered his face with his hands. Stunned by the act, he looked back at Neal. "What are they trying to do, kill us?"

A look of shock and horror flashed from Neal's face so fast Freddy wasn't sure he had seen it. Trying to cover up his feelings, Neal waved his hand down. "We don't have to worry about that."

Freddy stood rooted in awe. "But they shot at us with a shotgun." He pointed to the holes the lead pellets had made in the front fender of the dump truck. "What do you mean, we don't have to worry?"

Acting as if getting shot at was an everyday thing, Neal shrugged. "When they shoot something with a shotgun, it's only a message. If they were going to kill us, they would have blown us to smithereens. But then again, if they had, we wouldn't have to worry about getting shot."

Freddy didn't believe there was nothing to worry about. Mike Walker, one of the old owners of the Mafia's most infamous gambling den, the Jungle Inn, had been killed by the third shot from a shotgun, but that may have been a warning that turned into an accidental shooting. Shot below the waist, Walker had made it to the hospital but died. But the twisted bodies of Cadillac Charlie and his eleven-year-old son tangled in the auto wreckage and building material that littered Charlie's backyard yard was no warning. It was just one of eighty-two unsolved underworld car bombings that created the phrase "Youngstown Tune-ups".

Calming down a little, Freddy asked, "Can't they use a pencil and a piece of paper to send a message?"

"That wouldn't scare us enough to do what they want us to do."

"What do they want us to do?"

Patting the few dollars in his pocket, he had collected from the customer, Neal watched the blue Dodge tear away down the road. "They want protection money, but they're not going to get it."

Freddy knew the gangsters could make it hard on them. "Couldn't we just pay them and keep them from putting holes in the truck?"

"No way." Neal violently shook his head. "Once you get in with those guys, they become a part of your life, and you can't get rid of them. They just keep on collecting more and more. Pretty soon they're trying to collect more money than you make." He made a face and shuddered. "If we start to pay them, it'll be like trying to feed a baby elephant. They'll never get enough."

"Yeah, but they don't call Youngstown 'Bomb Town' for nothing. They shot our truck. Maybe they'll give it a Youngstown tune up. You know, blow it up."

"Let them blow it up. We're trading it in anyway."

Freddy gestured to the shot-up front fender. "Won't they shoot up the new truck?"

"Johnny Hudson's going to get a Master Freight Agreement for the truckers' union."

"What does that got to do with us?"

Neal sighed. "Truckers take care of their members. With a single contract for the whole country everybody has to go by the same rules. If they don't, they'll have a nationwide strike. That'll stop those idiots from trying to get protection money. We'll pay it to the union, but it won't be as much, because we'll be in the system. Then the union will pay it to them."

Searching Neal's face for a hint of doubt and finding none, Freddy shrugged. "I guess you're right, but we're not in the truckers' union."

"I'd rather die on my feet than live on my

knees," Neal said with conviction and smiled a mischievous smile. "Besides, I never liked the idea of having flat knees and a round mouth. With a new truck, we'll make enough money to join the truckers."

"Are you sure about that?"

Neal's face beamed with confidence. "Heck yeah!" He kicked the front tire of the truck to see if it was going flat. "Today, we'll have enough money to buy a new truck. With the money we make with a new truck and our new contracts, we'll be able to buy another truck."

Freddy nodded. "If Blondie hadn't cheated us out of Capone's vault, we wouldn't have to go to the bank."

Acting like he didn't want to be reminded of the vault, Neal grabbed the door handle of the truck and hesitated. "What did Smeal say?"

"You mean that old guy in the Dodge?"

Neal turned serious. "That guy's not as old as he looks. He was a prisoner of war. While he was captured, a rat ate half his ear off. He was young then, but he came back with gray hair."

"Anybody that asked me if I punched his milk horse has to be some kind of a nut."

Neal nodded heavily. "He could be crazy. They say he's killed a lot of people."

"No wonder he looks like he just crawled out of a grave." Freddy shuddered. "He gives me the creeps."

"Don't worry about the little things, Freddy. He's gone now." Neal jerked his head toward the cab of the truck. "Get in. We got to change clothes and get to the bank. Rafferty's waiting."

57

Shaking off the creepy feeling, Freddy climbed into the dump truck and smiled about Rafferty's ability to amuse himself with the simplest things. Before Rafferty had met Neal, he had been somewhat like Freddy, feeling sorry for himself and going nowhere fast. Way back in grade school, Neal already had charisma and charm, and he had used it to comfort Rafferty.

Rafferty only had one pair of socks. The heels were worn and torn almost in half. He had folded the tears down into the inside of his shoes to conceal the holes. But a well-dressed kid who had enough money to get a haircut every week reached down and ripped the socks off Rafferty's ankles. In front of the whole class, the rich kid held the socks between his lily-white fingertips and pointed to Rafferty's crimson face.

Almost yelling, he said, "How many more years are you going to wear the same dirty socks?"

Neal, who had been leaning against the wall picking his teeth with the corner of his ID card which showed his age as twenty-one so he could buy beer, jerked away from the wall and headed for the kid. Girls placed their hands over their mouths and gasped. Other kids laughed and joined in the jeering and pointing. Encouraged, the kid reared back to throw the socks in Rafferty's red embarrassed face. Neal stepped up and grabbed the kids' arm. The kid tried to move his arm. Neal's grip kept it solid.

Without turning, the kid playfully pleaded, "Come on, man, rub these in his face."

Neal jerked on the kid's arm and lifted him off the floor. While the kid's feet dangled a foot off the floor, Neal whispered in his ear, "Who's gonna make me?" The confused kid turned to Neal. In a low and even voice, Neal said, "Get out of here before I reach down your throat and pull out your lungs."

Neal pushed on the kid's arm and let loose. The kid stared at Neal in helpless disbelief. Then he dropped the socks, stumbled sideways, caught his balance, and slunk away.

Neal's parents had moved around a lot, and the constant moving had caused him to start school a year later than other kids. And he had been held back a year for missing school. In the quiet that enveloped the school room that day, Neal stepped up and put his arm around Rafferty's shoulder. Being a few years older, bigger and stronger, he was in charge now. He didn't have to say a word. His compassionate actions showed the hateful kids he had taken the orange-headed, freckled-faced Rafferty under his protective wing.

But as Neal stood there, a tall kid, who usually had his way, made a face and pointed to Rafferty. "Don't waste your time with that skinny creep."

Neal's cold-eyed stare told the kid the jeering was over. It was understood that Rafferty's new friend was the tough kid with the black leather jacket and slicked-back hair. After that, as sort of a payback for all the years of abuse, Rafferty became a smart aleck with a scatterbrained sense of humor. In addition to being strangely enchanted by childish pranks, he seemed to always be screwing around with something. In a drug store, he had stepped onto on a belly vibrating machine, put the belt on, and turned on the machine. As the machine vibrated his torso, he laughed, waved his hands, and swung his hips doing a hula dance.

A stout lady wearing shoes too small for her plump feet huffed past, waving her hands in the air, saying, "Oh my God, he's an idiot."

Rafferty smiled with an eloquent air of benign and generous forgiveness.

Sitting in the seat of the garbage truck, Freddy smiled at the thought of Rafferty's ability to amuse himself and others with the simplest things. Neal grasped the steering wheel and turned toward Freddy. "I know why you're smiling."

Freddy wondered if Neal knew he was thinking about Rafferty. "What are you, a mind reader?"

"I don't have to be," Neal said. "By tonight we'll have a new truck, and you'll be in Julie's arms."

Freddy lit up at the thought, but he felt his face flush with embarrassment. Although there was nothing he would like more than to hold Julie's lovely body in his arms, he wasn't as outgoing as Neal. Neal had tried to date Julie's sister, Samantha, and for the first time in his life he had struck out. Freddy wasn't surprised. Neal and he had a different set of values than the girl's. Although he would never admit it, Freddy figured it was because they were more emotional than the girls.

Sophistication of the girls caused them to have no real feelings. They had more than they wanted and couldn't want anything else, but still looked for something new to want. Hiding behind a wall of aloofness, they were careful not to let their real selves show through. Even if the new truck deal went as planned, Julie was so beautiful that she wouldn't date just anybody, and Freddy didn't want to take the chance of being too aggressive and alienate her. If he did, she would surely say no to anything he asked. No matter what Neal said, Freddy would have to raise his social status and then take measured steps to date her.

When they dumped their last load of garbage, the dump truck threw a rod right through the engine block. After the bulldozer operator at the dump had pushed the truck off to the side, Neal said, "It could stay there. Every time we drive our new trucks to the dump, it will serve as a reminder of how just how poor we had been."

Chapter 5

Assured they had orchestrated everything for appearance and effect, Freddy and Neal donned their expensive suit jackets, stood on the sidewalk outside the bank, and waited for Rafferty to show up.

Freddy felt good dressed up. Like most kids from Patagonia, he had a reputation of being a greasy-haired hood. Even if he didn't steal things, mug people, and get boozed up, he was still considered a hood. He used to pretend to be proud of that. But more and more he didn't care for the reputation.

When it was time to go into the bank, Rafferty was nowhere to be seen. As they waited, a clean-shaven man with a reed like figure, emphasized by form-fitting clothes, carried a briefcase and walked out the front doors of the bank.

Neal smiled at him and said, "Hi."

The man didn't acknowledge their presence. Watching the "dressed-for-success" businessman walk down the street, Freddy felt the man's taste and intelligence was beyond his, and that the man believed he was too good to talk to them. It made Freddy feel inferior.

When a man wearing a white shirt and tie walked toward the man, the man turned his head, smiled, and freely exchanged pleasantries with him. Freddy figured the man wearing the white shirt and tie was one of the more important citizens of the town. This snobbery bothered Freddy, but with the new fleet of trucks they would eventually get, some day he would have more money than that man ever thought of having. He shrugged off the inferior feeling and looked at the clock above the bank. The big black hour hand jerked right in front of the twelve. The appointment was a minute away.

Freddy checked the street again and turned toward Neal. "Rafferty should've been here by now."

Neal gave Freddy a concerned look. "Maybe he couldn't get out of the house."

Rafferty's house was never quiet. The radio or TV was usually going full blast. While Rafferty tried to sleep on a lumpy mattress, with springs poking him in the rear end, his older brothers yelled at each other. Tipping over chairs and tables in the process, they may have grabbed Rafferty and wrestled him to the floor. If they had, Rafferty would wiggle out of it, but it would take time.

"Rafferty's always late," Neal said. "Why that little rotten..." He went on and called Rafferty every cuss work he could think of. It was his way of showing his affection. He patted the front pocket of Freddy's suit coat. "Is it in there?"

"It bulges too much. I put it in my back pocket."

"That's a good idea. We want to look like businessmen. As long as we face him, he won't see it."

Freddy reached into his back pocket and pulled out a piece of brass and rolled it in his hands. The flat metal was half an inch thick, seven inches long and L-shaped. The body of the L was three inches wider than its bottom that was only an inch high and stuck out two inches like a little foot. Four notches ran down one side, and the top of the L came to a dull point. In various places, other little rectangular slots had been cut into the brass. Freddy held it by its L-shaped end and shook it. "This key brought us luck before. Maybe it will again."

Freddy pressed his forehead against the glass window of the bank and looked in. "Rafferty's not in there."

With his hand resting on the door handle, Neal looked up and down the street. "You want to wait for him?"

Freddy stepped away from the window. "No way, man. The deadline's today. If we wait, we'll be late. We'll forfeit all the money we already paid."

Once Neal started something, he hated turning back. Even though Freddy didn't like it, the only way the loan had been approved was when they shook hands on what the bank president claimed was an irregular contract. If they missed the deadline, they forfeited the money. Freddy didn't want to be right back where they had started: broke. He turned to the door and checked the street one last time. Rafferty was a no-show. With a tilt of his head, Freddy gestured to Neal. "Let's go."

They strode into the bank and stopped ten feet away from a small brass-framed gate that was connected to a low wooden railing that ran in a semi-circle around the vault and kept people from getting too close. As if he were measuring it, Neal scanned the bank lobby. "It's kind of small in here. It looks like they're going to have to build on to handle all the money we're going to make."

"That would be nice." Freddy stared at the bars that protected the bank's shiny silver vault. "If

64

Blondie wouldn't have taken the vault they would be digging a new foundation right now."

Neal nudged Freddy's elbow and pointed to his right. A long-nosed, stone-faced man wearing a pinstriped suit stood next to a tall plant at the side of the wall. He reached up and touched the gray fedora on his head. A tattoo of a skull and cross-bones flashed from the back of his hand. As if he didn't want anyone to see the tattoo, he quickly lowered his hand. When he glanced up at Neal, his wrinkled high brows accentuated the length of his long nose. As if he were ashamed of his long nose, he turned away.

At first, Freddy thought it was odd that someone that looked like a gangster with a tattoo would be standing in the bank. But on second thought, he figured the man was probably collecting protection money or paying off a gambling debt.

Usually Freddy and Neal went to the desk of the secretary of the president or to the teller. But today, a barrel-chested, armed guard, dressed in an impeccable uniform, stepped in front of Neal. His granite jaw swung open and he spoke. "Are you gentlemen here to see Mister Cathcart?"

Neal presented his hand to the guard. "Yes, we are, sir. Glad to meet you. My name's Neal McCord and. We're here to…"

Before Neal could finish, the guard held up his hand in a protesting gesture. Ignoring Neal's hand of friendship, he turned on his heel and ushered them between a purple velvet-rope maze and across a thick-piled rug until they stood in front of a teakwood desk big enough to support an armored truck. Right away Freddy noticed the air. It reeked of alcohol and iodine and seemed to be filled with tension.

Without saying a word, the guard slightly bowed and left the room.

The bank president stood extra erect, pulled a gold watch out of the vest of his three-piece rumpled suit and cleared his throat. "You're thirty seconds late." He slapped a manila folder down on the desk and sat down. Although presidents of banks usually were tall and generally well proportioned, this president's wide hips and pot belly sloped upward to his narrow shoulders and made him look like a timid man who had not earned his position but had been promoted at the whim of a moron relative or as a political favor.

The last time Freddy had seen the president there hadn't been a hair out of place on his head. His forehead had been dry. His white shirt had been pressed, a stiff clean collar accented his clean-shaven face, and his shoes had glowed with a recent shine. All his movements and precise speech had conveyed superiority.

Now Freddy wondered what had happen to him. A gravy stain stood out on the left side of his wrinkled shirt. Oily hair topped what seemed to be an oversized head that glistened with sweat, making him look sneakier than a weasel.

As if he couldn't decide if he wanted to sit or stand, the president wiped his forehead with a wadded up, gray handkerchief, stood up, and stepped back. Freddy took his eyes off the president's unshaven face and looked at his shoes. They looked as if they had been buffed with sandpaper.

The president propped his fists on his hips and sneered under the strips of white first-aid tape that ran down the bridge of his nose and zigzagged between his two small dark eyes that broadcasted greed. With his mouth moving like a bottom-feeding catfish, trying to get at the white first-aid tape above its lip, he waved impatiently. "Come on, boys. Get on with it."

Neal bent over the massive desk and thrust his hand out. "Just in case you don't remember us, my name's Neal McCord, nice to shake your hand again." Reading the triangular walnut name plaque displayed on the desk, Neal tried an engaging grin. "Ah, yes. Very nice to meet you again, Mister Cathcart."

Although Neal held his hand out longer than necessary, the president didn't offer his hand in return. Neal sloughed off the disrespectful gesture and tilted his head toward Freddy. "You remember my business partner, Freddy Crane?"

In an act of friendly introduction, Freddy politely nodded. But the president didn't even look at him.

Neal continued, "We came in to make our final payment."

The president pyramided his fingers under his chin and talked over them. "Mister McCord," he said with a nasal sound to his voice from the taped nose, "you haven't brought in the money to make your first down payment. We have given you ample time to come and make a payment but you haven't."

A pleading look emanated from Neal's puzzled face. "What are you talking about?" He reached into his shirt pocket. "I have the receipt right here." He held it in front of the president.

The president reached out and took the receipt. "I'm sorry, boys. This isn't a receipt from this bank."

Neal bent over and snatched the receipt from the president's hands. "There has to be a mistake. You gave us this receipt just last week. You said the truck would be ours just as soon as we made the last payment."

As if he were waiting for a reply, Neal stared at the president. The president didn't reply.

Neal raised his voice. "You said, 'Although it was an irregular contract, we would have no problem. And that the receipt was just as good as any contract."

"I don't remember doing that."

"What do you mean, you don't remember? We shook hands on it."

The president reached under his desk and seemed to press something. "You boys weren't going to start trouble, were you?"

Neal held up his hand in a halting gesture. "I'll be right back." He turned and walked out of the office.

Freddy stepped to the doorway and watched. Neal walked to the teller's window and slammed down the receipt. A red-haired girl with a tight pink sweater turned from an adding machine and stepped toward the window. Neal's rage softened. "Excuse me, gorgeous. Is this receipt from your bank?"

The girl's face blushed to the color of her red hair. Smiling, she picked up the receipt and examined it. Looking toward the president's office, she slowly placed it in front of Neal. "No, sir." She reached under the counter and pulled out a receipt. "Our receipts look like this."

Neal picked up the receipt. "Thank you, sweetie, but something's wrong." He stormed back into the office and stopped in front of the desk next to Freddy.

As if they weren't there, the president lowered his head. With a timid nasal voice, he began talking to the manila folder in front of him. "I'm sorry, Mister McCord, but since you never made a down payment, your garbage truck has already been sold." Still looking at the folder, he leaned back and turned his empty palms up. "It's out of my hands."

With a threatening slant, Neal leaned toward the president. "I can't help it if the crooked garbage men got you and the crooked politicians in their back pockets." He thrust out his hand. "Give us our money back, and we'll be out of here."

A little light came into the president's eyes. No way could the president be faking that kind of sudden look and surprise over something he had already known about.

Freddy felt his resentment boil like acid. Trying to keep his emotions in check, he groaned. He knew Neal was right. But to make matters worse, when someone got on the wrong side of Neal, his mood could change rapidly. He was usually welcomed anywhere he went, but his rebellious attitude could become something apart from the known properties of a normal human being. Right now the slightest touch in the wrong place or an authoritative tone of voice would throw him into a rage. And a bank with an armed guard wasn't a place to cause a ruckus.

The president cleared his throat and kept his eyes turned down. "I can't give you what isn't yours."

Neal withdrew his hand, glared at the president, and tensed for action. "We brought the money in here and laid it right here on this desk." He slammed the bottom of his fist on the top of the desk.

The president held up his hands in defense and leaned back.

Leaning over the deck, Neal jerked the receipt in front of the president's face and shook it. "You signed this receipt."

Emitting a helpless self-pitying sniff, the president stared at the receipt. "That's not my signature."

With his head bobbing with sadistic laughter, Neal raised his voice. "What do you want to lie for?" He placed the receipt on the desk and jammed his finger down on the signature. "You know this signature is yours. Did somebody break your nose to make you steal our money?" Like a mad bull about to charge, he let out a rasping grunt. "That truck should be ours."

The president jerked his head up with resentful distrust. "That's not the receipt I need to see."

Neal pulled his arm back to strike. "The only thing you need to see is the inside of an ambulance."

The president rose to his feet in terror.

"That's it," Neal thundered. "Be scared. For every dollar you weaseled us out of, you're going to spend three days in the hospital."

70

Freddy grabbed Neal by the arm and pulled. "Let's go, Neal."

Neal shrugged off Freddy's hand. "Right after I take our money out of this guy's ass."

The president tensed. In helpless horror, he put his hand on his bandaged nose and backed away. Between labored gasps, he managed to speak. "We have armed guards here."

"Big deal." Neal thrust his arm into the air. "Pennsylvania's a big state. If your broken-down rent-a-cops shot at it, they'd probably miss."

From the doorway, a deep baritone voice of authority boomed across the office. "That will be enough."

Neal turned toward the voice.

The barrel-chested guard walked up to Neal, stood in front of his face, and placed his huge hand on his pistol. "You boys will have to leave Mister Cathcart's office. You are not wanted here."

Holding the receipt at arms-length in front of him, Neal stepped toward the guard. "Just the man we want to see."

The guard pulled his gun halfway out of the holster. Freddy reached into his own pocket and gripped the big, brass, decoding key. If he had to, he would throw it and hit that guard upside his crew-cut head.

Neal held up his hands. "We're not trying to rob the bank, sir. We just want our money back."

The guard's head tilted with mock suspicion. "What money?"

Neal held out the receipt and cautiously stepped toward the guard. "Here, read it."

The guard let the gun fall back into its holster,

took the receipt, and glanced at it. "I'm sorry, boys. I've worked here for over twenty years. This receipt isn't from our bank."

With an air of intolerable despair, Neal reached up and slowly took the receipt. "So that's how it's gonna be?"

As a sly smile formed at the corners of the president's mouth, his breathing smoothed. He gestured toward the guard. "If you still have a problem that man will gladly paint your house."

Freddy turned toward Neal. "I don't even have a house. What's this guy talking about?"

Keeping a wary eye on the guard, Neal talked in a whisper. "It's what the gangsters call killing someone. The paint's the blood that gets splattered on the walls and floors."

Smiling a better-than-thou smile, the guard added, "And I do my own carpentry work, too."

Again, Freddy turned to Neal.

"He gets rid of the bodies, too."

Freddy gave the guard a withering look. With the look all dishonest people give when they thought they had gotten the best of a situation, the guard stared back.

As if he were deciding to jump the guard or the president, Neal's eyes filled with contempt.

Still clutching the key in his pocket, Freddy stepped toward the door. "Come on, Neal. Gangsters are taking over the garbage business." He looked at the President and then the guard. "They're on the take."

With defiance radiating from every pore in his body, Neal stared at the guard for a long moment.

The guard casually leaned against the

72

doorframe, folded his muscular arms across his chest, and looked down at Neal. "Don't even think about trying something."

"What are you going to do, if I do? I have a receipt."

"We don't need an excuse to call the cops. You're trying to pass a forged receipt."

"Remember, Neal," Freddy said, "don't sit when you can stand."

A look of recall filled Neal's face.

Freddy hoped Neal remembered the saying, Don't crawl when you can walk, don't stand when you can sit, don't walk when you can ride, and don't push when they got pull. These people had pull. For the moment, it was best not to push.

A furrow appeared between Neal's eyebrows. "I should have known better than to come to a bank. During the depression, after poor people worked and saved for a lifetime, smug-faced bastards like you caused thousands of people to become flat-ass broke and laughed about it."

The guard turned his head away.

Neal jammed his hands into his pockets. His face relaxed, but his angry expression remained. Then as if he had just thought of something, his face lit up.

Since he had taken the suit jacket Blondie had given him off the coat hook at the Peacock Alley Bar, Freddy had never seen him put his hands into the pockets. Now for the first time, he did. As Neal felt around in the pocket, his angry expression changed to inquisitive. He pulled out a folded piece of paper and a penknife.

The guard stepped away from the doorframe

and placed his hand on the handle of his gun. "You don't have to get violent."

Neal faced the president and held out his hand. "Look, it's only a piece of paper and a penknife. He put the knife back into his pocket but held on to the paper.

An inquisitive look came to the president's face. "I told you boys, it's out of my hands. What do you want from me?"

Neal held up his hand. "Just wait a second." He placed the paper on the gleaming desktop.

The president tilted his head to the side and stared at the paper. "What's that, another phony receipt?"

Smiling at the pear-shaped president, Neal smoothed the paper out on the desk. "You people act like you got more muscles than brains."

The bank president reached up, straightened the already perfect knot in his tie, and growled. "Don't scratch that desk."

Freddy ignored him, horned in close to Neal, and looked at the paper. It seemed to be an old business letter with a "Zephyr Manufacturing" company header. It was the same kind of header on the top of an encoded letter that had previously led them to Al Capone's vault.

Neal turned his head toward Freddy. Freddy knew they should wait until they were outside the bank, but he wanted to decode the letter. And he wanted to do it right now. He shrugged and took out the seven-inch brass key that had decoded the original letter.

The president held up his hand in a shielding gesture and backed away.

With his right hand, the guard reached down, pulled his gun out of its holster, and pointed it at Freddy. "Drop it."

Freddy felt the tension of the moment mount, but it didn't seem to bother Neal.

Neal looked back over his shoulder at the guard. "What's the matter, buddy? It's only a key."

Keeping the gun aimed at Freddy, the guard held out his left hand. "Let me see it."

Freddy held out the key.

The guard's forehead wrinkled with bewilderment, but he didn't take the key. "Oh, it's just a paperweight." He returned his gun to his holster.

Neal rolled his hand in an encouraging gesture. "Come on, Freddy. Try it."

Freddy laid the key on the paper. The guard stretched his neck to see what Freddy was doing, but Freddy blocked his view.

The president pointed at the key. "I'm not telling you again. Don't damage my deck with that paperweight."

"Don't worry about it." Neal reached down and repositioned the key. "Try this way."

"That isn't it." Freddy turned the key over.

Neal's eyes widened. "Ah, ha!"

Before the guard or the president could read what the key had decoded, Freddy pulled the key off the paper and pulled its pointed end across the mirror finish of the desk. It plowed deep into the teakwood, leaving a scratch seven inches long.

"Oh, sorry about that." Freddy stepped back and slid the key back into his pocket.

The president thrust his finger toward the

gouge. "You'll pay for that."

"Take out of our down payment," Freddy snapped back. "We'll give you a receipt." Ignoring the president, he turned toward Neal. "I'll be damned."

Neal looked up from the paper and turned toward Freddy. "You thinking what I'm thinking?"

Freddy stared at the pocket of Neal's suit jacket. It was as if some random synapse in his brain had just connected. During his reign in Chicago, Al Capone had made over one hundred million dollars a year. In 1929 he earned one hundred and five million. The big brass decoding key and Blondie, the gentle gangster from Buffalo, had enabled them to find Capone's secret vault. Even after they had found it, they didn't know how valuable it was. The thin layer of brass that covered the outside of the vault had made it seem worthless. If an inquisitive person peeled back the brass, they would have only fond a thin layer of cement that concealed a gold vault, worth almost a million dollars. Although Blondie had cheated them out of the vault, Freddy knew there was much more money to be found. And again, the key was going to show them where to look.

"That was Blondie's jacket," he said.

Neal nodded and smiled big. "We're in the game again."

As a show of disrespect, Neal intentionally placed his foot up on the edge of the president's desk. With his lips spread into his famous smile, he leaned toward the president. "Sorry, buddy. But you can stick that truck and our money you stole right up your arrogant ass."

He dropped his foot and turned toward the guard. "And it'll probably fit."

Freddy followed Neal out of the bank. Although Neal had always managed to keep him in a state of keen excitement, their last great adventure over the Canadian border that had led to the vault had almost gotten them burned to death.

Now that they had found a new message, Freddy knew Neal's unending quest for adventure and his uncanny ability to change the mundane world of those around him, would surface again.

Months ago, in the grapey dawn, they had found the gold vault in the abandoned coalmine at the triangular tract of land called Petroleum. They had also discovered that Al Capone never went to prison. A look-alike had gone for him, but the great switch was short lived. Someone or something in the mine had killed Al Capone, and his skeleton was still hidden there.

Freddy stopped on the sidewalk and leaned his back against the concrete side of the bank. "Too bad we thought the vault was worthless."

Choosing comfort over dignity, Neal took his suit jacket off, flung it over his shoulder, and held it with his forefinger. "I thought we were going to be rich. I don't believe we were so stupid." He ran his hand along the front of his chest. "At least we got these expensive suit jackets and an envelope full of money."

Freddy nodded. "That extra money sure made my mom's life easy for a while."

Freddy had known the money wouldn't last. Now he wondered if they he had done the right thing. When Neal applied for the new required permits, they were denied because the dump truck they used to haul garbage was deemed outdated. They figured that expanding the garbage business with a new truck and joining the truckers union could keep them in the money. Without a new truck, the corrupt politicians would give the higher bids to the mob-controlled garbage collectors.

So… Freddy, Rafferty, and Neal had agreed to pool their remaining money and make a down payment on a new garbage truck. Now that they couldn't get the new truck, they couldn't get the new contracts, and they automatically lost the old contracts, too. Someone in power had turned a win-win situation into a loss. Now if they went to the dump, their broken-down truck wouldn't remind them of how poor they had been, it would remind them of how gullible they had been.

Walking down the sidewalk outside the bank, Neal put his hand on Freddy's back. "We lost a new truck and our garbage business, but let's look at that note again?"

Freddy longed for the feeling of being rich. Trying to subdue his excitement, he shrugged. "I saw 'big shoebox.' It has to have money in it."

Neal shook the paper in front of Freddy's face. "That's not all. Look at it!"

Freddy bent to the paper and placed the brass decoding key on it. "It still says 'big shoebox'"

With a look of amazement, Neal held the paper with both hands and stared at it. "This message is different from the one that was in the bank bag we got from Blondie."

Wondering what Neal was getting at, Freddy squinted at the paper. "What are you talking about?"

"Remember that shoebox in the gangster's office in Buffalo?"

"Yeah, it was full of money."

As if unable to believe what he was reading, Neal cried with delight, "That was only a little shoebox. This note here says, 'Big shoebox, Peacock Alley.' There's more money in that foundation." He placed his hand on his forehead and gleefully whirled around in a circle. "There's a whole lot more."

In the clandestine process of digging up the encoding key at the old burned down Peacock Alley foundation, a gangster called Nose, had been killed by a hit and run driver. Freddy figured if they went back there, they would be connected to the crime.

"We can check it out," he said. "But the cops are still investigating Nose's death. We'll have to wait until the place cools down."

Neal gave him a quizzical stare. "Nose was killed months ago. And the cops still think it was an accident. We'll get Rafferty and dig up the foundation at night, just like we did before."

Freddy stepped away from the bank wall. "I don't know," he started to say, but before he could finish, the click of high heels on the sidewalk echoed toward him. He raised an appreciative eyebrow.

Walking with her long-legged sensual sway, Julie headed toward Freddy. He figured since he was wearing a suit coat, he would surely make a lasting impression on the girl of his dreams. Staring right at him, Julie fluffed her hair and smiled brightly. His heart fluttered with anticipation.

Nervously wanting to do something, he smoothed out his suit coat and waited for her to come near. When she was right next to him, he uttered a friendly, "Hello."

She didn't answer. She acted as if he didn't exist. She kept on walking. Her long-legged sensual sway had been for the benefit of someone else. Freddy hadn't noticed it before, but a 1932 five-window Ford hot rod had pulled up the curb. Even though the car was coated with a thick grayish-blue paint and looked like it had been painted at the cut-rate Earl Scribes one-day paint store, it was something better than he could buy. Julie's social stratum was still beyond his reach.

He sighed so deeply that it brought tears to his eyes. He didn't want to let Neal see him in such a state, but he had.

Neal patted him on the back. "Cheer up, Freddy. We're going to have enough money to buy ten of those Fords. Then she won't act like that."

Freddy gained back his composure. "I'll buy a five-window coupe, but mine's going to be professionally painted a pagan gold color."

When Freddy turned from the sight of Julie getting into the coupe, Neal's attention was already elsewhere. Blond hair flowing from a gorgeous girl's head had caught his eye. It was Julie's sister, Samantha. A red dress accented her sensuous curves. Her tanned legs flowed down to her baby doll shoes. With her hair swaying lazily behind her and her face partially hidden by sunglass, she slipped lithely past and stopped at the door of a white Cadillac convertible.

Neal was the person everyone secretly wished

they could be. And he seemed to be every place at the same time. Trying to catch up with her before she pulled away, he flashed his engaging smile and hurried toward her.

Freddy ambled toward them and watched. Samantha opened the door, hitched up her skirt, and slipped behind the wheel. Waiting for a hint of recognition, Neal stood alongside the Cadillac. But as if he weren't there, Samantha shifted the transmission into gear and tossed her head. With her hair cascading over her shoulder, she pulled away. She never turned back to see Neal. If she had, she would have seen his baby blue eyes and a smile that could sell toothpaste. She would have felt his incandescent presence that emanated an unseen power.

Neal turned his back to the fleeing Cadillac. Looking dejected, he walked back to Freddy and stopped.

Freddy raised his hand slightly. "I never saw you strike out like that. What happened?"

Neal shrugged. "Who knows? But I'm not worried. Dames are like streetcars. You miss one, there's always another one right after that." He regained his bright outlook. "And anyway, would you rather work on the garbage truck or chase pretty girls?"

Freddy didn't answer right away. Although he wouldn't be back on the garbage truck, lifting heavy cans and smelling noxious fumes, he could imagine what was in store. Just to make something happen, if he had to, Neal would slyly put his hand behind his back, cross his fingers, and shake hands with the Devil. No matter how great the reward, Freddy sensed he would end up in a precarious position. And although he was never ready for it, he couldn't stay away from Neal and the excitement he generated from living on the edge.

Neal crossed his arms and tugged on Freddy's shoulder. "Are you going to answer me?"

"I'm not thinking about girls or that garbage truck," he said. "I'm thinking about the last time you talked me into going to Canada just to get a cup of coffee and a souvenir."

Neal's eyes lit up. "Yeah, wasn't it great?"

"If you call almost getting killed great, then it was the greatest thing since they started putting back seats in cars."

Neal waved his hand in the air and flamboyantly put up one finger. "With the right babe, those back seats are terrific." He patted Freddy on the back. "We didn't get the receipt, but we got the flag and we didn't get killed. And we got enough money to live the good life for a while."

The boulevard sound of dual exhaust pipes thundered in the distance. Freddy's ears perked up. Neal's 1940 hot rod Ford eased around the corner and pulled next to the curb right in front of them. The orange-headed driver cut the engine, slid across the front seat, opened the passenger side door, and grinned an extra wide toothed smile. "Who's running this lunatic asylum?"

No one answered.

It was the other third of the trio: Rafferty Allnut.

Before Freddy had joined up with them, Rafferty and Neal had traveled to South Carolina with big plans to get into the moonshine hauling business. With the intention of hauling one hundred twenty gallons a trip and making seven runs a night, they had planned to clear at least five hundred dollars a day.

Neal bought the 1940 Ford coupe. Then they hung a block and tackle from a tree branch and snatched a big V-8 engine out of a Cadillac Ambulance. When they dropped it into the Ford, with the turbo charger, the engine got an extra one hundred horsepower. This was more than enough to outrun any revenue officer.

Neal usually managed to sweet talk his way into anything. But the big problem was that they were not from the South. And their Yankee accents caused still operators to treat them as if they were federal agents, trying to get enough evidence to shut them down.

With no moonshine to haul, they limped back to Patagonia, bought a broken down dump truck, and used it to haul garbage. Much to their surprise, they turned a profit on a business that was legal.

Sitting on the edge of the front seat of the Ford, Rafferty pulled up one knee, placed his elbow on it, and propped his forehead on his palm. With his green eyes peering from under the wave in his carrot-orange hair, his contagious smile beamed across his freckled face. "Did you guys go in the bank yet?"

"It doesn't take an hour to collect one garbage fee," Neal said. "Where were you?"

With an idiotic look on his face, Rafferty formed a large oval with his mouth and dropped his jaw in mock astonishment. "I haven't been on what some people would call a picnic," he groaned. "I had a flat tire. I would've been here on time, but right after I got the tire changed, some old guy pulled over and wanted to know if I punched his milk horse."

Neal shot Rafferty a playful expression. "Well, did you?"

Rafferty returned the gesture. "No, but I told him that if he was looking for milk horse punchers he should look in the Yellow Pages."

Turning serious, Freddy lifted his hand and pointed at Rafferty. "Did that old guy have a blue Dodge?"

"Yeah."

Freddy reached to the side of his head and adjusted an imaginary hat. "Was he wearing a gray hat turned down on one side like a gangster's?"

As if waiting for Freddy to get to the point, Rafferty tilted his head upward and talked to the ceiling of the Ford. "Yeah, why?"

"That guy asked me the same thing."

Rafferty could always be counted on to sit back and poke fun at serious or terrible situations, and this time he sounded like he was doing just that.

With his mouth ajar, Neal nudged Freddy with his elbow and stared at Rafferty. "What are you guys punching defenseless milk horses for? Are you nuts?"

"We're not punching milk horses." Rafferty took a defensive stance. "That guy was Smeal. He's crazy."

"He looks like he is," Freddy said ignoring Neal's rag. "He reminds me of those gangsters we ran into in Buffalo."

"All those guys from Buffalo are gone." Neal

placed his foot on the running board of the Ford. "And I'm not worried about some nut punching horses."

With a questioning slant, Rafferty leaned his head toward Neal. "Did you go in the bank yet?"

As if he were trying to get the image of Rafferty punching a milk horse out of his mind, Neal shook his head. "We've been in and out."

Anticipation beamed from Rafferty's face. "Did you get the truck?"

"No!" Neal sagged and took his foot off the Ford's running board. With condemnation, he jerked a piercing finger in the direction of the bank. "That broken-nosed sleaze-ball took our down payment."

"They can't do that," Rafferty said, shaking his finger toward the bank for emphasis. "We have a receipt."

Making no effort to disguise his wounded feelings, Neal frowned. "The mob broke the bank president's nose. They got him to rig the system. We're out of the garbage business."

As if he were letting what he had just heard sink in, Rafferty sat still and showed nothing but a blank stare. Talking to the steering wheel, he softly said, "The only thing good about banks is that they are idiots." He was quiet for a while, and then, with tears forming in the corners of his green eyes, he gripped the steering wheel and looked to Neal. "We can't work in the mills. They're laying people off. What are we going to do for money?"

Neal pulled the note from his pocket and handed it to Rafferty. "I think we can dig something up."

As Rafferty quickly read the note, his eyes widened. He looked up. "Peacock Alley?" He snorted with quizzical amusement. "They're going to widen the road there. Maybe the road crew already dug up the foundation."

Neal flashed Rafferty a look of excruciating pain. "Don't even think that."

Chapter 6

After the bars closed and darkness could cloak their actions, Freddy, Neal, and Rafferty jumped in the Ford and hightailed across the state line into Masury, Ohio. As the Ford's headlights lit their way down Standard Avenue, Neal kept the engine purring until they came to a sign that read,

MEN WORKING

Here, he slowed the Ford to a crawl.

Cannon-ball-shaped oilcans with thick wicks nourishing orange flames sat at each end of wooden sawhorses. Black and white striped boards, secured on the tops of sawhorses, blocked the right side of the road and marked the construction site. Beyond the flame's orange glow, a gravel parking lot stretched across the foundation of the former Peacock Alley Bar that had burned down. At the edge of the road, moths flew around a single light bulb glowing above a sign on a tall metal pole. The sign advertised the new bar that had been built further away from the highway. Freddy looked up and read the words, "Melody Lane."

Sitting in the parking lot, a yellow road scraper, a green steamroller, an orange bulldozer, and a five-ton dump truck, waited to be started up and roar into the next day's task of feeding the appetites of the work zones.

As Neal eased on past the parking lot, the outline of the old foundation came into view. Gravel usually covered it, but the construction workers had apparently scraped it away. Now, scarcely visible tops of cement blocks lay exposed in the dim moonlight.

Neal gasped and pointed toward the foundation. "Look over there!"

Two men in suits watched a man with a long nose poke the blocks with a stick.

"Looks like those guys beat us to it," Rafferty said. "But how did they know where to dig?"

Trying to make out the shapes of the men, Freddy strained his eyes, but all he could be sure of was that one of the men had a long nose. "Maybe it's the road crew."

"No way," Neal said with his hand resting on the Koehler beer-tap floor shift knob. "A road crew doesn't work at three in the morning, and the only place I've seen a nose that long was on the guy that broke the bank president's nose."

Rafferty leaned over the seat. "I've never seen anybody with a nose that long. I'd bet he can smoke a king-size cigarette in the rain without getting it wet."

Shaking his head, Neal smiled faintly, gripped the Koehler beer-tap floor shift knob, and hit second gear. "We'll turn around and come back."

"If those guys see you turn around," Freddy said, bending crookedly to watch the men, "they'll get suspicious. Take the long way around." He pointed out the back window toward a semi-secluded wide spot at the side of the road. "They won't see us if we stop above that little hill. Then we can get out and sneak close to the foundation and listen to what they're talking about."

Neal snapped his fingers and shifted into high gear. "That's a good idea. They'll never suspect anyone to park above that little hill."

After a few right turns, they were back on

Standard Avenue. Fifty feet from the wide spot at the side of the road, Neal cut the engine and quietly coasted the Ford to a stop. Making sure not to slam the doors, they all got out. Neal opened the trunk, fished out two long-handled shovels, and whispered to Rafferty, "Here!" He threw a shovel at him.

Rafferty caught it.

Holding the other shovel, Neal continued to whisper, "Those guys don't have any shovels. They'll probably quit looking. When they do, we'll go dig out that shoebox." He inclined his head toward Freddy. "Since you're part Indian, you should go first."

"Wait a minute," Freddy said and held up his hand. "Indians can get shot just as easily as anybody else."

Neal gave Rafferty a secret wink. "That may be so, but the Indians didn't get shot at Little Big Horn."

Neal made a shooing motion with his hand toward the semi-darkness of the field between the parking lot and them. "Go ahead," he said. "We'll be the lookouts."

Nodding weakly Freddy headed into the semi-darkness. With night hugging the land, he crawled through the tall grass of the field that lined the meanders of the stream that cut through the land. Beyond that, a small tangle of blackberry bushes grew on the embankment that led to the gravel parking lot of the replacement building of the Peacock Alley Bar: the Melody Lane Bar.

As tall stands of grass swished with his guarded movements, Freddy hoped he was too far away for the long-nosed man poking the foundation to hear him. When the man lifted the stick and looked toward him, Freddy stopped and got ready to run. He looked back toward Neal and Rafferty. Although they roved the darkness and stopped briefly at strategic vantage points to observe, it didn't look like the long-nosed man had seen them.

Freddy stood still until the man went back to poking the foundation. Then he dropped down and waited a few minutes. Hearing nothing, and without Rafferty knowing it, he crept next to him, lay on his side, and looked up. Leaning on the shovel handle, Rafferty peered into the darkness, but he didn't look down. Freddy tugged at his pants leg and whispered, "Rafferty!"

Rafferty jerked his foot away and jumped about a foot into the air. Grasping the shovel as if he were choking it, he looked down at Freddy and half whispered, half squeaked, "Damn! You scared the crap out of me." Then he wisecracked, saying, "Did I get any on you?"

Freddy ignored Rafferty's attempted humor. "You see anything?"

Rafferty held his finger to his lips and pointed toward the parking lot.

Freddy slowly rose to his feet and squinted into the semi-darkness. The three men had gone, but across the stream and on the other side of the parking lot, the brake lights of a dark 1957 Chevy flashed bright red. Freddy slipped on something. His feet flew out from under him. With a muffled thump, he landed on the soft ground. The fragrance of spearmint gum drenched his face. If any one of the three men were chewing spearmint gum, they would be close enough to spit on him. He tensed and searched the darkness. Nothing moved. When his searching eyes lowered toward the vegetation next to the stream, strips of spearmint plants lay broken on the bank. He let out a sigh of relief and rose to a crouching position.

The taillights of the Chevy dulled to taillight red. It slowly pulled next to the road and coasted to a stop.

With the shovel on his shoulder, Neal crashed through the bushes and stopped in front of Freddy. "Okay, they're leaving." He jerked his thumb toward the foundation. "Let's get up there and dig out that money."

Rafferty burrowed his fists down deep into his pockets and slouched. "I don't mean to get pushy. But wouldn't it be a good idea to wait until they're gone?"

Neal pointed the shovel handle toward the Chevy. "In a second, they will be gone."

With the throaty roar of its duel exhaust purring into the night, the Chevy pulled out of the parking lot. As it sped down the highway, its taillights vanished into the dark.

Without regard to the noise he made, Neal splashed through the little stream, crashed through the berry bushes, rushed up the embankment, and stopped at the foundation. He turned toward Freddy and Rafferty. With one hand leaning on the shovel, he continually swung his arm around and around, signaling for them to come on.

Shaking his head, Freddy smiled at Rafferty. "He'll never change."

"Yep," Rafferty said and hopped over the stream. "Still crazy as ever."

At the foundation, Rafferty stood next to Neal and clunked his shovel into the gravel alongside a cement block. Keeping a wary eye out for the Chevy, Freddy watched Neal feverously sling dirt away from the foundation. In the distance, a jagged shaft of lightning slanted across the heavens and slashed at the dark sky. A rippling crash of thunder followed. Rafferty stopped his enthusiastic digging, leaned on his shovel, and looked at Neal. As if he were a machine with the switch jammed on wide open, Neal didn't stop.

"What are you going to do?" Rafferty asked. "Dig the whole place up?"

Neal kept right on digging. "If I have to, I will. We got to get that big shoebox before those guys come back."

Freddy pointed to a cement block. "The last time we were here, we kicked a block over before we found anything."

Neal continued his frantic pace, but looked up just long enough to say, "So what?"

Just as Rafferty jammed his shovel into the gravel, a web of lightening exploded right above the parking lot. For a moment, a purple and straw-colored haze filled the air. The wind picked up, and thunder pounded louder than before.

"The sky's going to fall on us." Freddy said to Neal. "Instead of digging the whole foundation out, why don't you put the shovel on the end of the block and pry it up. That way you won't have to dig around it."

As if a great realization had entered his mind, Neal stopped his frantic digging. "Ah, um, ahem, of course," he said, as if in thought. "I was just going to suggest just that very thing."

He placed the blade of the shovel under the end of a cement block and pried. The block moved but the block next to it stopped it from coming up. He went to the other side of the block and pried.

Freddy placed his hand on Neal's shoulder. "Let me try it." He bent over, grabbed the block, and pulled. It broke free from its years-old hiding place, but there was nothing underneath but another block. Rafferty brushed his hands together and re-gripped his shovel.

"That's one. Let's get another one."

Neal did the same. Ten blocks later, they hadn't found anything. Neal wiped his brow with the back of his hand. "Maybe those guys in the suits already found it."

"I doubt it," Freddy said with hope. "All they did was poke around with a stick."

Rafferty's face wreathed with a smile. "Maybe that guy with the anteater nose sniffed it out."

Freddy looked at Rafferty and shook his head. Then he stepped down into the narrow opening where the first course of blocks had been pried out. "Let's try this second course."

Neal and Rafferty pried the first block on the second course. It let out a metallic squeak and eased up out of the ground.

"Hey," Freddy said with alarm. "Cement blocks don't sound like that."

"That's right," Rafferty agreed. "That's metal."

Neal leaned over the hole and brushed the dirt away. On the third course down, flat rusty metal glared back at them. Before anyone could speak, Neal grabbed the shovel and pried three more blocks off the top of the metal. He reached down and pulled on the metal. It stayed solid. "Come on, Rafferty," he said. "Let's shovel some dirt away so we can get at it."

Rafferty and Neal jammed their shovel blades into the dirt, scooped it up, and flung it into the air. The metal slowly became what they were looking for: A big metal shoebox.

A great gust of wind whipped down the parking lot and kicked up a cloud of dust. Rafferty squinted against the dust and threw his shovel onto the gravel-covered ground. "That box should come out now."

Neal bent over, pulled the box from its tomb, and sat it on the ground.

At first, Freddy didn't know if it was his heart beating because of the excitement of wanting to know how much money was in the box, or it was someone approaching. But faint vibrations of feet padding on the ground traveled through the thin soles of his shoes and gave him a feeling someone was watching. He shuddered. Fighting the urge to stay and watch Neal open the box, he tiptoed around the bulldozer and hid in its shadow. If someone were watching, their eyes wouldn't be on him. They would be on the box.

Rafferty horned in close to Neal. "Come on, Neal. Open it."

Neal put his fingertips under the edge of the box and pulled. "It's stuck."

Rafferty offered him a shovel. "Whack it with this."

A deep authoritative voice barked out of the dark. "I'll take it from here."

A man wearing a fedora and a pinstriped suit walked from behind the steamroller. "That's right, boys," he said and rubbed his Pinocchio nose. "No use wearing yourselves out."

Rafferty glared at the man. "What do you want?"

With a carefree flick of his hand, the man motioned for them to get away from the box. "Sorry, you boys have to leave."

Grinning and snickering, as though the situation were comic, Rafferty stared at the man's long nose. Then he put his fist on his own nose and made it look like his nose extended down his forearm to his elbow. "We don't want to, Mister Durante," he said, referring to the long-nosed comedian, Jimmy Durante. "It's just getting interesting."

For a moment, the man's mouth dropped open, but he showed no other facial expressions. Rafferty's remarks must have flown over the man's head.

Neal assumed a fighting stance and tensed. "You may have stolen our truck, but you're not taking our box."

As if he were sure he had the power to do anything he wanted, the man reached into his suit jacket and patted under his arm. "I *am* taking *my* box."

As a light rain began to fall, Neal held up his hands in a submissive gesture. "We know when we've been beat." With the look of a kid who wasn't going to get anything for Christmas, he looked down at the box. "We'll go, but just let us see what's in that thing."

The man lifted his hand. Lightning lit the sky.

Its light revealed the tattoo of a skull and crossbones on the back of his hand that Freddy had seen at the bank.

As if shooing a fly, the man waved his hand. "Just back away."

Neal and Rafferty backed away a few feet. When Neal stopped, he placed his foot close to the upturned shovel blade.

Freddy stayed behind the bulldozer and thought about the tattoo. In addition to looking like a fourth grader had drawn it, no one in a good gangster organization would put a tattoo or any identifying marks anywhere on their body. If this guy were a gangster, he wasn't a very smart one. As a signal to Neal, Freddy slowly lifted his hand. Neal saw it. As Freddy watched Neal's foot slowly rise, he crouched to leap.

The man stood over the box, looked around, hunched over, and lifted the box. Just before he straightened up, Neal tromped down on the shovel blade. The long handle flew up and whacked the man in the nose. Bone and cartilage snapped. The man dropped the box, stood up, and barely flinched. As if he had enjoyed getting his long nose broken, a smiled widened across his face. Then as if it were a delayed reaction, he grimaced and grabbed his blood-spurting long nose.

Neal stood over him. "That's for stealing our truck."

The man reached for his gun, but a blinding flash of lightning arced between the steamroller and the bulldozer. In one smooth motion, Freddy performed his favorite move. He sprang from behind the bulldozer, grabbed the tail of the man's suit jacket, yanked it up over the man's back, and pulled it down over his head.

Rafferty picked up a shovel and arched back to swing. "Hey, Pinocchio, if you want to play in the dirt, you have to dig it." He swung the shovel. It whooshed over the man's head and flew out of Rafferty's hands.

Trying to struggle free, the man windmilled his arms. As great drops of rain tumbled out of the sky, Freddy lifted his leg. With one great effort of balancing on one leg, he kicked the arm-whirling man away from the box. The man tumbled backwards and landed on his rear end. Freddy figured they had the man outnumbered three to one. For a moment, he thought about jumping on the man and maybe tie him up. But headlights from a car pulling into the parking lot illuminated the area. Without stopping, Freddy scooped up the box and hightailed down over the embankment and towards the stream. Neal and Rafferty sprinted right behind him.

With gunshots barking into the rain-filled night, they sloshed through the swollen stream and rushed toward the Ford.

When they got to where the land rose to a hump, they stopped just below the Ford and looked up. A dome light illuminated the area around a car parked right next to the Ford. It was the black '57 Chevy that had been in the parking lot. Its headlights beamed across the land, making it impossible for anyone to pop up from the cover of the hump in the land and sprint away without being seen.

A shirtless man with muscles bulging out in

hard swells stood at the driver's side door of the Chevy and breathed deeply. The breadth of his chest and shoulders expanded on a level with another man's head.

Holding a pump action shotgun at the ready, the other man slumped over the trunk of the Chevy. As he shifted his head from side to side, the lights on the Chevy caused the searching eyes on his toad face to glint with death-like silver flashes.

In the dim light, Freddy crouched next to Neal and whispered, "Now what are we going to do?"

Neal wrinkled one eye and wiped the water from his forehead. "They won't hear us in this rain. We'll sneak into the passenger door. I'll start the engine, and we'll be out of there before they know what happened."

Freddy squinted at the shotgun. "We might get shot."

With wide inquisitive eyes, Neal turned his head to the side and stared directly into Freddy's face. "You got a better Idea?"

Holding the metal box, Freddy glanced back toward the parking lot. If they went back there, the man with the broken nose would be just waiting to get even. And he wouldn't hesitate to use his freshly loaded gun. As the rain pattered on his face, Freddy shifted his gaze behind him. The stream had swollen over its banks and created a mushy swampland. Evidently the land upstream had been bombarded with rain. If he tried to run through there, his feet would be sucked into the soft mud. Worse yet, it would be impossible to outrun a shotgun blast.

Neal looked toward the swampland. "You're

not thinking of running through that, are you?"

Freddy turned toward Neal. "I guess not."

Getting ready to crawl, Neal dropped to his belly. "When I get the door open, you guys grab a handful of mud and throw it into the weeds. While they're looking toward the weeds, run up and jump in. I'll already have the motor started. Before they know what's happening, we'll be gone."

In the rainy darkness, Freddy and Rafferty nodded. Neal crawled toward the Ford. At the passenger side door, he rose to all fours and reached up to open it.

But when Freddy and Rafferty clawed at the mud and scooped up handfuls. Then they hunched down and got ready to spring up the hump, the rain stopped. All became quiet.

Neal nodded in their direction. They slung the mud into the tall grass at the side of the road. Before the splat of the mud hitting the ground could be heard, Bam! Whoosh! A shotgun blast blew out the Ford's triangular back windows. Neal jerked back away from the door and slid down the muddy hump.

The shirtless muscular man yelled at the silver-eyed toad-faced man with the shotgun, "Hey, Toad. What the hell did you do that for?"

Toad smiled. "Take it easy, Muscles, I just wanted to make sure it was loaded."

"Shoot out the radiator. If those little bastards sneak back here and try to drive away, they won't get far."

As if to say, "Thank you!" Toad tipped his hat and walked to the front of the Ford. As if it were an everyday thing, he pumped three shotgun blasts into the grill. Steam hissed into a scalding cloud, and for a second, water from the lead-shot-peppered radiator squirted through the freshly perforated bars of the chrome grill and traveled three feet into the night air. The corners of Toad's mouth curled into little yellow-white crescents and formed an ugly satisfied grin.

Neal cussed under his breath and whined, "They killed our car."

Freddy winced. He hated what the man had done to the hot rod Ford, and he didn't like the idea of having to walk back home. Now it was worse than a simple walk in the rain. Between the hump in the land and the Ford, the Chevy blocked their escape, and someone in the Chevy was holding a hand-held spotlight scanning the area right behind them.

Lightning flashed. The land across the road was illuminated for a moment and revealed hundreds of weeds and small trees. In the distance, two long buzzes of a diesel locomotive's horn split the dark night. Beyond the small trees, the dark shaggy outlines of bushes spread as far as Freddy could see. As the steady rhythm of the powerful engines of the diesel locomotive pounded, the light from the lightning flashes stopped, but spaces between the bushes flickered dim-yellow from the headlight on the locomotive. On the other side of the bushes, a railroad track waited for the train to lumber on down the line.

Freddy tugged on Neal's shoulder. "Do you see it?"

"It's just starting to move, but how are we going to get there?"

100

Rafferty whispered close. "Diversion, throw the box."

The box and the promise of money in it, was making Freddy forget feeling like the bank president had stomped him down in the mud. If he threw the box, the feeling would pop back up. He hugged the box close to his chest. "No way."

Neal put his hand on the box. "Take what's in the box out, and throw the box. They won't know it's empty."

"If there's money in it, it'll get wet." Desperation surged throughout Freddy's entire body. "And we don't have time to separate it and stuff it into our pockets."

As if confused, Neal nodded weakly and leaned back. "I got it," he said with relief and elation. He grabbed the bottom of his T-shirt and pulled until it was over his head, and off. Then he leaned over and spread his shirt on the ground. "Open the box and dump whatever's in it on this."

Freddy pried at the lid on the box. It didn't move. "It's stuck."

Neal glanced up at Rafferty. "Keep an eye out while we get this thing open." He looked back at the box, reached over, placed his hands next to Freddy's, and gripped the lid. "Let's both pull."

Freddy and Neal pulled. The box opened with a faint squeak.

Alarmed, Rafferty grabbed Freddy's shoulder. "Somebody's coming."

Without seeing what was in the box, Freddy dumped what was in it onto the shirt. It landed with a muted thud. He pulled the ends of the shirt around it and tied them in knots.

Neal grabbed the empty box and arched back to throw it.

"Wait," Freddy said. "Close it first."

Neal placed the opened box between his hands and pushed. It closed with a loud squeak.

Toad squinted his silver eyes and pointed the barrel of the shotgun in their direction. "The little goons are down there!"

Someone in the Chevy directed a bright beam from the spotlight right into Neal's eyes. As if Neal were the Devil himself, Muscles began yelling.

Blinded by the light, Neal lowered his head and held up his hands. "We give up, mister. You can have the box."

Toad pumped a shotgun shell into the chamber. "Get your asses up here."

Freddy shoved Neal's shirt that had the contents of the box into the front of his shirt and placed it under his armpit. He squeezed the shirt to conceal it. It crunched under the pressure and felt like fresh-from-the-bank, crisp dollar bills.

Like whipped pups, Neal, Freddy, and Rafferty marched up the hump in the land, stopped in front of the Chevy, and stood in the brightness of the headlights.

Freddy waited for Neal to try some of his soft-tongued affability on the duo. Before he could speak, the back door of the Chevy opened. Under the yellow glow of the car's dome light, a man with basset-hound eyes and blond hair turned on the edge of the seat and placed his feet on the ground. He studied Freddy. His eyes shifted to Neal, then to Rafferty. "Are you the kids that stole that key?"

Freddy knew he was referring to the decoding

key they had found and opened the secret vault at the little strip of land called Petroleum, but with Toad holding the shotgun at his back, he wasn't going to admit anything.

The horns on the diesel locomotives buzzed. The train was going to increase speed.

Freddy tried not to look at it, but just for an instant, he felt the revealing sign of a troubled smile flit across Hound Eyre's face. "We didn't steal anything."

Methodically rolling a cigar between his fingers, Hound Eyes grunted with satisfaction. "And you never met a man called Blondie?"

"We know a lot of people who could be called Blondie," Neal butted in. "That doesn't mean a thing."

Hound Eye's lips curled into a sarcastic grin. "Oh... so you admit you know him?"

"Don't put words in my mouth," Neal shot back. "We don't know what you're talking about."

Hound Eyes aggressively jerked his finger at the box in Neal's hand. "And I suppose you have no idea how that box got into your hand."

Rafferty leaned forward and held out his chin. "So what if we don't know how it got there." He giggled. "Maybe we want it to be a surprise."

Hound Eyes growled at Rafferty, and Toad poked the barrel of the shotgun into Neal's back. "Tell the man what he wants to know. Tell him where Capone is."

Neal flinched but didn't jerk away. "Everybody knows Capone died after he got out of prison."

Hound Eyes stared at Neal for a long moment.

"That's a pretty good theory, but we're not buying it."

Freddy knew the man was right. Al Capone's body was hidden under a trap door in the caved-in coalmine where they had found the vault. But if he told them the truth, their value to them would be over. They would be killed immediately, and the train was picking up speed. If they couldn't get on it, keeping their mouths shut would be their only chance to stay alive.

Freddy looked to Neal for a sign. Neal tightened his grip on the box. Freddy knew Neal was going to throw it. He looked to Rafferty. Rafferty blinked his eyes once. He knew Neal was going to throw the box. They were ready to run, but Freddy figured they would have a better chance of getting away if he made the man and his thugs believe the empty box contained something they really wanted.

He pointed to the box in Neal's hand. "We never got a chance to look in the box. Why don't you look in it? Maybe there's a note from Al Capone inside."

All eyes turned toward the box. The headlights of a car flashed down the road.

Adding to the distraction, Rafferty let out a triumphant, "Whoop!" Waving his arm wildly, he motioned for the car to come ahead. "Here he is!" he cried, reached out and pulled Hound Eye's pants down until they were around his ankles. Standing in his underwear, a befuddled, Hound Eyes stood as if his feet had been glued to the road. Rafferty continued. "Your master knows you broke your chain and ran away." He waved his arm at the car.

"Come and get him." He pointed to Hound Eyes. "He's right here!"

As if he had just been slapped and wanted immediate revenge, Hound Eyes lunged at Rafferty. At the last second, Rafferty merely skipped aside and helped Hound Eyes along past him with a strong shove. With his pants down, Hound Eyes stumbled but didn't fall. As if the looming car were going to hit him, Neal leaped sideways and yelled at the top of his lungs, "Watch Out!" He threw the box onto the road, right in front of the oncoming car.

Jolted by Rafferty's smooth move, Neal's unexpected leap, and his booming voice, the mouths on the three thugs went agape. For a precious moment, they froze, their eyes fixed on the box and what the oncoming car would do to it.

Freddy wheeled around, grabbed the barrel of Toad's shotgun, jammed it down into the mud, and took off running. In a blur of action, Neal and Rafferty were right behind him. They sprinted right in front of the oncoming car. With the car's tires squealing and sliding sideways on the wet pavement, the escaping trio sprinted to the other side of the road. Behind them, tires from the oncoming car thumped over the box. After that a muffled shotgun blast sent chills up Freddy's spine. A whining like a wounded animal caused him to look at Neal and Rafferty. They were still running. Freddy figured the mud in the barrel had caused the bullet to explode in the chamber. Toad wouldn't be using that shotgun to ventilate their bodies.

On the other side of the road, they blindly leaped down over the embankment. At the bottom, their feet slipped on wet grass, and low-lying bushes tangled their feet. They tripped and went down like tall grass being cut with a scythe. But they jumped back up and kept on running. Now they were out of the low lying bushes, but supple branches, from little trees, whipped at their bodies and stung their faces. Up ahead, the light from the approaching diesel locomotive brightened the steel tracks in front of it. With his lungs aching for air, Freddy slowed to a trot. Neal and Rafferty slowed and panted to catch their breaths. Thirty feet from the railroad tracks, they stopped.

The train's horn blasted two longs, one short, and one long deafening blare that brought ringing to Freddy's ears. With dirty exhaust fumes spewing into the night air, the engines of the lumbering and rasping diesel locomotives drew near. Pulling a string of grimy tank cars down the twin steel tracks, the engines rose to a throaty roar. As the train increased speed, the engines pounded past and were followed by the tank cars.

Neal looked to Freddy. "Those tank cars are too hard to grab onto on, and there's no place to hide."

Rafferty grinned and broke into a nervous laugh. "It's better than getting shot."

Freddy looked down the line of approaching cars. A tall Westinghouse transformer was riding on a low flatcar. Fresh gray paint covered the six-foot by eight-foot metal sides of the transformer. Cooling louvers protruded around the top, and the bottom was anchored with steel ropes bolted to fasteners that had been welded onto the car's heavy steel floor. On one end of the flatcar, an oily tarpaulin covered another component of the transformer. Freddy pointed to the flatcar. "Let's jump that one. We can get behind the transformer. Bullets won't go through it."

When Freddy looked toward Neal and Rafferty, their heads snapped around. They peered apprehensively in the direction of the road.

Freddy had caught a glimpse of their wary looks. "What's the matter?"

Rafferty put his finger to his lips and pointed to movement in the darkness.

Freddy looked back toward the road. Muscles and Hound Eyes crashed through the tree branches. Apparently, their interest in the box hadn't slowed them down enough, and leniency surely wasn't one of their noticeable attributes.

Without saying a word, Freddy rushed toward the moving flatcar. When he was alongside, he grabbed the grab-iron and swung onto the floor. Neal's balled-up shirt with the contents of the box rolled out the front of Freddy's shirt. Just as it was about to fall off the edge of the car, he grabbed it. With the contents crunching under his grasp, he tucked the balled-up shirt back into his own shirt. To keep a low profile, he rolled and flattened his body against floor of the car. Neal and Rafferty swung on and flattened out in the shadow of the transformer. As the caboose clacked on past the place they had jumped on, a long flash of lightening lit up the night. Freddy focused on the land between the moving railroad cars and the road. Beneath tree branches swishing forward and backward, Hound Eyes and Muscles smashed through, over, and around bushes trying to get to the slow moving train.

Freddy placed his hand on the balled-up shirt that held the contents of the box and let out a sigh of relief. Rain pattered on his head, but it didn't matter if he got a little wet. The train would be gone before Hound Eyes and Muscles had a chance to grab on and follow.

Chapter 7

In the township of Masury, Ohio, a battered fifty-year-old man, known as Smeal, sat on the front porch of his one story house coughing so hard tears ran down his cheeks and jowls. After the spasm passed, he wiped his face and blew his nose. Breathing easier, he let the warm rays of the setting sun stream down on him. He didn't know what had happened to Blondie or the vault, but he was working on it.

He stretched out, got comfortable, and tipped his chair up on two legs. With the knowledge that most gangsters were fools, incompetents, and preferred to stay in familiar surroundings, he was waiting for this common flaw to work in his favor. It would eventually bring someone back that he could follow to the location of Capone's vault. It was a dangerous game, and he wondered if he would live long enough to find out what Blondie had done with the vault. Right now there was hope that he would. He was waiting for the phone to ring.

With a drooping, lined face, seething with rage, hatred, and cruelty, he looked like some sort or apparition out of a Halloween night. On his face, purple scars crisscrossed patches of discolored skin. Although his hands were twisted and ruined, he was still capable of holding a weapon. He could still kill, but the human mind had a way of punishing itself for killing a person. It remembered and relieved the killing again and again. And it never stopped.

Even though Smeal was an old man from the

old days of crime, and his constant coughing signaled that his life was running out, he didn't want to be one of those old stooped-over guys who shuffled around in old secondhand clothes waiting for nothing while they let their ancient bodies get flabby and their minds grew dull and useless. Every chance he got, he stood in front of his black-and-white TV and exercised with the TV fitness guru Jack LaLanne. To keep up his arm strength, he curled a set of ten-pound dumbbells every day. Although this exercise kept his weight down, his rear end remained big and wide.

He rolled up his left sleeve and massaged the reminder of what had happened to him when he was a ten–year-old kid who had tried to fight fair: A bluish knife scar on his wrist.

He reached up, took one last drag off the remains of a cheap cigar, and blew tobacco smoke at a moth flying toward the glow of the yellow light coming from the window of his living room. Then he spit the spent end of the cigar from his mouth. It landed atop a heap of other discarded cigar butts and took its place at the base of a dying azalea bush. He ran his tongue over the left side of his teeth. It felt as if someone had carved half-moons between his upper and lower incisors. When he closed his mouth, the teeth formed the round hole that was the shape a cigar. Years of clamping down on cigars, impregnated with minute granules of sand in their leaves, had worn his teeth into this convenient cigar holder. On his head, a silk band ran around a light gray fedora that matched the hair on the sides of his baldhead. Its brim was turned down on one side, gangster style. He believed his intellect and mobster image made up for his ugly broken-down body.

He took another cigar from his vest pocket, clinched it between his teeth, struck a wooden match, and laid the flame to the tip. Lying back with a half-smile, he exhaled a stream of smoke. Underneath his bushy eyebrows, dark eyes stared thoughtfully into the deepening shadows of dusk.

Even though he was fifty years old, he had lived through a hundred-year carnival of evil doing, but he suffered no bitterness or regret. Long ago he had given up on trying to be an honest person. He had tried but it only reminded him of just how strong the real people in control were and how weak he was. He learned that in this so-called civilized world, it was absolutely no good being on the right side when he could never prevail over those financially favored people who were in the wrong. And police were of no help. They kept jails full just to keep weak people scared.

As if it were a warning from God, the remains of the setting sun sank behind a dark cloud and threw a long dark shadow across his scared face. He tipped the chair back to four legs, defiantly stood up, and faced the black sky. With his hands locked behind his back, his thick lips curled his wrinkled face into a satisfied smile. He had seen and suffered things many people had not.

Eighteen years ago, as a prisoner of war, he was shipped to the Japanese POW camp, Hotel Tacloban. Here he saw the cynical exploitation of the weak by the strong. Mingling with men with missing teeth, missing ears, and missing eyes, he watched fellow soldiers limp around, lame and twisted from unset broken bones, while others were immobilized with infected wounds from being used as ashtrays, punching bags, and bayonet practice. He figured he could make it through, but the Japanese guards set him up. They gave him extra food. Although he shared the food with fellow prisoners, he was much healthier than them. Because he was able, he cared for the sick and helped in any way he could. But all this didn't matter. The guards circulated rumors that he was giving information about his fellow prisoners in exchange for the extra food. When he tried to tell his fellow prisoners what the guards were doing, they didn't believe him. The guards not only stopped his extra food, they took his meager ration and left him to fend for himself. The guards laughed about it, and his fellow prisoners that he had helped wouldn't even talk to him. When he had been sick and helpless and a rat was chewing part of his ear off, he had watched his fellow soldiers steal his meager ration of food and water. When other prisoners were sick, others clustered around them, fed them weak soup, and came away with tears in their eyes. Not one ever came to feed him anything. Even though some prisoners saw God and the American flag as one and the same, not one prisoner visited him or said a simple, "How are you doing?"

He found it hard to believe that prisoners, he had helped, would take advantage of the weak. Incredible overcrowding, filth, and drinking water — the guards had playfully pissed in — caused him to turn into a mere skeleton of his former self. Ankle-deep shit covered his bony feet, and when night fell, the place crawled with worms. But he never whined about it. He had a good reason to play the hand he was dealt. He had seen Capone's vault. If he didn't stay alive, he would never find it again. He battled rats. He battled the essence of death. He fooled the guards and his fellow prisoners. He ate worms, bugs, maggots, snakes, and anything he could find.

When he could stand erect again, he couldn't move faster than a painful shuffle, but when he confronted his so-called friends, they all swore they had not taken anything of his. And the Japanese guards had laughed and went along with them, but Smeal could smell out a bullshit story in any language. He became amazed at how people all around him tried to cash in on every decent impulse and every human tragedy. This glaring face of evil destroyed all hope and any degree of faith he had in his fellow man.

He told himself, "So this how I get repaid for helping people?" Right then and there, he vowed to distrust everyone. He would never give anyone a fair shake. He had become a very cold and different person.

When agony was all he had left, for a while, he did not want to give up the agony because he would have nothing at all. When he learned not to care about anything anymore, he figured no one could do anything worse to him. But he was wrong.

When ragged prisoners lined up for a pitifully small breakfast, one smug Japanese guard lifted a shiny brass bugle to his thin lips, turned toward Smeal, and belted out a sour string of taps. As his so-called fellow prisoners laughed and pointed at Smeal as if he were some kind of idiot, a fellow guard danced on top of a tall rock and sang along in broken English, but instead of singing the words, "Go to sleep. Go to sleep," the guard looked at Smeal and mockingly sang, "You dumm-ee. You dumm-ee."

At first the act didn't bother Smeal. He knew the guards were looking for a reason to shoot him, and knew better than to give them a reason. But when his fellow soldiers laughed, pointed, and jeered him, he needed to fight back. Army training had taught him how to handle guns, memorize maps, break open safes, and kill people with his bare hands, but if he fought back, it would be instant death. But it didn't matter. He decided he was a dummy for not doing something about the mocking guard and his fellow prisoners.

So... on a night when shabby black clouds streamed across an orange moon, he snuck up on the smug-mouthed, bugle-blowing guard, stuck the bugle down the his throat and made it look like he had been dancing around on top of the stone and had fallen face first, causing the bugle to be forced into his throat.

At first, the killing and the coppery odor of fresh killed bodies that followed him into his sleep bothered him. But he knew he couldn't let his life be dominated by fear, and he couldn't lapse into a feeling of being safe. A sense of fatalism may have helped, but he considered himself the master of his fate. He decided to lash out, and he did. When he strangled the prisoner who had caused him to almost starve to death, he knew he had found the easy solution to any problem. He killed it. In doing so, another side of the human will to survive surfaced. He became a coldly efficient killing machine that seldom made a mistake and often withdrew into himself. At times remote and aloof, he had gotten used to death.

After he had successfully escaped from the prison camp, the war was over. Although the Army suspected he had intentionally murdered men for food to survive, they could never prove it. To save the trouble of a lengthy report or a court martial, they gave him a general discharge. After which he had had tried to get help from the Veterans' Administration, but the lazy, uncaring people in that corrupt organization wouldn't even acknowledge he had been a Prisoner of War.

All he had wanted to do was go home, go straight, marry a nice girl, and settle down to enjoy the land he had fought for. But when he told of the conditions at the POW camp and what he had went through, the Veterans' Administrations' doctors nodded, turned away, and whispered to each other as if he weren't there.

One doctor said, "This guy's sick. We can't believe a cockamamie story like that."

Rumor was that Army investigators had been paid so much money that they wouldn't talk if they had their mouths opened with a crowbar. Those in the know called it gratuitous collateral damage. Looting, bribes, and payoffs took precedence over prosecuting people for prisoner abuse. So, no one was convicted.

Smeal had wanted to change. Although he had the symptoms of what they called battle fatigue – headaches, nightmares, flashbacks, difficulty sleeping, and always on edge – the Army offered no lectures on what to do after he got out. In fact they called his symptoms malingering. It was incapable of helping him.

Fed up with the rigged system of the government, he knew he couldn't go straight without pretending to be ignorant of the real system that controlled people. He joined up with a gang of men who did not stop at murder. They had been one of the first underworld powers around Youngstown, Ohio. For years they operated without the law's outside interference at Halls Corners. Here handpicked underworld rulers protected a sprawling gambling empire. Every type of illegal gambling imaginable was inside, even cover-all Bingo, for the older folks, could be played at The Jungle Inn Casino.

Rumored to be secretly backed by the Jewish members of the ruthless Purple Gang out of Detroit, twin Walker brothers, Jack and Bob, operated the Jungle Inn. Although Jack Walker had been sentenced to twenty years for murdering a man near Chardon, Ohio in 1931, a year later he was granted a full pardon.

Having a military background and known to keep his mouth shut, Smeal manned a machine gun behind one of the gun turrets in the Jungle Inn. Not only did the turret room kept him out of sight of law enforcement and anyone who might recognize him from his crime days before the war, it provided him a room where he would be away from crowds that made him uneasy, and it kept him away from people when one of his uncontrollable coughing spells erupted.

The Inn generated more than enough money to

bribe people in positions of authority. But no matter who was paid off or on the take, most people loved the Jungle Inn. It was plush and the cordial atmosphere had a stylish tone. After all, illegal gambling wasn't hurting anyone, and when the police treated Jack and Bob Walker tenderly, no one complained.

People like Elliot Ness and Melvin Pervus, looking for a reputation, dubbed the successful casino a den of blatant gangland rebellion, where gangsters with the syndicate had helped rule the underworld, including Buffalo, Cleveland, Chicago, and Detroit. They literarily defied law enforcement officers, and it seemed as if no strong counter action would ever be taken by people in authority.

During the John Dillinger depression days of the thirties, bank closings, mortgage foreclosures, and thrift scandals caused many people to root for bank robbers. After all, the banks had taken many people's life savings and returned pennies on the dollar. Multitudes of people hated banks and said that Dillinger was only using a gun to do what the banks had done with pen and paper to the working people of America. Newspapers played fast and loose with the facts and blew up stories, sometimes making legends out of sociopaths. But those days didn't last.

Eventually, bombings and murders amongst the gangsters projected an image of the Jungle Inn as a source of danger from which no one was safe.

On the thirteenth day of August 1949, Smeal walked beneath the fluorescent lights that illuminated the spacious thirty-thousand-square-foot gambling section of the Jungle Inn. Sturdy wooden legs of handsome leather chairs and poker tables rested on the large red and black blocks of linoleum that conceal a cement floor. Light brown veneer paneling covered the walls, ceilings, and pillars of the inside of the building. To the right of the cashier's cage, two gun barrels pointed out of semi-circular slots of a gun turret in the wall.

Smeal stepped through a side door, climbed a three-foot ladder, and stepped into the gun turret room. After relieving the man in the room and being updated on the goings on of the Inn, Smeal took off his suit coat and sat on a specially built wooden highchair. To his right, two blackjacks hung from the top of the chair. Beneath his feet, a foot-high platform with slanted legs supported his feet. Behind him a fly swatter with a wire handle hung from a wooden shelf support. He leaned over, placed his head into the semi-circular space of the metal gun turret, and peered through the four skinny slits just big enough for the barrels of his Thompson machine guns to stick through and fire.

At the rear of the night club, three bingo players entered the only entrance to huge building and passed long rows of sixty slot machines that included two fifty-cent type, seventeen twenty-five-centers, eighteen ten-centers, and twenty-three five-centers.

A few teen-age boys and girls who looked to be seniors in high school intermingled with older people who probably came to wager their pension checks to win five hundred, and three hundred dollar jackpots, playing bingo games that cost a dollar for sixteen games and ten cents for each extra card in the final game. Chuck-a-luck games and slot machines attracted mostly women, but men dominated the poker and crap tables.

On the walls, in back of four chuck-a-luck tables, huge boards not only posted results of the horse races at the country's major horse racing tracks, they also gave complete information on the names of horses, jockeys, scratches, times of races, and the mutuals.

Two huge crap tables and two poker tables with a seating capacity of eight players and the dealer completed the scene.

As Smeal watched, he noticed that everything inside the inn was going as usual. That was until Sophie Tupper, the wife of the inspector in charge of the State Liquor Department's Cleveland district walked in with her husband Rowan. The first thing Smeal noticed was Sophie. She kept watching the moneychangers at the rear of the casino, who were emptying money from their aprons and putting it into bags. Figuring something was about to happen, Smeal yelled through the turret's slots and asked for Jack Walker.

Wearing his tailored suit, Walker climbed the three-foot ladder, stepped into the turret room, and looked to Smeal. "What's the problem?"

"Sophie Tupper and her husband are in the building. They look suspicious."

"Thanks for the sharp eye out," Walker said. "But I wouldn't worry about it. Everybody's been paid off."

"But they keep looking around."

Walker laughed. "They're probably a little nervous because they don't want to be seen gambling. Like everybody else, they're just here to have a good time." He looked at the gun turret's slot. "If you see somebody starting trouble, just stick the shotgun thought the slot and rattle it."

Smeal smiled. "Many times when he had rattled the shotgun's barrel in the turret's slot, people had stopped in their tracks. Scared for only few seconds, they always continued to gamble.

Although Walker didn't seem to be worried, Smeal didn't like the way the Tuppers were acting. "Are you sure?"

"We'll be okay," Walker said with agitation creeping into his voice. "I did a lot of political favors and shelled out a lot of money. We'll continue to operate as usual."

Smeal nodded in agreement, but he was still uneasy.

At 8:30 in the evening, as a mob of bingo players, trying to win a one thousand dollar prize and large home appliances, watched and waited for the winning numbers to be called, nineteen men dressed in brown suits and various colors of ties with their top coats open, entered the gambling room. To Smeal, they looked like lawmen. Although they didn't seem to be there to cause trouble, Smeal kept a wary eye on them.

At exactly 9 p.m., two men who had the same shape mouths and noses entered the gambling room side by side. From their ill-fitting ties and off-the-rack white shirts, Smeal recognized them. State liquor enforcement officers, Chief Dunham, and his sidekick, Lenis, had been on other raids.

Dunham asked the man standing at the door something, but Smeal couldn't hear what it was. The man took a defiant stance and didn't answer.

Dunham stared at the man for moment, then walked to the center of the room and stopped in front of the man wearing a harness supporting the bingo microphone in front of his face.

Annoyed at having the game interrupted, the man stopped calling bingo and looked to Dunham. "What do you want?"

Dunham pointed to the microphone. "Announce to the patrons that they should leave the premises."

The bingo caller boldly stood his ground. "What for?"

"I have a search warrant for liquor and gambling equipment."

The bingo caller held his hand over the microphone and whispered to Dunham, "Let me finish the game."

As if he didn't hear the caller's request, Dunham persisted. "Announce to the patrons that they should leave the premises."

The caller's eyes narrowed. "I'll have to have orders from the boss."

Dunham arrogantly tilted his head to the side. "Just where is your so-called boss?"

The caller pointed toward the doorway. Dressed in a blue suit, Jack Walker was standing there.

Pointing to Walker, Dunham faced the bingo caller and told him, "Go to your boss and get your orders."

The bingo caller hesitated. Then removed the microphone from its holder, placed it on the table, and walked over to Walker.

Dunham picked up the microphone, held it to

his mouth, and addressed the people, "Ladies and gentlemen, I am State Liquor Enforcement Chief Dunham." He gestured toward Lenis. "I am in the company of State Liquor Director Lenis and other inspectors."

Waves of muffled grumbling surged through the crowd. Dunham glared at the crowd and continued. "We have a search warrant to search this place for intoxicating liquors and gambling devices."

"So what?" Someone yelled from the crowd. "We came here to play bingo. There's nothing illegal about that."

A hint of frustration crossed Dunham's face. He exhaled and continued. "Unless you leave the premises, we will be unable to perform our duty. I request that you all leave."

A loud howl erupted from the patrons.

The slot machines quit rolling and ringing.

The bingo players stood up.

A gray-haired lady in a purple sweater shook her fist and screamed. "Give us a chance to get our money back."

A cussing man wearing a brown vest and a white shirt stood in front of the long row of horserace results blackboards. He picked up his chair and held it, ready to throw. Looking directly at Dunham, he yelled, "You're not wanted here, go home."

A man's voice from the crowd yelled, "Shoot the son-of-a-bitch, Jack."

All the agent's eyes turned toward the man. With one shirtsleeve rolled up, he pulled the arm on a slot machine. It jangled with a payoff. The agents looked toward the slot machine.

The man hollered back over his shoulder, "Go away. This thing's paying off."

Table game players folded their hands, threw down their cards on the green felt, stood up, and watched. The chuck-a-luck operator paid off his last roll and reached under the counter.

A lady in a gray housecoat stood up, shook her fist and yelled, "We want our money back."

"Yeah," a man with thick glasses added, "what are you trying to pull?"

Other players joined in, demanding their money back.

Dunham held up his hand. The crowd calmed down and listened. Dunham talked into the microphone. "I cannot answer your questions."

Another ear-piercing howl came from the bingo players. In the other section of the inn, people at the bar quickly downed their drinks, stormed into the gambling section, and began cussing. People seated at the various two hundred dining tables threw down their silverware, ripped the napkins from their chests, and stood up.

Pandemonium erupted.

Walker looked to Dunham. "See what you started. Why don't you just leave?"

As if expecting pity, Dunham held up his hands. "I can't leave now. There's too much trouble."

An inspector, Smeal didn't recognize, walked up to Dunham and whispered in his ear.

Dunham turned toward the microphone and announced, "The owner will refund your money. Go to the cashier's desk."

The crowd calmed to a grumbling multitude.

Still grumbling, the bingo players got up in an orderly fashion and walked to the cashier's cage. While Dunham watched from inside the cage, Jungle Inn employees began refunding money.

As dust and exhaust fumes from the many cars leaving the gravel parking lot filled the night air, like tongue-less wraiths, the bingo players stood in a long line.

After a thousand nightly gamblers cashed out and filtered out of the building, Dunham could find no liquor in the gambling section of the building. With no liquor found he had no authority. He called the Trumbull County sheriff for assistance. While they waited for him to arrive, Jack Walker's brother, Bob came into the room wearing his signature black and white shoes and blue suit. He stood directly in front of Dunham and violently cussed at him and other agents. When he turned to leave, an agent blocked his path.

"Get the hell out of my way." Bob physically plowed the agent out of his way and left the building.

Smeal figured Bob was going to get help or find out why the payoffs were being ignored.

Encouraged by Bob's aggressive action, a Jungle Inn employee approached Dunham. "Where's your authority to search the premises?"

Dunham held his hand over the breast pocket of his brown suit coat. "I have a warrant. If you can identify yourself as the owner or a manager, you can examine it."

"I don't have to identify a damn thing to your stupid ass." The employee turned, stopped and turned back. "I'll find out who has authority here." He turned and walked toward the main entrance. An inspector blocked his exit. The employee forcefully pushed the inspector out of the way.

Dunham shouted to the inspector, "Hold that man."

The inspector regained his balance and reached for the man.

Jack Walker yelled at Dunham, "Hey, you rotten son-of-a-bitch, where's your authority to do anything?"

When the inspector looked to Walker, the employee avoided his grasp and rushed outside.

Dunham puffed up and held out his chest. "I have a warrant from Trumbull County Common Pleas Judge. It makes me an officer of the Trumbull County Court."

Walker did not ask to see the warrant. Instead, he shouted at Dunham, "I don't give a rat's ass what you have or don't have, you shit-eatin' weasel. This is not Trumbull County. It's Halls Corners."

Smeal felt Walker was correct in claiming that Dunham did not have legal authority in Halls Corners. Although the little village was called Halls Corners, it was situated on two hundred acres on the southeast corner of Trumbull County. Originally it was incorporated to secure a liquor license and defeat the Liberty Township electors, who had made the sale of liquor by the glass illegal. Halls Corner's nine voters were all Halls Corner city officials who were personally connected with the Jungle Inn. The mayor operated the bar at the inn. He appointed councilmen and two marshals to enforce the law. The county sheriff claimed he had

125

no right to interfere with local government unless the village's officers called for help. Establishments with state liquor licenses were not permitted to have any form of gambling on the premises. No one was permitted to bring in or drink alcoholic beverages into the gambling hall. But gamblers could walk five feet away from the casino, exit, and step into a separate building not technically connected to the casino. The Jungle Inn nightclub. Here they could legally absorb all the gambling pleasures they wanted.

As if he knew something Walker didn't, Dunham smiled a mocking smile. "We'll see who has authority."

In order to continue the Jungle Inn's gambling operations, Walker had not only paid large amounts in cash to key people, he had also provided services to authorities. After the Hollyhock Gardens Night Club had been eliminated, the Jungle Inn was no longer in competition with that gambling hot spot. As a result the gambling business at the Jungle Inn had greatly improved. The inn had spent over seventy-five thousand dollars to remodel. Smeal knew Walker was in no mood to let some arrogant agent shut him down.

Walker yelled back at Dunham. "You bastards welshed on your deal."

Dunham defiantly shot back, "We had no deal. We don't accept bribes."

Walker's anger rose. He shouted to his employees, "We're being robbed by the assholes we pay to protect us." He waved his hands around in the air. "Who's the crooks now?"

Dunham gestured to his agents. "Okay, boys,

126

let's fill up the van and haul this illegal gambling equipment away."

Walker thrust his finger into Dunham's chest. "What do you mean haul away?"

Dunham began to answer, but Walker cut him off. "You started this mess. I fixed it by giving money back. Now you want to shut me down?"

Dunham stepped back one step and assumed a high-and-mighty attitude. "I'm shutting you down, and I'm taking anything I want."

Walker's loud strained voice echoed in the huge room. "Your liquor control agents, not gambling agents." He spread his arms and gestured to the gambling section. "There's no liquor here. You have no right to take anything."

A self-satisfied smile beamed from Dunham's face. "It doesn't matter."

Walker's eyes opened wide with alarm. "Get the hell out of here."

Smiling, Dunham reached into his vest pocket. "I don't have to. I have a search warrant." He pulled out the warrant information and waved in front of Walker's face. "This gives me the right to look for alcohol and gambling devices." He turned his nose up triumphantly. "I'm not going anywhere. This rat hole is officially shut down."

Walker didn't look at the warrant. As his face darkened with mountainous wrath, he launched into a string of vulgarities. With his fist waving in the air, he screamed to Smeal behind the wall, "Kill him! Jock, kill him!"

Constrained silence filled the inn, but nothing happened. Even though Jock was the name Smeal was using, he didn't respond.

With his eyes flaring up with fiery fury, Walker pointed at Smeal's gun turret and screamed rapidly in succession, "Jock, don't let this crook rob us. Shoot the son-of-a-bitch."

Smeal place his finger on the trigger of the machine gun and began the slow squeeze. He almost opened up with warning bursts over Dunham's head. But with at least nineteen agents inside and more outside, he would need the help of the other turret men. But his POW days wouldn't let him trust anyone. He had to put up with the nightmares and flashbacks of what his fellow prisoners had done to him, but there was no way he was going to trust the other turret men. He knew they wouldn't fire. If he fired, he would take the whole wrap. Even if he didn't kill anyone, he would still go to jail. The agents would dig into his past. They would discover he had been wanted before the war. Then just like they had done when he was a POW, his so-called friends would watch. The agents would painfully jerk his hands behind his back, clamp their so-called silver wrist jewelry on his wrists, and give him a free trip to jail. He had suffered enough when he was a POW. He could no longer live a claustrophobic life like that. He had sworn he would never be locked up again. He didn't shoot.

Smiling, Dunham looked to the right of the cashier's cage. In an attempt to scare Dunham and the agents out of the building and end the fiasco, Smeal thrust the machine gun barrel out of the semi-circular slot of the turret.

Instantly, Dunham's smile was replaced with a look of terror. While Walker ran toward the cashier's cage, Dunham inched his way away from the threatening turret.

George Crafton, one of the liquor agents Smeal recognized, stepped to the side door to the turret. Then he climbed the three-foot ladder leading into the gun turret and stepped into the turret room. When he looked into Smeal's face, Smeal tried to turn away, but he was too late.

A familiar look of recognition filled Crafton's face. "I know you," he said. "I could arrest you right now."

Smeal scooped up two shotguns and pointed them directly at Crafton. "Go ahead. Try it. I'll blow your guts out. After you suffer a while, I might feel pity for you and blow your head clean off."

Gripped by a sudden coughing seizer, Smeal felt his face reddened and his broken POW body shake violently.

As the barrels of the shotguns in Smeal's hands dropped with each cough, Crafton held up his hands in surrender. "I'm not here to arrest you, Smeal." A slight smile formed on his lips. "Hell, you'll probably die on the way to jail. I'm only following orders. Give me the shotguns and you can disappear."

Smeal quit coughing, regained his composure, lifted the barrels of the shotguns, and trained them on Crafton's stomach."

With the smile gone from his face, Crafton talked in a no-nonsense manner. "Face it, Smeal. You're outnumbered. You shoot me, you'll go to prison for life."

The agony of his POW days flashed in Smeal's

mind. There was no way he was going to get sent back to any type of confinement. There were too many agents. He would not get away with killing anyone. He lowered the guns. Crafton reached over and gently took them from Smeal's hands. Nodding in approval, Crafton stepped out of the turret room.

Seeing Walker in the private office next to the cashier's cage, Crafton waved the two shotguns in his direction and ordered him to, "Get out of that cage."

Walker didn't come out. He yelled at Crafton, "Get rid of the shotguns, and I might come out."

After a few tense minutes, Crafton reached into the gun turret room and handed the shotguns back to Smeal.

Five minutes later, Walker came out of the office and talked to Crafton and Dunham. "You're state liquor agents, you have no authority here."

Dunham seemed to be gaining some of his arrogance back. He leaned back, crossed his arms across his chest, and looked directly at Walker. "The sheriff is on his way."

"Don't hold your breath," Walker said. "He won't go back on his word."

Smeal knew the sheriff would take his time or not show up at all. He had to be miffed that he had not been notified of the raid.

As if he weren't concerned, Dunham waved his hand down. "The state police will cover until he gets here."

Smeal laughed. He knew the state police wouldn't assist the agents either.

While the agent's waited for the sheriff, the

parking lots outside emptied. The only thing the state police did was to aid disappointed patrons as they left the area. When that was done, the state police left. This left the twenty-man liquor force on its own.

A little before 10 p.m., carloads of underworld overlords and their obedient underlings arrived. The overlords and employees from the inn placed crates, sawhorses, pieces of wood and anything they could get their hands on and barricaded the entrance to the parking lot. This kept cars out and blocked in the two trucks the liquor agents had brought to remove the gambling equipment. The employees took up positions around the buildings and surrounding grounds. Anyone not connected with the underworld was barred entry to Jungle Inn property.

The liquor agents had no telephones inside. A two-way radio in one of the agent's car was their only communication.

Using the radio, Dunham broadcast several messages asking for support. One request went to the Youngstown police chief, but he sadly replied that his police force could not legally make any arrests in Trumbull County. But the police chief assured Dunham that he would keep a full shift of men on call, just in case some of the Trumbull county men could be deputized.

Dunham tried to contact the Governor. The governor was at Cleveland Municipal Stadium, where the Indians were losing to the Chicago White Sox by the score of six to five.

As the agents continued to wait for the sheriff, Walker and other members of the Jungle Inn

131

management taunted the liquor agents.

"You're licked," a strong-armed employee told an agent. "You haven't found any liquor. You're not going to make any gambling arrests."

"Yeah," another broad shouldered employee added. "You might as well take your big trucks and drive back to Columbus."

"You can't mess with us," Dunham said with authority. "How many times do I have to tell you? We're from the Ohio Department of Liquor Control."

Walker stood in front of Dunham. "You're beat. Get out of my club."

Dunham stubbornly stood his ground. "We're not going anywhere."

The standoff continued.

Outside, newspaper employees from The Youngstown Vindicator had been notified that state liquor agents had raided the Jungle Inn. A reporter, the acting city editor, and a staff photographer had raced to Halls Corners to cover the story. They were trying to get into the Jungle Inn. When they tried to enter the casino, several scowling Jungle Inn employees forcefully stepped in front of them. One employee with a voice of authority said, "You can't go in there. It's private property"

The acting city editor stood his ground. "Who's in charge here?"

"A burly employee dressed in a brown suit coat and purple tie stepped forward. I'm in charge." He pointed to the parking lot, and then jerked his finger at the city editor. "Now, you! Get out."

As the unruly Jungle Inn employees shoved the newspaper people around, one of the disgruntled employees attempted to take the photographer's camera. The Jungle Inn employee didn't get it, but other employees managed to steal the photographer's file holders and break the flash attachment on the camera.

Just before things got out of hand, a voice with authority called out, "No rough stuff."

The employees backed off. The newspaper employees breathed sighs of relief and made their ways to their automobiles. When they called the state highway patrol and tried to get them to retrieve the stolen file holders, the state highway patrol told them that the law only permitted them to intervene in traffic law enforcement.

When the sheriff arrived, the clock on the wall read 11:30 p.m. With his gray fedora cocked to the side, he peered through his black, plastic-framed glasses and said, "We don't want any Vindicator men in here."

After adjusting his black tie and clearing his throat, the sheriff didn't give the state liquor men the help they had been waiting for. He took the cap off a bottle of liquor that had been confiscated and smelled it. The liquor agents waited for him to announce it was alcohol, but he announced, "It's only wine vinaigrette. They use it for salads."

Not wanting to be photographed or take a chance of getting arrested, Smeal managed to sneak out of the building and make his way through the wooded area behind the Inn. He found out later that the agent raiders had confiscated eighty-three slot machines and all the gambling equipment. The sheriff arrested clerks, bartenders, and a maintenance man. After he had charted a bus and transported the fifteen employees to the county jail, it was three a.m.

At 9 o'clock Saturday morning, as the birds of morning finished their first songs of the day, twenty Jungle Inn men stood in front of the Judge.

Their council was quick to defend them. "Your Honor, no liquor has been found." He lowered his gaze and shook his head. "The liquor agents had no authority to arrest anyone. Gambling law enforcement is strictly up to Turmbull County officials." He gestured to the men. "These honorable men should be set free and the equipment released."

No one was ever charged with paying or accepting a bribe, and no one went to jail. "Confiscated money," from the slot machines, paid fines ranging from one hundred to one thousand dollars. Although a standoff, unmatched in the history of the country had happened, on the thirteenth and fourteenth day of August 1949, the law closed the doors to the Jungle Inn Casino and nailed them shut.

***

When word of the Jungle Inn reopening occasionally surfaced, it always excited Smeal. The rumor that the nephew of the former Halls Corner's mayor, who had been treasurer for the Jungle Inn, still had political pull, excited a lot of people, but Smeal knew better. The nephew had only worked as a parking lot attendant at the Jungle Inn, and his so-called financial expertise had come from his ability to make change.

Although former patrons of the Inn wanted it to re-open, the media had convinced the general public and law makers that the Jungle Inn must stayed closed because it brought gangsters into Trumbull and Mahoning counties and corrupted public life.

The passage of time showed the closing was no deterrent to crime. Jack Walker was told to quit the gambling business, retire and live the easy life. But he didn't listen. He started to get back into the gambling business, maybe start another Jungle Inn and make millions again. On a Saturday morning in June of 1961, while waiting in his front yard for a golfing partner to arrive, Jack Walker was putting golf balls on the lawn of his Warren, Ohio home. A 1959 Chevrolet sedan stopped at the corner of Kenilworth and South Avenues. A man in the back seat stuck a shotgun out the window and fired three rounds of 12-gauge double-O-buckshot. The first shot tore up the ground at his Walker's feet. The second blasted the basement window casing on his house, but the third shot hit him in the abdomen, hip and thigh. Even though he made it to the hospital, he died.

People in power wanted Jack Walker and any other enterprising individual out of the gambling business, and they had proved they had the means to do it. On top of that, the river gang from Detroit was passing themselves off at the vicious purple gang. They had even monopolized the Jukebox business.

Smeal figured he would be next, but he lived on. Being a bullshit artist who hung around men who lived on the outside of the law, made their own rules, stole anything, and hurt anyone who got in their way, Smeal had never believed he would live to be fifty years old. The Mafioso oath he had taken: "You come in alive and you go out dead. The gun and knife are the instruments by which you live and die," should have made his life short. But it hadn't.

In 1954, his house had been blown up, but he wasn't home. In 1955, a bomb was placed in his car, but it failed to explode. In 1960, he survived two shotgun blasts. By all percentages he should be have been dead years ago. He was sick of the killing and had tried to stay away from it. But when two big laughing bastards said he was nothing but an elephant-assed runt and threatened to break him in half, and then laughed and pointed at him as if he were some kind of an idiot, they reminded him of the Japanese prison guard with the bugle. And he hated them for it.

He had planned to shoot them both, but when he wore his expensive wig to cover the hair loss from his POW days, one of the men had said a fifteen-pound rat had died on his head. So, he sent a message that shooting was too good for the two laughing bastards. That night he choked one of the men to death, cut off his head, and dumped the man's body in the driveway of the other man's home. Then he tossed the man's head on to the front porch. They never laughed at him again. And his house or car was never blown up again.

Every day he wondered if he had been killed and his long life was only a dream. To make sure he wasn't dead, he reached up and tapped himself in the forehead. The pain from the tender bullet scar signaled he was still alive.

Then his thoughts would drift to the sad fact that it was no good to be alive when he had no big money to do anything? Sure he had made money, but what most people did not know was that over fifty percent went for protection and taxes to the families who run the Mafia territories. The other fifty percent should have been more than enough for twenty men's retirements. But back then the money had been so easy to get that he had not worried about how he would get more. So he had spent it freely. He figured he could always open up a gambling joint, a miniature version of the Jungle Inn. But the sheriff was cleaning up Youngstown. Jack Walker had been shot for his troubles, and with the Detroit river gang having a reputation of the vicious purple gang, they were now in charge. Smeal had no real way to make easy money, and he needed a source of income. He had never paid taxes, and he was too young to collect Social Security. There was no retirement fund for him.

The existence of Al Capone's vault was supposed to be a myth. But Smeal knew different. Like warm light from a friendly sun filtering through dark clouds, a few loose ends that could pull him to the vault had beamed through. If he could tug on a few of them, it would be better than hitting a slot machine jackpot at the old Jungle Inn. Then with the money the gold vault would bring, he'd regain something of his youth and begin to live again.

His telephone inside his house rang. "It's about time," he said out loud, jumped up, and grabbed the handle to the screen door. The phone quit ringing. A sly grin spread across his lips. One ring was the signal that they had some information and they were going to call again. He sat back down and waited

137

for the next call.

Although he looked old and inactive, he lived near Brookfield, Ohio, and never got completely out of the crime loop. In the 1920's and early 1930's the township had easy access to whiskey and gambling and was referred to as "Little Canada." Mill workers, railroad men, gamblers, prostitutes, burglars, con men, drunks, derelicts, cutthroats, and murderers called this place their home. It was all there, debauchery and degradation, poor people, rich people, working stiffs, misery, and death.

Bar, gambling-house, and brothel owners bribed crooked politicians who allowed the infamous area to freely exist. Secretly proud of their unwritten reputation as the wickedest city in the Western Hemisphere, few citizens complained about these carnivals of vice and corruption.

If Smeal took a short drive down South State Line Road, hung a right turn on Route 62, crossed the Ohio state line, and rumbled across a little bridge, he would be in the old, promised land of brothels and bars. Here the Green Parrot Tavern still existed. Although it was only a neighborhood bar now, back in the 1930's it had been a four thousand square-foot casino surrounded with a frame built from the thick planks taken from the wood floors of railroad boxcars. To stop bullets, steel plating, three quarters of an inch thick, lined the walls. Steps that led upstairs to the club had a buzzer, and the doors were opened and closed electronically. Before patrons were let in, two big ape-like fellas with machine guns frisked them. Inside, the notorious gangster, John Dillinger, occasionally dealt cards.

138

Although, John Dillinger's boss, "Legs Diamond, was killed by the mob that was backing him in the club in the "Forty-nine" District of Masury, named after the streetcar, stop there, Dillinger openly lived there. He could jump on just about any train and go anywhere he wanted. And the police and the FBI never figured it out.

His neighbors on Edmund Street knew him as Smitty, the man who gambled and played cards at the Green Parrot Tavern and at Torma's Tavern on Brookfield Avenue. Even though Dillinger wore his hat tilted to the side and walked with a mobster swagger, local residents fondly remembered him as a regular guy. If you were caught up in the throes of the depression, he would give you the shirt off his back.

The girl that did housework for him said that he was a real nice gentleman, but FBI Director, J. Edgar Hoover, said Dillinger was a cheap, boastful, selfish, tight fisted, pug-ugly gangster. Even though Hover was in charge of the FBI, people didn't put too much in faith in him. He had never been out in the field, had never been in the line of danger, and he had never made a single arrest. Some people believed the FBI was nothing but an organized bunch of nitwits, making excuses to keep from meeting up with this brilliant criminal.

Just a jaunt down the road from The Green Parrot, establishments like The Blue Danube, The Gray Wolf — also called Pete Myers's Place — and The Clover Club, with its nearby green cement block house of prostitution, known as "The Block House", had operated without interference from anyone. When police raided these places, Smeal figured the only reason the government interfered with these enterprising businessmen was because they weren't getting tax money from them. And he reasoned that the government wasn't the ones putting their asses on the line all the time, so they weren't entitled to a damn cent.

After Smeal had dozed off on his front porch, sirens mourned far away. He jerked awake. All around him, from every side, the sound immediately soared to a braying onrushing cacophony. He jerked to his feet and peered into the darkness. Out on the main road, just down from his house, a lone black and white police car, with red lights flashing, sped past. He was glad the police thought of him as a useless old man and were no longer interested in him. But it hadn't always been like that.

Chapter 8

Hiding from the law early in July of 1934, Smeal had spent three days tossing and turning on a damp coffin-sized cot. Looking for a diversion, he had waited until the streets were in shadow. Then he had gone to the Green Parrot Tavern. Before he could walk up the stairs to the gambling den, a man put his hand on his shoulder and tried to push him away from the door. With a flick of his arm, Smeal slammed the man across the parking lot. A man in an expensive suite laughed and patted him on the back. Smeal flexed his right hand and turned toward the man.

The man held up his hand. Although a little portly, the man was stiff-spined with square shoulders and he held his head high. His eyes surveyed the scene as though he not only owned the building, but the people inside. "Don't get excited." The man smiled. "I like the way you operate."

Smeal cast a suspicious look at the man. "Do I know you?"

The man smiled big. "I can spot an old five-point gang man a mile away."

Smeal studied the man. The five-point gang was a ruthless gang out of New York that would kill a person for his shoes or a sandwich in a lunch pail. He had never been in that gang. Maybe the man was mistaken. When Smeal recognized the man, he was taken aback. "But they sent you to prison."

"Almost," the man said, bowed slightly at the waist, and opened the door. "Go on up. My friends and I will follow."

As usual, Smeal was stopped at the top of the

stairs by two thugs with machine guns. With their eyes full of fire, they raked back and forth at the man who had come with Smeal. As the glow of an overhead light bulb mushroomed against a haze of cigarette smoke, the man tipped his white fedora and nodded. Below his fresh haircut, the man's tailor-made dark suit fit his rotund body perfectly. A silk tie accented the center of his white-shirted chest. The familiar smooth ash line, burning on the cigar he had tucked in the side of his thick smiling lips, told the world it was an expensive Cuban import.

Without speaking a word, the man projected the image of a well-mannered man. Two big men who could have been bodyguards stood at his side. Holding their hands in the pockets of their long overcoats, as if they were hiding pistols, they flicked open the front of their overcoats, and the real threat rose: two Thompson sub-machine guns. These guns didn't have the fifty-round drums but had the twenty-round clips that could be stashed under long coats.

The man in the fedora looked at the raised guns. Then he nodded and held up his hand and signaled to the men beside him. "These gentlemen have nice hardware, too."

As if caught off guard, the fire in the thug's eyes extinguished. They immediately dropped their Thompsons to their sides. With large smiles on their faces, they recognized the man who was supposed to be in prison since 1931. One of the big men nodded in approval. "Good evening, Mister Capone."

As Al Capone nodded back, almost falling over

himself, the thug hit the buzzer. The other thug reached over, opened the door, and held it open.

When Capone, his two bodyguards, and Smeal walked in, the dim-lit place wallowed in smoke. Hundreds of cigarette butts had been stamped out on the wooden floor, and the smell of beer and whisky floated into their faces. A few customers cradled their glasses and bottles in their hands and slid backward toward the far wall. As if they were afraid to leave and afraid to stay, they huddled together, hunkered down, and stared at the Capone.

Getting set to run, a few men slipped off their bar stools, stood up, and tried not to stare. A bartender with a bar rag in his hand slid off a swivel stool behind the bar, bowed his head, and talked to a cop in uniform. Smeal knew the cop from before. This cop was big, dumb, and crooked. So, he was no threat. A few stools down, the local constable sat in front of a boilermaker, a mug of beer with a shot glass full of whisky dropped into it. Smeal wasn't worried about the constable. He usually came in to gamble. And if things got out of hand, Al Capone had both of his bodyguards with him.

John Dillinger sat at a round table dealing cards. His white shirt was open at the neck and his tie was loose. His dark vest fit perfectly, and he seemed to be comfortable. He looked up at Capone and called him by his preferred nickname. "You playin' Snorky?"

Capone walked to the table and stood. "I'll wait until you finish the hand."

Trying to be sociable, Smeal walked up to Dillinger and smiled. Using Dillinger's alias, he said, "Good afternoon, Smitty. Can I get you a fresh drink?"

Dealing with his left hand, Dillinger waved his right hand to the side. "No thanks. When you rob banks, you can't do a lot of drinking."

As he dealt the cards, a half-inch scar that swept across his left ring finger was apparent. His medium chestnut hair was neatly trimmed, and on his clean-shaven face another half-inch scar decorated the right side, but his moustache almost completely covered the scar on the middle of his upper lip.

As he sat back in the chair, he had a slight tilt to his head. The brown mole between the eyebrows of his gray eyes was hardly noticeable, and his permanent smile and prominent cleft chin did not resemble any of the pug ugly gangsters Smeal had known.

Smeal glanced under the table. Cradled in Dillinger's lap, ready to fire, was a 38-caliber Colt, automatic pistol.

Dillinger held his hand over his cards, looked at the player across the table, and smiled. "What do you got?"

With his face filled with delight, the player's pointed Adam's apple jumped up and down inside his scraggly neck. He spread out three fours. "Beat this."

"Nice try." Dillinger laid down a straight.

The player stood up and shook his head. "You cleaned me out again. You win all the time."

As the player walked away from the table, Dillinger stretched to scoop up the cards. The Colt slid from his lap. It clattered across the floor and came to a stop at the feet of the local constable. The constable picked up the Colt. The air in the tavern chilled with terrifying silence. Holding the Colt, the constable stood for a long moment.

Dillinger lifted his glass, rocked back in his chair drinking slowly, and then bought his chair down with a crash. Staring at the constable, he said, "What you do here today is going to be a story to tell your children and great-grandchildren. This could be one of the big moments in your life. Don't make it your last!"

The constable held the Colt by the barrel, hunched over, and offered it to Dillinger. "I think you dropped this."

Dillinger kept a steady eye on the constable but extended his hand. Shaking, the constable placed the Colt into Dillinger's hand. Dillinger tucked the Colt into the holster under his arm.

As the room returned to its normal sounds, a man at the bar whispered to the constable, "You just missed a golden opportunity to make a name for yourself."

Capone glanced sideways at Dillinger. Dillinger slipped his hand onto the handle of his Colt. Although the mirror behind the bar was fogged with years of alcohol fumes and cigarette smoke, Smeal could see the reflection of the constable and the man at the bar. They froze in silence. Conversation droned on down, punctured by one harsh laugh and the sound of glasses clinking.

With shaking hands, the constable looked at the floor. As though he were taking an oath, he lifted his hand. "The only name I would have made for myself would be on a tombstone."

Dillinger nodded in agreement and took his hand off his Colt.

The constable's hand slid toward the bottle on the bar. The bottle was empty, but he clinched his quivering fingers around it. It seemed as if he couldn't pick it up. He reached over with his other hand, clamped the empty bottle between his palms, picked it up, and tilted it to his lips.

Standing next to his bodyguards, Capone placed his hand on the back of a chair at the table and looked to Dillinger. "Gentlemen, is this game still open?"

Dillinger shuffled the cards and looked up at Capone. "Have a seat, Snorky. Your money's just as good as anybody else's."

Capone motioned for his bodyguards to back off. They grabbed Smeal by the shoulder to pull him away. Capone held up his hand. "He's okay. He's old five-point gang."

Still standing, Smeal held his breath to see if one of the bodyguards would know he had never been in the five-point gang. They stared at him for a long moment, nodded, and retreated to the bar.

Capone scraped the chair across the dirty wooden floor until it was next to Dillinger and sat down.

Dillinger threw a suspicious stare toward Smeal.

Capone lifted his open hand toward Smeal. "He's okay."

Capone leaned close and whispered, "You've been causing the FBI a lot of trouble."

A tinge of excitement shone in Dillinger's face. "What do you want me to do about it?"

146

"All you have to do is let the FBI kill you," Capone broke into a thunderous laugh.

Dillinger looked at Capone as if he were crazy.

Capone laughed so hard he started coughing. When he settled down, he took on a serious face. "They want you to go along with the idea of faking your death."

Dillinger's face brightened. "If I decide to do this, they'll need a body." He held up his hand and made the classic thumb and forefinger gun sign. "Who's the lucky guy that's going to take my place?"

"Jimmy Lawrence, he has a rheumatic heart condition. He's dying and agreed to do it so his family would be taken care of for the rest of their lives."

"Does he look like me?"

"Not really. He has brown eyes and he's a little shorter. But the FBI knows how to lie out of that."

"Dillinger took on a confused look. "My eyes are gray. How will they explain that?"

"They'll claim postmortem caused chemical changes in the eye and made them turn brown."

Dillinger touched his chin with his finger. "What about this?"

"They have a man who will testify that you have had plastic surgery to eliminate that clef in your chin."

Dillinger scrunched down in his chair. "This Jimmy Lawrence guy is shorter than me. How are they going to lie out of that?"

"They're going to shoot him on a hot day." Capone smiled and waved his hand in the air. "They'll simply say that the heat caused your body to swell up and made you look shorter."

"That sounds pretty good, but when the people actually see the differences on the dead body, won't they ask questions?"

"Nobody investigates anything the FBI does. The people are gullible. They'll babble for a while. Then they'll only echo what they read in the newspapers and what they hear on the radio."

A sly look came into Dillinger's eyes. "How much are they going to pay?"

"The people in charge are going to give you a million to fake getting shot in Chicago. After that, if you're seen, you'll be considered a Dillinger look alike with the name Ralph Alsman."

"Whoa," Dillinger said with a toothy grin. "That's a lot of money to be called Ralph. How do I know they'll pay?"

"I'm going to personally put the million in the vault. Half now and half after you're officially dead."

"I don't understand," Dillinger said with a sweep of his hand. "Hoover really wants me dead. Why the sudden change?"

"The FBI doesn't like the public thinking you're a hero for taking from the rich and giving to the poor." Capone let his words hang in the air for a few moments. "But the main reason is that congress is talking about eliminating the FBI. Hover wants to stay in business by building it on your back."

Dillinger leaned toward Capone and rolled his hand in encouragement. "How?"

"They want to change a lot of laws."

"That doesn't sound right."

"Don't kid yourself. They already use headlines about you to discourage politicians who want to get rid of the FBI."

"I never thought of the headlines that way before but it makes sense."

"Even FDR's getting worried. When he read about you robbing the Greencastle bank where you told the farmer to put his life savings in his pocket because you were there to rob the bank not people, FDR called Hoover and told him you're becoming a national hero."

"Wait a minute." Dillinger held up his hand in a halting gesture. "I'm no hero. All I ever wanted to be was a bank robber. I guess I'm just about the best bank robber they ever had."

"People are saying that you are standing up to the banks that have robbed the poor people. FDR's afraid you'll be considered a Robin Hood."

"So, they have to get rid of me?"

"You get the picture." Capone held his hands over his face and smiled through his fingers. "You'll have to have a death mask made. Hoover wants to hang it outside his office."

"I'm not getting plastic surgery. The mask won't match the body.

"Experts will change your death mask. It'll look like you had plastic surgery. That way, if anybody gets nosy, the size and basic shape of your skull will be the same."

"It seems it would be cheaper and easier just to kill me for real. Why all the trouble?"

"You made them look so silly the last time you escaped that the public started calling the FBI the Keystone Cops."

A foxy grin spread across Dillinger's face. "When you're trying to escape, money does open a lot of doors."

"That's true, and you have escaped so many times that they aren't sure they can catch you before congress gets rid of the FBI."

"Dillinger wrinkled his brow as if in deep thought. "I'm having a hard time believing they're going to give me that much money."

Actually there's a lot at stake," Capone said. "They want to be able to chase bank robbers across state lines and make robbing federal insured banks a national offense. That way, bank robbers will be placed under the jurisdiction of the FBI."

"It's still hard to believe."

"I didn't believe it at first, either. But they need you to be killed by the FBI so they can make people believe they need more laws." Capone jerked his head downward. "They even want to give firemen guns and make them special police deputies. Then they want to let the National Guard use tanks, troops, and planes to fight criminal gangs."

As if in thought, Dillinger let out a long sigh. "I'll be free, but that will be the end of bank jobs." He looked to the floor. "It's just as well. The president of the last Indiana bank I robbed said I got ten thousand. I only took three, and it was a made-to-order job."

Capone tapped his finger on the table. "That's too much for a made-to-order job. If you want, I'll check into that for the usual fee."

"Go ahead," Dillinger said. "Take your cut and put the rest in the vault."

150

Leaning back in the chair, Capone took a roll of money out of his breast pocket and laid it on the table. "No problem. Anytime you need to make a withdrawal, you know where the keys are."

Dillinger nodded without looking up. "When I use them, to keep our records straight, I'll leave the usual I.O.U."

As Smeal stood next to the table, waiting to be invited into the game, he made a mental note to remember that Dillinger would leave an I.O.U. But even more interesting, was the fact that Dillinger had said "made-to-order job." That meant the rumor of Dillinger's collusion between crooked bankers begging him to rob their institutions to mask their own thefts was true. Now Smeal knew why Dillinger robbed so many banks in Chicago and never got caught. With Capone running Chicago, and paying off its police force, Dillinger had no reason to fear getting caught. But for this service, the bankers had to give Capone and Dillinger a percentage of the money they made off the phony bank robberies. And now they were going to go one further. With the FBI on the verge of being disbanded because Dillinger had made them look like the keystone cops, Capone had arranged for another man to be killed and passed off as Dillinger.

Capone looked up at Smeal and pointed to the chair. "You playing?"

Smeal nodded, sat down, and looked to his right. A man with a black beret that seemed to be glued to the side of his skull with the fold draped over down to his ear, sat at the end of the bar and downed a double shot of whisky. As the man's mind reeled in a haze of alcohol, he motioned to the bartender. "Fill it up again."

The bartender held up one finger. "Coming up, Frenchy."

A blowsy whore with thick makeup and body odor covered with too much perfume placed a cigarette between her red lips and stepped up to Frenchy. "How about a light, honey?"

Frenchy swung around and faced her. In an on-the-verge-of-crying tone he pleaded, "Get away from me."

She turned on her scuffed high heels, tossed her frizzy blond hair, and walked away.

Frenchy placed his elbows on the bar and held his head in his hands. The bartender came over and poured another double shot. "What's the matter, Frenchy?"

Frenchy looked at the drink and then at the bartender. "I've been thinking about where I've been and where I might be heading, and I suddenly realized I was there. Shit Crick."

The bartender flashed a cautious smile. "It's not that bad, is it?"

Frenchy nodded. "I'm thinking about givin' myself up. You know, plead guilty and get a lesser sentence."

Capone turned his head toward Dillinger. "I know someone who did that once. Why don't you give the man some advice?"

Dillinger's face clouded over. He shifted in his chair and turned toward Frenchy. "I robbed the dinky Mooresville grocery store and got caught. Maybe you read about my buddy, webbed-fingers, Eddie Singleton."

Frenchy shook his head thoughtfully.

"He pleaded not guilty." Dillinger resentfully clenched his hands on his hips. "He was sentenced to two years. I figured if I pleaded guilty I'd get probation or fewer than two years for being honest." In a gesture of disgust, he threw his arm out to the side. "The great legal system convicted me of assault and battery with intent to rob, and conspiracy to commit a felony. I got joint sentences of two to fourteen years and ten to twenty years in the Indiana State Prison. I was lucky I got out in eight and a half years."

Capone hunched over. As his eyes swept through the gloom, his manner took on a sharp significant air. "I know the feeling. Look at how many people I fed with my Chicago soup kitchens. It didn't matter how many people I helped, they still tried to send me to prison on a trumped up tax charge."

Dillinger turned back to the table, shuffled the cards, and held them in his hands. "They'll only help if there's something in it for them." He began dealing. "I don't know why robbing a bank is illegal for only some people. When thousands of working men lost their jobs, the banks robbed their savings and then took their houses." He unbuttoned the cuff on his shirt and began rolling it up. "And then they blamed it on the depression."

As Frenchy nodded with approval, Smeal cautiously entered the conversation. "My Aunt and Uncle were late for their mortgage payment by only one day. You think the bank cared about that one day or the fact that they had paid on the farm for twenty years? The bank didn't care. A sheriff came with a piece of paper and threw them out."

Dillinger lifted his glass, but put it back down. "I know people who only had a few hours to pack up all their stuff and get out. Those greedy bloodsuckers wouldn't even give them a break. And they call us crooks."

Once again, Dillinger held up his hand and made the classic thumb and forefinger gun sign. "I take from banks what they steal from the people."

As if he were holding a baseball bat, Capone clinched his fists. "Those so-called exemplary American businessmen are nothing but cannibals. My lieutenant, Joe Batters, could give them a break with a baseball bat and they'd never forget it."

The blowsy whore shook out her hair, walked over, and stopped next to Dillinger. As if she were waiting for him to buy her a drink or take her home, she stood waiting.

Dillinger didn't look up. As he dealt the cards, he politely said. "Sorry, honey, I don't go for blonds."

She jammed her hands on her hips, cocked her head, and talked out the side of her mouth. "Just because you people come in here dressed in your fancy suits, you think you're better than everybody else." As she stared at the drinks on the table, her eyes bugged out. "I ought to call the cops and tell them about your illegal booze. Then we'll see just how high and mighty you are."

The bartender stopped wiping a glass and pointed to a calendar taped to the mirror behind the bar. "Where have you been, lady? It's June 1934. Prohibition's been over since March of 1933."

Smeal raised his shoulders in a gesture of

indifference. Then he turned his palms up and stretched his arms toward the whore. "Hey, lady."

The whore threw a scowl in his direction and held it. "What?"

Smeal smiled a big mocking smile. "If you still want to call the cops" — he pointed to the constable — "there's one right there."

With her eyes blinking with amazement, she looked toward the constable.

The constable stood next to a bar stool, innocently looking toward the ceiling and nonchalantly drumming his fingers on the bar.

The whore took one step toward Smeal and stopped. "You think that's funny?"

A muffled ripple of laughter spread throughout the bar.

Smeal innocently shrugged. "Everybody's laughing. You tell me."

With her face turning the color of her red lips, she turned on her high heels and stomped out the door. Her blend of body odor and cheap perfume lingered in the air.

Hours later, the game broke up. Before they left, Capone and Dillinger shook hands with everyone.

Smeal was amazed at how similar Capone and Dillinger's personalities were. The images the news media constantly printed about being ruthless killers with no feelings didn't fit. It was as if they were two regular guys just out for a usual Saturday night poker game, nothing more. Finding it hard to believe that he had just had a friendly game of cards with Capone and Dillinger, Smeal stuck around.

As he had one last drink, he thought about the

keys Capone had mentioned. He didn't know if Capone had wanted him to hear that he was going to make a five hundred thousand dollar deposit, but he had heard it. And if Capone were going to make that much of a deposit, then wherever he was going to deposit it, there had to be millions already there. If Capone had said, "Key," that would have meant one key. But he had definitely said, "You know where the *keys* are." That meant there was more than one key. The deposit place couldn't be a safety deposit box at a bank. Dillinger only made withdrawals. It was rumored that Capone had caught syphilis when he was a kid. Maybe his mind was going. If it were, and he made a slip and revealed the location of the money, Smeal wanted to be around when he did.

And Smeal didn't have to wait long. Less than a month later, he greeted Capone in the parking lot of the Green Parrot Tavern. The plan to fake Dillinger's death must have worked. In July of 1934, a G-man supposedly shot him in the base of the skull at a range close enough to leave powder burns. The three thousand dollars Dillinger usually carried was never found, and police claimed he had only seven dollars and seventy cents in his pocket. Even though people said the man killed was Dillinger, Smeal knew better. And he knew the only reason Capone had come to the Green Parrot Tavern was to deposit Dillinger's other half of the million into the vault. But before they could climb the steps of the Tavern and be buzzed in, like a thunderclap, a loud voice boomed next to his ear. "Jackass, stop right there!"

Smeal's first inclination was to shove a gun in

the man's gut and order him away. But because he was next to Capone and felt safe, he stopped and turned toward the irritating voice. The big dumb cop that had been in the bar before, stepped from around the building smiling. He was dressed in full uniform. With his eyes boring into their skulls like shots of acid, his smile fled and his words ripped out, "Give it to me."

Smeal looked left then right. Capone's bodyguards were nowhere in sight. Smeal lifted his hand but instead of reaching for his gun, he made a fist. The cop jumped in front of him, flexed his knees, and threw out his chest. With one hand locked on his hip and the other behind his back, he said, "Go ahead, try and knock me down. You won't even make me step one step back." He stuck out his massive chest and bumped into Smeal.

Smeal stumbled back but caught his balance. "If you didn't have that gun behind your back, you wouldn't be so tough."

The cop reached out toward Smeal. "Don't worry about what's behind my back. Just hand that gun over, slow and easy."

Smeal wanted to shoot the cop, but he didn't know what the cop was hiding behind his back. He placed his hand on his Walther PPK, double-action, semi-automatic pistol, but didn't take it out.

Capone moved his hand toward his shoulder holster.

"Don't even think about it." The cop pulled his right hand from behind his back. In it, he held a forty-five caliber Thompson machine gun.

Smeal pulled out his PPK and held it in front of the cop. With his left hand, the cop took it, flipped it in the air, and caught it coming down. He pointed the Thompson at Capone. "Yours too."

Staring into the cop's eyes, Capone reached into his suit coat and pulled out his gun. "If I were you, I wouldn't do this."

The cop made a face and growled. "What makes you think you you're so important that I care about what you think?"

Capone glared at the cop for a moment, then shrugged and handed him his gun.

Smeal wondered why Capone was being so calm and cooperative.

The cop waved the Thompson in an arc, and pointed it in the direction of an approaching car. "Okay, boys, get movin'."

Before they could take a step, a 1932 Chevy Phaeton with full white-wall tires and flashing spoke wheels pulled next to Smeal and stopped. The car's light-blue body sat on top of dark blue fenders that ran the length of the running boards. On the passenger's side, a spare tire was nestled in its mount. Next to the tire, a man with his collar turned up and his hands in his pocket stared at Smeal. The cop jabbed Smeal in the ribs with the barrel of the machine gun. "Get in. You're going to take a ride in style."

Smeal opened the back door of the Phaeton, slipped under the beige convertible top, and sat next to a man. From behind a full-face black mask, the man's eyes peered from two holes. Capone was prodded in, too.

Inside, the masked man leaned over and clinched a blindfold around Smeal's head. Smeal didn't know if Capone was blindfolded. But movement from the masked man seemed to indicate that he had also been blindfolded.

Twisting around turns and sailing down straight-a-ways, they rode around in the Phaeton for what Smeal thought was an hour. When the car stopped, they walked a short distance. After tall weeds and grass whipped at their legs and the smell of used oil entered their nostrils, they descended down a narrow set of steps. When the blindfolds were taken off, they discovered they were in one of the many abandoned coalmines of the area.

A lot of work had been done to the mine. Before them, at the other side of a concrete floor, a long brass vault, as big as a coffin, lay on a stone pedestal. Smeal turned and looked back. "What are we doing here?"

The man with the machine gun jabbed Capone in the ribs. "Walk over there and make a withdrawal."

Capone immediately threw his hands in the air so hard they hit a wooden crossbeam in the ceiling. "I'll do anything you want." He kept his hands on the beam and smiled a mischievous smile.

Out of the corner of his eye, Smeal watched Capone snake his hands over the ceiling beam and pull out two lightly rusted guns. Now he knew why Capone had been so calm.

Capone kept his hands and the guns above his head. When Smeal lifted his feet to take a step onto the concrete floor, Capone turned and aimed both guns at the machine gun man. "Okay friend. Drop it!"

The man dropped the Thompson.

Capone waved the gun in his right hand toward

the ceiling. "Okay hands up."

The man reached up, grabbed a handful of dirt from the crossbeam. Smeal squinted his eyes against the threat.

Capone didn't.

The man threw the dirt at Capone's face.

Too late, Capone turned his face away from the flying dirt and blindly pulled the triggers on both guns.

They didn't fire.

With surprise, the eyes of the man flew wide open. Instead of reaching for the Thompson, he reached up and pulled a lever. Making a grating noise, the concrete floor vibrated for an instant. Then it opened up. Gripping the guns in his hands, Capone tried to keep his balance. At the last moment, he windmilled his arms, tumbled forward, and landed face down into a deep pit.

Smeal dove forward and just managed to snag a handhold and hang onto the edge of the moving floor. Before he could throw his leg up and scramble to the top of the floor, Capone rolled over and started pulling the triggers on the guns. After three snaps they fired. Then after three more snaps they fired again. A bullet punctured Smeal's side. The man who had pulled the lever snatched the Thompson up off the floor and fired at Capone, the aimed at Smeal. But he didn't fire. His face grimaced with pain. He grabbed his own stomach. With a metallic clatter, the Thompson fell onto the edge of the concrete floor. With blood flowing from between his fingers, the man bent over, ran up the steps and out of the mine.

In rapid succession, Capone continued pulling

the triggers on the guns. Every two or three pulls, the guns fired.

Smeal yelled at Capone, "He' gone! Stop firing."

But Capone continued to wave the guns around and constantly pull the triggers. Between clicks, the bullets zinged around the mine, just missing Smeal. Not wanting to get shot again, Smeal jumped over Capone's head and pulled the lever. The floor closed over Capone. Hoping the man wouldn't come back, Smeal stood perfectly still and listened. He didn't hear the man, but he wanted to wait longer to be sure. Watching the blood ooze from his wound, he knew if he didn't get it patched up, and soon, he would die. He didn't have time to open the floor and wait for Capone to run out of bullets. He may have reloaded. He decided he had to leave the mine. If he survived, he would come back and get Capone out.

Holding his bleeding side, he clumsily struggled toward the blood-soaked steps. With loud grunts and wheezes, he crawled up the steps and emerged into total darkness. Being lightheaded from lack of blood, he held onto a tilted steel pole. It moved to an upright position and a dull clunk filled the night air. He found an unfamiliar road and staggered along it until a black 1933 Hudson Terraplane Eight stopped and a stranger searched him, found nothing, and then dragged him into the back seat.

As the car traveled down the highway, through blurred vision, Smeal tried to see who the stranger was. He wasn't positive, but the man could have been John Dillinger. The Terraplane automobile

161

was his favorite set of wheels. The luxurious, state-of-the-art model could blow away anything the cops had. Smeal remembered it well.

The stranger drove over the Ohio state line and stopped at the front of the Columbia Theater in downtown Sharon, Pennsylvania. A light wind blew down the street scattering cigarette butts and a few scraps of paper. At this late-night hour, a few bargoers and night-shift workers who frequented the night and shunned the daylight were still out.

The stranger who resembled Dillinger looked to his right and said, "Watch him for a minute, Billie."

A sleepy woman's voice answered, "Don't be long."

When he had been dragged into the Terraplane, Smeal hadn't seen the woman.. He figured she must have been slumped down in the front seat, sleeping.

As if he were trying to hide his identity, the stranger crammed his hat down hard on his head, stepped out of the car, and walked into the alleyway next to the theater. Usually it was washed in neon from the gentle buzzing Arcade Bar sign, but it was out. He stopped in a darkened doorway and faced the brick side of the theater. A man with a large forehead and horn-rimmed glasses came walking down the sidewalk and started to turn down the alley next to the theater, but when he saw the stranger, he stopped and awkwardly stood next to the corner of the red brick building. The stranger looked back over his shoulder. With a drooping head, the horn-rimmed glasses man twisted his hands, tried to hide his face, and pretend he wasn't looking. As the stranger relieved himself, steam curled up from his hands. Just as the dawn

162

shouldered the black night aside, the stranger zipped up his pants and walked toward the horn-rimmed glasses man.

With a crooked smile, the horn-rimmed glasses man eyed him steadily. "Sometimes a good piss is better than a piece of ass."

The stranger slightly smiled, got back into the car, drove up State Street, pulled next to the curb, and stopped. Smeal looked out the window. He was in the front of the white entrance of a three-story red brick building. Two-inch thick pipe railings ran along the sides of six concrete steps that led to two doors with grids of windowpanes. He didn't know why he counted the windowpanes but he did. On each door, skinny white strips of wood held fifteen panes of rectangular glass, three wide and six high. Two long windows with eight panes of glass, two wide and four high, framed the ends of the doors. There were so many windows Smeal thought it could be a greenhouse attached to the building. But two brass coach lights on the outsides of the windows told him the white and glass structure was something else. And he was right. Stretched across the top of the doors, a row of ten windowpanes sat below black letters against a white background. With his vision still blurred, Smeal could barely read it, but it spelled out "Christian H. Buhl Hospital".

He broke into a hopeful smile and expectantly turned toward the stranger. Instead of getting out, opening the back door, and helping Smeal up the six flights of concrete steps, the stranger pulled his hat down and covered most of his face. Then he opened the door, grabbed Smeal's arm, and dragged

163

him out of the car. Unable to stand, Smeal crumpled to the cement sidewalk at the bottom of the steps. The stranger slammed the door, leaned his head out the window, and looked down at Smeal. "Get out of this business before you can't turn back."

The stranger hopped into the Terraplane and frantically blew the horn until someone came to the hospital doors. Then he sped away.

Before Smeal lost consciousness, two white uniformed Nurses came running down the steps and helped him hobble inside.

Smeal never saw the 1933 Terraplane again, and he never found out if the stranger that had saved his life was the "Robin Hood" of bank robbers: John Hubert Dillinger.

Smeal figured the man Capone had wounded in the mine must have died from his wounds. But before he died, to keep the big dumb cop silent, the man must have expended so much energy to kill the cop and dispose of his body that he had died before he could be treated for his wounds. And those had been the only people, except Dillinger, who knew where the mine and the vault were. Hoping Dillinger didn't know about the gold vault covered with a thin layer of brass and concrete, Smeal had tried to find the mine. But after months of trying and dodging the cops, he had failed to turn up a single clue.

Even though the police were looking for him, he kept looking for the vault until Pearl Harbor was bombed. Then World War II offered him a way to stay away until things cooled down. Like many men of the era, he got caught up in the feeling that it was his patriotic duty to defend his country before there was no country left to defend. He joined the Army, was captured by the Japanese, and became a prisoner of war.

Now, thirty years later, a few young garbage men who he considered nothing but a bunch of noisy, overconfident, empty-headed smart aleck kids may have found a box of bootleg money somewhere at the old Peacock Alley Bar location. If they were smart enough to figure out where that box had been hidden for so many years, it was a sure bet that they had found Capone's gold vault and hadn't been fooled by its cheap brass and concrete layers. Judging from their expressions when he had asked them if they had punched his milk horse, they knew Blondie, and they knew where he was. And wherever Blondie was, the vault or the money for the vault would be there, too. Being a former POW, Smeal knew how to do just the right things and make those kids unknowingly show him where the vault was.

Thirty years ago, he could have easily found out whatever he wanted at the Green Parrot Tavern. But now, the thugs with Thompson machine guns no longer stood at the top of the stairs of the Tavern, and John Dillinger would never play cards there again.

For years, Smeal had believed that after Dillinger had faked his death, he had taken the second half of the million from the mine. But now, as he sat on his porch, he realized, if the man who had searched him and driven him to the Buhl Hospital had been Dillinger, it was a sure bet that he had not found the other five hundred thousand

Capone was supposed to have put in the mine. Apparently Dillinger didn't know about the sliding cement slab. That meant the five hundred thousand was still in the mine, hid under the sliding cement slab and in the pocket of the suit coat on Capone's body. Now Smeal had two reasons to find Blondie: The gold vault and the five hundred thousand.

He figured if he made the kids forfeit the down payment for their new truck and eliminate their contracts, they would have no money coming from their garbage business. If they had somehow gotten the cash value for the vault, Blondie would not have given them their full share. He believed in not putting all his money in one place, and he wouldn't let the kids do it either. Those kids would need to contact Blondie and get some of the money he was holding for them.

Smeal hadn't wanted to use force with the president of the bank, but he didn't want to cooperate. He wasn't qualified for the job, but his relatives had pulled strings and gotten him the position. So he thought they could protect him. But he was wrong. Smeal had Schnoz, the man with the long nose, flash his skull and cross-bones tattoo and break the stubborn president's nose. The president did what he was told to do. Right away, the kids lost the new truck and the contracts, too. They hadn't contacted Blondie yet, but Smeal was having the little weasels followed.

Still sitting on his porch, waiting for a call from Schnoz, Smeal leaned back and fell asleep.

When the phone rang, he stumbled into the house and yanked the receiver from the wall. "Go ahead."

166

"Bad news," Schnoz said with a nasal sound to his voice. "Those kids, you told us to follow, dug a metal box out of the old foundation at Peacock Alley."

Smeal knew bootleggers always played it safe. In case of a raid, where the Feds would destroy all the alcohol and take all the money, the bootleggers would hide thousands of dollars in metal boxes, burry them, hide them in concrete foundations, or slip them under little secret trap doors. He tried to hold back the excitement in his voice, but he couldn't. "Well bring it on over."

There was a pause on the on the other end of the receiver.

Even though Schnoz couldn't see him, Smeal rolled his hand with encouragement. "Come on, talk."

"We could bring it over," Schnoz said. "But it's empty."

"What do you mean it's empty?"

"Those kids took whatever was in it and threw the empty box onto the road. While we went after it, they got away."

Smell felt frustration fill his chest. "How can they outrun a bullet?"

Hesitating, Schnoz didn't answer. Then with his voice quivering, he whined, "Toad's shotgun blew up, and they ran down to the railroad and jumped on a train."

Accelerating with emotion, Smeal's voice rose. "How can a shotgun blow up? Didn't he clean it?"

The whiny tone immediately left Schnoz's nasal voice. "That black-headed kid jammed the barrel into the mud. Toad never took the time to see

167

if it was clogged."

" "What's the matter with your voice?"

"That older kid stepped on a shovel. The handle flew up and broke my nose."

Smeal paused and let what had just happened sink in. Regaining his composure, he calmly spoke. "Okay, Schnoz, thanks for the information. I'll be in touch."

He replaced the receiver to its cradle on the wall, went through the door, and sat on his porch. Sighing, he thought about how everything had been going just fine. He was just about to have a box of money, but incompetent help had let those smart aleck kids fool them with an empty box, hop a train, and ride away. Comforted with the fact that he knew where the slow train was going, he leaned back and fell asleep.

Chapter 9

As the train sped into the night, the steel wheels of the flatcar clicked and clacked in a steady rhythm on the steel rails of the railroad. Above the rails, huge raindrops plunked on the solid steel floor of the flatcar and plinked off the sheet metal sides of the tall gray transformer. With the downpour blasting into their faces, Freddy, Neal, and Rafferty hunched miserably, looking like drowned rats shivering in the sudden cold.

Freddy glanced to his left. An oily tarpaulin sat folded next the transformer. Gesturing toward it, he shook Neal's and Rafferty's shoulders.

Neal flicked the water off his shirtless arms and looked toward the bulge of his T-shirt that Freddy had tucked under his arm.

Freddy reached in for the shirt. "It's pretty cold. You want the shirt?"

Neal hurriedly shook his head. "If there's a paper map in it, I don't want it go get wet." He reached into his wet pocket and took out his penknife. "I can make something better."

He unfolded the tarpaulin and cut a piece big enough to cover his upper body. Then he folded it, cut a slot for his head, threw the makeshift poncho over his head, and tucked the ends into his pants.

"Hey," Rafferty said. "That's a good idea."

They all tugged at the remaining piece of tarpaulin, pulled it over them, and sat down. It was too short to cover them completely, but with Freddy sitting in the center and Neal and Rafferty holding the ends tight under their chins, they pulled the top edge forward and formed a little hood to keep the rain off their faces.

As the night rain slowed and the train clacked on down the railroad tracks, Freddy figured he would have a chance to dry off, but a long explosive sound of thunder rumbled in the dark sky. Holding his wet shirt with the contents of the box next to his chest, he slumped down on a dry spot next to the transformer, looked out from under the hood, and focused forward. As the train rolled through an exceptionally dark stretch, black branches of trees arched over the railroad cars and made it look like the train was going through a tunnel of leaves. Out the other side, the train's bell clanged in monotone clangs. Then two long blasts, one short blast, and one long blast of the diesel locomotive horn blared "train-coming" warnings into the pre-dawn darkness.

Before the train came to a crossing, sudden excessive swaying of the flatcar rocked Freddy's body side to side and caused the tarpaulin to cover his head. At the crossing, the train's wheels rumbled over uneven tracks that ran across the highway where loose metal components on the moving cars jerked and banged with a repetitive, one, two beat.

A half a mile down from the crossing, the swaying and banging slowed. Freddy stuck his head out from under the tarpaulin and looked ahead. On the side of the tracks, a lone light, on a metal pole, cut through a foggy mist and brightened what looked like a stretch of grass. It would be a place soft enough jump off and land without getting scraped up. He motioned to Neal and Rafferty and pointed ahead. "How about there?"

With his makeshift tarpaulin shirt hanging loosely on his lean and sinewy frame, Neal shed the tarpaulin from his head and stood up. Swaying with the rhythm of the car's rocking motion, he squinted into the gray darkness ahead. "That looks like a good place to see what was in that box."

For support, Rafferty stood up and grabbed onto a cable connected to the transformer. "I'm out of the sightseeing mood. Let's go."

Before the train got to the jumping off spot, it picked up speed. Like an invisible plow, wind from the train cleared away ghostly trails of rain vapor that huddled along the tracks for miles.

"We're going too fast," Neal said. "But we should be all right if we land in the grass."

They all stood on the edge of the flatcar and flexed to jump. As the grass under the light neared, the train went faster. Thirty feet before the grass, Freddy stepped back from the edge of the car. "Wait!'

Crouching, ready to jump, Neal shot him a puzzled look. "What for?"

Freddy pointed to the grass. "Look!"

Like demons waiting in ambush, old brake shoes and pieces of rusty steel with sharp jagged edges peeked between the tall grasses. Beyond that, rays from the lone light revealed glistening edges of broken bottles winking between bone-breaking boulders.

Neal's shoulders sagged in defeat. He stepped back, sat back down, and covered his head with the tarpaulin. "I guess we're not getting off here."

Rafferty folded his arms across his chest and leaned against the transformer. As if the rainy night's ethereal beauty had soothed him, he looked ahead. Then they all piled forward in a helpless heap and dozed off.

172

Chapter 10

When Smeal awoke, he was still sitting on his front porch. His mental clock told him the sun would be up any time now. This was the usual time people in his business went to sleep, but he couldn't go to bed. He had to follow those kids.

Even though he could kill any of them without hesitation, he sort of liked them, and he knew he could control them. They weren't like mobsters or the phony fellow POWs that had almost caused him to starve to death. The orange-headed Rafferty kid had a smart mouth, but these kids had a little respect for their fellow man. Smeal hoped nothing would ever happen to them that would force them to change. He had started out just like them. God-fearing, believing in the law, and trying to follow the golden rule, but his many bad experiences revealed that most people weren't like that. They follow the golden rule only as long as it doesn't affect them.

Smeal knew the train the kids had hopped onto would stop on the Mahoning River Bridge. If they didn't jump off before that, a healthy man could easily catch them, but his body was too broken-down for these cat and mouse games. He would have to have help. Hound Eyes and his buddies were lazy and didn't like to work in the mornings.

Smeal sighed and stood up. Hound Eyes and his buddies would follow him if he gave them a good enough reason. He took off his fedora, placed a black wig on his head, covered his eyes with his mirrored sunglasses, and walked out to his blue Dodge.

When Smeal pulled off the road, Hound Eye's '57 Chevy was parked at the old Peacock Alley foundation. Toad was probably at the hospital getting his wounds tended to from the shotgun that had blown up in his face. Hound Eyes and Muscles were probably inside the Melody Lane Bar collecting or losing gambling money.

Smeal laid on the car's horn. It blasted into the early morning's red sky. "Red sky in the morning, sailor's warning," came to his mind. There was a good chance that it would rain on those kids today and slow them down. He looked to the door of the bar. Nothing moved. He laid on the horn and held it there. Still nothing. He put his blue Dodge into reverse and hit the gas. The car spun around backwards in a semi-circle, and the tires kicked up gravel, until, Bam! The back bumper of the Dodge crashed into the rear end of the Chevy.

The door of the bar opened. A stripe of weak light rushed through the opening and filtered through the early morning mist. Like hung-over soldiers late for formation, Hound Eyes and Muscles stumbled through the opening and rushed toward Smeal and his Dodge.

Smeal jammed the accelerator to the floor and sped on down the road. In the distance, squealing tires of the Chevy coming after him was music to his ears. He knew they would follow.

Chapter 11

A long slow roll of thunder filled the air. The train slowed. Neal raised his head and blinked sullenly. The sun cut through a string of clouds and sent white rays of light through a morning mist that huddled close to a big bridge ahead.

Freddy stood up and prepared to jump off, but before he could, the concave brake shoes mashing against the steel wheels of the tank car in front of them shrieked and spewed sparks from the wheels. As the train slowed, the new light of dawn illuminated a bridge that spanned the Mahoning River. Like big, rounded buttons, rivets ran up both sides of two three-foot wide heavy steel I-beams of the bridge.

As if fighting gravity and reaching for the distant sky, the great structures leaned inward and up. At first glance, the cross-member at the top of the bridge looked skewed, twisted by time. Freddy shook his head to make sure he was seeing straight. The bridge still looked skewed, but he noted the left side was further away than the right side. It had been built at a crossing where the banks on the sides of the river sat at an angle, making it looked skewed.

Grinding along rusty rails, the flat car rolled onto the bridge. After a continuing clash of couplings, the train ground to a halt. The flat car was in the center of the span.

Freddy looked up. Above his head, more rows of rivets held steel lattice that crisscrossed at a sturdy X. Connected to that, smaller beams, all riveted, too, supported a zigzagged, see-through lattice of more steel beams with slanted V's that separated two long angles. It was a heavy duty-bridge.

Freddy searched for a place to step down off the flat car. Beneath both sides of the car's coupler, two shining snakes of steel rails held down railroad ties spaced far enough apart for a man's leg to fall through. Iron ore and coke lay on and around the ties, remnants of a very busy place. Almost touching the sides of the car, the side rails of the bridge were taller than a man, and their wide openings offered no protection for pedestrians. If people had to walk across this bridge, they would hold their breath while crossing. It was definitely not a public bridge. It was a railroad trestle used by trains going to the steel mills in Youngstown, Ohio.

Rafferty stood up and looked down at Freddy. "You want to get off here?"

Sitting on the floor of the flatcar, Freddy picked up a rusty bolt and tossed it over the side rail. It rocketed toward the dirty water far below and hit with a dull plop, sending oily blue and green rings outward.

Freddy looked at the narrow space between the car and the bridge railing. "There's no place to walk, and I don't want to fall in that water."

Rafferty held out his arms as if he were a tightrope walker. "We can balance on the ties."

"We could," Neal said. "But if the train starts up, we'll get knocked into the filthy, stinkin' river."

With his smiling face shinning like a lighthouse beacon of hope, Rafferty turned toward Neal. "So what? We can swim. And if we hold our noses, the water will only be filthy."

Beneath the tarpaulin shirt, Neal's shoulders shook with laughter. "There's so much oil in that water, it's a wonder it doesn't catch fire."

Freddy stared at the floating oil with a mixture of awe and amazement. "I've never seen that much oil on water before. I heard that it does catch on fire, and I can see why. I wouldn't want to be in there when it does."

Rafferty suddenly seized Freddy's arm. "Hey," he said with sudden excitement. "While we're waiting for the train to start why don't we see what was in that box?"

Pulling away from Rafferty's hand, Freddy jumped up. "That's right." He reached across his own chest, and felt Neal's T-shirt that contained the contents of the box. "I've had this thing under my arm so long I almost forgot it was here." He took out the shirt.

With dark clouds rolling across the sun, Rafferty and Neal horned in close.

Standing, Freddy bent over and laid the shirt on the flatcar floor. He untied the knotted shirt and slowly folded the ends back. Something wrapped in fire-scorched newspaper secured with a gray string appeared. Freddy pulled on the string. It snapped. A little cloud of gray dust puffed up, hovered for an instant, and dissipated.

As Freddy peeled back the charred newspaper, it was so dry that it broke at the folds. After the last piece had been peeled away, a pile of seared money sat before him. Although the fragile money was cracked into many pieces, Freddy could make out denominations. None were fewer that one hundred dollars.

"Whoa!" he groaned with delight and straightened up. The blackened and broken bills fluttered in a slight breeze. He bent back down and looked closer. The money looked so ancient that it seemed to crumble before his eyes.

Neal stared in amazement. "That's a lot of money, but what happened to it?"

"It's old and the fire that burned down Peacock Alley must have been so hot that it heated the money so bad that it just falls apart."

"That doesn't matter," Rafferty said. "We can take it to a bank. They'll exchange old money for new money."

Neal nodded in agreement. "There's thousands of dollars there." He nudged Freddy in the elbow. "With that much money, Julie will forget about that guy in the '32 Ford coupe.

Freddy stood upright and let his lips spread into a huge smile. Although Julie was way above his social status, he knew the money at his feet would fix that. Just the thought of going out with her sent excitement into his chest. "It'll be great," he said, "but first, we go to get this money to the bank."

Neal held up his hand and waved it in a dismissive gesture. "But we're not taking it to that bank creep that cheated us out of our truck."

Freddy knelt on one knee, reached down with his right arm, grabbed a corner of the shirt, and lifted it to pull the money closer.

Clunk! The train jerked into reverse. As it began to move, a banshee shriek of metal against metal pierced the air. Freddy jerked his head around to see where the shriek had come from. The unexpected shriek and the sudden reversing movement knocked Freddy off balance. He lunged over sideways and landed on his right shoulder. Before he could let loose of the end of the shirt and regain his balance, he jerked the shirt out from under the money. Breaking into many pieces, the money scattered across the floor of the flatcar and headed for the edge. All at the same time, Freddy, Neal, and Rafferty scrambled to catch it. In their haste, they crashed into each other. Before they had a chance to regroup and grab the money, the flatcar traveled out of the protection of the huge I-beam and right into the path of a crosswind. As if it were being sprayed with a high-pressure water hose, the wind blasted the fragile money pieces into tiny fragments that flew off the edge of the flatcar and sailed into the air. Like ancient crumbling leaves, the fragments broke into thousands of particles. As if it were a tickertape parade of sadness, a fortune of particles snowed down onto surface of the oily water.

With mouths agape, they all watched. The particles floated on top of the water and seemed to be headed for shore.

Neal crouched on the side of the moving flat car, ready to jump off. "I don't care how much oil's on that water, I'm going in after that money."

As if Mother Nature were showing off with one final crowning achievement, lightening flashed, followed by a single crack of thunder. Clouds opened up and huge drops of rain hammered the particles into the oily surface until they were gone.

Neal straightened up and stared at the water. His jaw pulsed with anger. "Damn it!" he rasped over the rush of the rain. "We'll never get it now."

As the flatcar inched its way across the bridge, Freddy felt as if the kid in the '32 hot rod Ford coup had just picked up Julie and taken her a thousand miles away.

With water running down Rafferty's cheeks and over his lips, he dejectedly shook his head. "There goes my chance to move into the ghetto."

Freddy flipped his sopping hair away from his face, cocked his head to one side, and stared at Rafferty. "Don't you mean, 'there goes your chance to move out of the ghetto'?"

"Oh no," Rafferty said and forced a smile. "I never had enough money to move into the ghetto. I always had to live behind it."

Visibly fighting back tears, Neal reached up, held onto the cable that ran from the bottom of the flatcar to the top of the gray transformer, and looked toward the sky. After a long pause, he managed to ask, "If we still had the money what would we do with it?"

Freddy knew Neal was trying to subdue the disappointment of losing the money but he didn't answer.

Draped in soaked clothes, Rafferty rubbed the water from his eyes and said, "I'd invest it in real estate."

"You mean land?" Neal asked and took one hand off the cable. "The last time I heard, they weren't making any more land, but they can make houses anytime."

"No," Rafferty said, "The other real estate, you know, houses and lots."

Neal reached up and playfully hit himself on the side of his rain-soaked head. "Oh, you mean

180

whorehouses and lots of whiskey."

"That's the one," Rafferty said and paused. "We could still open a whore house, but we'd have to run it by hand until we got enough money to hire the girls."

Neal managed a slight smile, but in a silence like the one that comes after a bad joke, no one laughed.

As the train pulled away from the bridge, Freddy was glad Rafferty had kept his sense of humor, but now, without the money and the garbage business gone, he was afraid he wouldn't even be able to work in the steel mill. They were laying off workers. And even if he could get a job in a mill, Julie would never consider going out with a lowly steel worker.

As the flatcar rolled toward the end of the bridge, Freddy stared at the rain pounding on the oily surface of the river. That was a lot of money," he said. "But it was nowhere near the one hundred million Capone made every year."

As if the loss of the money didn't bother him, Neal reached down and scooped his shirt up off the flatcar floor. "At least I got my shirt back." He slipped off the tarpaulin shirt and pulled on his black T-shirt. "That feels better." He shook the water from the tarpaulin shirt and put it on over his T-shirt. Hooking his thumbs in the sides of the tarpaulin shirt, he leaned back. "This is almost as classy as the suit coat Blondie gave me."

Lifting both hands toward Neal, Rafferty made a face and faked being impressed. "Oh, just elegant."

Shaking his head at Rafferty's antics, Freddy

watched the rain slow and patter through the trees that ran alongside the tracks. When the train approached a switch, a tinge of fear crawled up his spine. He looked to Neal. "The bad part is that those gangsters don't know we lost the money."

Neal waved his hand in the air. "Maybe they didn't know it was in the box."

"I hope they didn't," Freddy said. "I don't like the idea of them coming after us."

"What are you worried about?" Neal bolted upright. "The greatest thrill in the world is dancing along the edge of the unknown. We might live dangerously. But whatever we do, it'll payoff."

As the train carried them on down tracks, Freddy leaned forward in a helpless heap and hoped Neal was right.

Chapter 12

About a mile from the Mahoning River Bridge the train stopped at a switch and the rain stopped. As the tracks glistened under the hazy glow of new sunlight, Freddy, Neal, and Rafferty jumped off the flatcar and onto the gray ballast that ran along the tracks. After the line of railroad cars had gone through their noisy sequence of clunking couplers and had taken up the slack, they started moving forward.

When the train and its noise were gone, in a new silence that filled the air, Neal turned toward Freddy. "Are you sure Capone made one hundred million a year?"

"That's what the newspapers said. But I'd say he made more than that."

"We had a piece of it," Neal said and stared down the empty tracks. "But there has to be more."

As their footsteps crunched in loud unison on the ballast, an unusual strong odor of creosote, from the wooden railroad ties, plagued Freddy's lungs. It reminded him of the stinking smells of a steel mill. He wondered if he would ever be free of the threat of wasting his life in such a place.

"We took a chance and lost," he said. "If we wouldn't have tried to buy a new truck, we'd have enough money to fix the old truck."

Neal rubbed his brow and threw his hands into the air. "Even if we could fix the old truck, it would only be a glorious pain in the ass. We lost all the contracts." He pondered in silence for a moment. "But it just doesn't matter. No one can make money without taking a chance. The difference between a rich man and a working fool, is knowing when to take a risk and when not to."

Freddy struggled not to show his disappointment. "I guess we didn't pick the right time to take a risk."

Neal tilted his head back and looked Freddy in the eye. "The money we spent on the new truck didn't actually vanish like the money that went into the river."

"Oh yeah? Then where did it go?"

Neal held up one finger and jerked it to the rhythm of his speech. "Ah, ahem, ah, yes," he said and rubbed his chin. "It was actually an investment in our future education. We learned not to trust a bank."

Freddy glanced uncomfortably at him. He felt a loyalty to Neal, a loyalty of one who knows that what he is doing might be wrong, but feels he owes his friend too much to back out, no matter what might happen.

Looking down, Rafferty toyed with a stone with the toe of his shoe. His skinny body suddenly shuddered with quiet laughter.

Neal glared at him. "What are you laughing at? It was your money, too."

Rafferty raised his orange-haired head and smiled an exaggerated tooth-filled smile. "I think I know where we can get some more money."

Freddy and Neal looked at each other.

Freddy spoke first. "Did you find another note?"

"I didn't find another note, but we never finished looking in the coalmine."

Freddy felt a tinge of hope, but waved his hand

down. "There's no money there. John Dillinger got the half million, and the FBI killed him at the Biograph Theater in Chicago."

Rafferty squinted one eye and arrogantly tilted his head. "Maybe he got the money and maybe he didn't."

"What are you talking about?" Neal asked with concern. "I saw some old newspapers. Dillinger was in them. They had pictures of his body and everything."

Rafferty's face took on a sly look. "Think about it." He pointed to his own head. "When we were in the coalmine going after Al Capone's vault, you guys said the skeleton was dressed in a brown suit and had a dirty-white gangster hat on its skull. That skeleton could be Al Capone."

"So, what?" Freddy said and gave Neal a conspiratorial wink. "To keep you guys from being scared out of your wits, we pulled the lever and let the trap door cover him up."

Rafferty playfully poked Freddy in the chest with his finger. "That's the point. The five hundred thousand, John Dillinger was supposed to get, wasn't in the vault. That skeleton that could be Al Capone may have been shot before he had a chance to put it in there."

"We already found the I.O. U. Dillinger left it in the vault. So that proves Capone put the money there and Dillinger got it."

"Maybe it does and maybe it doesn't." Rafferty crinkled his freckled nose. "What if Dillinger wrote the I.O.U. but Capone never had a chance to give him the money?" He lifted his arms, leaned back, grinned from ear to ear, and stared directly into

Freddy's face. "How do you like that idea?"

Freddy turned his head from Rafferty's stare and looked to Neal. "The skeleton's bony hand was holding a gun. Before the man died, he could have shot at anybody in the mine."

"That almost makes sense," Neal said and held up one finger to emphasize the point. "If he shot somebody and they closed the trap door and never came back because they died—" He paused and suddenly lit up with excitement. "Then the money's still in Capone's pocket."

"I'm glad you guys figured that out all by yourself," Rafferty said in mock praise.

As if digging up the skeletal remains of a well-known gangster was a common thing, Neal nonchalantly said, "We gotta go back to the mine and dig out the cave-in."

Freddy took a few steps, turned, and looked back at Neal. Neal's profile silhouetting against clouds of the steel mill's red smoke, reminded him of the nightmares he had had the last time he had seen the skeleton. When the concrete floor had yawned open, the skeleton has spilled gloom throughout his entire body. He didn't like the thought of seeing it again. "We could dig it out," he said, and then shuddered. "But we should still try to get our truck money back from the bank."

Neal grimaced as if he were swallowing oily water from the river. "I don't like the way that bank creep took our money any more than you do." He jerked his head to the side one time. "But the thing is, we all know those thugs got the system rigged."

"So what are we supposed to do?" Freddy asked. "Just take what they dish out?"

"We're not going to take anything they throw at us," Neal said in a tough clipped tone. "But I do know that if you don't like certain things the system does to you, the way to beat it is to not look back." His mouth twisted into a determined grin. "We got to keep moving ahead. There's always a new bend in the road, and the rotten bastards can't rig everything."

With the sun struggling to beam through the recently red smoke-filled sky, the thumping of a locomotive engine filled the air. A train with three diesel engines pounding under the strain of pulling a long string of ore-loaded hopper cars labored over the bridge.

"The train's going back the way we came," Rafferty said. "Are we going to jump on?"

As the steel wheels under the hopper cars clacked on a loose rail and slowly rolled on down the tracks, Freddy studied the sides of the maroon cars. Except for the different digits of the dusty white numbers, they all looked the same. The car's high sides swayed gently. And on the bottoms, triangular doors pointed down toward the tracks. As if it were magnetized, dark-red iron ore dust stuck to the paint and almost matched the cars' darker maroon colors.

Freddy turned toward Neal. "It looks like a unit ore train to me."

Neal bobbed his head in agreement. "With all the hopper cars coated with ore dust, I'd bet on it."

A look of panic crossed Rafferty's face. "I don't care what kind of train it is." He pointed to the clitter-clattering cars. "They're going our way. Let's get on before they're gone."

Watching one car lumber past, Neal's head slowly moved from right to left. "If we want to ride to some steel mill around Pittsburgh, we can jump right on." He jerked his head back to the right and watched another car go past. This time his head moved a little faster. "Once those trains get up speed, they don't stop for nothin'."

"That's right," Freddy said. "If we get on, and it keeps going too fast for us to get off, we'll have to wait until it stops. And when that red ore dust gets into your skin, it doesn't come off for days."

As the long line of cars continued to clack past at a snail's pace, Neal looked down the tracks and to where the train was headed. "There's a railroad crossing a ways down there," he said. "Let's hang onto a car and ride back to the road. Then we'll hitchhike back home."

Rafferty ran his hand across his wet shirt. "I've had enough of railroad life. Let's get back on the real road again."

"I'm tired of this hobo life," Neal said and grabbed onto a slow moving hopper car. "Let's get back to that mine and make a withdrawal."

Rafferty and Freddy grabbed onto cars, too. When they came to the crossing, the train picked up a little speed. They jumped off and started walking toward the automobile that was waiting on the train to pass. Next to the crossing, a blue Dodge waited. Inside, a man with thick lips, mirror sunglasses, and black hair that looked like a wig, sat behind the steering wheel.

Freddy slowed and tugged on Neal's shoulder. "That's the crazy guy who wanted to know if I punched his milk horse. It's Smeal."

188

Neal hurried to the car and stopped at the window.

Smeal glanced in his rearview mirror and looked toward Neal. "Do I know you?"

Rafferty stepped up to the window, looked right in Smeal's face and smiled. "We want to know if you punched our milk horse."

As if he were expecting someone, Smeal stared into his rearview mirror and bit down on his cigar. He turned to Rafferty. With the cigar flapping on his lips, he talked through clenched teeth. "Are you making fun of me?"

With the train's ore cars increasing their clacking and speeding up, Rafferty shook his head excessively in mock amusement. "No, we're not making fun of you. Why would we do that?"

A '57 Chevy rushed down the road and screeched to a stop right at the bumper of the blue Dodge. Freddy jerked back with a start. The doors on the Chevy flew open. Out jumped a muscled man.

Inside the car, a hound-eyed man pointed out the window. "Hey, Muscles, is that him?"

Muscles pointed to the back bumper of the Dodge. It was bent into the shape of the Chevy's bashed in back bumper. "They don't call you Hound Eyes for nothin'. That's Smeal."

Freddy, Neal, and Rafferty slowly backed away from Smeal's Dodge.

Stepping out of the Chevy, Hound Eyes walked to Smeal's window, stopped, and waved his hand in a dismissing motion. "Don't worry about a thing, Smeal," he said and jerked his finger toward Freddy. "We'll get those kids this time."

As Freddy, Neal, and Rafferty kept walking backwards, Muscles ran around the side of the Chevy, stopped next to Hound Eyes, and reached into his suit coat. "Let's get rid of them once and for all."

Hound Eyes nodded in agreement, but held up one finger. "Don't kill them all. Keep one alive. We'll make the little bastard tell us what they took out of that box."

As if coming from a deep tunnel, Neal's voice whispered low and secret. "Get on the train."

Freddy turned back toward Neal. All he saw was Neal's and Rafferty's backs and their running feet, rushing toward the train.

Freddy sprinted after them. Before he caught up, Neal grabbed the ladder rungs of the side of a moving hopper and climbed to the top. Rafferty was right behind him. When the car was three car-lengths away from the crossing, Rafferty was halfway up the ladder, but Freddy was nowhere near him.

Rushing to catch the fleeing hopper car, Freddy thought he was out of danger, but behind him, the report of a gunshot smacked in his ear. Neal grabbed the top of his head and fell into the hopper car.

Freddy knew that if he didn't catch the fleeing car and get out the range of the bullets, he would be next. He increased his speed and made his jump. He landed awkwardly and missed his grip. For a moment, his breath caught in his throat. Bent over, he stumbled close to the moving steel wheels of the car, but he regained his footing, ran after the car, and jumped again.

This time, one of his hands snagged a rung on the ladder. But his hand began to slip. He hooked his arm around the side of the ladder and slapped his other hand onto the rung to stop his fall. Keeping a firm grip on the rung, he pulled himself up. Now that Muscles was close, the car that had seemed to race down the tracks when he was chasing it seemed to ponderously move along. Waiting for Rafferty to move up the ladder, Freddy entwined his legs in the ladder rung.

From behind his back, Hound Eyes shouted, "Don't shoot the black-headed bastard. Get that orange-headed smart ass before he gets in the car."

Rafferty was right at the top of the car. One more pull and he would be able to crawl over the top and drop behind the safety of the steel wall of the car. Freddy hoped he wouldn't land on Neal's body. Right next to Freddy's foot, Muscles ran alongside the train and aimed a gun at Rafferty's orange-headed head. Freddy kicked at the gun. Muscles didn't fire but jerked the gun out of the way. Freddy missed. Keeping the gun out of Freddy's kicking range, Muscles took aim again. Freddy squinted with apprehension and braced for the shot that would surely kill Rafferty.

Before the gun fired, like a jack in the box, Neal jumped up above the top of the wall of the car with his hand held high. Freddy's heart filled with joy. Neal was still alive.

Before Neal popped back down, he slung a handful of iron ore pellets right at Muscles. A few of the pellets bounced off the top of Freddy's head. But the lion's share rocketed into Muscle's upturned face. Still running, Muscles lowered his gun, grabbed his eyes, and turned away. Rafferty scrambled over the wall of the car and dropped over the side to safety. Neal jumped up again and slung more pellets down on Muscles.

As the train increased speed, Freddy struggled to cling onto the ladder. With a tremendous burst of scared energy, he grabbed the upper rungs of the ladder, placed his foot on the bottom rung, and pulled himself up.

From behind him, Hound Eyes shouted to Muscles, "Grab his legs. Make him fall off. I'll try to wound him."

Freddy heaved with all his might and pulled himself upward. He was halfway up the ladder. Even though Hound Eyes was only trying to wound him, Freddy could feel the gun aiming at his back. Something tugged at his leg. He looked down. Muscles had climbed onto the bottom rungs of the ladder and clamped a hand onto Freddy's ankle. Muscles yanked down. The unexpected jerk caused Freddy's feet and his left hand to slip off the rung and make his body turn sideways. The first joints on the fingers of his right hand slipped just over the steel rung. Kicking at Muscles with his free foot, he clamped the ends of his fingers down as if they were claws of an eagle and held on. With his arm stretched to the limit, his body settled against the wall of the car. For a moment, he felt the overworked muscles in his back and shoulders painfully burning. He ignored the burn and tightened his grip on his right hand until his fingers crawled back onto the rung and attained a palm grip. With a solid grip, he immediately re-gripped with his left hand.

But the train's increasing speed and Muscle's weight was tugging him off the ladder. His left hand slipped off again. This time it was too far down to re-grip. He closed his eyes. With his right hand, he held onto the ladder with all his might. He strained so hard to keep hanging on that tiny silver stars exploded behind his tightly closed eyes.

Just before his hand was about to slip from the iron rung and send him crashing onto the tracks and under the rolling steel wheels, Neal and Rafferty popped up over the other side of the car. While Rafferty slung down iron ore pellets, Neal threw his tarpaulin shirt at Muscles. It caught between the ladder and the car and waved in the wind. With his eyes wide with fright, Muscles let loose of Freddy's ankle. With the tarpaulin shirt flapping in his face, Freddy re-gripped with his left hand, and placed his foot on the ladder. Gasping for air, he climbed upward.

Muscles came around the ladder on the inside of the car and grabbed Freddy's knee. Freddy lifted his other foot and kicked at Muscle's face. Muscles jerked away, and pellets rained down from above. Muscles lifted his hands to protect his face. Freddy grabbed the tarpaulin shirt and flung it over Muscles head. This time, when Freddy kicked, he made a direct hit. Muscles reached for the ladder rung, but with the tarpaulin shirt covering his eyes, his hand only grazed the rung. The train swayed. Muscles fell toward the coupler that connected the two cars together. His head hit the cutting bar. As his body rolled under the moving wheels, his head hit the steel rail and cracked open in a sickening splat.

Running alongside the train, Hound Eyes lifted

his gun to shoot, but as if it had been launched with a spring loaded device, Neal's tarpaulin shirt sailed out from under the train and flopped onto the ground, right in front of Hound Eye's feet. He tripped over the tarpaulin but stopped his fall with his hands. Muscle's foot and the stump of his bloody arm flung out from under the train and landed in front of Hound Eye's face. As horror filled his face, more pellets rained down on his head. Blinded by the rocketing pellets, he shielded his face with his arms. In the process, he swung the gun away from Freddy and the car.

As the train pulled away, Hound Eyes stayed on his hands and knees and blindly fired his weapon. With bullets ricocheting off the steel sides of the car, Freddy climbed up the ladder. Just before the top, he paused and sucked in a much-needed breath. Before he could exhale, one final bullet zinged the skin on his forearm and burned like a hot match. Without stopping to breathe, he pulled himself upward, got a knee over the edge of wall of the car, and worked the rest of his body up onto the narrow top. He threw his other leg over the wall and dropped down.

Outside the wall of the car, another volley of shots whacked the air. But Hound Eyes was too far away. The bullets weakly plunked into the side of the steel wall and harmlessly dropped onto the railroad bed.

Shaking from seeing Muscles fall underneath the car and being rolled and cut into chunks and pieces, Freddy sat down on the steel hump in the center of the hopper car and looked at his hands. Red iron ore dust coated his skin.

Neal kept in a crouch, made his way down the slanted floor of the hopper, and stopped at the little mountain of iron ore. He placed a reassuring hand on Freddy's back. "How did Muscles fall off?"

Freddy looked up at Neal. "I kicked him and he fell under the car and got cut to pieces. I don't feel too good."

Sitting on the iron ore, Rafferty folded his arms across his chest. "Don't feel bad about it. We didn't have a choice. It was him or us."

"The worst part of the situation," Neal said and forced a smile, "is that I lost my tarpaulin suit coat. I was just getting attached to that thing."

Freddy nodded in agreement and tried to smile, but a rotten feeling stayed in his chest.

As the train stormed down a grade, its whistle moaned one long blast. Freddy tried to get the image of Muscles falling under the wheels and being cut to pieces out of his mind. He looked to Rafferty. "I know I shouldn't feel bad about it, but if I wouldn't have kicked him, he wouldn't have fallen off."

Easily swaying to the motion of the car, Neal placed his hands on his thighs and looked toward Freddy and Rafferty. "If I wouldn't have thrown the tarpaulin, he could have pulled you off. It doesn't matter how it happened, it could have happened to anyone of us. The main thing is, we're still alive, and we're about to become rich." Attempting to change the subject, he glanced at his own red hands. "Looks like we're going to have red hands until we get to wherever this thing's going."

Rafferty shifted his weight from one side of his rear end to another. "If we don't get out of this thing pretty soon, we'll have more calluses on our asses than a two-bit whore."

While Freddy held his head in his hands, the train sung through high tree-covered hills, over a dusty bridge, and kept right on rolling.

Chapter 13

The long wail of the locomotive's whistle came from ahead of the long string of moving railroad cars, and Smeal continued to wait at the railroad crossing. Although Muscle's body parts that were strewn along the tracks were about fifty yards away, Smeal didn't want to look at them. He decided to use an old trick to take his mind off what had just happened. He would concentrate on something else. It didn't have to be anything important, just something to give his mind a break from the horror of the present. Adjusting his mirrored sunglasses, he lowered his head, peered out the windshield of his blue Dodge, and concentrated on what was to his right. A cross buck, railroad crossing sign stood next to a long curve of tracks. The word "Railroad" on one half of the rectangular tin sign, slanted downward at a forty-five degree angle. On the other half of the cross-buck sign the word "Crossing" read upward at another forty-five degree angle and formed an X. Light from out of a clear blue sky poked through bullet holes in the letters. Two rusted bolts held the sign to a splintering wood post. Dark-red grime, from years of diesel engine's exhaust and iron ore dust, coated the entire structure. Beyond that, coarse gray gravel lay between the creosote soaked ties and lined the outer area along the tracks that formed the railroad bed that ran between tall weeds and grasses.

As one of the railroad cars raced over the crossing with a staccato burst of its steel wheels, movement along the tracks caught Smeal's eye. He snapped his head toward the movement. Hound

Eyes trotted up the path next to the tracks. Then he slowed, walked along the side of the road, and headed toward Smeal.

Although death had never bothered him before, Smeal felt a familiar feeling of anticipation and fear. Sitting in his Dodge, he bent over and pretended to be fixing something under the dashboard. Without saying a word or acknowledging Smeal's presence, Hound Eyes huffed past Smeal's opened window.

Smeal sat up and looked into the rearview mirror. Hound Eyes placed his hand on the chrome handle of the door of the Chevy. As if he had forgotten something, he stopped, turned around, and came back to Smeal's window. With a strange, contented look on his face, he whispered, "As soon as the train goes past, we got to get out of here before they find what's left of the Muscles. That black-headed kid kicked him under the train and got away." He hastily walked back to the Chevy, got in, slammed the door, and sat behind the wheel, laughing.

Smeal hated the feeling that someone was laughing at him behind his back. There was a time when everyone respected him, and he had marveled when people became anxious when he walked into a room. Hound Eyes hadn't known him then, but if he had, he wouldn't even think of laughing at him. After all, in 1949, there had been a big elimination the public knew little about. When honored mobsters had failed to punish someone who clearly deserved punishment, Smeal had gotten rid of Eddie O'Hare, the man who Capone had let run his dog and racetracks, but ratted to the IRS about where to find Capone's financial records. Eddie's little stunt had cost Al Capone two hundred fifteen thousand in back taxes, and generated a sentence of eleven years in Federal prison.

Smeal never knew the identity of the big man in charge, but for some reason, someone had spread it around that if the cops took Smeal in for the killing of Eddie, he was going to rat, too. Back then most mobsters had self-respect, integrity, justice, and honor. But even if Smeal had not killed Eddie, and they thought he had thought about exposing crime members to the law, then that was a good enough reason to have him killed. The reasoning being, "When in doubt, take them out." The big man in charge had slated Smeal to have his house painted, but Smeal had lucked out again.

The public never knew Capone had arranged a look-alike to take his place in prison. When it was reported that his look-alike's mental and physical condition were severely deteriorated, the look-alike was released from prison and sent to a Baltimore hospital for brain treatment.

A few years after his discharge from the hospital, the Capone look-alike died of a stroke and pneumonia. The public and most authorities believed the look-alike was the real Al Capone, and he was the one who took the blame for killing Eddie O'Hare. So the big man canceled the contract to paint Smeal's house.

Smeal didn't want to do anything to arouse the big man's suspicions again. If he did, it would be the end of his life, and the big man would take his fortunes from the vault. Smeal hoped using those kids to find the vault would help keep him out of the picture and safe, but he could never be sure.

As the train continued to rumble over the crossing, he nervously twitched his thumb against the steering wheel and watched in the rearview mirror. Two cars pulled up and stopped behind Hound Eye's Chevy. As if he were on a casual Sunday afternoon drive, Hound Eyes sat with his arm propped on his window, smoking a cigarette.

In front of Smeal, the train swayed and clacked faster and faster. As the long string of hopper cars rolled across the crossing, he thought about calling the police or an ambulance to pick up the pieces of Muscle's body, but he figured the New York mob would take the heat for this one. So he shrugged off the feeling.

When the New York mob had gained a toehold in the garbage hauler's unions, they did what they always did to make money. First they asked someone to do something. Then they told them to do it. If they didn't do it, bones would be broken. If that didn't work, the killing would start. Their actions were just a tool used in the business that created a shroud of fear that usually kept everyone in line. Because of the mob's reputation, the investigation into Muscle's death would be short lived. To keep the news media happy, the police would make a pretense of working while doing nothing.

Hound Eyes took a long drag off his cigarette and flicked it into the weeds at the side of the road. The constant clacking of the steel wheels of the hopper car began to fade. When they dulled to a few single clacks, a red caboose clattered across the crossing.

Quiet returned to the crossing.

Smeal shifted his blue Dodge into first gear and took one last look at the scattered body parts. He figured Hound Eyes was watching to see if he were going to throw up. He looked straight ahead and squared his shoulders, but all the while, what he really wanted to do was cry, not for the dead man, but because the kids had gotten away with the money. He let out the clutch, rumbled across the railroad crossing, and sped down the road.

Hound Eye's slow-wittedness was maddening. Smeal had wanted to keep things simple. That way, fewer mistakes would have been made and fewer people would have been involved. But Hound Eyes had botched the job again. The people in the cars that had pulled behind Hound Eyes may have seen Smeal sitting in his blue Dodge. It they tied the Dodge in with the body parts, he could go to jail. He needed to get rid of the Dodge, and fast.

Any other kids would have surrendered, given Hound Eyes the box, or at least shown Hound Eyes and Muscles where the mine was that had held Capone's vault. But these kids weren't your everyday gullible types that think they know everything and know nothing. Their little bit of common sense and a stronger will to stay alive, kept making his plans precede at a slow creep. But another thing was bothering him. He was beginning to like those kids. How they had outsmarted Muscles and Hound Eyes had been clever. It was actually humiliating, but Smeal appreciated the sheer nerve and ingenuity of the kids.

He drove to a run-down housing district in Youngstown and stopped in front of a grassless lot where kids were playing stickball. Smeal considered them lucky. The squalor around them could motivate them toward something better, but they were too naive to realize their luck.

He looked to his right. Days and nights of airborne grime from the steel mills had lightly coated the roofs, causing them to have a uniform color of gray grease. A slight breeze urged fine red dust to gently swirl on down the filthy streets that surrounded clusters of small tumbledown houses. A few yards from where Smeal had stopped the Dodge, a fierce dog ran from between two garbage cans and chased a rat over a pile of garbage. With the dog's mouth nipping at its tail, the rat barely stayed ahead of the dog. It raced across the toes of barefoot children playing on the cracked sidewalk. As they screamed in fright, the rat jumped over a pile of refuse and escaped through a hole in a rickety wooden fence. The dog whined and pawed at the fence. Then it turned and lay on the only patch of grass in a foot-hammered front yard.

At the intersection of a brick-paved street, a 1957 two-tone Ford, sputtered to a stop and stalled. Harsh Ohio winters, salted roads, poor steel, and rust had eaten the body of the car so badly that it looked as if it could have been carved from a huge piece of cheese that giant river rats had gnawed holes into. Three men, dressed in grimy mill clothes, got out and slammed the doors of the Ford. The flimsy body of the Ford shuddered and looked like it was going to shake apart. While the other two men watched, one man lifted the hood. He held his hand on something next to the engine and yelled to the driver. "Try it now!"

The driver hit the starter. The engine backfired

once and coughed to life. The man slammed the hood and smiled. As tiny pieces of rusted metal dropped off the body of the Ford, it sputtered away.

Carrying metal lunch boxes, the men briskly walked down the sidewalk. One by one, they turned, waved a good-bye, and disappeared into old but freshly painted houses.

Around the corner, a slanted wooden pole had been nailed to a front porch post. Hanging from the pole, the tattered red-white-and-blue of old glory fluttered above a rotting wooden step that led to a broken washing machine sitting the porch.

Youngstown being the third largest steel producer in the world, the men were probably just getting off midnight turn at one of the Republic Iron and Steel Works or from Youngstown Sheet and Tube. Smeal reminisced how he used to sell men like this instant winner gambling tickets, but he had never forgot the sweaty man carrying a lunch box who reeked of sulfur. When Smeal had asked him if he wanted to buy a ticket, the man had growled. "Those things are illegal. Quit sponging off society. Join the Army or get in the mill and go to work. You'll become a part of the human race for the first time in your life."

Smeal believed men like this would never change. It wasn't his fault that they were ignorant. If they hadn't got caught up in the stupid American dream of having a family, which demanded money to feed and clothe an ugly wife who would pop out a kid every few years, they would have raised their standard of living faster than they ever could by working in a filthy steel mill. He had seen the results of men working for big companies and believing the people in charge cared about them. In the end, the companies or the banks always found a way to steal their financial futures and call it good business. Deep in his heart, Smeal believed that someday these men who were loyal to the steel mills would be just like the many out of work people Capone had fed with the many soup kitchens that he had helped pay for in Chicago during the depression. They would be unemployed and hungry. All these men had the same things in common. They believed in God and fighting for their country, and they bathed in the belief that the police were honest.

If Smeal parked the car here, these working people wouldn't steal it. They would try to find out who it belonged to. When they couldn't, they would call the police. Eventually they would come, and Smeal didn't want anything to tie him in with the car that could lead to Muscle's body parts. Being close to the Day of Judgment, he didn't want to spend the remaining years of his life in a jail cell for petty car theft. He wasn't going to take a chance and leave the Dodge in this honest neighborhood.

He drove to the busiest section of Market Street and parked next the curb. Sitting behind the wheel, he felt tired and emptily weak. And he felt old, too old in a way to care, but he sloughed it off. There was nothing a long hot shower, followed by a night on his porch with a bottle of Scotch, wouldn't fix. But like it had been in the old days when he hardly ever drank or smoked, he was going to have to be like the high-powered gangsters who needed to stay in control of their senses and reflexes at all times. Tonight, he wouldn't be sitting on his porch with a bottle of Scotch. He would be in full control of his faculties.

He looked out the window of the Dodge. On his right, a man standing on the corner looked his way. Then he turned and talked to another man who kept his face concealed on the other side of the dirty-yellow brick building. The man had small dusty-green eyes and a pale completion that made him look like he had taken too much dope. And when he spoke his eyes narrowed.

In the old days, if Smeal had parked the car here, nothing would have happened to it. Back then he had a powerful voice and a presence that would intimidate any adversary. Back then some of the mob still had some fire in their veins, but after prohibition it had been lost, especially when they saw a large lack of concern among their fellow members. His easy days of getting something or keeping people at bay with just a mean look or a growl were gone. Now he had to live by his wits.

In a show of defiance, the green-eyed man standing on the corner made a fist with one hand and punched his other hand. Smeal cringed under the threat. He knew an old man is helpless unless people are afraid of him, but right now, looking old had an advantage. In a matter of minutes the man would take the Dodge. Then if it were traced back to Muscle's body parts, the green-eyed man would be a prime suspect.

Smeal left the keys in the ignition and the motor running. As the man on the corner pretended not to see him, Smeal stepped out of the car and quietly closed the door. Making sure the man was watching him, Smeal stood slightly hunched as if he expected to be flogged. Keeping a wary eye on the man, he walked a few blocks down the street, went into a bar, and called a cab.

Chapter 14

A few miles from the railroad crossing the train stopped. Freddy and his friends peered over the wall of the hopper car. On both sides of the tracks there was nothing but swampland.

Freddy turned toward Neal. "Are we getting off here?"

"You can if you want," Neal said, "but it looks like it's a long way to another crossing. I'm not walking down those tracks when I can ride."

Freddy rubbed his hands together and tried to rub the red ore dust from his skin. It didn't come off. "I guess you're right," he said, "but what if the train doesn't slow down again?"

"We'll end up in Pittsburgh."

Rafferty slid back down into the car, laced his hands behind his head, and lay back. "I can wait."

Freddy and Neal slid down the wall and began the wait.

When the train started up again, the sun was past high noon. Between taking turns watching for the unit ore train to slow down enough for them to jump off, they tried to get comfortable, but the iron ore hopper kept buffeting and swaying, kicking red ore dust through cracks in the car's wall. At first, the ore dust hadn't bothered Freddy, but now the air was hot and dry, and he couldn't get the taste of ore dust out of his lungs. It clung to his skin and stung the back of his throat. And the train never slowed down.

With the front of his shirt pulled up over his mouth to filter out the ore dust, Neal sat in a solemn mood.

Freddy stood up and peered over the edge of the hopper car. As the orange rim of the sun kissed the horizon, innumerable shards of brilliant color exploded and shot through the purple and orange clouds. When the sky grew darker in the west, the clouds turned to feathery purple fingers, and the train finally slowed.

Neal let the front of his shirt fall from his smiling face. His natural exuberance had returned. He jumped up and looked over the top of the car. "It looks like there's a road just across a field." He reached up, grabbed the top of the wall of the car, pulled himself up, and threw his leg over the side. Straddling the wall, he gestured to Freddy and Rafferty. "Come on up. We'll jump off, get on that road, and hitchhike back."

Rafferty reached up and rubbed his ore-stained red face with the back of his hand. "If I look like you guys, I could pass for an Indian." He pulled himself up onto the wall. "Let's get out of this red stuff."

Freddy climbed up and straddled the wall. "Let's wait until the train slows down a little bit more."

Neal nodded in agreement. "We are going a little too fast. But let's get ready." He climbed down the ladder on the outside of the car and poised to jump off. At the other end of the car, Rafferty did the same. The wheels under the car clacked faster. Freddy climbed down the ladder and stood above Neal.

Neal jerked on Freddy's pants leg. "It's picking up speed."

Freddy was sick of the ore dust, the constant

banging, and the constant clacking. He looked down at Neal. "If we don't get off now, we might end up a million miles away."

Neal gave him a questioning glance and looked toward Rafferty. Rafferty let loose of the ladder and jumped.

Neal gave Freddy a thumbs-up and leaped from the car.

Freddy needed to jump before the train picked up more speed. He stepped down the ladder and got ready to jump. Just before he was about to let loose of the ladder rung, a shudder of revulsion rushed through his body. A line of sharp stones and thorn bushes came up along the track. He hung on and waited for a clearer spot to jump. The train picked up speed. Just as he was about to climb back up and drop into the car, a stretch of tall soft grass came into view. He took a deep breath and leaped. He flew through the air. Like a soft green rug being pulled out from under him, the grass slipped past. His feet plopped down into a soft yellow mud embankment. He thrust his hands out to break his fall. One foot caught on a tree root. His chest slammed forward and thumped against the ground. His breath escaped in one sudden whoosh. He couldn't breathe. Struggling to catch his breath, he slid, headlong, down a steep, slimy slope of yellow mud.

At first, it wasn't bad. It was like sled riding down a snow-covered hill with no sled. Catching his breath, he felt confident that he would come out of this unexpected ride unscathed. But when he looked up, the trunk of a fallen tree, as wide as a weightlifter's rock hard shoulders, lay across his path. Using his elbows and legs like sled runners, he tried to steer away from it. But he was too late. With all his might, he pushed with his arms and tried to steer his body around the trunk. The momentum helped. He turned and cleared the trunk, but on the other side was a thick branch. Clunk! His head hit it. He felt his body slide sideways and rest against the branch. Everything went black.

***

Freddy awoke to the fragrance of an oak tree. In a haze, chattering came from far away. He looked to his right. While he had slept, a white moon had beamed down and lit the area where he had slid down the hill. Now he knew why he had been unable to stop. The rain had washed away the yellow covering of mud and had exposed and lubricated the gray clay underneath.

As he rubbed the lump on his head, the unmistakable sound of a raccoon's chattering came from somewhere above his head. He jerked his head to his left and stared into the semi-darkness. The top of the fallen oak tree ran through an almost invisible narrow track of vegetation. On top of the trunk of the fallen tree, the raccoon stood on its hind legs. Its golden eyes stared Freddy right in the face. Freddy shook his head to clear his vision. The raccoon lowered itself to all fours and nonchalantly stepped down the tree trunk. The last thing Freddy saw of the raccoon was its bushy ringed-tail trailing into a dark tangle of bushes. Freddy's aching lungs felt like they were full of dust. Still a little dizzy, he coughed up a little ore dust phlegm and spit it on the ground.

To his left, an animal trail zigzagged into dense foliage. When he was a child playing hooky in the familiar woods of Patagonia, he had felt at home, but now, nothing looked familiar.

As his eyes adjusted to the night, he could see without the aid of a flashlight. He climbed around the tree trunk and dug his fingers into the wet clay. Clawing at the clay, he pulled his body up the steep slope and looked above the horizon. A spooky mist shrouded the top of a stand of trees. For a moment, the air felt like a graveyard in the winter. Hopping he could find Neal and Rafferty before dawn, he continued climbing.

When he stopped to catch his breath, he lay on his stomach and studied what was in front of him. As if they were waiting for a train to lumber on down the steel rails they were supporting, the dark rectangular ends of the railroad ties loomed above him. He crawled upward a few feet and held up his head. The shiny tops of the steel rails glistened with dewdrops. Just before the top, he looked to his right. The brush, clustered along the sides of the tracks, created a dark tunnel that seemed to stretch to infinity. Thinking how Muscle's head had cracked with a sickening splat and his foot and the stump of his bloody arm had flown out from under the steel wheels of the hopper, he hoped Neal and Rafferty had made it off the train in one piece.

With one final effort, he pulled himself up over the crest of the steep incline. After pausing, he stood up. Looking around, he slapped his arms against his sides to generate a little heat. Then he cupped his hands around his mouth and called into the darkness, "Neal!"

No reply.

He curved his tongue beneath his teeth and whistled, loud and shrill. Cocking his ear, he listened for a reply

Nothing.

He whistled again.

Still, nothing.

He threw his hands up defeat and walked down the tracks.

Beneath the overhanging branches of a dark tree, he picked up a stick to use as a weapon. Carrying it as he walked along the railroad tracks, he came to an opening that led into the forest. He turned and ventured in. In the shadow of an old maple tree, he dropped the stick into a patch of grass. Scanning the area, he whistled once more and listened.

Still, no answer.

He sat down, picked up the stick, and leaned against the trunk the tree. He had planned to close his eyes and take a short break, but laden with fatigue, he fell asleep.

In his dream, as he listened to the sound of water falling on a hard surface, the smell of urine invaded his nostrils. Then the sound of voices cut the silent night.

"I don't know where he can be," someone said.

"Let's keep looking," another voice said.

Then Freddy knew he wasn't dreaming. In a blazing fury, he jumped to his feet. With his right fist clenched and the stick clutched in his left hand, he was set to strike.

Holding his penis and spraying urine on his pants, Rafferty jerked away from the tree in fright.

As if he hadn't seen Freddy, Neal laughed and pointed to Rafferty's pants. "If you wouldn't hold you piss so long, it wouldn't blast you away from the tree."

Flushing with embarrassment, Rafferty turned red and squirmed, but managed to zip up his fly. With a quizzical expression on his face, he held his hand on his thumping chest and looked at Freddy. "You're covered with mud. Where were you? We've been looking all night."

Neal chucked Freddy under the chin. "This is the third time we went past here. We couldn't see you anywhere."

Freddy paused to let his heartbeat slow down. "After I jumped off, I rolled down a muddy hill and got knocked out. I must've rolled behind a big stump." He looked toward the horizon. "Did you guys go over to the road?"

Neal's face turned solemn. "There's no road there."

"What?" Freddy said with disbelief. "Just before we jumped off, I saw where one should be. It looked like it was just across that field of grass."

"We thought so, too," Rafferty said softly with his face lowered. "There's no road. That opening's a river."

"Maybe if we walk the tracks," Neal said with sudden enthusiasm, "we can come to a crossing."

Freddy was in no mood to force his tired body to walk the tracks, especially at night. With exhaustion, he helplessly dropped his arms. "I didn't hear the train blow for a crossing or blow for anything."

Rafferty looked puzzled. "What's blowing a

horn got to do with a crossing?"

"The railroaders use horn signals when something is about to happen. I don't know all of them, but I know when they blow two longs, a short, and one long, they are coming to a railroad crossing."

"I've heard that," Rafferty said. "It sounds like, here comes the bride. *Dah, Dah, Di, Dah.*"

As if in thought, Neal placed his palm on his chin. "Since we jumped off, I didn't hear a horn play, here comes the bride. I didn't hear a horn at all."

"Well," Freddy said and shrugged. "If there's a crossing, it's a long way off."

Neal looked around uneasily. "It's too dark to do anything now. Let's get some shut-eye. When it gets light, we'll check out that river. Maybe we can build a raft and float to a bridge where we can get onto a road and hitchhike home."

In the silver light of the moon, they walked away from the pee-soaked maple tree and stopped under a much-better-smelling oak tree. Here a soft blanket of brown leaves covered the ground making a comfortable place to stretch out. After they lay down, Neal laced his hands behind his head for a pillow and looked at the leaf-laden tree branches above.

"We'll only rest until light," he said and yawned. "Then we'll check out that river."

Freddy nodded, curled up, and tried to sleep. But he wanted to make sure he wasn't dreaming. He kept watching Neal and Rafferty. Sitting upright, he leaned his back against the oak tree. Peeking through slit eyes, he eventually he dozed off.

Chapter 15

Smeal had never thought a couple of kids could knock a strong man like Muscles off the train and ride away. In the old days, Smeal could have killed Muscles with a single blow just for being ignorant. And it wouldn't have bothered him in the least. Muscles was like all the rest of the gangsters with wrecked minds: He didn't deserve to live. He was blind to his flaws and summoned disaster upon himself. He had allowed the need for vengeance to cloud his thinking. Rather than do the job right, he had disgraced himself. But he couldn't help it. Men like him were born destined to be cowards. Cowards were already dead inside. By putting them out of their misery, Smeal believed he was actually doing these types of people a favor. Not to mention the service to mankind of making it impossible for these people to pass on their ignorance by fathering children. After all, survival was the name of the game. If killing a few people was what it took to get ahead, Smeal was glad to do it.

Right now, the thing that bothered him was that he didn't know where the train was going. He could just sit back and wait for those kids to spend all the money in the box and come back. If they did, and they knew where the mine or the vault was, they would go to it.

The problem was that if the train went all the way to the West Coast, those kids might get lost and never come back. They were young. Death to them was a distant reality that only happened to other people. It probably didn't bother them that if they tried to jump off the train, they could be cut to pieces just like Muscles had been. If they died, the location of the coalmine, the vault, and money in Capone's pocket would die, too.

If he could find out where the train was going, he might be able to find those kids. And when he did, it shouldn't be too hard to take the money that was in the box and get them to tell him where the vault was. After all, they were just like the rest of society. They were essentially people who wanted to be told what to do. When Muscles had trotted toward the train that had taken his life, he had looked tired and dispirited. He was one of the many wanna-be gangsters who thought they knew everything but were narrowed-minded and projected attitudes that went with their so-called professions.

Hound Eyes was a big man, but even if they were ignorant, big men usually gained power positions. And the worst part about Hound Eyes was that once he had what he wanted, he didn't want it anymore. It was all about the chase and the capture, getting one over on the other guy. Usually Hound Eyes would be about as easy to disturb as a block of granite. But if he found out Smeal was using him to find the vault and he wasn't going to get a share, there would be blood all over the mineshaft.

But he may not need him. Although not in the crime loop, as well as he had been in past, Smeal still had some connections, and valuable information could still be had at the Green Parrot Tavern. The railroad yardmaster that worked midnight turns always showed up there. Harry would know where the train was going.

***

At the Green Parrot Tavern, Smeal sat down on the barstool, wet his lips, and laid a twenty-dollar bill on the bar. "I've heard Harry comes in here."

The bartender glanced at the bill and nodded.

Smeal pushed it toward him. "Set me up with a seven and seven, and keep the change. If Harry shows up, let me know."

The bartender took the bill and put it in his pocket. "No problem. Harry's due any minute now."

The bartender set a glass half filled with ice on the bar, opened a bottle of 7-up and began to pour it over the ice. Smeal held up his hand in a stopping motion. The bartender quit pouring. Smeal held his hand in front of the glass and encouragingly waved it. The bartender tilted a fifth of Seagrams Seven. When the 7-up darkened, Smeal pointed his finger at the glass. The bartender stopped pouring the whisky. Smeal picked it up, walked to a table, and sat in a dark wooden chair with its arms supporting his elbows. With his drink setting on the table in front of him, he leaned back and rested his feet on the edge of the table. After five minutes, he let his feet fall to the floor and looked at the bartender. The bartended shrugged and waited on a patron.

A man wearing a dirty Yankees Baseball cap slid a bar stool across the floor and turned toward the bartender. "It gets worse every day." Rolling his sleeves up to his elbows, he continued. "The workingman always gets screwed over." Reaching into his pocket, his bare forearms arms danced with muscle.

Although the man projected the image of a hardworking man with dirt under his fingernails,

Smeal had no pity for him. Smeal believed that if the man had any brains, he would be the employer or the boss. He wouldn't be a whining crybaby impersonating a man sitting at the bar. He would a man who could take charge. He would take control of not only the duties of the job, but the human beings behind the other people that were less capable than him. Smeal took a sip from his glass and sighed. To him, the man had to be some kind of a loon to believe that the workingman was always mistreated or exploited, and there was nothing he could do to change it.

Looking at his glass, Smeal turned it with his thumb and forefinger and whispered under his breath, "Let the lazy bastard fight his way up like I had to."

The bartender looked in Smeal's direction. "You need another drink?"

Smeal waved his hand down. "Not yet." He wondered why Harry hadn't showed up. He should have been in by now. He worked six days a week, all midnight turns. He always came in first thing in the morning and played the bug number, the daily three-digit, tax-free lottery number ran by the mob.

When he had been in better health, Smeal didn't mind waiting. He could crouch all night on a rooftop and wait for a chance to make a little easy money. When there was a promising situation, his patience was infinite. He belched, stuck his finger in his mouth, and pulled out a wad of chewing tobacco. He glanced at the bartender. The bartender had his back turned. Smeal flicked the wad of tobacco under the table. Looking around, he stuffed his mouth with a fresh wad. When he got up and headed toward the restroom door, a man barged through the door and collided into him.

The man hesitated only long enough to say, "Out of my way, you elephant-assed clown."

The man's face was puffed, and his rosy cheeks showed that he had been up all night or had too much to drink. In the old days, Smeal would have thrown the man to the floor, but being imprisoned in his almost useless broken POW body, he shrugged the man off and went into the restroom.

After Smeal walked out the restroom, his eyes roamed the room. The man who had banged into him staggered to a table and leaned on its edge. He teetered above a chair for a moment. When he plopped into the chair, his breath hissed out. Then he stared at Smeal.

Smeal looked away.

But the man persisted. "Hey, you!"

Smeal spun around in bewilderment.

The man thrust his finger at Smeal. "Yeah, you! Pull up a chair. Don't be so goddamn shy."

Smeal turned his head away.

The man slid a chair away from the table far enough for Smeal to sit in. "Stop feeling sorry for yourself. Haul your ass over here and join the human race."

Smeal expanded his chest and turned toward the man. "Maybe I don't feel like joining you." He threw a scowl at the man and turned toward the bartender.

The man turned his semi-bald head to the side and growled. "Ah, forget it, friend." He turned to the bartender. Hey, Frank, your chicken pick any winners?"

The bartender shook his head. "Don't worry about that dumb chicken." He placed his hand on the Pabst Blue Ribbon beer tap handle. "You need another beer?"

The man's head bobbed with laughter. "Is there pigeon poop in the Vatican?"

Nodding, the bartender glanced toward Smeal and tilted his head toward the man. It was the man Smeal had been waiting for. It was Harry.

The bartender drew a mug of beer, carried it over to Harry's table, and set it down. "The last time I brought that chicken in, he crapped all over the place."

"See, I told you those were crappy numbers." Laughing, Harry picked up the beer. Referring to Smeal, he looked up at the bartender. "You gettin' so hard up for customers that you let anybody in here?"

Pointing to Harry, the bartender winked. "I let you in, didn't I?"

Harry laughed and looked toward Smeal. "No offense, buddy. I was only trying to rile you. Since Frank isn't going to bring his chicken in to pick a bug number, I got to do something to liven the place up a bit."

Smeal didn't believe he had almost ruined an opportunity to use the social lubricating abilities of a few drinks. His scowl changed into a smile. "What's a chicken got to do with the bug number?"

Harry pointed to the bar. Frank's got numbers painted on the floor back there. He puts pieces of corn on the numbers and lets the chicken in. Whatever numbers the chicken picks first, we play."

Smeal got up, walked over, and sat at Harry's

table.

Harry worked his legs out from under the table, stood up, leaned over, and extended his hand in friendship. "Name's Harry, Harry Staul."

Smeal rubbed his chin, stood up, and shook Harry's hand. "Smeal's the name. You been coming here long?"

"Just about every damn day. Steady midnight got me all wound up, got to come in here and get my sanity back."

Smeal sat down. "I know what you mean," he lied. "I had a friend who worked on the railroad, had the same problem."

As he sat down, Harry's eyes widened with interest. "Where did your friend work?"

"I think the Penn Central. Haven't seen him in years."

"I work for the Erie. We don't get to see too many people from the Penn Central."

"I'm not sure," Smeal said, fishing for more information. "My friend said he ran the line that took B&O coke hoppers down to Wheeling, West Virginia."

Harry held up his hand and waved in a stopping motion. "No, no, Fairmont, West Virginia is where the coke plant is, not Wheeling.

Smeal leaned back in his chair. Satisfaction filled his chest. He had gotten the information he had wanted, but he tried for more. "I always wanted to take a drive down there." He encouragingly rolled his hand. "You know, just to see what the place is like where all those cars go."

Harry held his hands chest high with his palms toward Smeal. "You can if you want. But I wouldn't. The place is about one hundred fifty miles away, sits between Clarksburgh and Morgantown." He shook his head as if he were getting an awful smell out of his lungs. "Even though it's right next to the Monongahela River, it's a hard place to breathe. That coke dust and smoke from the ovens gets in your throat, you can't get the taste out for days."

Smeal lowered his head and his voice. "I don't think a few hours would hurt." He exhaled and lifted his head. "What if I took a train?"

"No passenger train goes there." Harry's voice took on a tone of mischief. "You missed your big chance yesterday. Youngstown sent a unit ore train to Fairmont, it was supposed to go to Pittsburgh, but a big train wreck detoured it. It went right back to the B&O interchange in New Castle, and that was a big change. The Erie usually takes empty hoppers to New Castle." Harry took a large gulp of his beer, exhaled with contentment, and sat the mug on the table. "If you want, you can jump in an empty B&O hopper. It'll take the roundabout route, but eventually you'll ride right past the coke ovens."

Smeal smiled large. By highway, New Castle was only twenty miles away. Those kids could jump off the train when it slowed at the interchange. Then they would not get sucked under the wheels. It would be easy for them to hitchhike back to Sharon. He decided to order Hound Eyes and his flunkies to intercept them on the road out of the interchange, but if they didn't, the kid's '40 Ford with the shot-out radiator would still be sitting by the road at Peacock Alley. Eventually they would have to come back to get it. And when they did, he would be waiting.

Without dropping his false smile and phony cordiality, he looked at his watch and stood up. "I'm a little too old to be hopping trains, but thanks for the drink. I got to be going."

Chapter 16

A ways from the railroad tracks, Freddy, Neal and Rafferty were still sleeping under the oak tree. Somewhere in the dark, dry leaves rustled. Although the sound had awakened him, Freddy didn't want to open his eyes. All around him, the indifferent unfriendly sounds of the unfamiliar forest could be heard. He wanted to ignore the sounds of the night and sleep until the sun came up. Then he could see what might be lurking in the forest, but there was no use keeping his eyes closed and getting mauled by a bear or bit by a rabid raccoon. He opened his eyes. Turning toward the sound, he craned his neck and furtively glanced behind the tree. Nothing. He turned and searched the moon's silver darkness. Still seeing nothing, he looked to Neal. Neal awoke with a start and stumbled to his feet.

Rafferty peeked out from behind the tree, rubbing his eyes and yawning. "What's going on?"

Behind him, a black bear stood on its hind legs and growled. Rafferty turned around. The bear stood directly in front of his terror frozen face. With one gigantic leap, Rafferty jumped away from the threat. As if it were trying to defend itself in all ways at once, the bear swung around and swiped at the air.

Freddy swallowed and tried to quench the terror rising in his throat. He tensed to run.

Neal slowly reached over, slowly placed a restraining hand on Freddy's shoulder, and whispered, "Don't make any quick movements and don't run."

Watching the bear's exposed claws slashing at the air, Freddy froze. "Why not?"

Neal let his hand slowly slide from Freddy's shoulder. "Because he'll chase you." He stared at the bear.

The bear stopped swinging and stared back at Neal.

As if he were talking to a baby, Neal said, slow and gentle, "What's the matter, little bear? Did we scare you?"

Freddy couldn't believe his ears. A trapped feeling of terror invaded his chest, and Rafferty stood rigid with tension, but Neal managed to calmly talk to the bear as if it were a baby.

As if amazed, the bear continued to stare at Neal. Its eyes looked like it couldn't decide if it wanted to charge or run. Then it slowly leaned toward Neal. Freddy had seen tomcats do this right before they attacked. They would lean toward the other cat until they were close enough to bring up their paw and strike. Freddy had never seen one miss. He opened his mouth to warn Neal. Before he could utter a sound, Rafferty woofed out a deep, sickening, whooping cough.

The bear turned its head to the side and looked like it was going cry. Rafferty let out another gut wrenching cough. The bear dropped to all fours, turned, gave Rafferty one last sorrowful parting look, and ambled away.

Neal looked at Rafferty. "You sound like coughing your guts out. Are you sick?"

"Heck no." Rafferty woofed. "It took years to perfect that cough. Any time I wanted to get out of school, I'd go into the principal's office, cough a few times, and he would send me home."

"I don't care how many times you can cough and scare that bear away," Freddy said. "I don't want to stay up all night watching for a bear and listening to you hack your brains out."

"Thank you for the news flash," Rafferty said and toddled toward Freddy. "However!" He held up one finger. "I was under the impression that I didn't have any brains to hack out."

Neal chuckled and jerked his thumb over his shoulder. "Let's head for the river."

As they dubiously inched their way toward the river, despite the semi-darkness that surrounded them and the uncertainty of where they were or where they were going, Freddy felt like it was a holiday. They were together again, doing something together. When they had been separated, the holiday atmosphere had evaporated.

At the river and away from the cover of trees, the light of the moon momentarily sheathed the water with glitters of silver. Just beyond a stand of tall grass, a small peninsula jutted out into the silver river. At the shoreline, river water gently rolled past a rock-strewn, sandy shore.

Freddy glanced at the peninsula and then at Neal and Rafferty. "Whadda you think?"

Neal strutted fearlessly and picked up the pace. "Looks good to me. I don't think that bear will go in the water." He pointed to the end of the peninsula. "If we go out there, we can take turns watching while two of us sleep."

Rafferty lifted his hands to his face. "Maybe we can wash this red stuff off our faces and hands."

Rubbing his hands together in anticipation of

warmth, Freddy said, "Scout around for some wood. A good fire will keep that bear away."

Halfway to the peninsula, a definite snap cut the air. Rafferty tripped over something hidden in the grass and crashed to the ground.

Neal reached down to help him up. "Walk much?"

Rafferty took Neal's hand. "I only walk when I'm not falling down."

With Neal's help, Rafferty pulled himself upright and turned toward what he had tripped over: A ten-foot dead tree hidden in the tall grass. Its dry leaf-free branches hid amongst healthy growths of milkweed stocks and tall reed-like grass. Rafferty lifted the end of the tree. It pulled from the grass.

"You know what to trip over," Neal said. "Let's drag that thing to the peninsula. There's enough firewood on it to last all night."

Neal, Freddy, and Rafferty grabbed onto the heavy trunk of the tree and half muscled, half dragged it onto the peninsula.

While Rafferty and Neal ironed down tall grass with the sides of their feet, Freddy broke branches off the tree and stacked them in a pile, which blocked off the only land access to the peninsula.

"Hey, good idea." Neal pointed to the stack of branches. "That bear will never come near the fire. If he goes into the water, we'll hear him. We can all sleep now.

Rafferty faked a grimace of acute discomfort. "Ahh, man, I wanted to stay up all night and hack my brains out."

For a moment, Freddy started at Rafferty in quizzical disbelief. Then he went back to breaking off more tree branches for the fire.

Neal arranged small sticks into a pyramiding pile, pulled out his Zippo lighter, and crouched down. He held the tips of his fingers on top of the Zippo's case and his thumb on the bottom. With one quick flick, he snapped open the lighter, then ran his finger over the flint wheel. It spun. The wick ignited into an orange flame with a blue base. He reached out and held the flame under the small sticks. They sputtered for a moment then caught fire. Freddy fed the fire broken branches in a crisscross fashion. The flames caught and leaped around the branches. When the fire was about three feet high, he went to the water's edge and tried to wash the ore dust from his face and hands. But when he turned to Neal, Neal looked at him with a bewildered look. "It's still there."

Freddy bent over, dug into the river's edge and found a spot of soft yellow mud. Using the mud as if it were soap, he carefully washed the ore dust off.

While Neal and Rafferty did the same, Freddy gathered armfuls of tall grass and spread it onto the ground. Lying down on the soft bed, he watched the orange petals of the fire's flames lick toward the sky. Its continuous warm glow, relaxed Freddy. As he relaxed, Rafferty extended his hands to the fire. With the orange gleam flickering over his face, he sang Jimmy Rodgers song, "Waiting for a Train".

Neal idly prodded the flames with a long stick. Orange sparks winked up and spun upward in the river-scented breeze. When Freddy laced his hands behind his head, smoke funneled down and stung his eyes. He rolled onto his side, and a little gust of wind went past. It took the smoke and the scent of burning wood away.

As a light wind soughed through the forest around them, barks and whines of two wild dogs traveled on the warm night. From their whines Freddy knew the dogs had prey in sight. One dog kept signaling to the other dog the location of their victim. A rabbit let out a terrified cry, followed by sharp yips, then utter silence. Freddy figured the dogs had gotten something to eat and wouldn't be bothering him the rest of the night. And better yet, they would keep the bear away. He folded his hands and placed them under his head for a pillow. He had only planned to close his eyes for a moment, but once his did, being warm and comfortable, he fell fast asleep.

The next thing he knew, raindrops were falling onto his upturned face. He looked toward the fire. Hissing in protest, the few remaining flames went out, sending a wisp of smoke curling into the lavender light that had penetrated the fog and announced the arrival of dawn. As if it were an overture to a sun-filled day, the rain stopped and the sun's rays broke over the trees across the river, sending shafts of cathedral light down to brighten the peninsula. Before Freddy could begin to enjoy such a day, a wind kicked up. He could almost hear the cathedral light snap shut. The sky went gray. Rain returned with a fury, blasting against the water.

Neal jumped up. Trying to keep the rain from drenching the fire, he bent over and shielded it with his body. Waving his hand in Freddy's direction, he said something. But his voice submerged in a sudden surge of rain. As if God were slinging handfuls of pebbles from the sky, ice, as big as marbles plunked into the river's water and bounced off their heads.

The hail stopped only to be replaced by wind whipping across the water, followed by flashes of lightning zigzagging across the sky. A moment later, a long crash of thunder trembled in the heavens. The rain and hail stopped, but the tops of the trees, on the other side of the river, shook, and the tugging wind pulled on them until they bent over so far, the ends of their branches almost dipped into the water.

Rafferty jumped to his feet and batted the hailstones from his shoulders. "Hey, Neal, you think this rain's strong enough to get this red stuff off our clothes?"

Shaking the hailstones out of his long black hair, Neal nodded. "Looks like we're going to find out."

"Freddy reached up and peeled off his shirt. "We're soaking wet anyway. Let's wash our clothes in the river."

Neal bent over what was left of the dead tree, broke a handful of skinny branches off, and threw them onto the smoldering fire. Smoke billowed around the branches, but they were too wet to ignite. He mashed the little branches down with his foot, bent over, and blew on them. They puffed into flame and slowly grew. He hunched over the fire, put his elbows on his knees, and rubbed the palms of his hands together. "I might have been dreaming, but I thought I heard a switching engine last night."

Rafferty stepped out of his pants and underwear. While he washed them in the river, he looked to Neal. "What did you say about a switching engine?"

As if expecting a wise remark, Neal cast a suspicious glare toward Rafferty but repeated, "I thought I heard a switching engine last night."

Rafferty held his pants and began wringing out the water. "That's what I thought you said. I haven't heard an engine since we jumped off."

Freddy took off his pants, washed them in the river, and twisted them until most of the water eked out. "It would be nice if an engine was going back the way we came. After I dry these out" — he pointed off in the distance — "I'm going to climb that oak tree over there and get a look around."

After they wrung out their clothes, they pushed sticks into the ground around the fire. Then they hung their clothes on the sticks. As they waited for their clothes to dry, a few clouds in the east turned crimson, and golden rays shot toward the sky. The full light of morning had arrived. While the sun blazed the gray sky away and revealed a bright blue-sky morning, Rafferty skipped flat rocks across the surface of the calm river water.

***

Wearing dry but wrinkled clothes, Freddy and his friends picked their way through the tall grass until they came to the tall oak tree. At the trunk, Freddy jumped up but couldn't get a hold of the lowest branch. Neal laced his fingers together and held his hands at knee level. "Here, use this as a step."

Freddy placed his left foot in Neal's laced hands. "Okay, on three."

On the count of three, Freddy hopped his right

foot off the ground. While Neal lifted him, he pushed off with his left foot. The momentum shot him to the branch. He grabbed it, swung his leg over, and rolled until he straddled the branch. Then he stood on the branch and began to climb.

At the windy top, Freddy reached over his head and grabbed a skinny branch. Wind was usually stronger up high than it was on the ground, and today was no exception. Holding the branch, he walked out onto a foot wide limb. He tried to scan the area but could only stare into a leaf-filled branch that blocked his line of sight. A strong gust of wind kicked up and unbalanced him. Hanging onto the branch above his head, he teetered on the limb. The fear of falling dropped into his stomach and ran up his spine. He planted his feet firmly on the limb, took a deep breath, and let it out, slow and easy. Although his fear subsided, with one hand, he continued to cautiously hold onto the branch over his head. With his other hand, he moved the branch blocking his view out of his line of sight. As if he had pulled a switch, when he moved the branch, the wind stopped. Then, with the warm rays of the sun beaming bright and sunny, he searched for signs of civilization. No signs of life were close by, not even the bear. Way off in the distance, tall trees blocked his view. If he and his friends were going to get to a road, they would have to build a raft and float to a bridge or take a long walk down the railroad tracks. He turned to climb back down. For a moment, the wind kicked up. He held the branch tightly and stared at the surrounding forest. In the distance, a small clump of treetops swayed and created a small opening just big enough for him to see a switching yard. Off to the side, a dull-red railroad yard office with a green roof was a welcome sight. The yard office looked deserted until a locomotive sashayed down one of the tracks and stopped in front of the office. The wind stopped. The treetops clumped back together and blocked his view.

From under the tree, Rafferty yelled up, "What do you see?"

Freddy aimed his voice downward and yelled, "It looks like there's a little switching yard, but it's a long way off."

As Freddy climbed halfway down the tree, Neal yelled up. "Which way is it?"

Freddy quit climbing down and yelled back over his shoulder, "Further down the tracks, in the same direction we were going yesterday." He stepped on the branch above Neal's outstretched hand. "But if we take a short cut, it will be shorter than walking the tracks."

"Are you sure it's a switching yard?" Rafferty cupped his hand to his ear. "I didn't hear anything all night long."

Neal reached up and eased Freddy down onto the ground. "It doesn't matter what kind of a yard it is, there has to be a road close by."

Rafferty turned his back to the thick brush and looked toward the easy route through the tall grass that led to the river. "Which way is that short cut?"

Freddy tilted his head downward and pointed to the thick brush in front of a thicket of trees. "Straight ahead."

Rafferty turned back toward the thick brush. "It figures."

With the ore dust and railroad grime washed from their faces, the trio eased into the brush. As they weaved through the thorny undergrowth, the sun blazed onto the top of their heads, and heated the rain-soaked ground, causing humid air to wrap around them like a thick clammy blanket. Once out the other side of the undergrowth, they gingerly walked into the thicket of trees, where a welcome cool shade greeted them.

Neal reached up with the back of his hand and wiped the sweat from his forehead. "Stay alert, you guys." He took the lead. "That bear might be nosin' around."

Just then, they picked up a winding trail that moved gradually downhill. Hiking was easy, but in a matter of minutes they broke out of the cool shade of the trees and walked into a warm jungle of blackberry bushes. In the skeletal branches of a dead tree above their heads, black crows, as big as chickens, squawked an alarm, took flight, and lumbered off into the distant treetops. Although leaves rustled when the huge crows landed, Freddy could no longer see the crows.

Trudging through the blackberry bushes, the air seemed hotter and thicker. Breathing became harder. Tiny bugs and big mosquitoes leaped up off the dampness of the low-lying grasses and attacked their bare arms.

After Freddy and his entourage had finally picked their way through the bushes and tall grass, the trail straightened out, but a stretch of ankle twisting bright-gray boulders and loose stones that could cause an ankle to slip, heaved upwards and formed a sun-bleached hill. After carefully stepping between boulders, they were at the top of the hill. Here, the vegetation was heavy on both sides, and the scent of a plant, Freddy knew as skunk cabbage, hung heavy in the air. When they entered the coolness of the trees again, the sudden change from bright searing sun, bouncing off the bright-gray boulders, caused Freddy's eyes to see a glaring wall of grayness.

As they slowed down and bunched up, a strange feeling of fear clutched Freddy's throat. Like a little kid experiencing the effects of a bad dream, he could still see Terry's lifeless body lying in the alley. And he had a vivid picture of Capone's skeleton in the mine. Freddy had been getting used to those horrors, but Muscle's body parts being strewn across the railroad bed, clogged his thoughts and tugged at his sanity. He kept walking. His eyes adjusted to the shade of the dark trees and his fear subsided.

Up ahead, a stretch of trees crested the rise. After Freddy and friends past under the trees, they were back on the railroad tracks. With their heels crunching the ballast, they broke into an easy trot.

A few miles down the tracks, their tired feet plodded into the switching yard. Instead of walking on the ballast, Rafferty leaped onto a dusty path. Like a little kid, he dashed along with his head bowed and his hands in his pockets, deliberately kicking up little dusty clouds. Freddy shook his head in awe. They had just washed the grime and dirt from their bodies, and here was Rafferty, amusing himself by getting dirty again.

As the switching yard came into full view, Freddy noticed the only openings through the tall trees that surrounded the yard were ingoing and outgoing tracks and a one lane road. Two main tracks ran into the yard and branched into twelve sidetracks, some with loaded cars and some empty. It was a small yard.

A ways from the yard office building, a locomotive engine sat idling on one of the sidetracks. A light coat of railroad dust covered five automobiles parked on a slant next to the single track alongside the yard office, but there were no railroad people in sight.

Even though the sun's rays beamed right on him, Rafferty visibly shivered. "This place looks like a ghost town."

Neal gestured to the idling locomotive. "Ghosts can't run an engine like that."

A few steps later, they were in front of the yard office building. Many feet had trampled the grease-blackened ground all around it. A crack ran down the window of the door to the office. Although the window was thickened with grime, Freddy found a clean spot and peeked into the office. Two telephones, two typewriters, and a mechanical adding machine sat on a desk right below the window. Next to the office door, a tall black bill box towered over the back edge of another desk. White papers, folded lengthwise, stuck out of the pigeonholes of the bill box. In the far corner, a dark-brown Teletype printer, loaded with yellow paper, stood ready to print messages. In front of that, an oak desk, stacked with various piles of paper, spread to a distance of five feet. Behind it, a man wearing a white shirt and a tie, slumped in a chair. With his head tilted to one side clamping the receiver end of a two-piece black phone held to his ear, his mouth was fixed in a wide gape. Above his head, four-foot long fluorescent lights, coated with nicotine from cigar and cigarette smoke, were mounted in the ceiling. Barely buzzing, they threw down dull yellow light onto the man's sleeping head.

Neal stepped next to Freddy and whispered in his ear, "What do you see?"

Freddy backed away from the window and put his fingers to his lips. "The guy's sleeping. Let's see what's in the other part of this place."

They walked a few yards alongside the building and stopped at a door. It was opened just a crack. Freddy opened it a few inches and looked in. Although dark inside, he managed to make out a welcome sight. He looked back at Neal and Rafferty. "There's a candy machine in there. Let's go in."

Neal placed his hand on his stomach. "I haven't eaten since yesterday. I sure could go for a Milky Way."

Rafferty reached into his pocket. "I don't have any change. Do you?"

Neal's shoulders jiggled with held-in laughter. "No problem, I still got a few lead quarters."

They stepped into the dimly lit yard office locker room. As their eyes adjusted to the darkness, they feasted their eyes on a weird sight. Dark green blinds, coated with years of grime and railroad dirt, blocked out the yellow light from the few nicotine-coated windows, and the rank odor of warm bodies and chewing tobacco hung in the air. A lone dim-orange light lit one corner of the dark locker room.

In various positions, prone forms of sleeping men occupied benches. One man slumped in a chair and dozed with half-open eyes.

Neal stepped up to the candy machine, dropped a lead quarter into the slot, and slowly pulled the candy bar lever under a Milky Way candy bar. It dropped from the slot. Clunk! It landed in the tin bottom. He reached in, pulled it out, and handed it to Freddy. The change from the quarter clinked into the change return. Neal scooped it out with his fingers and dropped another lead quarter in the slot. He gave the second Milky Way to Rafferty, but after the third Milky Way dropped, a voice in the darkness complained. "Who's making that noise?"

The man slumped in the chair changed position. "Go back to sleep, Scotty. They can't have number nine track switched out yet."

While Neal put the Milky Way into his pocket, Freddy squinted in the direction of the voice coming from a bench. A man with powerful shoulders flashed a grumpy expression and waved his hand down. "Rossi, quit screwin' around with that candy machine and go back to sleep."

His command was greeted by several sleepy grunts. A thin man with a railroad lantern at his feet sat up. In a stupor, he looked around in the semi-darkness and lay back down on a long bench. After jostling for a comfortable position, he folded his hands, placed them under his face for a pillow, and turned his back to Freddy.

Freddy looked out the small opening in the door. Outside, a group of four men, clustered in a knot, stood next to the locomotive waving their hands and talking.

Freddy turned to Neal, turned his thumb sideways, and pointed outside. Neal grabbed the third Milky Way out of the machine and waved for Freddy and Rafferty to follow him. He tiptoed through the locker room. At the end of the room, a dirty maroon door with a broken brass latch led the way outside.

Outside, and out of view of the men at the locomotive, Neal shook his head. "No wonder we didn't hear anything all night, those guys were sleeping."

From the switching yard, the loud buzz of a switching engine's buzzing horn, mixed with dull explosions of shunted cars colliding, cracked the quiet morning.

Freddy peeked around the corner of the building and studied the four men standing next to the engine. They all wore dust-covered heavy work shoes and red bandannas hung from the back pockets of their baggy coveralls. A hangdog look filled one man's face. A droop to his upper body matched his mild eyes and his sagging gut. When his head suddenly reared up, he shot Freddy an unwelcoming expression. While the other two men talked and pointed to the engine, another man turned toward Freddy and curled his mouth into a vehement sneer. Being a muscular man with a red face, he looked like a man that if he got angry, steam would curl from his ears. Freddy didn't want to rile this man.

Freddy had dealt with men like this before. They usually started working a job right out of high school. They had never been laid off. They never had to go hungry a day in their working lives. Men like this never considered people who were not working as underprivileged victims of social inequity. Men like him felt the not working people were lazy and ignorant and just didn't want to work, and they hated them for it. Freddy knew the wrinkled unkempt clothes, he was wearing, would make the man believe he was a low life person. If he showed he was as mature and as intelligent as the man, the man would sense an air of undeserved superiority. He would become angry. The only way to treat these types of narrowed-minded working people was to pretend they were smarter than you were. Freddy wondered what he could say to the man. He hoped Neal wouldn't come around the corner with a big, crooked grin, walk up to the man, and announce a grand, "Hello".

He turned to Neal. "You're not going over there, are you?"

"Yeah," Rafferty added. "The guy that's running that dog and pony show looks mean."

Neal's smile displayed his brilliant white teeth. "Don't you know that when you smile and go toward someone with your arms wide open, they won't think you're a bad guy?"

With a wide grin on his face, Neal gave Freddy a conspiratorial wink and headed for the red-faced man. When he was face to face with the man, Neal stopped. The man glared at him, but before he could speak, Neal smiled broadly. As if welcoming a long-lost friend, he extended his hand. "Good morning."

A sense of hostility filled the air. The man looked warily at Neal's hand. "What are you doing here?"

As if he were a slow-motion symphony conductor, Neal tapped his finger in the air before him. "Well, ah, yes." He stopped tapping his finger and took on a helpless look. "You see, sir, our car broke down, and a truck full of chickens picked us up."

The man's stern face relaxed. It seemed to show that anybody that got picked up by a truck full of chickens was clearly beneath him. His forehead wrinkled with quizzical amusement. "So? What's the problem? Did the chickens crap on you?"

Going along with the man's attempted humor, Neal laughed a friendly laugh. "We fell asleep and the driver dropped us off last night. We have no idea where we are. Could you tell us the fastest way to get back to Sharon?"

With a sly look on his face, the red-faced man elbowed the hangdog man next to him. "The fastest way is to fly."

The hostility in the air softened, and the four men snickered in unison.

Neal started to laugh but said, "No, I mean which way do we go?" He leaned his head toward the gravel road that led from the yard office to the paved highway. "Do we turn right or left at that road over there?"

The door on the yard office slammed. The man in the white shirt and tie who had been sleeping behind the desk stood in front of the closed door. He held a mug of steaming coffee in his hand. Sleeping in the chair must have caused the bottom of his shirt to bunch up and cover his sagging belt. The shirt ballooned down over his waist, giving him an appearance of careless restraint and caused him to look shorter than he actually was. He yelled across the gravel road. "Ticky, quit givin' those kids a hard time. Get that track switched out. MC 3's due in half an hour."

Red-faced, Ticky gave a rueful laugh and waved his hand at the white-shirted man with the coffee cup. "Come on, Ducky. We was just havin' a little fun." He turned, stepped up on the engine step, and looked back at Ducky. He was about to say something, but Ducky interrupted.

"That's it. Get up in that engine where you belong."

Ticky scurried up the steps but stopped at the door to the cab and turned back toward Ducky. With his left hand, he grabbed the safety rail on the front of the engine and arrogantly pumped his right fist like a piston. "Ducky, you're the yardmaster. Why don't you call the railroad detective and have these kids arrested for trespassing?"

As if he were using them for a protective shield, Rafferty muscled between Neal and Freddy. "We're not trespassing." He flashed his smart aleck smile. "We're running away from home to join the circus. We stopped here just to see the clowns."

Ticky took a step down from the door of the engine. "I don't have to put up with idiots like him." He pointed to Rafferty. "I'll go in and call the railroad detective myself."

Rafferty smiled innocently. "Go ahead." He defiantly crossed his arms across his chest and leaned back. "We'll tell him how you guys slept all night long."

Ticky looked at Ducky. His expression changed from arrogant to concern. "Can they do that?"

Nodding, Ducky took a sip of his coffee and turned toward Ticky. "If that detective comes, they'll be able to tell him anything they want."

Ticky waved his hand down. "But we were just having a little fun."

At the railroad crossing, a train's horn blasted the morning quiet away. Freddy turned toward the sound. With wheels spinning and sanders hissing compressed air and sand onto the rails for traction, a locomotive with a long string of loaded coke hoppers inched its way toward the switching yard.

Over the thumping sounds of the oncoming locomotive, Ducky shouted to Ticky, "Have all the fun you want, but get the work done first." Shaking his head, he walked over to Neal. "I'm calling this little incident a draw, but you're not supposed to be on railroad property."

Neal lowered his head. "We're sorry, sir. We just want to get home. There was no other place to stop."

Ducky jerked his coffee cup down. The remaining coffee splashed onto the foot-pounded black ground. With concern, he glanced toward the road. "The general yardmaster is due any minute." He jabbed the crumpled folds of his white shirttails back down inside his trousers. "You better not let him see you here."

Freddy faced Ducky. "Just tell us which way to turn. We'll be gone in a flash."

Lifting his empty coffee mug, Ducky gestured toward the road. "Just make a right, then go up the road a ways and make a left. You'll be on route eighteen. It'll take you right into Sharon."

On the road, Freddy, Neal and Rafferty turned their backs to the yard office and drew their necks into their collars. If they could thumb a ride, the dirty-orange smoke from the steel mills of home would be just down the road.

Chapter 17

Smeal knew Blondie had gotten Al Capone's gold vault, and Blondie's girlfriend, Carolyn, had told him that Blondie was going to cut the vault into pieces, melt them down, and make little ingots, so she could cash them in at different banks. Smeal laughed at the plan, and then told Blondie that he could melt the gold down if he wanted to, but it had been illegal for anyone but jewelers, dentists, or manufactures to have gold since 1934.

Blondie was angry with himself for being ignorant, but he was so grateful that Smeal had saved him the embarrassment of having the gold confiscated by the federal government, paying a ten-thousand dollar fine, and spending ten years in jail, that he agreed to let him arrange a contact to take the vault out of the country and cash it in for money.

Smeal had no idea how heavy the vault was. Too late, he discovered he should have stolen a newer truck, but at the time, Blondie had called, and said, "Get a truck, and quick."

Smeal stole the first truck he saw: A green 1948 Chevy. It had bald tires and a broken spring, but it was the best he could do on such short notice. To keep anyone from tracing the truck, Blondie was going to get rid of it after the job was done.

As a security precaution, Blondie had planned to haul the vault along River Road until he came to the little village of Clark. In a cutoff, partially hidden in the trees, a semi-tractor trailer would be parked along the road. The hood would be up, and the driver would be pretending to be working on the engine. Blondie was instructed to ask the man if he needed any help. If the man turned and asked Blondie if he had punched his milk horse, Blondie was to answer that he did. When the man asked if he were going to pay for the horse's dentist bill, Blondie would know he had the right contact. Then the man would have unloaded the vault into the semi's trailer and closed the doors. Right on the spot, Blondie would have gotten seventy-five percent of the value of the gold vault in cash money, and Smeal would have gotten ten percent for himself. It was a simple solution. There should have been no problems. But Blondie never showed up.

While the man had pretended to be working on the semi, three kids in a 1940 Ford stopped and asked him if he needed any help, but when he asked them if they had punched his milk horse they looked at him as if he were crazy, turned and sped away.

Those three kids on the train had a 1940 Ford. Even though their suspicious behavior wouldn't have consciously registered in an unconditioned person's mind, Smeal had been in the business too long not to pick up on it. The first time he had seen the kids with their broken down garbage truck, he knew they had something to do with the vault. They were the same kids that had stopped at the semi. They were the same kids that had found the money at Peacock Alley. They may have double-crossed Blondie and taken the vault. Smeal had to catch those kids, find out what they knew about the key, find out what they knew about the coalmine that hid Capone's body, and find out about the money Capone had never deposited in the vault.

247

There was just too much money at stake to sit back and wait. Now he wasn't going to wait for Hound Eyes and his friends to drive to the New Castle B&O Railroad Interchange and find those kids. He was going himself.

Chapter 18

After Freddy, Neal, and Rafferty left the railroad switching yard, they walked down the highway eating the Milky Way candy bars. But the candy bars only increased their hunger. Just around a bend in the road, between a springhouse and a big red barn, a clean white farmhouse was nestled on a manicured lawn that was green enough to be a golf course. A soft breeze rustled through a gnarled apple tree with Red Delicious apples hanging down, waiting to be plucked and eaten. But the tree sat next to a white clapboard-sided springhouse plastered with a red and white sign. The sign were different from any Freddy had ever seen. It read,

NO TRESSPASSING
VIOLATORS WILL BE SHOT
SURVIVORS WILL BE SHOT AGAIN

Freddy figured some kind of a crazy person owned the land. He didn't want to go near that sign.

Rafferty stopped in the middle of the road and stared at the apples. "That's a big farm. Those people that own it, have to be rich. I don't think they'll mind if we take a few apples."

Neal turned toward the tree. "Stay here. I'll check it out."

With Freddy and Rafferty standing on the side of the road, Neal walked past the No Trespassing sign on the springhouse, reached up, and plucked three apples off the tree. Instead of coming back to the road, he placed two apples on the grass, lay on his side, and propped his head up on his fist. With his other hand, he took a huge bite out of one apple.

Holding the apple, he waved at Freddy and Rafferty and pointed to the two apples on the ground. "Come on over. Breakfast is served."

Freddy looked around uneasily. He didn't see any threat. He decided to chance it. Before he could take one step toward the tree, from out of the spring house — there! A man with a shotgun came, half running, half flying, with his sights on Neal. Neal jumped up and dropped the apple from his hand. Then he bent over, grabbed the other two apples, and started to run. Holding the shotgun in one hand, the man reached out with his other hand, snagged Neal's shirttail, and clinched his fist around it.

Neal continued to run, but, with the man holding onto his shirttail, he could get no traction. He wasn't going anywhere. As his feet slipped on the grass, the man tried to kick him in the rear end, saying, "You damn kids are weak because you fart around wasting your lives, gettin' your asses into slings like this."

The man missed six kicks at Neal's rear end, but one found its mark. Neal dropped the apples and turned toward the man. "Sorry, man, we were hungry."

The man let go of Neal's shirttail, but lifted the shotgun. Neal could have spun around, knocked the barrel of the shotgun away, and whapped the man right in the chest. He could have knocked the wind right out of him and taken the apples, but he didn't. He just stood there. His eyes misted over, and a guilty look appeared on his face.

Freddy figured that no matter how trivial the apples were, it was still stealing, and although Neal

250

broadcasted a tough guy attitude, deep down inside, he knew he was in the wrong.

As Neal fled away from the apple tree, the man's face screwed up into a grimace of acute discomfort. He yelled after Neal, "Quit stealing and get a job. Buy your own goddamn tree."

Neal ignored him, regained his carefree edge, and ran onto the road.

Rafferty yelled at the man, "We're sorry. We thought today was free apple day."

Cussing and shaking his head, the man's face contorted with bewilderment.

Jogging at a brisk pace, Neal motioned for Freddy and Rafferty to follow. "I just thought of something. Let's go back to the railroad. One of those guys getting off work might give us a ride."

They turned and headed back toward the railroad.

Jaunting down the center of the road, they slowed to a trot. Rafferty turned toward Neal. "What a cheap bastard." He took a deep breath. "He has a whole tree full of apples and won't let us have any."

Freddy slowed to a fast walk, and felt his hungry stomach growl. "He acts like he'll lose his farm if he lets us have one apple."

Rafferty moved his hands as he talked. "It's hard to believe that guy was ever a baby. I can't picture him on his back with a big smile on his face, gurgling, and kicking his legs, and full of gas."

As if he were trying to see something, Neal cocked his hand over his eyes and starred down the road. "Greed comes with wealth. It's just the way things are."

"I don't know about that," Rafferty said. "I don't' think that guy was even born. Somebody with a hangover probably manufactured him in a people-making place, but the machine that made him was out of whack. It didn't make a human being. It cranked out stingy imitation."

"Calling people names is the easy way to make you feel like you're getting back at someone," Neal said and rubbed his rear end. "But you're right. He's stingy."

"It doesn't matter how stingy he is," Freddy said with expectation. "When we get the money out of the mine, we'll be able to buy his farm."

Neal cupped his hand to his ear. "I hear something."

In the distance, a car kicked up a light cloud of gray dust.

Getting ready to stick out their thumbs and hitchhike, they all stopped walking and stood by the roadside. As the car neared, Freddy made out its front end. "Here comes a black '57 Chevy. Maybe it's one those guys from the Peacock Alley foundation."

Neal turned, walked backwards, and stuck out his thumb. "That's a long ways from here. There's thousands of black Chevys. Maybe this one will give us a ride."

Freddy and Rafferty turned, faced the Chevy, and stuck out their thumbs. The Chevy sped toward them and zipped right on past. Neal turned and hoisted his middle finger at the Chevy. "Here! Give this a ride." The brake lights on the Chevy burned bright red. The tires locked up, skidded across pavement, and sent a low cloud of blue smoke across the road.

Through the haze of smoke, Freddy stared at the rear end of the Chevy. As if it had been rear-ended, the back bumper was curled in. His heart skipped a beat. He grabbed onto Neal's elbow and shook it. "That's the same Chevy that was at the railroad crossing where Muscles got sucked under the wheels."

As he studied the Chevy, Neal wrinkled his forehead. "It can't be."

Freddy's body went rigid with tension. He looked at Neal. "I think you're wrong."

The Chevy hit reverse and backed up.

"See, I told you," Neal said. "He's coming back to pick us up."

The Chevy stopped next to Neal. Neal placed his hand on the door handle, bent over, and talked to the driver. "How far you going?"

The driver's eyes slipped toward Neal. "We'll take you to hell if you want."

"We're not going that far," Neal said, "but we'll take a lift to Sharon."

Freddy figured he had been wrong. He sighed with relief.

Keeping his eyes on Neal, the driver guided a cigar toward his mouth. When he placed his hand on the steering wheel, his hand flashed walnut knuckles, and his thick wrists ran to his knotted forearms. As if he were getting ready to reach over and open the door, he rolled his sleeves up to his elbows and clamped his square jaw on the cigar.

Freddy figured this square jawed man was someone who overcompensated for his intellectual inadequacies by pushing his excessive weight around but might be okay. But when Freddy noticed that the man's cramped face had permanent mean lines of hostility, he sensed something was wrong. Backing away, he tensed to run. His ears picked up the soft click of the passenger door being unlatched. He stepped close and looked into the back seat. To keep from being seen, Toad, the toad-faced man with the eyes that had been at Peacock Alley had flattened his six-foot, two hundred fifty pound body against the seat. Dirty-white gauze had been wound around his right hand. Freddy figured the gauze covered the wounds Toad had gotten when the mud in the barrel of the shotgun had caused the bullet to explode in the chamber.

Not noticing Toad, Neal opened the door and smiled at the driver. "Mind if I sit up front?"

As Freddy's chest heaved with anxious breaths, he pointed to the back seat. "Look!"

Wearing a wicked grin on his pale, unhealthy face, Toad lifted his foot and kicked the door. It flew open. He jumped out and tried to vault over the trunk of the Chevy, but his bandaged hand thumped on the tail fin. He grimaced with pain, and his face seemed to be wrapped in ugly, brown wax-paper skin. With the vigor of a boisterous boy, he sprinted around the car and stopped in front of Freddy and Rafferty. As he held his bandaged hand downward, the gauze unwound and fluttered in front of his leg.

Being the type of person that would tease a rattlesnake, just for the fun of it, Rafferty turned toward Freddy. "If he was one more grade below monkeys in a zoo, he'd be funny."

That's all we need, Freddy thought. These

guys are already mad because of the box and Muscles getting killed, and now, Rafferty has to make it worse.

Starring at Rafferty, Toad gnashed his teeth. "What did you say?"

Rafferty's gangly body shuddered with held in laughter. "It's not my fault everybody knows you have a lot of intelligence and no brains."

Before a bewildered Toad could answer, the roar of a V-eight engine drew near. Freddy turned his head to the left. A red 1955 Ford screeched around the bend and skidded to a stop behind the Chevy. A driver with a long crooked nose that seemed to have been broken more than a few times, stuck his head out the window. It was the man who had broken the bank president's nose. With a voice of absolute authority, he yelled in a steam-hammer like voice, "Get those little bastards. They're the ones that took the box."

Neal slammed the door on the Chevy.

Toad yelled back at the man with the long nose. "Come on, Schnoz. They're not getting' away this time."

As screams and angry shouts flooded the scene, Freddy caught sight of Rafferty whirling around to knee Toad in the groin. Before he could deliver the disabling blow, Schnoz jumped out the Ford and jumped him. Schnoz's weight caused Rafferty's skinny knees to buckle. He slumped down. Just as he was about to shed Schnoz off his back, Toad kicked him in the midsection. Rafferty grabbed his stomach and bent over. He fell forward. With a sickening crunch, his head slammed onto the pavement. The fight went out of his body. He curled into a fetal position.

While Schnoz and Rafferty lay on the pavement, Toad turned toward Freddy and reared back his big fist. Freddy braced for the blow, but just before it would have knocked his teeth out, he ducked. The huge fist swished over the top of his head.

As if he couldn't believe he had missed, Toad's eyes locked on Freddy's face.

Freddy smiled inwardly. He knew if a person didn't watch the other fighter's torso, he would not be able to anticipate his blows. Before Toad could react, Freddy managed three successive kicks to his ribs and a shot to the groin that didn't connect. But it was in vain. As if he had enjoyed it, Toad smiled. Then he savagely whirled upon Freddy. With a purpling face, Toad reached down and clamped Freddy's neck in a headlock. Freddy tried to slip free, but the muscles in Toad's arms felt like the jaws of steel vice. Freddy gritted his teeth and wondered what would come next. He found out real quick.

Toad tightened his arm around Freddy's neck and began punching him in the face and head. The blows intensified with each hit. And to make it worse, Freddy's air was cut off. Lightning bolts of pain shot into his head, raced down his neck, and into his back. Toad's arms covered his ears, but Freddy could still hear the bastard laughing. The sick laughter and lack of air caused Freddy to pull at Toad's hands. His arms strained. His tendons became tight as steel cables, but he couldn't budge Toad's death grip. The pain became so intense Freddy began to black out. He cast a slightly out-of-focus eye on Neal.

"Get off him!" Neal cried as he leaped forward, taking Toad's throat in a crushing grip. "Tell your buddies to stop!" He tightened his grip. "Now, or I'll rip your throat out!"

Toad clinched his mouth shut tight, and increased the pressure on Freddy's neck.

Neal tightened his grip. "You hear me?"

Square Jaw and Schnoz slammed into Neal like a speeding ore train. Before Neal's grip slipped from Toad's throat, Toad stumbled sideways and released the headlock from Freddy's neck. While Freddy tumbled to the pavement, gasping for air, Toad flopped, back first, onto the road. The back of his head clunked onto the hard pavement. The fight went out of him.

Square Jaw and Schnoz took a hold of Neal's arms and held tight. Struggling to get free, Neal wildly grabbed clothing and pulled. Gouging with his fingers, he found a weak spot he could use to escape. He reared back and brutally bashed his knee into the groin of Schnoz. Schnoz gasped and slumped to the pavement.

Square Jaw gripped Neal's hand and hung on. Neal twisted his wrist and broke the hold. He backed up, but only managed a few steps before Square Jaw hit him with a flying tackle. It sent Neal sailing backwards toward the rough asphalt road. It looked like Neal would have skinned or broken his elbows when he hit the pavement, but Square Jaw kept his arms clinched around Neal's midsection. When Neal hit the pavement a sickening crack filled the air. Freddy thought Neal was done for, but it was Square Jaw's elbows. They had absorbed the lion's share of the fall.

Square Jaw let loose of Neal's midsection, rolled over, and struggled to his knees. As he bent over and grasped his bleeding elbows, Neal jumped up, arched his foot back, and leveled a knockout kick to Square Jaw's jaw. His front teeth flew from his mouth He tipped sideways. His head thumped on the pavement. With his toothless and bleeding mouth open, his glazed eyes stared into the sky.

Schnoz came up behind Neal, twined his fingers in his hair, and wrenched him backward.

Freddy struggled to get upright and help, but Toad had recovered. He was standing in front of him. From a hand and knee position Freddy pushed off with his arms. Before he could get to his feet, Toad lifted his foot, stepped on Freddy's head, forced it to the pavement, and stood on it. With the pressure of Toad's foot grinding his ear into the pavement, Freddy caught sight of a 1957 magenta Oldsmobile. Its tires were thumping over the ruts at the side of the road and churning a cloud of dust into the air.

The Oldsmobile skidded to a stop behind the Ford. A man jumped out. A white plaster cast covered the lower part of his left leg. Freddy recognized Blondie's killer opal green eyes. Thinking he would have another man to fight, Freddy's senses heightened, but when he tried to pry Toad's foot off the side of his head, the asphalt dug into his face. He ignored the pain and twisted his head to the side. Toad's foot slid off and stomped onto the pavement. Freddy jumped up and looked toward Neal for help. But Neal was busy with Schnoz.

Neal and Schnoz struggled, kicked, and rolled over and over. When they reached the edge of the road, Schnoz gripped Neal by the shoulders and pushed him toward the culvert that ran into the drainage ditch at the side of the road. Neal stumbled and landed in the drainage ditch. Schnoz jumped on top of him and clinched both hands around his throat.

Blondie ran toward Freddy. Toad smiled at Freddy. Freddy was sure Blondie was part of the gang, and he going to hurt him. Freddy turned to run. Toad reached around, gathered him into a bear hug, held him secure, and said to Blondie, "Punch his guts out."

Freddy tensed for Blondie's onslaught.

But Blondie zipped right past and stopped in front of Schnoz.

Still trying to choke Neal to death, Schnoz looked up at Blondie. Their eyes met. It was as if the two of them were locked in a bitter combat of wills. With neither man flinching, Schnoz took one hand from Neal's throat. While Neal gasped for air, Schnoz reached into his pocket. When he pulled out his hand, his fingers were clamped around a set of brass knuckles.

Still maintaining eye contact, Blondie slowly lifted his hard-plaster-cast-encased foot. Before Schnoz could fit the deadly knuckles onto his fingers and bash them into the delicate bones of Neal's face, Blondie slammed the hard cast into Schnoz's chin. Teeth snapped under the impact. Schnoz grabbed his mouth and flew off of Neal.

Neal jumped to his feet and grabbed Schnoz by his ears. Pulling his face down, Neal jerked his knee right into Schnoz's face, pulverizing his nose. A jagged scream erupted. Schnoz grabbed his own face so fast that the brass knuckles on his hand smashed into his own cheekbone. Making an obscene cawing sound, he threw the brass knuckles at Neal. Neal jumped to the side. The knuckles hit Neal's shinbone, bounced off, and skidded across the pavement. Schnoz took two faltering steps and fell to his knees. Neal relaxed for a moment and rubbed his shinbone.

When Toad realized Blondie wasn't going to help, he tightened his arms around Freddy and squeezed. Freddy's breath was cut short. He tried to shake Toad's bear hug. He couldn't.

With Toad's chest glued to his back, Freddy curled the top of his right foot around Toad's ankle. With his other foot, he pushed with all his might. Their intertwined bodies hurled through the air and slammed backward onto the hard pavement. Being sandwiched beneath Freddy, Toad bore the brunt of the impact. As the breath was knocked from his lungs, he gasped. The vice-like clamp around Freddy's torso weakened. Freddy spun out of Toad's bear hug and leaped to his feet.

Toad rose to a crouching position. Swinging wildly, he lunged toward Freddy. Freddy took a blow to his forehead, but stood his ground. When he managed to get his left hand around Toad's neck, he placed his thumb on his windpipe and squeezed. He used his right fist to pop him square in the nose. Cartilage shattered and blood spattered. Toad backed away and stood still.

As if he had been playing possum, Square Jaw jumped up, spit teeth from his bloody mouth, crouched low, and came at Neal. In a renewed rage, Neal leaned down. Clenching his fists together, he hammered Square Jaw's skull again and again until he stopped fighting back. With his chest heaving from sucking in much needed air, Neal let up for a moment.

As if Neal's blows had no effect on him, Square Jaw reared back and prepared to thrust a knife into Neal's vulnerable throat.

With his thirty-eight Colt aimed at Square Jaw, Blondie's booming voice cut the air. "Don't make me have to shoot your dumb ass. Drop the knife."

Square Jaw looked at Blondie. Neal reared back. From the ground up, he swung his fist up under Square Jaw's chin. Square Jaw's head flew back. The knife fell from his hand. With his legs crumpling, he staggered backwards, landed in the ditch, and lay still.

As Freddy struggled to catch his breath, the blue-black sheen from the barrel of Blondie's Colt focused on Toad. Toad didn't seem to notice. He stood with his blood running from his nose, laughing.

With bloody smashed elbows, Square Jaw grimaced and pulled himself up of the ditch. Steadying himself, he held onto Toad's shoulder and waved his gun in Freddy's direction. "We need him!" He turned his gun on Blondie. "But we don't need him."

Getting out of the line of fire, Toad stepped back a few feet and stood next to Schnoz who was on his hands and knees coughing up blood.

Out of the corner of his eye, Freddy watched Neal jump over Rafferty's curled up form. Square

Jaw spun and re-aimed his gun at Neal's chest.

Freddy dove for the gun. His feet left the pavement. Sailing toward Square Jaw, he howled in rage like a wounded bear.

With both his arms stretched wide enough to body tackle two men, Freddy hit Square Jaw. As his arms encircled Square Jaw, the sharp point of the hammer on his gun sank into Freddy's right forearm. The hammer released. The gun fired. The bullet flew harmlessly into the air. Square Jaw jerked the gun away and re-pointed it at Neal. Just as he was about to fire, Freddy drove his right fist into Square Jaw's left kidney. Freddy felt Square Jaw's muffled grunt against his clinched fingers.

As Square Jaw bent over sideways, Freddy reached up and yanked the tail of his suit coat over his head. While Square Jaw windmilled his arms and tried to get the coat off his face, directly behind him, Blondie dropped down to his hands and knees and waited for Freddy. Freddy pushed Square Jaw. Blondie's body blocked the backs of Square Jaw's legs, causing them to be swept out from under him. His feet flew up into the air. Trying to keep his balance and keep his bloody elbows from hitting the pavement, he slumped over as if he had broken at the waist. But his actions did no good. He tripped over Blondie's body and flipped over backwards. His head thudded onto the pavement. He was out.

But the fight wasn't over. Schnoz jumped up. A haze of arms and legs flashed around Freddy. He vaguely glimpsed Neal kicking the unconscious Toad's gun from his hand. Then Freddy felt a blow strike him low on his spine. His legs went numb. He collapsed, landing hard on the road.

When he looked up, Schnoz was lying on his back and Blondie was standing above him, beating him unmercifully. Trying to shield his head with his arms, Schnoz withered. When he struggled to twist sideways and get to the Chevy and escape, Blondie delivered a stunning blow. It landed at the base of Schnoz's skull. Schnoz crumpled into a heap. Now, the fight was over.

Freddy looked at Schnoz and gasped. "Is he dead?"

Blondie reached down. With his thumbs pealing back Schnoz's eyelids, he whispered, "He's out, but he's still alive."

Huffing for air and with blood trickling from his nose, Freddy stood up and surveyed the grisly scene. It seemed that death had been right at his back door. But now that he knew he was going to survive, he felt they might have overreacted. "Do you think we should have beaten them so badly?"

Blondie looked at Freddy as if he were out of his mind. "Are you crazy? This isn't a game. Staying alive is the only way we'll beat these bastards. They think we'll give up without a fight. They make death available. If you let them, they'll shove it right down your throat and laugh about it."

Freddy thought about how his boxing trainer, Terry, had been beaten to death with a jagged pipe. He couldn't tell the police then because the loan sharks would come after him. He hoped it would be different now that he wasn't in Cleveland. He flashed Blondie a confused look. "But they tried to kill us. Shouldn't the law take over?"

Blondie flashed a bewildered look. "Did the law take over when they killed your trainer?"

Freddy shook his head.

Blondie threw his hands in the air. "It's the same everywhere. Those guys have pet judges on the payroll. They never serve time. If it weren't for the big man in charge, I would have killed them all." He thrust his middle finger into the air. "Just fuck 'em, Freddy, and fuck their pet judges, too. Stay alive."

Freddy knew Blondie was right, but he still wanted to believe that no matter how bad a situation became, giving a person an even break was the right thing to do. Even World War II had rules against mustard gas and shotguns. If a person did whatever and whenever he wanted to whoever he wanted, without regard for the feelings of others, it was uncivilized, and eventually the whole world would become uncivilized.

As Freddy felt the pain in his knees and palms that had been scraped raw from contact with the rough pavement, he remembered what a man back at a sweaty gym in the Boy's Buhl Club had told him. "Gentlemen who behaved decently and played by the rules weren't around anymore. They were already dead. When you know the other guy isn't going to play by the rules, hit early and hit hard. Don't be nice. Retaliate first." And now it seemed to be true

Freddy didn't know who the big man in charge was, that Blondie was talking about, but whoever the man was, he had to have some unknown power to control the men laying on the road. Toad was no longer laughing and giggling. He was gagging on something in his throat, and a small stream of blood oozed out his right ear that looked like a piece of raw hamburger. It would have been easier if Blondie had shot them all. But he hadn't. None of it made any sense. Freddy hunched his shoulders, and looked to Neal for some sort of explanation.

Neal smiled a half smile. "It looks like the picnic's over."

Freddy shrugged. "It may be over, but I don't like it."

Neal lifted his hand then dropped it. "When the rain comes it doesn't matter whether you like or not. Unless you do something, it will fall on your head."

The back door of the red '55 Ford flew open. From inside, a lady's melodious voice softly rang out, "The picnic could be just starting for one of you lucky men."

A bleached-blond woman clutching a bottle of gin in her pink-white, pudgy hand provocatively crossed her legs and kicked her shoes off. She swung around in the seat and faced Neal.

Shaking his head, Neal walked away.

Freddy turned toward the slightly overweight woman, but to avoid the blast of her alcoholic breath, he looked away. Blondie stood next to him staring into the sky. Slicing the air with the flat of his hand, he pounded out the words, "This is just the thing I wanted to get away from." He turned and looked at the woman.

As a stream of slobber ran down the side of her mouth, she pulled on her skirt until it was six inches above her knees and smiled a crooked smile. "Don't get excited, honey. I'll let you give me a thrill."

Blondie turned and looked toward Toad. With his belly flat with the road, he coughed and turned his face to the side. Blood trickled from his nose and mouth. With his hands over his eyes, Schnoz lay on his side, holding his broken nose and gasping for breath. Square Jaw sat on the edge of the ditch, holding his head in his hands.

Neal turned toward Blondie. "I know you're tired of the mob life, but wouldn't it have been easier to just shoot them?"

As if disgusted with the same question Freddy had just asked, Blondie gnashed his teeth, but answered. "If we shoot them, the big man might make sure we don't get near the vault. I learned long ago that if you shoot someone who has ties to the big man, he will show no mercy." He glanced toward the men sprawled on the road. "And I don't know what ties these creeps have."

Freddy nodded with understanding. For the moment, it didn't matter what kind of ties the creeps had. For a while, they would be down, writhing in agony.

The woman cleared her throat. "Don't look at that, sweetie. Look at something pretty. Look at me."

Blondie turned his head toward the woman. A sour look filled his face.

Trying to be sexy, the woman kicked one of her long slender legs into the air, but she slid off the car seat. She grabbed the back of the seat and barely kept herself from falling onto the road. Holding onto the door with one hand and holding onto the back of the seat with the other hand, she wobbled to a standing position. Using her melodious voice, she reached out to Blondie. "Come on, honey, give me a thrill."

Blondie ignored her and turned toward Freddy and his friends. "Come on, you guys. We got a vault to get."

Holding on to the door, the woman stretched out and placed a lithe hand on Blondie's arm. "Come on, honey. I need a ride. Give a girl a lift."

Blondie shrugged off her hand and walked toward his Oldsmobile. The woman teetered backwards but hung onto the door.

Freddy helped Rafferty up from his sitting position on the road. With Freddy supporting him, he hunched over and started to walk past the woman. In a voice filled with honey, she called out to Freddy, "How about you, strong man? Will you give a girl a lift?"

Exhausted from the fight and feeling the heat radiating from the asphalt, Freddy was in no mood to answer.

Holding his stomach Rafferty kept on walking. In a strange, slurred voice, he managed to call back over his shoulder, "Your breath can lift the tarpaper off the roof. Blow on yourself. It'll lift you right off that seat."

The woman's face scrunched up. "You know what I think about that?"

Rafferty painfully turned toward her. "What?"

Smiling, the woman seemed to be exerting extreme pressure on her stomach. All of a sudden, a rush of blubbery gas blatted from her chubby rear end and reverberated into the air. Erupting into a harsh laugh, she pointed at Rafferty. "That's what."

Shaking his head, Rafferty let a smile spread across his face. One of his front teeth had been knocked out.

Toad sat up and called through a cupped hand. "You people might be makin' jokes now. But it ain't over."

Freddy, Neal, Rafferty, and Blondie hobbled to the Oldsmobile and crawled in. Blondie started the engine, and whipped the Oldsmobile around. With a vicious spinning of the wheels on the side of the road, he sent a spray of fine grit into Toad's face.

Chapter 19

Smeal looked out the window of his house. Two bottles of scotch stood guard by the windowsill. He didn't have any real friends. Tomcats wouldn't even spray on his bushes. Even the local dogs were smart enough to avoid his yard. Animals always ran from him. To him it was just fine. As it had done in the past, money would solve all that. While he had spent most of his life working his tail off to avoid being killed, those garbage-collecting kids had been snug in their beds, reading dime store novels about cowboys and Indians. He knew his faculties were not what they used to be, but those kids had no idea how the system worked. Even though they were full of hopes and dreams of a better life, they shouldn't have even gotten close to something as valuable as the box. And now, if he didn't do anything about it, those kids were going to have Capone's vault, too.

After he thought about how they had started their own garbage business, he figured out a way to stop them from getting the vault. They were the type of people who believe hard work gets a person ahead in life. They had made the same mistake all honest people make. They had worked with their hands instead of their heads. He grinned wolfishly and talked to himself in the mirror. "Those dumb kids are trying to get ahead by being honest, but there's nothing I can't rig or pay off."

He glanced at the phone. Toad and his buddies should have called by now. They gave him the impression that they thought he was just a broken-down old man who couldn't back up his threats.

It was time to let them know who they were working for. When he went to the New Castle railroad switching yard, he would show them. But first, he needed to steal a car at a place where the owner wouldn't know it was gone for hours. He called a taxi and headed for the parking lot of Sharon Steel Corporation. There, the owner would not know his car was stolen until he had finished his eight-hour turn of work.

***

A ways from the railroad switching yard, Smeal drove a stolen 1949 Chevy around the bend and eased past a red '55 Ford with its door open and the motor running. Slobber ran down the side of the face of a bleached blonde passed out in the back seat.

Beyond the Ford, Toad lay with his legs splayed apart on the asphalt road. Smeal stopped the car and looked down at him. When Toad looked up and recognized Smeal, he struggled to stand but couldn't. With his legs still splayed, he managed to sit up. Breathing heavily through his smashed nose, his head sagged until his chin was on his chest. With his silver eyes almost shut, he lifted his head, took a deep breath, and looked up at Smeal.

Smeal cracked the Chevy's door open and looked down. "What happened?"

Rubbing the side of his bloody head, Toad's forehead wrinkled with confusion. "I can't remember. But just before I blanked out, I heard someone say something about the vault."

Smeal's heart rate accelerated with excitement. He had been right: Those kids still had the vault or the money for it. Without offering to help Toad,

Smeal quietly clicked the car door closed and looked to his left. Square Jaw lay in the ditch. His face was a bloody pulp, his eyes were staring at a little streak of blood on the shoulder of the road. In the center of the road, the clean blade of an unused knife flashed in the sun. A few feet from the knife, Schnoz lay on his back, his face to the sky, not moving. Just beyond his head, lay his gun.

Although Smeal was too old to bully these men, they had been beaten up. Now, they were too weak to stop him. The familiar dominating strength of his youth surged in his veins.

He laid on the horn. It blared across the road. Schnoz rolled over and looked up. Smeal leaned out the window and yelled, "Get your dumb ass off the road."

Schnoz looked up. Pain flooded his face. "But I'm hurt."

Being a veteran of months of real pain and the horror of a POW camp, where prisoners resembled skeletons, more than living humans, Smeal hated it when people exaggerated their pain and expected undeserved pity. He fixed an icy stare onto the wimpy man. "Don't confuse me with someone who cares."

Schnoz struggled to his feet, then reached down, picked up his gun, and walked toward Smeal.

Square Jaw who was sitting in the ditch began to stir. His sharkskin suit coat lay in the weeds, its smooth rayon and acetate fabric shinning in the sun. Dirt and dust covered his expensive thin shirt and pants, and they had apparently been torn and shredded during the fight.

Toad got up, screamed in pain, and crumpled

271

back down.

Smeal barked at Toad, "Get up!"

Toad didn't move.

With irritation in his voice, Smeal thundered, "I telling all of you. Get up!"

With his heels gouging the gravel at the side of the road, Square Jaw crawled out of the ditch, sat up, and grimaced. It was a great effort, and he managed to get to his feet. With his begging arms stretched out in front of him and his ragged clothes waving, he wobbled toward Smeal.

From somewhere in the dark reaches of Smeal's mind, a clear vision of ragged prisoners of war, wobbling toward him, came forth and flooded his mind with terror. As if he were back in the POW camp, the smell of death invaded his very soul. Fear of being trapped with no escape erupted. Chopping the air with the sides of his palms and jerking his head to clear the visions, he shouted. "Get the hell away from me!"

As he stood breathing heavily, the visions crawled back to where they had come from. Then anger replaced fear. He focused his attention on the pathetic men before him. "I was all set to have a lot of drinks to honor the occasion," he said, waving his hands in the air. "You would have had such a good time that the next day it would have been all you could do to slither off the bed and crawl to the bathroom." Surveying the situation, he slowly moved his head from side to side. "But no, hell no! You half-wits couldn't even take care of a couple of snot-nosed kids."

Square Jaw backed away from Smeal and shrugged. "Kids? They don't act like any kids I know."

Smeal looked at the knife lying on the road. "You could've slipped that shiv into their guts and drew it up nice and deep."

"But we didn't want to kill them," Square Jaw whined and wiped his red sweating face with the sleeve of his dirty suit coat. "Dead people can't tell us where the vault is."

"Your incompetence is becoming a habit. So what if you have to lame a few people or maybe kill one by mistake? That's the way it has to be." Smeal stared at Square Jaw. Although sun was not hot enough to cause a man to sweat, Square Jaw's face was sweltering. This sign of weakness greatly disturbed Smeal. He screamed directly into Square Jaw's ear, "And who in the hell cares what you think?"

A yellow pall of cowardice seemed to surround Square Jaw's face. He backed away from Smeal.

Weaving in his sitting position on the road, Toad spoke up. "We'll do better the next time."

"There may not be a next time," Smeal said with vehemence. "Those kids already got the money that was in the box. If they get that vault, they'll have enough money to go someplace where we'll never find them."

Still sitting on the road, Toad cautiously lifted his hand. "But their car is still down the road from Melody Lane. We can get them when they come back to get it."

Smeal didn't want to tell him something he already knew, but Toad had a point. That '40 Ford was something all young men wanted. He nodded at Toad. "For once in your life you may have

273

stumbled onto something."

Toad managed a slight smile. But when his face filled with pain, the frown returned. "What do you want us to do now?"

"You just said those kids would come back for the car. What do you think I want you to do?"

As if in deep thought, Toad paused and then looked up. An imbecilic grin filled his face. "Oh yeah, we gotta watch the car."

Shaking his head at the ignorance, Smeal slapped his hand onto the armrest and opened the car door. But he didn't get out. He tilted back until his head rested against the seat. With his eyes on Toad, he paused. He couldn't figure it out. In the old days, when he suggested someone to do something, people did it.

"Well," he said. "How come you can steer a semi-tractor trailer truck and not be able to steer your two hundred and fifty pounds of muscle to take care of those kids and pick up a simple box?"

As if shielding himself from a possible blow, Toad reached up and held his hand in front of his face. "We're sorry, boss, but another guy came. He had blond hair, so I guess it was Blondie."

A wave of excitement and expectation gushed into Smeal's POW crippled brain. Blondie was still alive. And the only reason he would be in the area was if the vault was, too.

Toad rubbed the white plaster mark on the side of his head. "Yeah, boss, I thought Blondie was helpless with that cast on his leg." As if expecting pity, he pointed to his own head. "But he kicked me in the face with it. He kicked Schnoz, too."

Like the calm before a storm, Smeal became

still. "I'm sick of all your lame excuses." Still sitting in the seat, he stretched his neck and looked down at Toad. "I think you should get up now."

As if in too much pain to stand, Toad shook his head and faced the pavement. He thrashed his arms across his chest a few times, turned his ruddy face up, and fixed defiant stare on Smeal.

Smeal was in no mood for disobedience. He opened the car door, placed one foot on the pavement, and cocked his other foot to strike.

Toad continued to stare at Smeal.

Smeal dropped his foot. "What are looking at?"

As if someone had to do something immediately or get hurt, the air filled with desperate haste.

Suddenly, Smeal was seized by a cough that came from the deepest, rawest cavities of his chest. As if he were about to throw up, he felt his face grotesquely contort. Trying to breathe through the congestion in his lungs, his tongue hung from his mouth.

Seeing his weakness, a revengeful grin formed on Toad's lips. For the first time in his miserable life, he seemed to have found the courage to confront Smeal. He flared up angrily. "Hey, puke face, I'm doing the best I can, but I'm getting sick of getting beat up." He waved a dismissive hand into the air. "Why don't you just cough your guts out and curl up and die?"

Smeal had been looking for an excuse to get rid if this incompetent. Toad thought he had it so bad. He had never seen the inside of a POW camp where half-naked filthy men stood around with their long, matted hair and scraggly beards covered with lice. He had never seen the scabs and running sores that dotted their skeletonized bodies covered with a veil of yellow-tinged skin. He never lived with crippled men who tried to see out of missing eyes, hear out of missing ears, and try to count on missing fingers and toes. He'd never watched deformed men with fever, move grotesquely as if they were already dead, just wandering around looking for a hole to fall into. Those starving men with terminal illnesses and broken limbs had done what they had to do. But this over-fed, toad-faced bastard couldn't do a simple task. Now he was on his knees whining.

Beneath a vast sapphire blue sky headed with low, isolated, puffy clouds, Smeal coughed out his last spasm and decided it was time to make a much-needed adjustment. After he wiped his mouth on the back of his sleeve, he reached behind his back and placed his hand on the leather cord in his back pocket. Awkwardly he stepped out of the car and painfully stood behind Toad.

"That's all right, old buddy," he said and patted Toad on the shoulder. "I know you're having a rough go of it. Let me get a good stance. I'll help you up."

A look of relief filled Toad's sun-brightened face. "Gee thanks, boss. Sorry to be so much trouble. I really appreciate it."

In one motion, Smeal whipped the cord out, and thrust it around Toad's unsuspecting neck. "You'll really appreciate this."

He placed his knee in Toad's back and jerked the cord. Toad's head snapped up high. He reached up and tried to pry the garrote from his neck. Smeal tightened the noose with all his might. Toad screamed,, but his voice was quickly snuffed out. As he squirmed and tried to pull off the garrote, his eyes bulged. His legs kicked so wild and strong that his shoes pounded indentations in the pavement. His arms dropped. Then he clutched at Smeal's arms, then back at the garrote. After one final effort to free the garrote from his neck, his hands quit moving. He limply fell to the pavement. A cloud rolled in front of the sun and turned the sapphire blue sky to gray.

Making absolutely sure Toad was dead, Smeal kept the garrote tight and increased the pressure. After Toad's face turned a bluish white, Smeal released the garrote, rolled it up, and threw it onto the front seat of the car. He brushed his hands together, sat behind the steering wheel, and closed the door with a definite clunk.

With his elbow on the window, Smeal stared at Square Jaw. Smeal didn't like him either. Square Jaw never had to work his way up in the system like he had. Square Jaw was just like all the warm, well-fed, comfortable, educated, establishment bastards in America. If he would have gone hungry a day in his life or bled a little, Smeal might have had a little compassion for him. You can't give an easy life to people. It's something they have to earn for themselves. If they don't want the easy life, bad enough to fight for it, they won't value it. Square Jaw was a poor excuse of a man. His relations had pampered, primped, and preened him for this type of work, but he still couldn't take care of the kids that had taken the box. His knife was lying on the road in front of him, but he was making no effort to pick it up. He seemed to be bred for defeat. He was a failure.

Smeal continued to stare at him.

Looking shocked and puzzled, Square Jaw stared at Toad's lifeless body. As if waiting in nervous dread for what might come next, he cocked his head at an insolent tilt and asked Smeal, "What did you do that for?"

Smeal flashed Square Jaw a dazzling professional smile. "It was about time you found out what can happen in the real world. And you did. If you know what's good for you, you'll do what you're told." He jerked his finger in Square Jaw's direction. "And another thing: If you don't quit being afraid and letting people scare the shit out of you, you're going to shit your life away."

Square Jaw seemed to be stunned speechless. His eyes blinked rapidly, and his jaw muscle twitched. With a shaking hand, he reached up and tried to wipe the blood away from his mouth, but it only smeared across the back of his hand. Staring at the blood, he seemed to be regarding the situation with total disbelief. He looked at Toad's dead body and nodded to Smeal. Schnoz tugged on his elbow. Square Jaw turned. They painfully walked back to the red Ford.

Smeal knew they would do something now. He was sure he had put on a good show.

But that was all it was, just a show. He didn't really want to kill anyone, but the deep-seated fear that always turned to hate had surfaced, causing him to become what he had been in the Army. A killing machine with no sense of right and wrong, and it had never bothered him. But this time it did.

Chapter 20

As Blondie steered his Oldsmobile around the bend on Chestnut Street in Sharon, Pennsylvania, Freddy sat in the back seat watching what was going on outside. The traffic from mill workers angrily rushing to and from work had diminished. People in automobiles no longer blew their horns and flashed grimaces of irritation. Rush hour was over. In the doldrums of late afternoon calm, drivers did not hurry, and only a few pedestrians strolled on the sidewalks.

When Blondie approached the intersection at State and Chestnut Street, the traffic light burned bright red.

He stopped.

Freddy looked up to his left. The rectangular four-faced clock attached to the side of the McDowell Bank building read seven o'clock. Off in the distance, the water of the Shenango River was not like it was upriver. Here, a huge, bloated dead carp floated on top of a stretch of blue-fetid sewer water. Slowly making its way south, the rotting fish would pass more mill towns that dumped sewage, industrial wastes, and any unwanted liquid, solid, or gas into the river's once pristine waters. Eventually, the dead fish would drift into a terribly defiled tributary that fed the mighty Ohio River. This disregard for nature's beauty and people's health that made a few people rich was another reason Freddy never wanted to work in the mills that ruined the river he loved.

On the sidewalk, just before the State Street Bridge, two girls sauntered by arm in arm. Their long flowing blond hair glowed wondrously. Their tight blouses and white shorts drew Freddy's eyes to their blossoming curves. Neal threw his arm over the front seat, turned toward the back seat, and winked at Rafferty. "Look at those honeys."

Freddy and Rafferty stretched their necks and watched. As the girls giggled over something, their sweet scent drifted into the windows of the Oldsmobile. When the girl on the right noticed she was being watched, she stretched her arms over her head in a lazy sensual manner that made her breasts strain against her blouse.

Neal gasped, placed a hand to the side of his face, and covered the blue and yellow bruises from the fight. "We should stop and pick them up."

The girl on the left licked her lips and flashed a saucy smile.

Blondie slowed the big Oldsmobile for a second but kept on going. "We don't have time for babes," he said with a dismissive wave of his hand. "We got to get that vault out of the river."

A pleading whimper escaped Neal's lips. "What's a few minutes?" he asked with hope in his voice. "We always got time for honeys like that."

As Blondie pulled away from the girl's tantalizing show, Freddy's face still hurt from being ground into the pavement. He wondered how bad it was swollen. He looked into the rearview mirror to check. Instead, he saw a 1932 five-window coup hot rod with thick grayish-blue paint. It pulled next to the curb and stopped. The girls ran up to it. Julie, the girl of his dreams, stuck her head out the window. Freddy turned from the sight. Just like after a boxing match, he knew his face would heal, but he didn't know if he would ever get over not being good enough for Julie.

Blondie turned his swollen jaw toward Neal and gave him a frosty smile. "Those girls are only having fun messing with your head."

With the girls fading in the distance, Neal squirmed around in the seat. "I like them to mess with my head."

As if he had a headache, Blondie leaned his head toward Neal. "We've got to get serious. Those guys almost had us back there. It won't be long before they figure out where the vault is. At thirty-five dollars an ounce, it's worth close to a million dollars. We got to get it out of the river before somebody else does."

Neal let out his breath in a long whistle. "Can we do that?"

"No problem," Freddy said. "Just get a tow truck and pull it out."

Blondie shook his head. "We can't do that. The brass and cement that concealed the gold is thin. When the vault went through the truck's window some of the brass may have peeled away, and the cement could have broken off." As he drove the Oldsmobile over the bridge, he waved his hand at the river. "We can't pull a big gold vault out of that river. Once a tow truck is spotted, people will think there had been an accident. They'll stop and ask questions. It'll cause a big traffic jam. Then the police will come." He paused. "I'm a wanted man."

Rafferty poked his head over the back of the seat and smiled his missing tooth smile. "I wouldn't let that bother you. You've been arrested so many times, the judge will probably give you a discount."

As thought he had been slapped, Blondie whirled to rage at Rafferty, but when he saw Rafferty's idiotic grin and his missing tooth, a short burst of laughter erupted from his lips. In a rare display of sarcastic humor, Blondie replied, "Maybe we could put your tooth under the pillow, and the tooth fairy could give us a million dollars for it."

"I tried that once," Rafferty replied without missing a beat. "But where I live, the tooth fairy took the pillow and left the tooth."

With his mouth agape, Blondie stared at Rafferty and muttered, "I'm glad you're on our side."

Freddy knew they would be taking a chance, but he couldn't think of any other way to get the heavy vault out of the deep river. "I still think we'll need a tow truck."

"If we use one," Blondie said, "we'll have to have a lot of money to pay people off."

At the intersection of North Water Avenue and State Street, Blondie stopped for the red light in front of the Corner News Stand. Like a miniature stockade wall, stacks of black and white newspapers surrounded the front of the stand. Two slanted racks, made of weathered wood, supported lines of colorful magazines. Between the racks, a gray-haired man with a blue work shirt and thick glasses leaped off his stool. He peeled a fresh newspaper off a stack and dashed toward the Oldsmobile. "Paper, mister?"

The light changed to green. Blondie reached out the window and waved his hand down. "No thanks."

The man snarled and turned back to his newsstand.

Glancing at Freddy in the rearview mirror, Blondie drove on. "If you want to share that gold vault with a bunch of crooked cops, or have the government take it from us, we could get a tow truck and pull it out."

Neal's left eyebrow lifted. "How's the government going to take it?"

As if he were in pain from repeating information, Blondie's closed his eyes for an instant. "They don't need a reason to take it. Owning gold has been illegal since 1934."

Rafferty's face broke into a wide grin. "Nothing's illegal until you get caught."

As the others tried to ignore Rafferty's attempted humor, Freddy's mind whirled. He already knew gold had been illegal, and he figured that was why Capone had hidden the heavy vault. He could feel Blondie's gaze reading Neal's reactions, and he wanted to see how much more Blondie would tell them.

Neal waved his hand in the air. "What's the big deal? I still say we don't need a tow truck." With a defeated look, he looked to Blondie. "But if you guys think we need one, I won't argue."

Blondie stiffened and his face took on a concerned look. "How much money do you guys have left from what I gave you?"

"Not a damn cent, "Freddy said.

Blondie jerked his head in Freddy's direction. "What?"

"Schnoz broke the bank president's nose. Then

283

the president sat behind his great polished desk and got men with their perfect haircuts and creased pants to steal it off us."

A grimace of acute discomfort filled Blondie's face. "Damn! He did it again." He raked his fingers through his hair and the discomfort lessened. He continued. "Smeal's got an uncanny way of getting his hooks into a lot of people. Somebody that owed him a favor probably arranged to have your money taken." With wide questioning eyes, he paused and looked at Neal. "Did you ever find that box of money at Peacock Alley?"

Neal bristled slightly at the question. "We found it."

Freddy shrugged indifferently and changed the subject. "There's gold lying on the bottom of the river. Let's get that tow truck and get it out."

"I would like to do just that," Blondie said and drove past the flying red horse painted on the sign of a Mobil Gas Station.

As Freddy watched the red Pegasus in the review mirror, Neal airily waved his hand in the air. "So let's do it."

Blondie steered the Oldsmobile around a bend and drove down River Road. "We could, but the problem is that there is too much money involved."

"What's the problem?" Neal wanted to know. "You got something against making money?"

"I want to make money, but I don't want everybody taking a cut. If we get a tow truck and manage not to attract attention, the driver won't keep his mouth shut without a share."

Neal threw up his hands. "You're right. If we get a tow truck, we might as well put a full page ad in the newspaper."

As if he were still groggy from the fight, Rafferty let out a weak laugh. "What's the difference?" he said with his missing tooth punctuating his mouth. "Blondie's going to take the money anyway."

Freddy cringed. The fact that Blondie had previously tricked them out of the vault was a sore spot with Neal, and Rafferty had just agitated it.

Neal leaned over the seat, and grabbed Rafferty by the front of the shirt. "Shut up! Just shut up."

"What for?" Rafferty said, trying to cover his missing tooth with his lips. "He gyped us once before. He'll do it again."

Blondie turned with a jolt. "I heard that."

As if he suddenly realized something, Neal let loose of Rafferty's shirt and turned toward Blondie. "So what? It's true."

With a pained face, Blondie ran his fingers through his blond hair. "Yeah, I'll admit I did that. But I left you guys enough money to live high on the hog for a while. I even left that key in my pocket with the letter to find the other moneybox. And to top it off, I saved you guys from getting burned up in Canada."

Freddy didn't even like to think about how they had almost been burned to death, but he figured Blondie only saved them because he knew they had mistakenly been given the decoding key and he wanted it back. And he couldn't blame him for wanting it. That key opened the secret entrance to the mine where Al Capone's vault had been hidden.

Freddy lifted his hand and gestured toward Blondie. "You probably saved our lives. But you still cheated us out of the vault."

Blondie pursed his lips in a businesslike manner. "Not really." He paused. "I never *said* I was going to share the vault with you. I only said we would share what was in it, not what it was made of. But it doesn't really matter. In that fight, I just saved your asses again."

Freddy still figured they were even and didn't owe Blondie anything. "So what?"

"So what, hell. You owe me."

Neal slumped in the seat. "We might owe you." His face scrunched with concentration. "But how about sharing a little wealth of that vault?"

"No problem," Blondie said, and his eyes seemed to peer at something way beyond the road.

Neal came erect. "What do you mean, no problem?"

"All we have to do is get the vault out of the river."

At the concrete bridge at the bottom of Myers Hill, Blondie slowed the Oldsmobile and looked to his right. The rock-strewn stream that ran under the bridge snaked its way into the Shenango River. Just above the roaring rapids, the water ran calm and deep. A silver shaft from the light of the sun highlighted the water below a rock outcropping near the opposite shore. As Blondie drove across the bridge, off to the left, gunshots rang out from behind a stand of trees.

Blondie tensed his shoulders forward and jerked his head toward the sound.

Neal turned toward Blondie and smiled. "Don't get excited, Blondie. It's only target practice." He pointed to his left. "Behind those trees, there's a shooting range. Police us it all the time."

Blondie's shoulders relaxed. He leaned back and steered the Oldsmobile up the dangerous curved road that led up the tree and brush-lined Myers Hill.

Near the top, he stopped at the only tree-free spot and said, "This is where the green truck with the vault was forced off the road and sent me into the river."

Freddy strained to look out the side window. Just before the curve in the road, the land sloped down at a steep angle. Tall weeds and grass covered the hill all the way to the muddy bank.

Blondie glanced in the rearview mirror and looked over his shoulder. "We can't stay here long. Smeal and his cronies can come around the bend and see us." He put the Oldsmobile into first gear and pulled away.

Turning his head, Freddy watched the river until it was out of sight. "I didn't see anything."

Blondie tipped his head at Freddy. "You won't. The truck and the vault's on the bottom."

Rafferty cocked an eyebrow and stared at Freddy. "If we could see it, someone else would have seen it, too. It wouldn't be there anymore." He stared into Freddy's face and smiled his missing tooth smile. "Do you have brain damage?"

Freddy didn't believe he had been so stupid. Dumbfounded, he sunk his head down and didn't answer.

Blondie smiled with a superior air. "Now that you gentleman have seen the situation, do you have any ideas how to get the vault out without a tow truck and a long cable?"

As if conceding an argument, Neal lowered his head and nodded. "No problem. We can get the vault out with a simple tool."

"No way," Blondie said with finality. "That vault's too heavy for a simple tool. We're going to need some heavy equipment to get that thing out of that river. We'll have to fake an accident and pay off the tow truck operator. It's going to cost a lot of money."

Blondie drove forward and steered the Oldsmobile around the bend at the top of the hill. "Do you think there is enough money in that box you guys dug out of Peacock Alley to cover the job?"

Neal looked at Rafferty.

Rafferty looked at Neal. "Should I tell him?"

Neal leaned back in the seat and laced his hands behind his head. "It's up to you."

Rafferty paused and turned toward Blondie. "The way you led us on about the vault being worthless, I don't think we should trust you."

One of Blondie's hands flew off the steering wheel. "If you guys don't want to help, don't." With sanctimonious anger, he shook his finger in front of Neal's eyes. "I don't need you guys. I don't need anybody." He stopped shaking his finger. His facade crumpled. As his face flushed with embarrassment, he placed his hand back on the steering wheel.

With an on the verge of crying look, Rafferty pulled his lips back, displayed the space of his missing tooth, and crossed his eyes. "You mean I won't be getting a new tooth?"

Blondie tried not to laugh at Rafferty's imbecile

look, but he couldn't hold it in. He laughed out loud and then whispered, "Sorry about that. If I had the brains of a nitwit, I couldn't cheat you guys out of the vault now. At first, I thought I could go on this thing alone. You know, every man for himself. But not any longer. I know those days are gone. It's our fight, and it's only beginning."

Neal dropped his hands from the back of his head. "The beginning of what?"

"Smeal and his halfwits want that vault, and they want that box of money you guys took."

Neal cocked his head to one side. "So?"

"So, hell. They'll send more tough guys with busted noses, big loose hands, and bull necks after us. We got to join up together."

Trying to be funny, Rafferty made another idiotic face and whistled, "Whee!" He turned toward Freddy and Neal. "What do you think we should do?" As if in a stupor, he held his mouth open and stared at Freddy. "Huh?"

Freddy ignored Rafferty's bird-brained effort to make him laugh. He knew the garbage hauling business was gone. He didn't want to work in the mill, and he hated the thought of not having any money. "That vault could set us up for life."

"You better believe it," Neal said with robust enthusiasm. "Let's get that vault out of that river."

Rafferty closed his mouth over his missing-tooth-smile and brought his hands together in a resounding clap of victory. "That's what I want to do, too."

Blondie steered around a bend and held up his thumb. "Okay, we'll use the money from that box you guys got at the Peacock Alley foundation."

"We could," Freddy said. "But that money was so old and dry, the wind blew it away."

Blondie let out a painful wince and jerked his head back. "What are you talking about?"

Rafferty formed a lopsided smile. "The wind blew the money away."

"What do you mean the wind blew the money away?" Blondie gestured impatiently with his hand. "Why didn't you chase it?"

Freddy shook his head in dismay. "It broke into a million pieces and went into the Mahoning River."

"Can't you swim?"

"Not in that oil," Freddy said. "And besides, the pieces were so small it would have taken a thousand years to find them and another thousand to put them back together."

As if it didn't bother him, Blondie gave a stoic shrug and slowed the Oldsmobile.

Neal slouched in the seat. "You look like you don't believe us?"

Blondie jerked his hand in a dismissive gesture. "Would you?"

Trying to get his point across, Rafferty lifted both hands and shook them. "The wind blew away the money that we dug up at the foundation."

Blondie held up one finger. "Hey, wait a minute." His forehead wrinkled with thought. "How could the wind blow money away if it was in a metal box?"

"Simple," Rafferty said. "Before Neal threw the box on the road for a diversion, Freddy opened it and wrapped the money in Neal's shirt. When we opened the shirt we were on a big bridge. Like we said before, the money was so old and dry from the fire that the wind blew it off the railroad car and it flew into a million pieces.

"You sure you didn't save the pieces?" Blondie said with hope in his voice. "The bank will exchange them for new money."

Rafferty held up his hands. "We couldn't save the pieces," he said and wiggled his fingers. "The money fell like confetti. When it hit the river, it floated on the top for a while, but a rainstorm pounded it to the bottom."

Blondie looked hurt. He jerked his head downward. "I can understand the money being gone, but what are we going to do now?"

After a brief silence, Rafferty spoke up. "Why don't just go out and dig up a hundred thousand dollars?" With an idiotic smile, he stared directly into Blondie's face.

As if expecting a joke, Blondie gawked at Rafferty with tortured wonder.

Rafferty continued with delight. "We think there's still a hundred thousand in the coalmine."

"What do you mean, we think?"

"We'll have to look in the coalmine to find out."

"We won't have to look," Blondie contradicted him belligerently. "Dillinger got the half million, and the FBI killed him at the Biograph Theater in Chicago."

Freddy leaned over the seat. "The way we see it, maybe Dillinger got the money, and maybe he didn't."

A spark of interest flashed in Blondie's eyes. He rolled his hand at Freddy in an encouraging gesture and increased speed. "Keep talking."

"When we were in the coalmine that skeleton was dressed in a brown suit and had a white fedora. It could be Al Capone."

Blondie looked inquisitively at Neal. "I didn't see any skeleton."

"We didn't want you to see it," Neal said and laughed. "There's a trap door just before where the vault was. We figured that if you or Rafferty saw the skeleton, you would get scared out of your wits and wouldn't help us dig the vault out. So, we pulled the lever, and the trap door covered him up."

"So?" Blondie said, rejecting the theory. "That doesn't prove anything."

"Sure it does," Rafferty said, his voice rising with emotion. "The five hundred thousand John Dillinger was supposed to get wasn't in the vault. Capone may have been shot before he had a chance to put it there."

"That's possible," Blondie said, his rejection turning to curiosity. "But John Dillinger left an I.O.U. in the vault."

"That's what we thought at first," Freddy said. "Maybe Dillinger never had a chance to get the money. Capone or someone may have scared him off right after he wrote the I.O.U."

Blondie's eyes widened with anticipation. "If that's true, the money's still in Capone's pocket."

"Now you're thinking," Neal said and held up his thumb in approval. "All we have to do is dig out the cave-in."

"It's not going to be that easy," Blondie said. "Do you know what the newspapers would do to us if we get caught digging out Al Capone's body?"

Freddy knew what would happen if they got caught, and he didn't like it. "They'd follow us wherever we went. We'd never be able to go near that vault."

"No problem," Neal said with the self-confidence of a man who knew he couldn't be wrong. "We'll dig the mine out at night, just like we did the last time."

As if a cold hand had crawled up his back, Freddy trembled. "I don't know about digging Capone up. It'll be like robbing a grave."

Neal jerked on Freddy's elbow. "What's the matter? Are you afraid of ghosts?"

Freddy leaned forward and remembered how Capone's cadaverous face had maliciously stared at him through sightless eyes sockets. "I don't know," he said. "Dead bodies give me the creeps."

Blondie reached over the seat and patted Freddy on the back. "Don't worry about it. Money will take care of all the little creepies your mind can conjure up."

"It might," Freddy said with the creepy feeling beginning to fade. "But how long do you think Capone has been in that mine?"

Rafferty interrupted with an impatient wave of his hand. "Long enough for you to rewrite the dictionary left handed."

Chapter 21

In the backseat of Blondie's magenta Oldsmobile, Freddy watched Blondie cut the headlights and pull alongside the road. With the sound of gravel popping between the tires, the car crunched to a stop. Wondering if it were going to rain and make their task miserable, Freddy stuck his head out the window and stared at the sky. No rain clouds, but the moon was playing hide-and-seek under a purple cloud. When it peeked out, it illuminated the little patch of land in the outskirts of Masury, Ohio. In the darkness, the dirty-white street sign with black letters stood in the middle of a bunch of tall weeds. It read,

PETROLEUM

Petroleum wasn't actually a town. It was a triangular shaped piece of land that separated two roads that merged into one. Although people drove past the little metal sign every day, few noticed it.

Freddy, Neal, Rafferty, and Blondie opened the Oldsmobile's doors and piled out. The smell of used oil filled the air. Off to the left, a pyramid of three leaking, 55-gallon, metal drums oozed oil onto the ground. Around them, rainbows of oil formed little puddles.

Blondie opened the trunk of the Oldsmobile and passed out four shovels, two buckets, and one pick.

Rafferty turned a bucket over and set it on the ground. As if he were a deity, about to sit on a throne, he spread his arms and graciously sat on the bucket. With one leg draped across his knee, he reluctantly rolled the handle of the shovel in his hands. "I'm still tired from the last time we dug this thing out."

"You might be tired now," Freddy said and leaned the pick against the side of his leg, "but that money in Capone's pocket will take care of all your problems."

Rafferty opened his eyes extra wide. "I'm ready to start digging any time you are." In eager merriment, he jumped up. "Let's go!"

Freddy placed his hand on the pole of the Petroleum sign. "Can you wait until we get the trap door open?"

Rafferty contorted his face into a dumbfound look. "Oh," he said and sat beck down on the bucket.

Neal held one of the brass decoding keys by its L-shaped end and placed it in the first slot at the bottom of the metal signpost. Freddy tilted the post forty-five degrees. A new slot appeared. Neal inserted the other key into that slot. Freddy pushed the signpost to its usual upright position. The ground grated. A grass-covered trap door slid open. Like a yawning monster inviting prey into its mouth, the open door revealed a four-foot deep hole with a wooden step half covered with dirt.

Blondie stabbed the step with the point of his long-handled shovel. "At least the first step's uncovered."

Freddy didn't like what he saw. "Hey," he said. "The last time we were here, the hole was filled almost to the top. Maybe somebody already got the money."

"I doubt it," Neal said. "The dirt probably settled."

Blondie placed his hands on his knees and bent over the hole. "I can't get over how there are no timbers holding up the mine roof."

Freddy tried not to show the fear beginning to creep into his spine. He made a dismissive sound and looked toward the Blondie. "I've seen hard rock mantel above mines that was twelve feet thick. They really don't need timbers to hold up a roof that thick."

"If that's true," Blondie said, and his voice raised a couple of octaves. "Then why did it cave in the last time we were here?"

"Sometimes the mantel ends for no reason. Then the miners put up timbers to hold up the roof. Maybe the timbers rotted away."

Still sitting on the bucket, Rafferty formed an O with his mouth and held his eyes wide open. "I don't want to go down there now. If those timbers rotted away, maybe Capone's ghost is the only thing holding up the roof."

"I can live with being in a mine that could cave in at any time," Blondie said. "But skeletons give me the creeps."

Freddy was getting tired of excuses. He wanted to go into the mine, get the money, and get out as fast as he could. Pretending he wasn't afraid of Al Capone's skeletal remains or the mine caving in, he jumped into the hole. "There's not much dirt in here." He started digging. After he had dug for about fifteen minutes, he passed the shovel to Neal.

Neal didn't hesitate. He grabbed the shovel and jumped into the hole. He jammed the shovel into the dirt and looked back over his shoulder. "I'm not afraid of a rich skeleton."

After Neal had tunneled near the room that contained the vault, Blondie and Rafferty fought their fears and took turns shoveling dirt into buckets and hauling them out of the mine. When they finally dug their way to the lever that opened the trapdoor, Blondie looked at his watch. It was four a.m.

Up top, they all sat on the ground in a circle, took in deep breaths, and drank coffee from paper cups.

Rafferty looked up with a questioning slant. "Is everybody ready to get rich?"

As if in deep thought, Neal caressed the cup in his hands. "We still don't know if the money will be there."

Blondie nodded and went on slurping coffee.

Neal crumpled his empty paper cup in his hands and dropped it on the ground. "We're about to find out." He reached out and grabbed Freddy's shoulder. "There's only room for two. Let's get below."

Neal led the way, and Freddy followed down the steps that led into the mine. Above the secret trap door, Neal reached up and grabbed the lever. "You ready?"

Freddy nodded.

Neal pulled the lever. The floor growled. An iron plate slid back. Only this time it didn't open as far as it did before. But it was open enough for Neal to see down into the pit.

Freddy took a breath of dank air coming from the pit. "Is the skeleton there?"

"I can't see. Hand me that flashlight."

297

Freddy handed Neal the flashlight.

Neal held the brightening beam and scanned the pit below the metal plate. He let out a painful moan and slapped himself in the head. "I don't believe it!"

Freddy figured Neal was seeing a lot of money. He tilted his head and tried to see into the pit. "How much money can you see?"

"None. The damn thing's empty."

Freddy horned in close and looked over Neal's shoulder. "Are you sure?"

Neal handed him the flashlight. "Here, see for yourself."

Freddy took the flashlight and searched every crevice and dark corner of the hidden hole. There was no skeleton in a brown suit with a white fedora. There was no gun in a skeletal hand. The entire secret pit was empty. His heart sunk.

Neal turned toward Freddy. "Let's get back up top and give them the bad news."

When Neal was waist deep in the hole, Blondie leaned over and looked up at Neal. "Did you get the money?"

Neal placed his hands on the rim of the hole and pushed himself up onto the top step. "There's nothing down there."

With hope in his eyes, Blondie made a slight nod in Neal's direction. "You got to be kidding."

Yeah," Rafferty said. "Quit foolin' around. Show us the money."

Neal stepped out of the hole and directed his voice toward Freddy. "Come on up and tell them what's down there."

Freddy placed his foot on the second step,

reached up, and grabbed Neal's hand. Neal pulled him to a standing position.

Freddy brushed off his pants and shook his head. "There's nothing down there. Somebody got to it before we did."

"I don't believe you guys," Rafferty said and jumped into the hole. He held out his hand. "Give me that flashlight."

Neal handed him the flashlight. "Knock yourself out."

Signaling for Blondie to follow, Rafferty waved his arm. "Come on. Let's see what's in this thing."

Blondie jumped into the hole behind Rafferty. Five minutes later, Rafferty and Blondie clawed their way up the steps and out of the mine. Except for the flashlight in Rafferty's hand, they also came up empty handed.

As he used his hands to brush the dirt off his pants, disappointment showed in Blondie's face. "I thought you guys were kidding me. But I can see that someone must have gotten here first and taken the skeleton and the money away."

Rafferty wiped his brow and slowly exhaled a long breath of air. Freddy figured Rafferty would seize the opportunity to throw some of his mischievous merriment into the situation. He waited for him to pick something out of his dazzling treasure-trove of puns, wisecracks, anecdotes, slanders, or idiotic sayings, but he didn't. He dropped his head and spoke lamely with a crooked smile. "We must be some species of idiot that likes to crawl around in dirt. We could be back in a bar having a cold beer."

Neal propped himself up on the shovel and

leaned to one side. "I'm glad you figured that out."

Disgusted, Freddy sat on the ground and looked at the entrance to the mine. It had offered new hope and quick riches, but now their spirits lay in the piles of worthless dirt they had hauled out of the mine. He put his head in his hands. "We should have looked in Capone's pockets the first time we were here."

Neal nodded violently. "That's right. We should have checked it out when we had the chance."

Sitting on an upturned bucket, Blondie held the flashlight in his hands and flicked it on and off a few times. Then he looked up at the dark sky. "Should've, could've." In a sudden frantic fury, he rose to his feet. "We don't have to think like that, and we're not going to."

"What are you talking about?" Freddy asked. "The skeleton's gone. The money's gone."

"I know the money's gone," Blondie said with a flick of his wrist. "We all know it's gone. In this world of crime, it's take or be taken from. That's what the real world's all about."

Neal flashed Blondie a questioning slant. "Are you talking about robbing a bank or something?"

As if he were in pain, Blondie's forehead wrinkled. "Before I ran into you guys I would have done just that. But I'm tired of living like a scared rat that has to steal and hide just to stay alive."

Freddy leaned on the long-handled shovel and thought about how the bank manager had used the corrupt system and taken their money. "How are we going to fight a rigged system?"

"I'm not sure, but one thing I've learned during

300

my wretched life is that if you don't like certain things that happen to you, and you want to beat the system, you never look back." His jaw set in a show of determination. "We got to keep moving ahead. There's always a new bend in the road, and I still believe whoever's in charge can't rig everything."

Rafferty sprang forward off his bucket. "That's right! That vault's still in the river. All we have to do is get enough money to get it out."

Neal nonchalantly turned his palm up and tilted his head to one side. "You guys are making a big deal out of nothing. Like I told you before, we don't need money to get that vault out."

"But that thing weighs at least two thousand pounds," Blondie countered. "We'll never be able to lift it."

Neal persisted. "Yes we will."

Blondie jerked one hand upward. "For cryin' out loud, I had to load it with a tow truck. Unless you're Super Man, you'll never get it out."

"I don't care how heavy that vault is," Neal objected. "The water will make it lighter." He shrugged. "Like I told you before, we can get the vault out with a simple tool.'"

"I don't mean to throw the monkey wrench into your logic," Rafferty said, and it sounded as if the life went out of his voice. "But if the vault is airtight, it may have floated away."

Neal snapped at Rafferty, "Don't talk like that. I don't care how much air's in that thing, it's still too heavy to float. We'll still be able to pull it out with a come-along."

As if he were hearing the word "come-along"

for the first time Blondie's face took on a puzzled look. "The vault probably *is* too heavy to float, but what's a come-along?"

Neal held his hands two feet apart. "It's about this big. Some people call it a hand winch. It has two hooks with quarter-inch aircraft cable that can pull four tons."

Blondie seemed interested. "Are the cables on it long enough to go into the river and back?"

"Heck no, the cables are only about five feet long, but we can attach a long rope to the vault and run it out to a tree on shore. Then we hook one end of the come-along onto the tree and the other end onto the rope that's tied around the vault." He curled his hands into fists and moved them as if he were pulling a lever. "A lever is connected to gears that are attached to the cable that makes it easy to pull things."

With an uncertain grin on his face Rafferty stared at Neal. "If it's so easy to use a come-along why do they have tow trucks?"

"Because the gear ratio is so low that you have to crank the handle about a million times to pull something a couple of feet. A little come-along has enough power to pull out the vault but only a few feet at a time."

"Then what?"

Neal looked at Rafferty as if he were insane. "Then what, hell. All we have to do is shorten the rope, reattach it to the come-along, and start cranking. We keep reattaching the rope until we pull the vault out of the river."

As if he were trying to picture what a come-along looked like, Blondie stared at Neal's hands.

"You sound pretty sure of that."

Lifting his hands, Neal tilted his head in a questioning slant. "If you got a better idea, I'm all ears."

With the space of his missing tooth showing, Rafferty flashed Blondie a mischievous grin. "If you don't want to do that then maybe we could get all dressed up, you know, take the wife and kids to church, get ourselves saved or something."

Blondie snarled, jerked his head away from Rafferty's attempted humor, and fixed a steady stare on Neal. "I still think we'll need a tow truck, but I'll try your so-called come-along."

Chapter 22

As if he were being interrupted, the man at the rental building stood behind a waist-high counter and cast an evil stare at Freddy. He seemed to be angry because they were interrupting him from doing nothing, and he would have to do his job and wait on them. His hair was cut extremely short on the sides, making the sides of head appear white. A scraggly goatee surrounded his thick pale lips and made his mouth resemble a monkey's butt. Although other customers may have entered and the man had made them feel unwelcome and caused them to cast stares of meek apology in his direction and left the store, Freddy and his friends were in no mood for it. The man had come-alongs for rent. And they needed one.

Walking into the store behind Neal and Blondie, Rafferty bumped Freddy's shoulder and surreptitiously imitated a monkey.

A glossy walnut cabinet, protected with thick panes of spotless glass, sat off to the side of the store. Inside, displayed like the most important things in the world, tennis trophies gleamed under bright lights. Freddy wasn't impressed. The trophies only signified the owner had done something that was of no benefit to anyone but himself.

Glowering at Neal with a blameful hatred, the man snapped, "What do you want?"

Rafferty interrupted. "Did those trophies come out of a dentist's office because you had no cavities?"

While the man forced a twisted smile, Neal

kept his upbeat attitude. "We need a come-along."

The man reached under the counter, pulled a come-along off the lower shelf, and slammed it onto the countertop in front of Neal.

"Here you go, long hair," the man said in a flat tone that indicated he didn't like Neal or his long hair.

Freddy didn't think Neal's hair was long. It was slicked back but was neat and wasn't hanging down below his neck. Although the man's eyes were downcast, Freddy sensed Neal was the object of the man's envy, suspicion, resentment, and malicious innuendo. But Neal's attention was focused on the come-along. Apparently he didn't hear the long hair remark. He placed his hand on the come-along and only gave the man a cautious stare.

Blondie stepped to the counter and reached into his pocket. "We'll need two ropes, too. How much?"

The man didn't answer right away. Swearing under his breath about long-haired hoodlums, he tore a page from a ream of rental forms. Then he placed the page in front of Blondie and held out his hand. "Before I give you the rope, I'll have to see your driver's license." Still holding out his hand, the man placed the finger of his other hand at the bottom of the page. "If you can write, you'll have to sign here, buddy."

Blondie cocked his right fist and took a half step backward. "What I got to say to you is simple, buddy! "Bug off!"

The man held up his hands and stood in a submissive position. "I'm sorry, sir. But we have to have identification, in case, you know, the come-along gets lost or stolen. It's only company policy."

Blondie was still wanted by the police. There was no way he was going to give the man any form of identification. He slammed his fist on the counter. "Look, you little monkey. We're not renting anything. We're buying this thing. And we're paying you twice what it's worth."

Confusion showed in the man's monkey-butt-looking face. "But, sir!" His upper lip curled up as if he smelled something awful. "This is not a store, we only rent things."

Freddy didn't feel the man was trying to cheat them, but he sensed that Neal did, and Neal hated people who did. Blondie has started something, and just to make things interesting, Neal loved to disrupt a simple thing. When he got this way, there was no telling what he would do. Freddy stepped back and waited for the onslaught.

Neal stepped between Blondie and the man. "So what happens if we rent this come-along and we don't bring it back?"

The man's lip curled up, more, almost touched his nose. As he lifted his arms in the air, a gold tooth shone out at Neal. "Why, you would have to pay for it."

"I tell you what, bright boy," Neal said with a hostile sneer. "We're renting the damn thing, and we're not bringing it back. So give us the come-along and some rope, and shut up."

A tremor of concern passed over the man's goateed face and his thick pale lips stretched into a thin line, but he didn't reach for the rope. Jerking his thumb over his shoulder angrily, the man roared,

"You're not going to tell me what to do. Get the hell out of here."

Blondie stepped around Neal, stood at the counter, and faced the man. "We're not going anywhere, you little creep. Why are you giving us a hard time?"

Blondie's voice carried so much vehement rage that the man held up his palms in a defensive manner and backed away. "Gentleman, there's no need to call people names."

Blondie's face tensed. "And there's no reason to make a big deal out of renting a simple come-along." He leaned toward the man and slapped a wad of cash onto the counter.

The man lowered his gaze and sheepishly fiddled with his fingers. "I think you're making a mistake."

A threatening sensation came from Blondie's very soul. "Perhaps you're the one making a mistake." As if reaching for his Colt, he placed his hand inside his suit coat. "Do you have enough life insurance to bury your sorry ass?"

The man's face took on an ashen shade. "I'm sure we can work something out, sir." He turned, reached up on the wall, and took down two huge coils of one-inch rope. "Here's the rope." He flopped the rope on the counter.

Freddy scooped up a coiled rope and put it over his shoulder.

Rafferty picked up the other rope and faced the man. "I'm impressed by how unimpressive you are." He turned, bowed his legs, and walking out of the store, he made noises like a monkey.

The man didn't say a word, but his face turned

purple with pent-up rage.

Shaking his head in disbelief, Freddy followed Rafferty out the door. Neal and Blondie came out a few moments later. Neal opened the trunk of the Oldsmobile and threw in the come-along. Freddy and Rafferty threw in the ropes. Then they all piled into the Oldsmobile.

Chapter 23

After they ate at the Dinner Bell restaurant in Sharon, Freddy, Neal, Rafferty, and Blondie sat back with the ruins of their meals before them and waited for dark.

When the sun finally set behind rusty-orange clouds of smoke, Sharon Steel's open-hearth furnaces had wheezed into the air, they left the restaurant and drove down River Road. The dark sky was clear for a stretch, and a quarter moon had replaced the sun.

At the bottom of Myers Hill, Blondie slowed the Oldsmobile to a crawl and looked to Neal. "If we park at the side of the road, someone might stop and see what we're doing. Where are we going to park?"

"No problem," Neal said. "Go up the hill, turn around, and go back down. We'll park at the shooting gallery. No one's there at night, and a crick runs under the bridge and leads right to the river."

Blondie drove up Myers Hill, turned on to Westinghouse Boulevard, did a U-turn, drove down Myers Hill, and onto the dirt and gravel road that led to the shooting gallery.

Neal reached over and pointed to the headlight switch. "We don't want anybody to see us. Turn off the lights."

Blondie cut the lights and drove back the rough road. Stray gravel haphazardly tapped the underside of the car until they were under a tree at the shooting gallery. Then the wheels crunched to a stop. Surrounded by tall trees, it was darker here.

Off to the right, a steep wall of yellow dirt and soft stones climbed to a height well over eighty feet. It reflected stray light and made it possible to see.

Green grass that took on a bluish hue in the moonlight ran up to a line of wooden posts with strong boards nailed across their tops. In the daylight, shooters rested their rifles on the boards and shot at paper targets set up in front of a stream that now babbled softly in the night. Just beyond the stream, the steep yellow dirt wall formed the backdrop that stopped the many bullets that flew thought the air.

With a look of concern in his face, Blondie looked to Neal. "You sure nobody shoots at night?"

"Look around," Neal said. "There're no lights in the place."

Rafferty turned his face toward Blondie and opened his eyes so wide that his eyeballs bugged out. "To shoot here at night, people would have to have cat eyes."

"I'll take your word for it." Blondie nudged Rafferty in the ribs and walked to the back of the Oldsmobile. "I just want to make sure we don't walk up that crick and have a storm of bullets rain down on our heads."

Blondie opened the trunk. Neal grabbed the come-along, and Rafferty slung a coil of rope around his shoulder. Freddy slipped his hand into the other coil of rope and picked it up. They all headed for the creek.

Flat rocks lined the banks of the foot deep creek, and slippery green algae coated the rocks that hid under the water. Being from the city, and not knowing how slippery the algae could be, Blondie took one step into the water. His feet flew out from under him. His blond hair tossed wildly. He splashed, butt first, into the shallow water. Faster than a blink, he was back on his feet. The hostile sneer on his face showed he was ready to fight. He looked around uneasily. No one was near him. "What happened?"

Neal, and Freddy tried to hold in their laughter, but Rafferty giggled with childish joy. "That stuff's slippery. You can't walk on it like you are on Main Street."

"That's right," Freddy said with a jovial chuckle. "Stay on the bank, or you'll fall on your ass again."

Blondie's hostile sneer faded. He carefully took a step toward the shore and turned toward Freddy. "Now you tell me."

As they made their way to the base of the bridge, their footsteps swished in unison on the grass-lined bank. Neal held up his hand and whispered, "Wait! I think hear I hear something."

With fear and alarm, they all froze in their tracks. Quietly, they stepped into the water, waded under the bridge, and leaned against the stone supports. With cocked heads and water up to their knees, they strained their ears trying to pick up the slightest sound.

Thinking they may have been followed and Smeal's henchmen were waiting in ambush, Freddy felt his whole body begin to tingle. He remembered that pursuers deliberately work to hide their upper bodies. When they cannot be seen from a standing position, sometimes a different prospective will enable a person to see their feet or legs moving.

Freddy dropped to a crouching position and peered toward the stream. Water falling from a pool next to the shore splashed and tinkled over a huge boulder, but no movement of feet or legs appeared.

Pretending to laugh, Rafferty quietly clutched his head with both hands and doubled over. Then he straightened up, displayed his missing tooth smile, and whispered, "It's only water."

After a few minutes listening to the water falling, in silence, they continued toward the river.

On the other side of the river, just above the rapids, yellow lights on poles flickered in the moving branches of the trees and illuminated the north end of the Ferrona Railroad switching yard.

Where the creek met the river, roaring water met their ears. On the right, swift water tumbled over jagged rocks and formed a dangerous stretch of rapids. On the opposite bank of the rapids, huge chunks of broken concrete pavement had been dumped onto the shore and formed an irregular wall, linked with tangled, twisted, rust-covered rebar. A ways beyond the chunks of broken pavement, rounded stones topped with unknown vegetation sat below a tall, latticed tower from which a dim light shone. The rest of the riverbank was barren except for one small stretch of trees and bushes that clung to a knuckle of rocks. Higher up on the shore, trees blocked the view of the switching yard, but Freddy thought he saw a dark form silhouetted against a billowing cloud of fog.

Hoping it wasn't Smeal, he looked to Rafferty. "What's the chances of anyone seeing us?"

Rafferty pointed to the raging rapids. "About as much chance as someone swimming up those things."

Freddy glanced at the rapids and the dark form vanished. He wasn't sure it had been there at all. He focused his eyes on a widening wedge of light that fell across the start of the rapids. When he looked upriver, not one ripple disturbed the surface of the giant dark mirror of the deep pool, but the hiss of air brakes and the clatter and bangs of yard locomotives switching cars at the railroad yard, traveled through the moving fog.

Freddy couldn't see the yard, but he knew twenty railroad tracks made up the switching yard. Two main tracks ran parallel to the river and fed back into the switching yard tracks at each end. This configuration of inbound and outbound tracks formed Ferrona Yard, an integral part of the Erie Lackawanna Railroad system. Here railroad cars loaded with coke, iron ore, coal, and scrap, headed for the Sharon Steel mill, were classified, weighed, and switched out. Other various cars, including flatcars, like the one they had ridden to the Mahoning River Bridge, boasted tall gray transformers from Westinghouse Electric Corporation, and they came and left here. Material for the Sawhill and Sharon Tube pipe plants came and went, too.

On any other night, Freddy and his friends would have been interested in railroad cars, what they were hauling, and where they were going. But tonight, all they wanted to do was get that vault out of the river.

Above the rapids, the water ran smooth and deep. Its velvet sheen reflected tree branches that gracefully dipped onto the surface and sent tiny waves toward a shore that curved inward, making the river four times wider than at the rapids, which was now right before them.

They turned left, walked along the curved shoreline, and headed upriver. As they made their way, the moonlit night filled with gnats, moths and mosquitoes. The mosquitoes buzzed around and bit viciously, but after five minutes they stopped.

"What's with these mosquitoes? Blondie said. "They bite like crazy, then all of a sudden they stop."

Shifting his eyes, Freddy searched for mosquitoes. "They usually quit biting at ten thirty."

"Why do they do that?"

"I spent a lot of time on this river, but I never could figure that out. All I know is that they do."

As if he were checking the time, Rafferty looked at his wrist. "Maybe they have a curfew and have to be home by ten thirty." With a flick of his hand, he batted a mosquito away from his smiling face. He leered at Freddy with maniacal mischief. "I think they'll stop biting when they're full."

Blondie held up his finger and jerked it one time at Rafferty. "This isn't a time for jokes. We have to stay sharp. Someone might be here waiting for us."

"I wouldn't worry about it," Rafferty said. "Smeal and his pals don't know about this place."

Blondie savagely whirled around and directed his raised voice at Rafferty. "In this business, if you take things for granted, you'll end up in a freshly dug grave."

As if he were going to make wisecrack, Rafferty crinkled is freckled nose, but he didn't reply.

"Think about it," Blondie said and lowered his voice. "We didn't think they knew where the Jungle Inn was, and they found us there."

Neal nodded. "You have a point there." Searching for movement, he turned his head from side to side. "But I don't see or hear anything."

Blondie stopped at the riverbank and moved his head from side to side. "I hope you're right. We're here."

Across the river, scarce light from the railroad switching yard tower scattered across the surface of the tea black water. Rafferty looked toward it. "Hey, I don't want to go in there at night. Why can't we just get a lawyer and get him to claim the vault for us?"

"Don't be ignorant," Blondie said with a careless flick of his wrist. "Lawyers are the secret backbones of the system we're up against." He turned toward Neal. "Okay, let's see if your come-along can pull that vault out."

Neal dropped the come-along on the riverbank. "Just as soon as we get a rope around that vault," — he pointed to the come-along — "I'll show you what that little thing can do." He tugged at the rope on Freddy's shoulder. "Okay, Freddy, are you ready to hook this thing up?"

Freddy shrugged the rope from his shoulder and let it fall to the ground. "I'm not going in with my clothes on."

While Freddy stripped to his underwear, Rafferty unwound his coil of rope and stretched it toward a strong willow tree near the bank.

Freddy grabbed on the end of the rope and

offered it to Blondie. "If the current takes it, this thing will get heavy." He pointed upriver. "Unwind it and lay it along the bank. If I find the vault, Neal will grab the end of the rope and swim it out to me. When he does, feed him rope little by little."

Blondie leaned toward the calm surface of the river. "I don't see any current."

"You won't see a current on the top." Freddy opened his hand and gestured toward the water. "Jump in. You'll feel it."

"That's all right," Blondie said and turned toward the rope. "I'll take your word for it."

Walking upriver, Blondie strung out the rope so that it was one long strand laying on the edge of the river. He walked back and stopped in front of Freddy. "It's pretty dark down there. How are you going to see the vault?"

Freddy shot him a confident smile. "I won't. I'll have to feel my way."

As Freddy eased into the water, its smooth quiet surface felt like velvet on his skin. Treading water, he looked back to shore. "Hey, Blondie, are you sure this is the place where you went in with the truck?"

"I'm not absolutely sure. It was raining then, and I didn't go in at night." He squinted toward the river. "I think you're close."

Freddy gave him a thumbs-up, did a surface dive, and shot toward the unknown bottom of the river. Feeling for the truck or the vault, he slit his eyes against the murky water and dove deeper. At the bottom, all he felt was thick mud. He swam back and forth, searching, but felt nothing but a few rocks. He surfaced and gasped for air.

Neal shouted across the water. "Did you find it?"

"Not yet."

Blondie pointed upriver. "I think it's up further.

Watching Blondie, Freddy swam upriver until Blondie held up his hand. "Try there."

Up on the railroad tracks, on the other side of the river, a diesel locomotive buzzed its horn. As it rounded a bend, its strong light beamed across the water. Again, Freddy did a surface dive and plunged into the inky darkness. Near the bottom, for a moment, the strong light from the diesel locomotive caused the darkness of the water to give way. The blurry outline of the truck was right in front of his face. He felt around and found the vault. It was still in the bed of the truck, but it wasn't wedged in the back window. One end was partially submerged in the soft mud bottom. He didn't know if Neal's come-along was strong enough to pull the heavy vault out of the quicksand-like muck, but he was going to find out. He surfaced and yelled across the water, "Okay, Blondie, get ready to start feeding Neal that rope."

Neal stripped to his underwear and stepped into the river until the water was up to his knees. He turned toward Blondie and Rafferty. "While I swim it out, you guys make sure the rope doesn't get tangled." He looped a section of the rope around his arm, clinched the end of it between his teeth, flexed his legs, and dove into the water. The last thing to enter the water was his toes and the plaster-white soles of his feet. After a few powerful sidestrokes, he was in front of Freddy. Treading water, he took the rope from his mouth and offered it to Freddy. "This rope's pretty heavy. You think you can tie it on?"

Freddy grabbed the rope. "If I can't, at least it'll be on the bottom. Keep the current from taking it, and feed it to me until I stop. When I yank on it twice, give me more slack."

Neal's face broke into a triumphant smile. "No problem."

Taking extra deep breaths to fill his lungs with air, Freddy held the end of the rope in his hand. After one big breath, he surfaced dove for the vault. Strong scissor kicks and the weight of the rope propelled him to the bottom. Now that the light from the diesel locomotive was gone, he could no longer see the vault. But as if he had planned it, the end of the rope hit the top of the vault and let out a dull thud. Neal quit feeding him slack. Freddy yanked on the rope twice. Neal fed him more rope. Freddy tried to loop the rope around the vault, but the upright end of the vault was leaning against the truck bed. He began to thread the rope through an opening between the bed and the vault but ran out of air. He stroked for the surface. Bursting through the top of the water, he gasped and breathed in.

Still treading water and fighting to keep the current from taking the rope downriver, Neal asked, "Did you get it on?"

Out of breath, Freddy didn't answer right away. As his breathing eased, he answered, "Almost, I think I'll get it this time." He breathed deep and relaxed for few moments. Then he took deep breaths to the point of hyperventilating and dove for the vault. Underwater, with his hands held in front of him, he groped blindly through the darkness, feeling his way to locate the vault again.

After he found it, he managed to thread the rope between the space between the back of the truck and the tilting vault. He almost had it wrapped around the vault, but the truck lurched toward the center of the river.

The vault shifted and slid onto his arm, trapping it. Wriggling against the pull of the moving vault, he managed to slide his arm free. He rushed to the surface, popped his head above the water, and gasp for air. As he caught his breath, an eerie feeling, as if he were being watched, ran down his back. He looked to his right. A threatening shadow passed behind him. Coughing out water, he turned toward Neal. But Neal was nowhere in sight. Freddy turned to see what was behind him.

Neal rose though the rolling water and held up his thumb. "I thought you'd never come up. I went down after you."

"That vault moved and almost trapped me. Can you swim down and hold it while I tie the rope?"

"I'm ready any time you are." Neal drew in a deep breath.

Freddy nodded, took in deep breaths, and dove for the bottom. As he descended, he felt Neal at his heels. On the bottom, he guided Neal's hand to the vault. Neal tapped on Freddy's shoulder. Freddy knew he was supporting the vault. He grabbed the rope, finished looping it around the vault and clinched it into a knot. To signal Neal he was done, he pounded on the vault and swam for the surface.

Freddy broke water just before Neal. As he

sucked in much needed air, he watched Neal's face beam into a huge, satisfied smile.

Rafferty cupped his hands to his mouth and shouted across the water. "Come on in. Only a crazy man would stay out there this long."

Neal turned toward the shore. "Then why aren't you out here?"

Rafferty pointed downriver. "Are you sure the vault's not full of air? I think I just saw it floating downriver."

Blondie gasped in horror. He snapped at Rafferty, "Don't talk like that." As if making sure Rafferty was joking, he scanned the river's surface.

Neal let out a wavering giggle.

Blondie relaxed.

Neal jerked his finger toward the shore and directed his voice across the water. "The rope's on. Take up the slack."

Rafferty and Blondie pulled the rope. It sliced through the water in an envelope of bubbles until it was pulled straight.

"All right," Neal said and looked to Freddy. "Let's get to shore and pull our future out."

On shore, Rafferty stood next to the willow tree. He had already attached one end of the come-along to the tree and the other end to the rope.

In one fluid motion, Neal heaved himself from the water. Moving his hands, he talked to Rafferty. "That come-along can only pull five feet at a time before we have to reattach it. If we leave the end of the rope where it is, we'll be all night just taking out the slack in the rope."

He unhooked the end of the rope from the come-along, walked a few feet from the willow tree, and stopped at a tree that was about a foot wide. Then he looped the rope around it, just above a low branch. Standing next to the tree, he motioned with his hand. "Come on, you guys, help me pull out the slack."

They all grabbed the rope, leaned back, and pulled. The rope zipped around the little tree and rose from the water at a slant. With the rope stretched tight, Neal reattached its end to the come-along on the willow tree. Smiling at Rafferty, he curled his hand into a fist and encouragingly rotated it. "Start cranking that thing."

Rafferty grabbed the come-along handle and began cranking in the rope. After a few cranks, Neal stared at the rope.. "Are you sure that thing's moving?"

"It's a slow bugger," Rafferty said. "My arms getting tired, but I think we moved it a little."

Still wearing only his underwear, Neal stepped next to Rafferty. "Let me crank a while."

Neal cranked, but it was difficult to see if the rope was moving.

Rafferty held his hand on the rope. It indicated that it was actually moving. But the rope moved so slowly that the vault rose in fractional increments. Cranking the come-along for what seemed the millionth time, Neal began to strain. The rope went taut and thrummed with tension. Neal grunted and pulled on the come-along's handle. "What's holding that thing?"

Rafferty stepped back from the rope. "I don't know. But that thing's tighter than a robin's ass at choke cherry time."

Blondie extended his hand and pulled on the

rope. "That vault was jammed in the back window. It had me trapped, but the truck moved and I got out." He shook the rope. "Maybe the vault slipped back into the window. This rope's about ready to break."

Freddy looked toward the river. "It wasn't in the truck's window. I think it's stuck in the mud."

Blondie took his hand off the rope and looked at Neal. "I told you, we need a tow truck."

"Come on," Neal said with a big encouraging smile. "Have a little faith. It'll come out." He grunted and pulled on the come-along handle.

Defending himself against the rope breaking and flying into his face, Freddy scrunched and held up his hands. Neal cranked the handle. Shivering with tension, the rope stretched tighter than a piano string about to break.

Freddy reached over and held onto the rope. "Maybe we can jerk it free."

"Good idea," Rafferty said, grabbed onto the rope, and sang, "Come along with me."

Rafferty and Freddy tugged on the rope. It moved a few inches, and was no longer at its breaking point.

Rafferty quit singing and Freddy jerked his head toward Neal and Blondie. "We need more weight. Come on, you guys, grab on."

Neal grabbed onto the tree branch just above the come-along. "If its weight you want, I'll jump on the thing." Holding onto the branch, and barefooted, he tightrope-walked out onto the taut rope and stopped. "When I jump, you guys pull."

He bounced on the rope, and Freddy and the others pulled. They struck up a rhythm, and the rope was soon bouncing up and down.

After three minutes of furious tugging and bouncing, Neal exhaled and stopped jumping on the rope. "It isn't going to come loose."

Plunk! The tension in the rope stopped. With Neal on it, it fell to the ground. Neal's feet hit the slippery mud and flew out from under him. Splat! He landed on the muddy bank.

Rafferty repeated what Neal had told Blondie back at the crick. "Stay on the bank, or you'll fall on your ass again."

Neal squatted down into the water and washed the mud from the seat of his underwear. "Very funny, Rafferty." He ran his hand through his hair and held his chin at an arrogant slant. "But no matter how hard you try, you'll never be like me."

Deliberately exposing his missing tooth, Rafferty smiled a big ear-to-ear smile. "I know. You don't have a missing tooth."

Blondie held in a laugh and pointed to Neal. "I told you it would break."

"So what?" Neal said and stood up. "We'll just tie it in a knot and try again."

Freddy picked the rope up off the riverbank and pulled. It moved easily but stopped. "Hey wait a minute. It isn't broke. Maybe it's snagged on something."

Neal grabbed the rope. "Come on, you guys, grab on. If it's a snag we'll pull it out."

Blondie and Rafferty grabbed the rope and they all pulled. The rope moved but it was difficult. They re-gripped and pulled again. This time the rope moved easier.

Freddy looked into the water and shouted.

"Look, there's something on the end of the rope."

Blondie waved his hand in a negative gesture. "It's probably just an old stump."

"Stump, hell," Neal said with amazement. "That's the vault. It's probably got air in it." A radiant grin of self-satisfaction filled his face. "See, I told you that thing would be easy to pull in the water."

With a mixture of awe and excitement, Freddy watched the gold vault shed water. It seemed to grow larger and get heavier.

Pointing to his missing tooth mouth, Rafferty vigorously nodded. "I can get a new tooth."

The excitement in Freddy's chest suddenly stopped. He quit pulling. "I don't believe we're so stupid."

"What are you talking about?" Neal said still, exhilarated by the discovery. "We got it coming out. All we have to do is pull harder."

Freddy slumped with disappointment. "We're like a dog that finally caught a car it was chasing."

Blondie glanced sidelong at Freddy. "What's a dog got to do with anything?"

"After the dog caught the car, he didn't know what to do with it."

Blondie rolled his hand in encouragement. "And?"

"After we get the vault on shore, how are we going to get it downriver, up that crick, and into the car?"

Neal dropped the rope. Rafferty and Blondie limply held the rope in their hands and sighed.

Shaking his head, Freddy said, "We were so caught up in getting the thing out, we forgot to make plans for what we were going to do with it once we got it out."

"I guess it was my fault," Blondie said and placed his palms on his chest. "I should have gotten a truck to haul it." He shrugged. "But I really didn't think we could get it out."

Neal rubbed the side of his face and looked along the bank of the river. "We can still get this thing to the crick. All we have to do is carry it."

Shaking his head, Blondie swept his hands open. "That thing weighs two thousand pounds. There's no way each one of us can carry five hundred pounds."

"Sure we can," Freddy countered matter-of-factly. "Everything's lighter in the water. All we have to do is carry it in the water."

"We can do that," Rafferty said and his downcast face turned forlorn. "But how are we going to get it up that shallow crick?"

"Well, ahem…ah," Neal said in a slow drawn out way and paused. "I'm working on that. By the time we get it to the crick, I may have an answer."

Rafferty held up the rope. "Are we going to need this?"

Freddy picked up the end of the rope. "We could tie the rope to the bumper of the car and drag the vault up the crick, but we'd need a lot of ropes."

"I don't think we can carry that thing up that crick," Blondie said. "So how are we going to get it to the car, and if we do get it to the car, how are we going to haul it?"

Taking on the look of a happy simpleton, Rafferty messed up his orange hair, crossed his eyes, and bobbed his head. "If you want to blow out the tires, Yuck! Yuck! Yuck! We can put it on the roof."

Referring to Rafferty, Neal winked at Blondie. "He's a winner, isn't he?"

Blondie acted like he was ignoring Rafferty's antics, but his torso shook with a muffled spasm of amusement. He let out a weird, wavering giggle. Shaking his head and smiling, he said, "Let's carry the vault to the crick but don't carry it up on shore. We'll get a truck someplace, come back, and figure out how to get it to the truck." He turned toward Neal. "Don't you have a dump truck you hauled garbage in?"

Neal took on a helpless look. "Sure, we have a dump truck. It's sitting at the dump. Right after we dumped our last load, it blew a rod right through the engine block."

Freddy pushed his palms away from his chest. "If the bulldozer guy wouldn't have shoved it off to the side, we'd have a big tow bill."

Blondie looked optimistic. "Can we fix it?"

Neal's eyes flew wide open. "Sure we could," he said with an upbeat attitude, but his forehead crinkled with disgust. "If we had a few days, a place to work on it, and a lot of money." He paused. "Sure we could."

Rafferty looked dejected. "Gee, Neal, if you not going to crawl under the truck and fix it, I won't get to throw some metric wrenches into your toolbox, and listen to you cuss?"

When Neal worked under a car or truck, except for a metric wrench, he could tell the size of the wrench just by looking at it. Metric wrench sizes were just a little smaller than a standard wrench.

Lying in dim light underneath a car or truck and having dirt and grime falling into one's upturned face while trying to fit a metric wrench on a bolt it wouldn't fit, would make any man go berserk. And Neal was no exception.

He gave Rafferty a stern look. "Don't even think about doing that."

Rafferty giggled at the thought.

After Neal and Freddy donned their clothes, they all stayed in four feet of water, carried the vault to the mouth the crick, and set it on the river bottom.

"Okay, gentleman," Neal said and began wading to shore. "Let's go rent a truck."

Blondie held up his hand. "We can't. Johnny Hudson's truckers could run the truck rental place loyal to Smeal. If we rent a truck and they tell Smeal, he'll figure out that we've found the vault."

Rafferty held up one finger. "Maybe we can get a truck at the free car lot."

Chapter 24

In downtown Sharon, the "free car lot" was the parking lot outside the Columbia Theater. Although nothing was free there, after an owner went in to watch the show, numerous vehicles could be stolen or borrowed. If the car was brought back before the movie was over, usually the owner never knew it had been gone. The problem with Rafferty's plan to take a truck from the "free car lot" was that there were no trucks there. Neal had another idea, but he would have to make a call and wait for an answer.

In the parking lot of the Diamond Café, Freddy sat in the front seat of Blondie's Oldsmobile. Through half-closed eyes, he watched the telephone booth. Red neon lights from the Café spilled onto the panes of glass making the booth look like an inviting place to be, but the inside smelled of urine. At two in the morning the telephone rang. Neal jumped up from a semi-sleep and flung the door of the Oldsmobile open. "See, I told you he'd call."

He leaped across the sidewalk in front of the parking lot, reached into the phone both, and jerked the phone from its cradle. Before the person on the other end of the line had time to say anything, Neal asked, "Did you get it?"

Freddy angled his head slowly around, but he couldn't hear what the person on the other end of the line was saying. Neal nodded and flashed a thumbs-up toward the Oldsmobile. Then he clamped the phone between his head and shoulder and pointed to Freddy. "Do you guys know where Seeguy's farm is?"

Blondie shook his head and Freddy and

Rafferty nodded.

Neal held the phone next to his mouth. "Yeah we got it." He leaned against the glass pane to listen and then said, "Sure we'll bring it right back. We only need it for about an hour." He paused. "Yeah, sure, and thanks." He hung up the phone and walked to the Oldsmobile.

With the door open, Freddy sat on the passenger side seat with his feet hanging over and resting on the black top of the parking lot. As Neal approached, Freddy slid off the seat and stood up. "What's the deal with Seeguy's?"

Neal placed his hands on the roof of the Oldsmobile and leaned into the opened door. "I don't know Seeguy, but my buddy said he's working midnight turn. He got a ride with a neighbor, and his truck will be in the barn all night."

With a look of concern, Blondie faced Neal. "Is that truck big enough to haul the two thousand pound vault?"

"No problem," Neal said. "It has extra leaf springs." He stepped back and smiled. "It'll be easy to take, too. But we'll have to push it away from the barn so his wife doesn't hear the motor running when we take it. Then all we got to do is get it back before daylight."

Neal stepped away from the door and let Freddy get in. Blondie started the Oldsmobile. With the dim light coming off the dash softly accenting the look of concern on his face, he turned to Neal. "You sure his wife won't see us? I don't want the cops picking us up for a stolen truck."

Neal held his hands out to the side and leaned back. "No problem." He slid into the front seat.

"This friend of mine takes the truck all the time."
He closed the door. "All we have to do is make
sure we disconnect the speed odometer and put gas
in the tank, so we don't ruin a good thing."

***

Slow and silent, Freddy and his friends walked
across a field of wheat until they stopped at the left
hand corner of Seeguy's barn. Although stout oak
boards covered the outside of the barn, the whole
thing looked like it had been made of old weathered
boards. Two main doors, made from tall boards,
baked and rotted by years of summers and winters,
were nailed together with square nails. At the top of
the doors, U-shaped channels, bolted to the barn's
structure, held little steel wheels that let the huge
square doors slide apart like theater curtains.
Although the doors looked like they had been blown
off-kilter by years of relentless use, they could still
be opened wide enough to get tractors and other
farming equipment in and out, and plenty big
enough to push a truck through.

As Freddy pulled the doors open, just enough to
peek inside, overhead, the wheels in the U-shaped
channels rumbled in their tracks. A pale stripe of
light from an overhead low-watt light bulb spilled
out onto his face. He blinked and readjusted his
vision. Inside, the saw-milled rough four-by-fours
of two deserted horse stalls stood next to a 1950
Ford F-100 pick-up truck. Time and trouble had
caused the once bright paint on the truck to oxidize
to dull-red. Searching for someone waiting with a
shotgun full of rock salt, Freddy opened the door
and stuck his head inside. Looking from side to
side, he scanned the barn. There was nothing

unusual, or anything that would signal a trap, but the absence of wind outside accented the quiet and desolate atmosphere.

Blondie came up behind him and looked over his shoulder. "I don't like it. I'm used to street noise when I work. It's too quiet."

Neal reached in front of Blondie, grabbed the doors, and slid them open. "We can't get that truck out standing around."

They all walked into the barn. While Neal crawled under the dashboard of the Ford to disconnect the speed odometer and hot-wire the ignition, Blondie nervously turned his head at every movement or sound.

Rafferty leaned against the horse stall, crossed his feet, and casually rested his elbows on a board that ran along the top of the stall.

"Relax, Blondie," he said and raised his arms in the air. "Old lady Seeguy won't come out."

Blondie's eyes flicked left then right. "I don't know about that. I heard country people are used to killing things. People born with a killer instinct never hesitate to shoot."

Neal slid from underneath the dashboard and rubbed his ear. "The wires have never been touched. How does he take this truck without hot wiring it?"

Rafferty reached around the post next to the horse stall, lifted an old seed-cap, and picked a brass key off a nail. He held it in front of Neal's face and chuckled. "Maybe he uses this."

Neal leaned back and nodded. "I don't care what Blondie says about you, Rafferty. You're all right."

331

Blondie stared at Neal. "I didn't say anything about him."

Neal smiled and ticked a finger at Blondie. "Don't worry. I won't tell."

Blondie stiffened with resentment. Fire flared in his eyes. "What are you trying to do?"

As if he had been pushed too far, Neal's face went rigid with tension. With hostility radiating from his body, he turned and looked Blondie directly in the face. Freddy hoped Neal wouldn't go off the deep end and do some nut house thing. It would be a hell of a fight, and he knew he would have to defend Neal. No matter who won the ruckus of a fight, it would bring the police. If that happened, Freddy and his friends would not take the truck. They would not pick up the vault. Rafferty was joking when he had said that the vault was full of air and could float away, but if enough rain fell, the river could rise, and the current could carry the vault into the rapids. If it got stuck there, it would be hard to find and damn near impossible to get out.

"Relax," Rafferty said and squinted at Blondie with undisguised befuddlement. "It's only a joke."

Blondie made no effort to disguise his wounded feelings. His lips tightened. "Where I come from, talking about someone behind his back will get you beaten or killed. If people leave me alone, I leave them alone. If they don't, then I don't."

Everyone stood still. Stunned silence filled the barn. Freddy couldn't believe Blondie had been agitated by Neal's attempted humor. He figured Blondie had been forced to live a life that didn't leave much room for laughs, and he began to understand why Blondie was the way he was:

332

always on the alert, always watching behind his back, always worried about what people were going to do to him, and never really being able to relax.

Rubbing the sides of his eyes with his fists, Rafferty gave the impression he was crying. "Waaah! He cried like a baby. "I wanna get the vault." Forcing a big missing-tooth smile, he wrinkled his forehead with quizzical amusement and faced Blondie.

The fire in Blondie's eyes went out. As if he couldn't ignore Rafferty's bird-brained effort to make his laugh, he made a resigned shrug, and his lips curled into a smile.

Neal took a few steps backward.

Freddy breathed a sigh of relief.

Standing with his back to the doorpost of the Ford, Neal placed his left foot on the ground and the other foot on the running board. With one hand on the steering wheel, he motioned to Rafferty. "Come on, you guys, quit foolin' around. Let's get this thing out on the road so we can get going before the captain gets back."

Blondie's hostility softened, but he stood perfectly still. "What captain?"

"Oh, that?" Neal said as if it were no big deal. "I thought I mentioned it. The guy that owns this truck is a state police captain."

Freddy knew he should have been surprised and maybe even angry, but he had long ago accepted the fact that Neal would do anything at any time that didn't fit with the usual flow of things.

With disbelief plastered on his face, Blondie stared at Neal. "What's the matter with you?" His face changed to one of wonder. "You said you didn't know Seeguy, and now you say he's a state police captain. What are you, some kind of a nut?"

Neal waved his hand down. "Don't worry about it. The captain has to drive thirty miles to get to work. Nobody around here will be awake to recognize the truck. And besides, who would be crazy enough to steal a state policeman's truck?"

Rafferty threw his hands into the air. "I guess we are."

Blondie slowly shook his head and succumbed to the task at hand. "Let's get going."

Neal placed his back on the doorframe of the truck, planted his feet on the floor of the barn, and began to push the truck backwards.

Blondie held up his hand. "Wait!"

Neal stopped pushing.

"We might need these." Blondie picked up the two-by-fours that were leaning against the stall door and gently placed them into the bed of the truck.

As if they had just been awakened from a daydream, Freddy and Rafferty stepped to the front of the truck and pushed. Neal slid behind the steering wheel and steered. The truck bumped off the lip of the brick floor and out of the double doors. With the dim overhead light from the barn falling on the front of the truck, Neal backed down the wheel-rutted incline. As the truck increased speed, he held his arm out the window and signaled a reassuring wave. Freddy slid the barn's doors shut, and the others kept on pushing.

Down the lane, a half a mile before the road, Neal hit the starter. The truck fired up. The engine purred as silent as a baby kitten. Neal shoved the floor shift into reverse and backed up onto the grass at the side of the lane.

Freddy and Rafferty climbed into the bed of the truck. Blondie climbed into the seat next to Neal, bent his head at an angle, and listened. "Boy, this engine's quiet."

Neal cut the wheel and stamped on the brake. "It just goes to show what an old, battered truck can do if the engine is taken care of."

He shoved the floor shift into low gear and took off forward. At the highway and just beyond where the Oldsmobile sat hidden in the trees, he turned right and pulled the light switch. The display lights in the dash came alive. The weak headlights beamed on the road ahead, and the truck headed toward Myers Hill and the vault.

Bam! The truck's back wheel hit a huge pothole. The steel side of the truck bed, Freddy had been leaning on, came up and hit him in the ribs. He dropped on to the floor of the bed. Breathing hard and grimacing at the pain in his side, he looked to Rafferty.

Rafferty held his rear end and looked down at the truck floor that had hit him. "Damn that hurts."

Neal didn't slow down. He kept right on driving down the arrow-straight gray road. With the wind whistling in his ears, Rafferty leaned over the side of the truck bed and yelled into Neal's window. "Go back, there's another pothole, you missed it."

Neal yelled back through the opened window. "Why didn't you tell me that thing was there?"

Rafferty yelled back, "How could you miss it. It was so big, me and the neighbor's kids pitched a tent and camped out in it for three days."

At the intersection of Orangeville Road and

River Road, a siren and red blinking lights, led by high beams that were like white flames in Freddy's eyes, came up from behind, and fast.

Rafferty leaned over and yelled into the window. "You won't miss this. The state police are right behind us."

Neal slowed and yelled back, "Okay, you guys. When we stop, jump out and take off. Everybody go a different direction so they won't know who to chase."

Neal downshifted into second gear, pulled off to the side of the road, and slowed. Freddy flexed his knees and tensed to jump. But right after Neal stopped, like a flash in the night, the police car blew past.

Rafferty jumped out of the bed of the truck and stood next to Neal's opened window. "You want to cancel that order to jump?"

Neal turned his head to the left. "Get back in the truck and go ahead and jump out if you want. Just wait until I get it up to a hundred and twenty. That way you'll fly further."

Freddy jumped out of the bed, opened the door on Blondie's side, and jumped in. "Move over, Blondie. If we hit another pothole I don't want to keep getting my ass beat with the bed of the truck."

Rubbing his rear end, Rafferty ran around the side of the tuck, squeezed into the front seat next to Freddy, and closed the door.

With Neal, Blondie, and Freddy shoulder to shoulder and Rafferty turned sideways, Neal hooked low gear but didn't let out the clutch. He turned toward Rafferty. "I thought you were going to wait until I got it up to hundred and twenty and fly."

As if he were about to leap into flight, Rafferty swooshed his hands over his head. "I was," he said, "but if this piece of gets past fifty, it'll fly apart."

Neal drove on. Up ahead, three sputtering red flares, set along the shoulder of the highway. As Neal drove the truck near, thin red lines of red light slashed into the dark night. Two police cars were parked so they cut the two-lane road down to one.

"It looks like an accident," Neal said, slowing the truck to a crawl. "Let's see if we can help."

Standing next to the police car, a policeman with a black uniform and a shiny chrome badge, reflecting the dancing red light of the flares, waved a flashlight. Its bright beam and red end signaled Neal to drive around. As he drove past, two tired looking men, whose faces glowed in the red flare light, wrestled with a mountain of tangled scrap steel. Their shoulders were slumped as if they had lifted so much weight it had pulled them downward into permanent sags. Beyond the scrap steel, an upside-down, yellow, dump truck lay on its roof. Steam hissed from its broken radiator, and the smell of burnt oil filled the night air. The bald tires on the truck stuck upward like fat stubby feet on a dying elephant.

Blondie stared at the wreckage. "That's what happens when you overload a truck."

"How do you know it was overloaded?" Rafferty asked.

"Because, that's what happened to me. In fact that's why we're going after the vault in the river. The truck Smeal got me was overloaded and had tires worse than that dump truck has."

Neal hit second gear and increased speed.

"Actually I'm glad that you did go in the river."

Blondie jerked his head toward Neal. "What?"

"I don't mean that I wanted you dead. But if you hadn't gone in the river, you'd been long gone, and we wouldn't have a chance to get our share of the vault."

As if being cautious about saying it, Rafferty nodded weakly. "And we would never have enjoyed the presence of your friendship."

A wave of compassion seemed to emanate from Blondie's face. "You got a point there," he said and a tint of red colored his cheeks. "For the first time in my life, I did feel a little guilty about using you guys. But I'm not sure I would have come back." He paused as if in deep thought. "Actually you guys are the only people I can trust."

"Oh yeah?" Neal said and steered through a long sweeping curve. "Then why didn't you tell us the whole story about the vault?"

Blondie looked at Neal as if he were ignorant. "You should know how it is. When there's a lot of money at stake, it's a good idea to hide part of any plan. This stops other people you can't trust from interfering and making schemes of their own." He swung his head around and thoughtfully stared out the windshield. "And even if they don't want to mess up your plan, they'll tell others who will."

Neal nodded in understanding.

Freddy squeezed away from Blondie and Rafferty and leaned toward the dashboard. "Sometimes things happen for the best."

"If that's true," Neal said with distress. "Then when's the best comin' our way?"

"We can't quit now," Rafferty said and stared

out the window as if in a spell. "We've been fighting the system since we fell out of the cradle. If we quit now" — a begin smile formed on his lips — "we'll die of boredom." His orange eyebrows arched over his wide-open eyes. "If that doesn't happen, we could get one of the good jobs in the steel mill."

A look of shock and disbelief filled Neal's face. "You got to be crazy. Every company boss I ever had was a jerk."

"You must've had some real winners for bosses," Blondie said in a matter-of-fact tone.

"I can't help it." Neal clinched his fist. "I just don't like company people. They're just industry suck-ups who throw their authority around and stand over people until they break their spirit. And when that happens, the people act like trained dogs, and they just put up with it."

Blondie nodded toward the windshield. "There're a lot of people like that out there just wishing their lives away. If you want to get out of the system, you have to have enough guts to take a chance once in a while."

"Taking a chance once in a while might be okay," Rafferty said. "But not every day."

"Our situation's only temporary," Neal said thumping his knee with enthusiasm. "If you don't take a chance once in a while, you'll end like those people who sit around all day and never do anything more exciting than crossing the street." He downshifted for a sharp bend. "I got to be free." He swept his hand in the air. "But for once in my life I would like to hit the big time." He leaned into the turn and smiled. "You know, have enough cash to take easy for a long, long, time."

As Neal drove down the worn gray road that had no centerlines, Rafferty pointed to the left. "There goes your chance. We just passed the shooting gallery."

A look of embarrassment filled Neal's face. He braked to a halt. "I just wanted to see if you guys were paying attention."

He reversed the truck to the turnoff, drove down the blue spruce tree-lined shooting gallery road, and stopped under the big oak tree. Here, the night air smelled of gunpowder and pine.

As a silver moon lit up the whole place, Freddy stepped out of the truck, stood back, and scanned the area. "Okay, Neal, how do we get the vault from the river to the shooting gallery?"

"I don't know, but I'm open to suggestions."

No one answered.

Neal started toward the stream. "Let's go look at it. Maybe we can wrap the rope around a tree and pull the vault up the crick."

The others followed.

Seventy-five yards from the place where the creek ran into the river, Freddy looked back toward the truck. It could not be seen, and there were no sturdy trees close enough to wrap the rope around and pull the vault. "Hey, Neal, that's a long way to carry a two thousand pound vault. Do you think we can make it?"

Studying possible obstacles of the creek, Neal slowly moved his head from side to side. "The rocks in the crick are slippery. If we managed to carry it, we could slip. That thing could come down and smash a foot or break a leg."

Blondie reached out and steadied himself by placing his hand on the side of a high clay bank. "What if we get more ropes and used the truck to drag it up the crick?"

"Ropes might work but there are too many bends," Freddy said. "The rope will dig into the clay bank you got your hand on."

Rafferty pointed along the clay bank and toward the river. "If we use long ropes and manage to pull the vault, it'll plow half the shooting gallery away."

Freddy looked across the river. As the headlight of a diesel train flickered through the trees along the riverbank, it blasted its horn and thundered down the tracks toward the Ferrona railroad switching yard, and a plan began to form in his mind. He looked at the crick. Then he looked across the river. Calm water ran deep and the surface stretched smooth. But right after the crick, the river narrowed and became swift. A few yards further downriver, the water roared white. Beyond that, choppy water formed irregular waves, heaved upward, and raced into raging rapids, where furious cascades of water surged, shooting, five, ten, fifteen feet, into the air.

"Hey," Freddy said. "We can take the vault across the river."

Rafferty squinted at Freddy. "What if we get swept down into the rapids?"

Freddy turned the flat of his hand down. Bending his elbow, he pulled the thumb side of his hand to his chest. "No way!" Keeping his hand horizontal, he slowly moved his hand away from his chest. "The water's smooth here. We'll be able to

341

pull the vault across with no problem."

Rafferty pointed across the river. "So what if we do make it across, how are we going to get it up that steep bank and over the railroad tracks?"

Before he could answer, a little locomotive, switching cars at the Ferrona Yard, snored in the distance. Freddy rolled his eyes toward the sound. "There're four tracks and a switch over there. If we drive the truck down Furnace Road and take the little cutoff out of Taylor Sand and Supply, we can be right at the tracks. Our rope is long enough to get across the river from there. All we'll have to do is tie one end of the rope onto the vault and tie the other end onto the truck's bumper. Then we'll drag it up the riverbank and load it on the truck."

"That sounds simple," Rafferty said. "But how are we going to lift it onto the truck?"

"We won't have to. We'll drag the vault to the top of that little sand pile at Taylor Supply. Then we'll back the truck up to the hill and push it onto the bed."

Blondie looked to Neal. "What do you think?"

"It's a lot better than trying to drag that monster up that crick."

Chapter 25

As Neal drove the state police captain's stolen Ford truck along Sharpsville Avenue, traffic was nil until an eighteen-wheeled semi-truck, coming from the opposite direction, blew its air horn. The red-haired driver wound down his window, flicked out a cigarette butt, and waved. As a backwash of diesel fumes filled the air, the butt skipped along and sent a tiny trail of bright orange sparks zigzagging across the dark road.

Neal waved back. "That's Tommy. He's a demolition derby driver, must've won about a thousand trophies."

Tommy smiled, shifted gears, and roared off into the night.

Rafferty slumped into a hangdog, hopeless look. "I've heard he always wanted to drive a dynamite truck."

"That's a dangerous job," Freddy said. "I wonder if pays big money."

"Who knows?" Rafferty shrugged. "Nobody ever lived long enough to collect a paycheck."

Turning away in bewilderment, Freddy let out a long, theatrical moan.

The unlit road to turn off to Taylor Supply was just ahead, but Neal didn't slow the stolen truck. Freddy jerked his arm up and pointed to the turn off. "Hey, aren't you going to turn?"

Neal kept right on going. "Someone's following us."

Dropping his arm, Freddy looked out the back window. "They can't be. We've only seen two cars all night."

Neal glanced into the rearview mirror. "That's the trick. They use more than one car. That way, the, person being followed doesn't expect anything."

In the crowded cab, Blondie craned his neck and peered out the side window. "A '57 Ford passed us twice," he said, "and an orange flat-bed truck followed us one time."

Rafferty turned and squinted toward the windshield. "There's no one following us from the front." Giggling with half-witted delight, he looked out the rear window. His half-witted face faded. "There's a '57 Ford behind us. It's down the road a ways."

Blondie glanced in the rearview mirror and turned his head toward Neal. "Do you think we can lose them?"

Neal leaned into a turn and forced a smile. "This truck's old and not too fast, but if it's still closed, we can."

"If what's still closed?"

"I'll show you."

Neal drove to the road construction site in Masury, Ohio and stopped. Bulldozers and backhoes were perched at the entrance of detours that consisted of two one-lane roads that ran in both directions. For about four miles, there were no exits. Right next to the freshly cemented detour roads, the ground had been graded to at least two feet lower than the detour road. Here, deep drop offs, debris, and scattered equipment of the construction site, made it impossible to turn around or get off. If a driver were caught behind a car doing the speed limit of twenty-five miles an hour, it would take him six minutes to get to the end of the one lane detour.

Neal hooked low gear, did a U-turn, and started back the way he had come. "We'll need to borrow a car."

"There was a '53 Chevy sitting in the 'free car lot' at Water Street," Freddy said. "It looked like it wasn't locked."

"It's probably sitting there," Rafferty added, "because it won't start."

Neal's face lit up with false excitement. "Gee… thanks for the helpful information."

On down the road, Neal rounded the bend and slowed to a crawl. On the left, the '53 Chevy sat in the "free car lot".

"It looks like it's been here a long time," Freddy said. "Some guy getting drunk in the Diamond Café probably owns it."

Jerking his head from side to side, Blondie screwed his face up with irritability. "Before you try anything that will get the police after us, why don't you drive past, pull into the Diamond, and find out?"

"Well, ahem…yes," Neal said as if intrigued. He looked toward the Diamond Café. "We just might do just that."

Blondie nodded and his face took on a calm look.

But Neal didn't drive past and pull into the parking lot of the Diamond Café. He pulled into the free parking lot on Water Street. Before anyone had a chance to complain, he jumped out, opened the door to the Chevy, and crawled under the dash.

"These things are easy to start."

The engine caught. Neal sat up in the driver's side and tried first gear. The car moved. He looked back at Rafferty. "It's not broke down."

Blondie stood next to the side door of the truck and eyed the entrance to the Diamond Café. "Now what?"

"Don't look around," Neal said. "But whoever's following us is probably watching. So, everybody get back into the truck. Freddy, you hide under the dash. After we get back out of the truck, wait for us to leave then drive the truck down the opposite way on the one lane road next to the construction site."

"Wait a minute," Freddy said. "Who's ever watching is going to know if I stay in the truck."

"How are they going to know?" Neal asked without looking around.

"Simple," Freddy said. "They'll count how many of us get into the Chevy."

"They might," Neal said and shrugged. "I'll park the Chevy close to the truck. When we all jump out in a bunch, they'll be in too big a hurry to count all of us."

Rafferty theatrically raised his hand into the air. "They probably can't count past two." He paused. "However, I think this will work better. He reached behind the seat of the truck and pulled out an old straw hat.

Neal smiled. "That's a good idea." He took the hat and turned to Freddy. "Put this on. When we get out, we'll huddle around you. Just before we jump into the Chevy, while Rafferty holds the hat, duck down and get back in the truck. It'll look like four people are getting into the car."

Neal gave Rafferty a dubious look and then ticked his finger at Freddy. "Are you ready?"

Freddy placed the straw hat on his head and thoughtfully nodded. "After you take off, you'll have to give me some time to drive past the detour and come back."

No problem," Neal said with haste. "I'll let them follow me up and down a few side streets."

Before the doors on the '53 Chevy closed, Freddy was back in the truck.

With Blondie in the front seat and Rafferty in the back seat holding the straw hat, making it look like the Chevy held four people, Neal roared out of the parking lot and headed for the side streets.

Freddy stayed under the dash of the truck and watched through the rear view mirror. In less than a minute, the '57 Ford that had been following them took out after the Chevy. After waiting a few minutes, he slid behind the wheel of the truck, and took off.

At the construction site, Freddy grabbed the floor shift and tried to shift smoothly but grinded the gears. He double clutched, caught third gear, and drove the six minutes it took to get to the end of the one lane detour. Then he turned around and started driving back on the opposite side of the road. Just as he barreled around a sharp bend, up ahead, in the opposite slow moving lane, Smeal and his boys were in the '57 Ford, two cars behind Neal and the '53 Chevy. At a place where a two-foot drop off alongside the concrete road made it impossible to drive through a barrier without wrecking the underside of a car, Neal hit the brakes. The Chevy skidded to a stop. Neal jumped out. As if he were having engine trouble, he lifted the hood and stared at the engine.

Right across from the Chevy, on the opposite road, Freddy slowed the truck to a halt. The doors on the '53 Chevy flung open. Blondie and the others jumped out. Neal joined them and they leaped over the barriers. Freddy opened the driver's side door and slid over. Neal jumped behind the wheel. Blondie and Rafferty jumped into the bed of the truck. As the truck pulled away, Freddy craned his neck and got an angle to see through the rear window. While Smeal mopped his forehead with an oversized handkerchief, his boys were gathered around the '53 Chevy with the hood up, shining flashlights off to the side of the road.

Giggling like a crazy freak watching some kind of morons, Rafferty stuck his head out the side window and yelled at them. "Oh, by the way, boys, are you going to follow us or what?"

Smeal slowly let his hand with the handkerchief fall to his side. Realizing that they had been had, he and his men only stared in awe."

Freddy stuck his head out the window of the truck and yelled back at Rafferty, "I think we made them very unhappy."

With the wind blowing in his face, Rafferty let out a goofy giggle. "They don't have enough brains to be unhappy."

As a light rain fell and began tap dancing on the roof of the truck, Neal turned off the road that led to Taylor Supply and bumped down off the blacktopped road. Traveling toward the east end of Ferrona Yard, the truck bounced over the usual ruts and potholes found in all railroad switching yards.

After Neal had driven through the black cinder-covered parking lot of Taylor Supply, he stopped the truck under a light. The rain stopped, but raindrops looked as if a thousand diamonds had formed on the windshield.

Just past the little sand pile, Neal pulled a tight left and nosed slowly toward the railroad tracks. With the front bumper almost touching the tracks, Freddy looked out the side window. To his right, the night sky gleamed on the shiny rails of the two main tracks. To his left, in the switching yard, railroad cars, headed in both directions, waited to be hooked up and formed into a train. In a few places, plants, stunted by the harsh environment of the railroad, struggled to stand upright in front of a string of black tank cars with white letters that read GATX, followed by white numbers. Another track with various railroad cars was interlaced with rust-colored gondola cars loaded with crushed scrap waiting to be plucked out with huge crane magnets at the Sharon Steel Mill, where it would be dumped into open-hearth furnaces, and be melted into some of the best stainless steel in the world.

On another track, huge rectangular bales of crushed steel peeked over the tops of green gondola cars. Other gondola cars had been piled so high with scrap from demolished skyscrapers that it reached upward and made a jagged silhouette against the night sky. One gondola car stood out from the rest. Rust bloomed like a skin disease all over its sides. Paint had oxidized and peeled, and years of wind and rain had washed most of it away. Inside the car, rusted industrial hulks and a myriad of things like railroad wheels, old tricycles, bicycles, and parts of ships, had been heaped high and caused the sides of the car to puff out. And all the scrap would be reduced to molten metal.

But the only metal Freddy and his friends were concerned about was the gold the vault was made of.

The familiar throbbing of a diesel locomotive traveling down the railroad tracks pounded in Freddy's ears. He reached over and grabbed Neal's shoulder. "Hey, Neal, get this truck away from the tracks. A train's coming."

Neal grunted in disgust, but backed the truck away from the tracks and stopped. "We'll probably be here all night waiting for that train to pick up a bunch of cars."

"Yeah, you never know how long those trains are going to be."

A bright cone of light, from the headlight of the train, bored through the dark night and became brighter and brighter.

Blondie and Rafferty jumped out of the truck, ready for action, but Neal sprawled sideways on the seat and rested his head on the side of the door. "Wake me up after that train goes past."

The train pounded down the tracks. Its headlight beamed across the still river water and reflected like a black mirror. As the brass buzz of the diesel's horns filled the air, a single locomotive engine zipped past.

Rafferty reached into the truck and shook Neal's shoulder. "The train's gone."

Neal jerked his head off the window and sat up. "What?"

"Your great train didn't have any cars. It was a

single engine."

Freddy nodded. "Some hostler's probably hoss-lin' engines."

Neal lifted an eyebrow. "Hoss-lin' what?"

"Hoss-lin' engines. It's when a hostler runs engines from one yard to another for repairs or service."

"What for?"

"If an engine needs repairs or service, a hostler is what they call the guy that delivers the engines."

"Why don't they just say moving engines around?"

"My uncle said it's something left over from the war. So the Germans and Japanese couldn't sabotage the railroads or blow them up, they called things by different names. It made it difficult for them to find out what the railroads were doing."

Grinning broadly, Neal reached out the window and tapped Rafferty on the shoulder. "Why didn't you guys tell me that before I stretched out to relax?"

"I don't know," Rafferty said with a fresh grin. "Maybe we don't like the sound of your voice and wanted you to go to sleep."

Shaking his head, Neal sat up, placed his hand on the door handle, and looked toward the sky. "Let's just hoss-el our asses across that river and get that vault before it rains and the river gets too high to get across."

Blondie held up his hand in a halting motion. "What if those railroad workers come up here and see us with the vault?"

"The yard crew does most of their work at the other end of the yard," Rafferty said and pointed to

351

the darkness of the south end of switching yard. "That's about a mile away. And midnight turn comes out two hours early so they can get the work done and go to sleep."

Blondie's forehead wrinkled in confusion. "I've never heard of people getting paid for sleeping. Are you sure about that?"

"I should be," Rafferty said. "My uncle worked there for twenty years. He told me all about it. He said because they get to quit when all the work's done they work like crazy and get more work done on midnight turn than all the other turns combined."

They walked across a set of four tracks and stopped at the steep riverbank. Neal looked to Rafferty. "Who wants to go first?"

"That looks like a pretty steep drop off," Rafferty said and backed away. "But I have a good idea."

Neal flicked his finger at Rafferty, "Shoot, man, we're all ears."

Leaning back and clasping his hands comfortably over the top of his head, Rafferty smiled a lopsided grin. "Why don't you guys buy me a case of beer?"

Neal shot him a look of puzzlement. "Are you crazy? What kind of an idea is that?"

Chuckling at Neal's look of puzzlement, Rafferty said, "While I watch you guys go across the river and get the vault, I'll sit in the truck and drink beer."

Before Neal could reply, something splashed into the water. Alarmed, all eyes turned toward the sound. A muskrat swam along the shore and plopped its head under the water.

Rafferty lifted his hands in a helpless gesture. "I'll even share a beer with that muskrat."

Everyone laughed affectionately.

"All right, you guys," Neal said and glanced nervously toward the sky. "Let's get to work before that rain comes down."

He pulled the rope over the side of the truck and dragged it to a tree at the top of the riverbank. "I'll tie one end to this tree. We can lower ourselves down the bank and get to the water."

Freddy started toward the riverbank. "I don't need a rope. All you can do is fall in the water, and we're going to get wet anyway."

"Wait," Neal said with caution, "That water's too swift right here. It'll suck you down the rapids."

Stumbling down the steep embankment, Freddy looked back. "What?"

Neal grabbed the end of the rope and rolled it toward Freddy. "Here, grab it."

Freddy looked toward the river. In the darkness, he had misjudged just how close he was to the rapids. He reached for the rope to pull himself to safety. Before he could grab it, his foot jammed between a rock and the muddy bank. He slid sideways and fell on his side, but his foot was still jammed. He curled to a fetal position and tried to free his foot. It wouldn't budge. He took his other foot placed it on the rock and pushed. His foot slipped free, but the momentum of the push sent him sliding down the muddy riverbank. Before he could stop himself, he splashed into the dark water.

Neal yelled down, "Are you all right?"

Freddy stood up. The roar of the rapids made it difficult for him to hear. The whirling water was up to his waist. "I'm okay," he yelled back. "But I got to wash this mud off."

He hunched over and rubbed the front of his pants. A stray streak of lightening lit the sky. He jerked his head upward. A dark shadow appeared downriver. He wasn't sure what it was, but Smeal could have somehow followed them. To get a better view of the movement, he took one step and turned. A churning wave from the rapids exploded and slightly lifted him out of the water. Moving to regain his balance, he stepped on a slanted rock and began to fall. He jerked his other foot to catch his balance, but that foot found no footing, only a deep-water drop off. "Ah man."

He slipped into the swift water. It was over his head, and the roar of the rapids canceled out all other sounds. Taking one stroke toward shore, he found that the current was pulling him away from the riverbank.

He had swum in strong currents before and decided he could easily swim upriver and get into the shallow water. But the darkness of the water, the heaviness of his clothes, and the fact that he had his shoes on, caused him to misjudge the strength of this current. Three futile strokes later, he was at the mouth of the rapids, the deafening roar of crashing waves pounding in his ear. The controlling current drew against his whole body. The mouth of the rapids yawned wide and sucked him in, pulled him down, and fast.

A few feet down from the mouth of the rapids,

the current rolled into a powerful hump. He went over it. As if he was on a carnival ride, his body rose and fell, sending an up-and-down sickening sensation into his stomach. A huge round rock bumped into his side. It didn't hurt much, but he knew if he went fast enough, a sharp rock or hidden tree branch could tear away an arm, a hand, or a leg.

The water sped up. Barreling through a curve at thirty miles an hour, he felt the turbulent wake of the water. Just as he thought the worst was over, and he would safely float to the end of the rapids, his hip crashed into a submerged boulder. It was a glancing blow that sent his body sideways.

Sailing down a trough of white water, a tree branch, six inches off the surface, turned and jumped out at him. He reached out and grabbed it, but the current pulled his body so hard the branch slid from his hands. Swirling down the river, the dark figure of a man standing in the shadow of a river willow appeared. Before Freddy could get a good look at the figure, a huge rolling tree stump thudded into his rear end. He tried to cry out in agony, but a huge wave engulfed his face and muffled the sound. He spun sideways and continued on down the raging water. Waves chopped and roared in his ears. In the center of a foaming uprising, a huge surge formed a geyser-like column of whirling white water and shot him upward. Before he could take a breath of air, the heavy curl of a dark wave crashed on top of him, pulling him under, and holding him there.

Figuring he would eventually come up, he patiently held his breath. But the whirling water continued to hold him down. For a moment, he managed to grab the edge of a rectangular rock and claw his way to his knees. Before he could draw a breath of air, the tree stump rolled up from the bottom and raced toward him. Making powerful strokes with his arms to swim out of its way, the stump hit him on the shoulder, sending him head over heels and charging down the river, making him feel like a runaway flopping flat tire. A sunken branch slammed into his stomach. It stopped his rollovers, but the force of the water caused his body to bend at the waist and be pinned to the branch for many long seconds. With his lungs screaming for air, he fought the violent flow and palmed his way to the end of the branch. The force of the water swept him off the end of the branch and on downriver, right into a new exploding wave of froth and white water.

He needed air but he couldn't get to the surface to sip one breath. He rolled one more time, surged past another hump of an exploding wave and felt his feet hit a rocky bottom. As if running to a stop, he crouched and gained footing on the bottom. Then he straightened his knees and stood up. Standing in four feet of water, in the middle of the river, he sucked in great drafts of much needed air.

The deafening sound of the roaring water faded, but it was still strong enough to sound a warning not to ever try that again. In the distance, the rattling chug of a diesel engine idling drowned out what seemed to be footsteps crunching over ballast along the railroad tracks.

Faint sounds of Neal calling his name drew closer. He looked across the river. Neal, Blondie, and Rafferty came running alongside the tracks.

Freddy whistled once. They all stopped and looked toward the sound. Freddy whistled again and waved. "I'm over here."

Neal led the way and picked his way down an incline of jagged rocks on the shoreline. He stopped at the edge of the swift water and cupped his hands to his mouth. "Are you okay?"

Freddy felt his legs and arms. They weren't broken, but he was tired, and his side ached where it had been hit with the boulder. He wanted to say he needed a little help, but that would be a show of something he and his friends had learned not to show weakness.

Neal called again. "Are you okay?"

Freddy still wanted to ask for help, but they didn't have time to waste. If the threatening rain fell, muddy water from the many streams that ran into the river would cause it to quickly rise. The vault would be swept downriver in a yellow mud colored current. He grimaced, rubbed his sore side, and yelled back, "I'm okay, nothing to it."

Rafferty stepped his way next to Neal and yelled across the water. "We know you wanted to get across, but you didn't have to take the express route."

Freddy had almost drowned and here was Rafferty making jokes. He shrugged it off and realized the attempted humor made him feel better.

Neal turned to go but looked back. "You sure you're okay?"

Freddy nodded. "Yeah, I'll see you up at the crick."

He splashed through the shallows and walked to the opposite shore. Bruised and dripping, he drew his damp shirt across his shoulders and began his trudge upriver. Ten feet from the shore, jagged rocks, fallen trees, and a rectangle of rusted bedsprings, caught in the Y of a fallen tree, blocked his way. He walked around the conglomeration, and his foot was sucked into a pool of thick slimy mud. He pulled his foot out, but his shoe remained in the mud. Kneeling down, he felt around, found his shoe, and pulled it out. Walking without shoes was an option, but stones with sharp edges surrounded the pool. After banging the mud from his shoe on an upturned tree stump, he put his shoe back on his foot and stepped around the mud pool.

Here, rocks worn smooth by years of spring floods, made the going easier. As he walked across the clean water of the crick, the mud was washed from the bottom of his pants and shoes.

On the tracks across the river, a diesel locomotive, pulling a string of coke hoppers, buzzed its horn and swayed into the switching yard. Freddy watched it go past and looked upriver. Just above the crick, where the vault rested under four feet of water, Neal was waiting with the rope in his hand.

As Freddy neared, Neal asked, "What took you so long?"

Not wanting to be a crybaby, Freddy said, "I missed the train. Didn't you see it go by?"

Making a crazy sign, Neal rotated his hand in a circle next to his ear. "I thought wise guy Rafferty was on the other side."

Across the river, Blondie lifted his arm and held the end of the rope in the air.

Neal flashed an okay signal back and turned to Freddy. "He's getting impatient."

"I can't blame him," Freddy said and looked around. "Smeal might be snooping around."

A look of confusion crossed Neal's face. "What are you talking about? We lost those guys."

"I know, but when I was going down the rapids, I think I saw somebody."

"Yeah, we saw him, too. I think he's a brakeman from the railroad."

Freddy breathed a sigh of relief, bent over, reached into the water, and tried to lift the vault. It didn't move.

"What's the matter?" Neal said. "That thing too heavy for you?"

"Freddy stood up. "Just a little."

Neal squatted in the water and grabbed the end of the vault. "You have to use your legs."

Squatting in the water, Neal and Freddy lifted the end of the vault and used their feet to snake the end of the rope under it. After they set the vault down, Neal sloshed to its side and pulled on the rope until he had enough slack to tie a knot. Handing the end of the rope to Freddy he said, "Make sure it's on good. We don't need it to slip off and have to chase it down the rapids."

Freddy tied a square knot, pulled the rope snug, and yanked on it. "Yeah, I know. I don't need another thrill ride." He placed his foot on the vault and pulled the rope tighter. "That should hold it."

Neal reached down and felt the knot. "You sure?"

"The harder the truck pulls the rope, the tighter the knot gets." Freddy looked across the river. Making a what's-taking-you-so-long gesture, Blondie held his arms to his sides and hunched his

359

shoulders.

Freddy turned his attention back to Neal. With water glistening on his chin, Neal motioned to Blondie. "Let her rip."

Blondie climbed up the riverbank and got into the truck. Rafferty stood on the shore and relayed signals to Blondie. As the truck stole out of sight and into the shadows, it tugged on the rope. The rope slanted out of the water in a long splash. As Capone's old vault was about to begin its journey across the river, for a moment, Freddy felt they were resurrecting the history of the 1930s. He and Neal grabbed the rope and hung on. Towing Freddy and Neal with it, the vault turned and crawled toward the center of the river.

At the opposite side of the river, Rafferty waved for Blondie to keep on pulling. As the vault cut through the river in a foamy arc, Freddy and Neal kept a hold on the rope. As the vault neared the shore, they jumped on the vault and hung on. With the vault beneath them, they rose out of the water, sledded up the muddy bank, stopped at the top, jumped off the vault, and stood up.

"See, nothing to it," Neal said and brushed his hands together. Freddy looked at the end of the vault. On one side, the thin brass had been pealed back about a foot, and a thin layer of concrete was gone. The gold end of the vault could now be seen.

"Hey,' Freddy sad. "What happened?"

"That must be where it went through the back window of the truck," Neal said. "From now on it'll be pretty hard to pass this vault off as worthless."

Purposely exaggerating his missing tooth,

Rafferty smiled. "It doesn't matter." With his whole body radiating merriment and his orange hair tossing wildly, he excitedly danced around the vault. "We got it out." He hopped on one foot. "We're rich!" He switched and hopped on his other foot. "We're rich!"

Freddy had never seen this much gold. Now, more than ever, he was glad he had not taken his mother's advice and gone to work in a steel mill. Tonight, while the mill workers of Patagonia dreamed about what turn they would be working, or slobbered over last call in one of the many bars, or worked the fiery hell of a midnight turn, sucking in obnoxious dirt and dust, he and his friends had make it across the river with a gold vault. Breathing the clean night air, he felt like a rich man.

At the railroad tracks, like a long tired snake not amused with Rafferty's antics, the rope lay limply across four sets of tracks. Sitting in the truck, Blondie turned and looked at the slack rope. He let out the clutch and continued to slowly pull the vault until the first rail stopped it. The rope pulled straight. Rafferty quit hopping, held up his hand, and signaled Blondie to stop. But Blondie kept on pulling.

The rope stretched tight.

Thunk! It broke at the bumper.

Blondie stopped the truck, opened the door, and looked back at Rafferty. "Come on, you guys," he said with excited enthusiasm. "I want to get out of here before it starts to rain."

With both arms spread and with his palms upward, Rafferty flashed a helpless gesture. "What are you looking at me for? This is not a railroad crossing on a highway. I signaled for you to stop."

"That's all right," Neal said. "We had to stop anyway."

"What for?" Rafferty asked.

"So we can put something in front of the track so the vault can ease on over."

"That's stupid," Rafferty snapped with caustic resentment. "All we have to do is lift it over."

Neal bowed. Slowly uncurling his arm, he gestured to the vault. "Knock yourself out."

As Neal watched patiently with a glimmer of delight, Rafferty bent over and tried to lift the vault. He grunted and groaned. His face tightened with strain, but the vault stayed on the ground. With a whoosh of defeated air escaping from his chest, he stood up and held his back as if in pain.

Freddy gave him a comforting pat on the shoulder. "I think it's too heavy."

Breathing heavily, Rafferty pointed to his own head. "Nice deduction, Einstein."

While Blondie re-tied the rope back onto the bumper of the truck, thunder rumbled in the distance. Although the ground was still a little wet from the previous rain, a gust of wind sucked a gray cloud of railroad dust out from under a string of railroad hoppers and tossed it into the air. As a little, densely-branched bush skittered from between two railroad cars, Freddy squinted to keep the dust out of his eyes, but when lightening streaked across the sky, he opened them. Touching Rafferty's shoulder, he pointed down the tracks. "What's that?"

Rafferty pointed to a little twirling cloud of dust. "That's just a baby whirlwind on its way to

362

Kansas." He eyed Freddy with a funny expression. "When it grows up, it'll be a big tornado and visit the monkeys in the Land of Oz."

A crumpled piece of shining sheet steel came tumbling down the tracks and right at them. It clattered along the tracks, ran into a switch stand, and banged to a stop at Rafferty's feet.

Rafferty made a face at the sheet steel. In a cartoon voice, he mocked the steel. "Ha, ha, you didn't get me."

Neal gaped at him in undisguised befuddlement, until — there! A bolt of lightning zigzagged out of the sky and caused the thin brass covering on the gold vault to wink in the flash of light.

"Hey," Freddy said and backed away from the vault. "Lightening might strike that thing."

"Don't worry about it," Neal said, but shifted his eyes uneasily. "That lightening was miles away."

Rain began to fall, and another bolt of lightning struck. As it sought ground, it danced across the tracks, split into green fingers of fire that sizzled on down the tracks, and stopped at an open switch.

"See," Neal said as if trying to convince himself. "There's too much metal around here for it to hit us."

Freddy didn't know whether to believe him. But when a torrential of rain poured down on the railroad ties and bounced up to his knees, he forgot about the lightening.

Searching the area for something to put in front of the tracks so the vault could be pulled over them, he walked alongside the railroad bed. With each step, yellow mud piled up on his feet and made him feel taller, but his shoes stuck to the mud and almost pulled off. He slogged onward and finally found a piece of a fallen tree, but he couldn't move it. He looked to his right. As if they were seeking shelter from the rain, stones, scattered in a haphazard pattern, rested under a dark-green bush. Freddy looked back through the sheeting rain. Neal and Blondie stood hunched over with their backs turned toward him. Freddy wasn't sure but it looked like they were laughing. Rafferty smiled at Freddy. Freddy motioned for him to come forward.

As if looking for approval, Rafferty glanced at Neal and Blondie. Neal shrugged. Rafferty nodded and slogged through the fresh mud until he was in front of Freddy. "What?"

"Help me carry these things."

"If you need help, hire yourself a partner."

"You're hired. You'll get paid when we cash in that vault."

Rafferty willingly cradled his arms and Freddy loaded them up with rocks. With both arms cradled with rocks, they slogged back to the vault and dropped the rocks next to the rail.

"It's not enough," Freddy said. "Let's get some more."

With a questioning slant, Rafferty tilted his head toward Freddy. "What for?"

"Quit foolin' around. We got to get this vault out of here before another train comes."

Neal and Blondie looked toward the bed of the truck.

Rafferty laughed. "Why don't we use the two-by-fours we got out of Seeguy's barn?"

Freddy shook his head. He couldn't believe how ignorant he had been, and he found it hard to believe Rafferty had carried an armful of rocks in the falling rain just to pull a joke.

Rafferty folded his arms across his chest and took on a look of superiority. "Do you want to carry more rocks, Einstein?"

Freddy didn't answer. They all walked to the truck. As the falling rain pattered on the roof of the truck, they took out the two-by-fours and carried them to the tracks.

When they had the two-by-fours in place, Freddy thought about the shadow he had seen when he had been washed down the rapids. He looked to Neal. "It's a good thing it's raining."

"What's so good about it? We can only see a few yards."

"If Smeal's snooping around that means he can only see that far, too."

With his face streaming with rain, Rafferty stood next to the vault and signaled Blondie. Blondie gave the truck's engine a little gas and eased out the clutch. The rope went taut. He gave the engine a little more gas. The vault bumped up onto the two-by-fours, slid over the first set of tracks, and stopped.

"One more to go," Rafferty said, bent over and helped Freddy and Neal set the two-by-fours in place for the last pull.

As Freddy watched the vault ease over the last set of tracks, rainwater snaked its way down his back and sent cold shivers up his spine. He bent over to wipe the mud from his shoes. But it was unnecessary. The hard rain had washed it away.

Blondie backed the truck up to the vault. Neal shortened the rope and retied it to the bumper. While Neal and Freddy walked behind the moving vault, Rafferty turned his feet to the side and playfully jumped into puddles, sending slanted sheets of water onto Freddy's pants. But it didn't matter. It was raining anyway.

After Blondie dragged the vault through the mud, over the little gravel road, and into the yard at Taylor Supply, he tried to tow the vault up a little pile of sand. But the end of the vault plowed into the wet sand and stopped solid.

With rain spilling down his nose, Rafferty shook the water from his face and grinned. "Now what?"

Freddy wiped the rain from his eyes and looked to the loading dock. Three cement steps led to it, and its thick wood planks rose to the height of the bed of the truck. A corrugated steel roof protected the entire length of the dock, but the falling rain hammered on it, sending echoes through the night. He noticed Rafferty staring at the dock.

Rafferty looked at Freddy and then back at the dock. "You think we can load it there?"

"I doubt it," Freddy said. "It's too heavy to lift the end and drag it up the steps."

Blondie stuck his head out the window. "Get those two-by-fours and make a ramp on the steps."

Rafferty flashed Freddy a playful stare. "Are you sure you don't want to use rocks instead?"

"Are you crazy?" Freddy said, shaking an annoyed finger in front of Rafferty's eyes. "Let's get this thing loaded."

While Rafferty chuckled, Neal positioned the

rope up and over the dock. Then Freddy and Rafferty placed the two-by-fours onto the steps. Blondie pulled the truck onto the other side of the dock. Neal hooked up the rope, and Blondie easily towed the vault up the two-by-four ramp. Then he backed the truck up to the loading dock and, in the falling rain, they finally slid the vault into the bed of the truck.

Freddy let out a sigh of relief. "It's about time."

Blondie pointed to the two-by-fours. "We're going to need those again. Put them back into the truck."

Neal turned toward Freddy. "Are you sure you saw someone along the riverbank?"

Freddy shook his head. "I'm not completely sure, but I wouldn't take a chance."

Neal let out a disgusted sigh. "Just in case someone tries to follow us, we're going to take a roundabout way.

As they pulled back onto Sharpsville Avenue, the rain stopped. A glimmer of cloudy moonlight faded, and a golden dawn chased the truck down the road.

Chapter 26

In a cold dawn, the tires on the dull-red truck slashed a groove through the water-covered blacktopped road and rocketed onward. As Freddy and Rafferty sat in the bed of the truck next to the vault, a slit of sunlight scraped through a new crimson sky and brightened a road that curled around fields of uncut hay. As Neal shifted through the gears to negotiate the turns, the wind whipped at Freddy, flattening his shirt against his body and his pants against his legs.

Rafferty turned toward the cab and shouted something into the wind, but the characteristic symphony of the usual highway sounds of wet tires rolling over wet pavement drowned out his words.

Traveling down Broadway Avenue, they came to the National Castings foundry. Here, the air seemed dry and smelled of alkali. As they passed the stinking place, a rotten egg odor invaded Freddy's nostrils and sank right down into the bottom of his stomach.

Rafferty's eyes twinkled with humor. "You ain't seen nothin' yet." He closed his eyes, and Freddy wondered why he had.

When the smell was just about gone, he found out why. Air, full of grit, blasted into his face. He closed his eyes and clinched his teeth. The grit in his mouth felt like sand. He spit out the offending particles and looked to Rafferty. "I'm glad I don't work in that place."

Rafferty spit over the side of the truck. "If you did, you'd never have to wash your face. You would get it sand-blasted every day."

Freddy wiped his eyes with the front of his shirt and looked into the cab. Neal was waving his hand around in an excited motion and Blondie was nodding. They were talking about something.

Rafferty tilted his head to the side and leaned his head close to the cab. "What are they saying?"

Holding his hand to his ear, Freddy shook his head. "I can't hear but it looks like Neal is starting to trust Blondie."

"I doubt that," Rafferty said and waved his hand down. "After Blondie cheated us the last time, I don't think Neal could trust him again."

Freddy lowered his head and didn't say anything. Although his shirt had been blown dry from wind whipping into the bed of the truck, his wet pants stuck to his skin. He thrashed his arms onto his chest. "I didn't think it would get this cold."

Rafferty put his hand on the vault and patted it. "When we cash this thing in, you'll be able to buy all the heat you want."

The truck approached a slumbering Mobil gas station and slowed to turn. Two red, brush-painted gas pumps with thick rectangular glass that protected the black and white dials from the weather, stood in front of the station like square men standing at attention. Rubber hoses tucked into the sides of the pumps resembled one-armed men with fingers stuck in their ears.

Above Freddy's head, a stray gust of wind blew through the treetops and split the morning peace with a discordant flapping of small triangular blue and white flags that hung on a long rope strung from the roof of the gas station to the telephone pole at the corner of Clark Street. He looked back the way they had come. No cars were following.

Neal turned left. As the tires of the truck buzzed over the steel grating of the Clark Street Bridge, small pebbles that had caught in the treads of the tires dropped off, fell through the holes, and splashed into the green waters of the Shenango River.

At the Ferrona railroad switching yard crossing, a crossing watchman dressed in gray-striped coveralls came out of a little watchman shanty. He carried a tall round white sign on a long pole to a place in the center of the road between four tracks. With one hand, he held the wooden post that supported the sign and planted the bottom of the pole on the pavement. Black letters on the white background of the metal sign spelled,

STOP

Neal stopped the truck.

The buzz of a locomotive warned of its approaching danger.

Freddy looked to his left. Next to the tracks, a white-shirted man with thinning hair rolled up his sleeves and rested his forearms on the raining of a small porch that led to the yard office. He looked back over his shoulder and shouted, "Hey, Jimmy, get that mail."

A blond-haired man wearing a blue shirt rushed out of the side door of the yard office and placed a leather mail sack on a stanchion.

Freddy propped his back against the wall of the bed of the truck and turned to Rafferty. "If we were on the other side, we could watch the train snatch that mail off that hook."

Rafferty rubbed his hand over the vault. "The only thing I want to see snatching something, is my hand snatching up the money we get from this thing."

Blasting its diesel horn, the lead engine came into view. It was the Erie passenger train, called the flyer. Although it was early morning, the light behind the rectangular glass illuminated the train's number: 7101. On the swept-back front of the behemoth of steel, a maroon square turned in the shape of a fat diamond outlined a white circle that highlighted a big yellow E. A broad horizontal maroon stripe, accented with skinny yellow lines, ran the full length of the sides of two gray locomotive engines. Designed to look strong, these streamlined engines conveyed to people that this train could get them to where they were going, and in style. Inside, up top, behind a slanted windshield, an engineer wore a red flannel shirt and a gray and white striped railroader's cap. The train had a strict schedule to keep, and running at seventy miles an hour, it didn't stop or slow for anything.

As it zipped past, rushing air howled along the sides of the passenger cars. The wheels thumped and clattered on the expansion joints under the steel rails until the tail end of the train swept on down the tracks and revealed that the crossing watchman, dressed in gray striped coveralls, holding the stop sign, was gone. Another man had replaced him. Baggy pants draped his legs, and a huge red bandanna hung out of his back pocket. Broadcasting the characteristics of a circus clown, the man looked at his pocket watch, swung a dimly-lit-red kerosene lantern, and signaled for Neal to drive across the tracks.

Neal hooked first gear and eased over the tracks, but the exposed rails and beat up pavement thumped under the tires, causing Freddy and Rafferty to bounce in the bed of the truck. Past the tracks, the road smoothed out. Neal slowed the truck and crept past the Westinghouse transformer-manufacturing factory where a sleepy-headed security guard in a little shanty waved to him. Neal nodded and after coasting through a red light, he went straight. He started up the Clark Street hill, but when he hit second gear, the engine groaned under the strain from the weight of the vault. The truck slowed to a crawl. He double clutched and shifted back into low gear. The overloaded truck moaned and labored up the steep hill that led to the Oakwood Cemetery.

On level ground, an iron picket fence encircled the graveyard. Black clumps of spruce and fir stood guard above a row of tombstones. Neal drove the truck up the winding gravel road and rolled to a stop. They were in front of an ancient mausoleum. Heavy stones that had been carved into rectangular blocks formed the walls. A steep thick slate roof, with copper ridges that were oxidized the color of dull green, pointed toward the sky. The structure had no windows. Two double doors made of iron bars stood ten feet tall and blocked a tarnished brass door. A foot above and a foot below, the brass door, ornate iron straps reached across its length and studded round rivets ran around its edges.

Freddy jumped out of the truck. To his surprise, the lack of meaningful sleep and the continuing anxiety was catching up with him, and he was a little stiff from the ride. Wondering why they had stopped in a cemetery, he looked in the window at Neal. "What happened? Did you run out of gas?"

Neal turned toward him with a glimmer of mischief. "No, we're just fine."

Rafferty bent around the cab of the truck and pointed to the mausoleum. "Hey, this place wasn't on the vacation brochure. You're not thinking of putting the vault in there are you?"

Chuckling at Rafferty's look of puzzlement, Neal jumped out of the truck. "Where else would you put a vault?"

Rafferty drew back into the bed of the truck. "This place gives me the creeps."

"Good," Blondie said with an air of authority and stepped out of the truck. "We hope it gives everybody else the creeps. We're going to hide the vault here until we arrange to cash it in."

"Why don't we just cash it in now?" Rafferty said as if he had been insulted.

Shaking his head, Blondie held up his hand. "We can't. We don't have the connections to get the gold vault across the border."

"Why do we have to take it across the border?"

Blondie jerked his head violently and cussed. "How many times do I have to tell you guys? Before you were born, Roosevelt made it illegal for U.S. citizens to buy, sell, or own gold."

Rafferty tapped the vault with his finger. "So... are you saying that if the police catch us with this vault, they can take it?"

Blondie's words came out crispy and to the point. "They can, and they will take it. And they don't care who they take it from."

Rubbing the top of the vault, Rafferty flashed Blondie a shifty grin. "They wouldn't take it from someone with enough money to pay them off."

Blondie's eyebrows arched in surprise. "I wouldn't say that. In 1963, federal agents walked into the Witte Museum in San Antonio and took gold coins they had on display." He placed his hand on the vault. "This thing weighs at least two thousand pounds. Even at the frozen price of thirty-five dollars an ounce, it's worth at least eight hundred forty thousand dollars. I don't think anybody is going to accept a bribe when they can take the whole vault?"

Rafferty looked at Blondie with awe and adulation. "No wonder Capone hid it."

"It's a good idea to hide it here, "Freddy said, "but how are we going to unload it?"

Blondie looked toward Freddy. "You'll think of something."

Rafferty stared at the iron bars of the double doors that blocked the second door to the burial chamber. He tilted his head from one side to the other and pulled on one of the iron handles on the door. "Even if we unload it, how are we going to unlock the doors?"

"Those locks are so big just about anything will open them." Blondie held up one of the brass keys they had used to open the trapdoor at Petroleum. "This should open them."

He stood in front of the steel bars of the first door, inserted the key and turned it. As if a body's

374

sprit had been released, an ancient squeal cried from the lock. Blondie shuddered. "It's unlocked."

As he opened the steel-bared door, the hinges behind the ornate iron straps squealed eerily. He pushed on the latch on the brass door. It slid down with a small squeak. It wasn't locked. He pushed it open. As the musty smell of death escaped, Freddy couldn't take a deep breath without the urge to cough. Inside, dust, grime, and cobwebs filled the air, but there was no vault with a dead body. Except for a three-foot high stone platform, layered with dust, there was nothing inside.

With his face filled with amusement, Rafferty stood at the edge of the door, covered his head with his shirt, and acted like a ghost. "This thing's quiet as a tomb."

Freddy gave him a withering look and peered over Blondie's shoulder. "The guy this thing's for didn't die yet."

"Let's hope he doesn't kick the bucket before we cash this thing in," Rafferty said, changing his mood to a more somber one.

Dropping the truck's tailgate, Blondie looked to Neal. "Okay, back it up."

Neal jumped in the truck and hit reverse. With Blondie directing him, he slowly backed up until the corner of the tailgate was inside the crypt. He leaned his head out the window. "Okay, you guys, push that thing off."

Freddy, Rafferty, and Blondie heaved in concert and pushed the vault. It slid to the end of the tailgate and stopped solid.

"Don't stop now," Neal said. "It's almost off."

Straining from the weight of the vault, Freddy

took a deep breath, leaned on the vault, and looked at Neal. "Get your froggy ass back here and help."

Neal shot back a contemptuous look. "I'm sorry. I didn't know you guys were that weak." He jumped into the bed of the truck, and they all started to push.

Blondie held up his hand. "Wait." He picked up the two-by-fours and handed them to Freddy. "Put these onto the tailgate and make sure the other ends are on the stone."

"These things sure come in handy," Freddy said and placed the ends two-by-fours on the stone pedestal and the tailgate. They all pushed. The vault easily slid off the truck and onto the dusty stone platform.

Blondie brushed his hands together. "Okay, let's lock it up and get out of here before someone sees us."

"Let's get this truck back before Seeguy gets home from work. We might need it again."

After they closed the doors to the crypt, they jumped into the truck. Just as they were about to leave Rafferty spoke up. "What about the two-by-fours? Are we just going to leave them there?"

"Yes, we are," Neal said, gunned the truck, and sped away from the crypt.

Chapter 27

After Neal stopped at the Mobile gas station and filled the gas tank of the truck, he drove to the thicket where they had hidden the Oldsmobile and dropped off Blondie, Freddy, and Rafferty. Then he drove the truck back into Seeguy's barn, put the speed odometer cable back on, and hung the key back under the seed-cap. Then he walked back to the thicket, jumped into the Oldsmobile, and they all began the trip to Sharon.

Freddy wanted to go home and sleep a few peaceful hours in his own bed, but if Smeal or any of his cronies knew where he lived they might do something to his mother. No matter how difficult it was, it was best for all of them to stay completely away from their homes.

After waiting at a railroad crossing for a unit ore train to slowly rumble pass, they went to the Dinner Bell restaurant for a much-needed breakfast. After they ate, Blondie drove the Oldsmobile to a high-tension tower maintenance road, where they were jarred from the tires rolling over exposed rocks and ruts from past rains. When they stopped, they were well hidden behind a grove of trees. With full bellies, they tried to sleep, but the growing expectation of cashing in the vault caused excitement to surge through their veins. After hours of tossing and turning in torment, they gave up trying to sleep and headed toward Masury, Ohio and the Blue Danube bar on Budd Street.

Even though the sun was heading toward the horizon, the Blue Danube bar was closed, so Blondie drove down the road and stopped at the

Green Parrot Tavern. Here, a yellow dirt parking lot, speckled with about fifty packs worth of cigarette butts, stretched out for forty feet in front of the tall building. Making a third story and a perfect lookout point for a gun turret, a single cupola sat on the slanted side of the peaked roof. On the right side of the building, under a little green hood, a lone light bulb directed light to three-foot-high green letters that read "The Green Parrot". Painted under that, a green parrot with a yellow beak stood seven foot high with its big eyes looking toward the entrance.

Off to the side of the bar, crates of bottles, a single metal beer keg, and one lone garbage can sat next to a broken down Hudson with bricks wedged under its back axel.

It was difficult to see the extent of the remodeling of the bar from the outside, and a padlock denied entry to a door that opened at the bottom of a set of stairs. Blondie wondered if it was the door that led to the machine gun protected room where John Dillinger had dealt cards.

Neal opened the door of the Oldsmobile to step out. Blondie reached over and held his shoulder. "Wait."

"What for?"

"To see if Smeal and his boys are around."

After five minutes, Blondie checked the rearview mirror for the tenth time. Then he flopped his arm over the back of the seat and turned toward Freddy. "Freddy, you and Rafferty stay here and watch for Smeal." He swung has arm back over the seat and looked directly at Neal. "Anything can happen in a place like this. I'll need you to watch, but we can't be seen going in together."

"No problem," Neal said, "I'll I go in after you do and pretend to be making a call in the phone booth."

"If something looks fishy, we'll need a signal."

"Good idea," Neal said. "If something looks out of the ordinary, I'll cough three times."

Rafferty made a helpless gesture. "Then what?"

"Then, you glorious pain in the ass," Blondie said with a surge of compassion and joy, "I'll see if we can find someone to give us some big money for the vault."

Rafferty nodded in pleasant amazement.

When Blondie stepped inside the building, there were only two men sitting at the bar. He took a stool opposite the two men who were conversing under a cloud of cigarette smoke and ordered a scotch and water. When the drink came, he lifted his glass and saluted the men. As they nodded in false recognition, he knocked back his drink in two quick swallows.

Apart from owning the tavern, the bartender ran a rather lucrative illegal sports book. He was suspicious of strangers, but Blondie had used him before when he had gotten the vault the first time. This time when the bartender talked to Blondie, his voice came out like the threatening growl of an animal being fed meat on the end of a pointed stick. To someone not accustomed to danger or idle threats, it would be a chilling thing to hear.

Three minutes later, Neal walked in. He went into the wooden phone booth, closed the glass doors, took out a little notebook, and pretended to be making various calls.

Blondie shoved a large bill across the bar. "If you can keep your mouth shut, it'll be the same deal as before. I'm looking for anyone who wants to buy gold, but it can't be Smeal."

Terror filled the bartender's eyes. He glanced right then left. Hunching his tall narrow body, he reached under the bar. "Smeal said you'd show up."

Blondie wasn't ready for Smeal's influence. Not knowing what to expect, he grimaced.

The bartender pulled his hand out from under the bar. In it, he held the front pistol grip of a Thompson sub machine gun that had been apparently looted from some small town police station. The rear stock had been taken off to allow one hand operation, freeing the other hand to carry bank loot or anything else the holder wanted to carry. With a cyclic rate of fire of seven hundred rounds per minute, the ten-pound, one hundred round drum magazine could feed the barrel and spray down any adversary. The bartender waved it menacingly.

The two men at the bar quickly crushed their cigarettes out in the ashtray and stepped back.

"I don't want to use this," the bartender said. "But we don't want no trouble with Smeal. If you want to sell gold, you have to deal with him."

With such a large amount of gold Blondie hadn't counted on Smeal scaring everyone away, but he had. He casually draped his hand across his shoulder holster. He could whap the bulky machine gun barrel to the side. Before the skinny bartender would have a chance to fire a single round, Blondie would shoot him right between the eyes. But Blondie wasn't looking for revenge or to make a name for himself. He was looking for someone to buy the vault. He held up his palms in a helpless gesture. "Anything you say, partner."

Leaving the large bill on the bar, he turned on the stool, stepped down, and briskly walked out.

Forty-five minutes later, still waiting for Neal, Blondie drummed his fingers on the side of the steering wheel. "There's something wrong. Neal shouldn't be in there that long."

Freddy got out of the car and stepped to Blondie's window. "I'll go in and get him."

Before Freddy could take a single step, Neal came out and eased his lithe frame into the front seat of the Oldsmobile. Blondie turned and stared at him for a long moment. "What are you smiling about?"

"I figured while I was in there I should have a beer. You know, make it look natural."

"So, it took you over a half hour to drink one beer?"

Neal slouched in the seat and grinned. "To make it look really good I had a few. When the bartender was out of earshot, I asked a guy next to me what he would do if he had a lot of gold and wanted to trade it for cash."

Rafferty eagerly leaned over the front seat. "What did he say?"

"He asked how much gold I was talking about, and I said a couple thousand pounds." Neal broke into a huge smile. "He about fell off the stool." He let out a sputtering laugh. "Then we went over to a table where no one could hear. The guy said that if

I was serious, I could meet him tomorrow at Radkowski's bar in Patagonia."

Still standing outside, Freddy poked his head into the open window of the Oldsmobile. "That's a mill worker bar."

"Yeah, I know. That's why he wants us to meet him there. He said, 'Everybody in the place knows how to keep their mouths shut.' He likes the place because, when John Dillinger sat right at the bar and showed the owner how to play cards, not one person even thought about calling the cops."

Blondie lifted his wrist and glanced at his watch. "What time should we be there?"

Before Neal could answer, on the other side of the parking lot, a blue '58 Chevy plowed into the yellow dirt and skidded to a dusty stop. Right behind that, a '57 Ford with a knocking engine and cancer-like rust holes along its sides shuddered, backfired with one loud bang, and died. The back door to the '58 Chevy opened, but no one got out. A moment later, Blondie recognized the form of a man running around the back of the bar. As the man's jacket flapped, Blondie caught a glimpse of a leather shoulder holster.

Rafferty cringed and slumped down in the seat. "If that's Smeal, what are we going to tell him?"

Neal slid has arm over the front seat and looked at Rafferty. "Don't join the panic parade yet. Smeal can't run that fast. It could be the people working on a tin roof in the back. But if it's Smeal, we'll tell him we think the vault's in the dump?"

"He'll never believe that. Why don't we just take off?" He gestured toward the '58 Chevy and the '57 Ford. "This Oldsmobile can outrun both those pieces of junk."

Blondie shifted the Oldsmobile into reverse, started to back up, but stopped. "Wait a second." He sat back in the seat, calm but cautious. "I had a deal with Smeal before. If Radkowski's bar doesn't pan out, we might have to make a deal with him."

"So," Rafferty said and smacked his hand over his eyes in frustration. "What are we going to tell him?"

Suddenly Blondie felt belittled. Why was he letting Smeal push him around? He had taken care of men worse than him. He thrust his jaw out and let out a resentful snarl. "We don't have to tell him anything." Thinking about the dump story, he paused, and said, "The dump story might work. When we first found the vault, we thought it was worthless cement covered with thin brass. Anybody who doesn't know it's gold will throw it away or break off the cement and think they can cash in the brass for scrap."

Freddy nodded. "That's so far-fetched it might work."

Trying to be funny, Rafferty looked at Neal with mock astonishment. "What if he makes us take him to the dump and it gets dark?"

"So what?" Neal said and spread his hands apart. "We'll use a flashlight."

"At night?" Rafferty questioned with a trace of alarm. "When it's dark, there's so many rats they'll eat you alive. Will the light scare them away?"

"No," Neal said and chuckled. "But we'll be able to see them come after us."

Rafferty's usual easygoing expression faded. "Oh, that's just great."

Neal leaned back in the seat and clasped his hands behind his head. "Quit griping. If Smeal's here, we'll lead him to the dump. After he gets a whiff of the stinkin' place and wallows around in that filth for a while, he might give up."

Rafferty shot him a pained grimace. "Maybe we can tie him up and let the rats eat him."

"I wouldn't wish that on anyone," Blondie said. "But if nothing else, it'll give us some time to figure out how to get rid of him."

Off to the right, a man stepped around the corner of the bar laughing. He turned and shuffled toward the road in a festival of inebriated ecstasy.

While Freddy watched the man, a hand dropped on his shoulder with such force that his knees buckled, and his face filled with painful shivers. He turned around. Smeal's iced-over face appeared.

Chapter 28

When Smeal had pulled into the parking lot of the Green Parrot Tavern, he had planned to threaten to kill Freddy and his friends. Usually the enduring fear of the threat was enough to make people do what he wanted them to do. But when he saw the defiant look on Blondie's face, he knew a threat wouldn't work this time. Blondie would never talk.

At first Smeal thought his only hope was to keep at least one of the kids alive to find out where the vault was. But when he figured there was a possibility that not all the kids knew where the vault was, he changed his mind.

With yellow parking lot dust covering his shiny shoes, Smeal kept his hand on Freddy's shoulder and peered into the window of Blondie's Oldsmobile. Now for the first time, he saw the kids up close. He was old enough to be their father. Except for Blondie, they were all young men with adolescent faces starting to take on lines of weariness and cruelty. They reminded him of the recruits he had hung out with in the army before he had been captured and put into a prisoner of war camp. Those recruits had seemed to be good friends but they changed. After he had escaped, on his own initiative, these same friends had told him, "All right, so what? You were a prisoner of war. That doesn't give you the right to do whatever the hell you like for the rest of your life."

But as far as Smeal was concerned, it did give him the right, because he had earned it, and why should he believe those so-called-friends who wouldn't lift a finger to help him when the times were tough. Nobody had cared about him when he was a prisoner of war, and civilian life wasn't much different. It was all dog eat dog. Now that he had found the secret of survival, nobody liked it. Well, it was just too damn bad. He had the right to do whatever the hell he wanted, for the rest of his life, because he had learned how to kill and they hadn't.

As he held his hand on Freddy's shoulder, he felt familiarity and trust. For a moment, he wanted to be friends with these kids, but he wasn't going to be fooled into thinking a bunch of young kids could be his friends. He dropped his hand from Freddy's shoulder.

Freddy backed away.

The feeling of familiarity and trust vanished.

Smeal felt a sudden loss, but told himself that it didn't matter. He knew any promise of wealth generates greed. When he was in the Tacloban Prisoner of War Camp, a single scrap of bread had caused so much greed and jealousy that rather than give in and lose the bread, two men had grabbed each other by the throats and strangled each other until one of them was dead. He figured the kids and Blondie would eventually fight for dominance. It was an ugly truth of a basic cause of human conflicts. And besides, if you don't get close to people, when they die, it won't play on your mind.

Smeal jerked his head to the side and signaled to Greenie. Greenie sauntered up to the Oldsmobile. Tall and heavily built like a brawler, knots and scars on his bony skull stood out underneath his short blond hair. His green eyes had the glare of a combat-trained Marine just out of boot camp. His very presence sent the message: Stay away from me.

Smeal wasn't worried what Greenie would do or wouldn't do. Smeal had considered himself dead long ago. He had stayed alive for a long time, and he hadn't done it by being nice. He glared at Freddy. Freddy looked like a kid, but he didn't move like a kid. His eyes tirelessly flicked left and right. This kid could be trouble.

Smeal reached into his suit coat and pulled out his Walther PPK. A 22-caliber long rifle shell was locked in the chamber, ready to fire. No use having a gun unless it's ready to fire. Using the double action semi-automatic action of the PPK, he could empty the eight-round clip and make short work of them all. And it would be clean. The heat from the 22-caliber bullet would cauterize the entry point, and little blood would flow from the wounds. He flashed the steel blue barrel at Freddy. "What are you going to do now?"

Freddy gave a little shrug of exasperation. "I guess whatever you say."

Smeal figured he had them, but from around the corner of the bar, a metallic pulse came and went. Just about anyone could tell the sound was a sheet of heavy tin being hit with a hammer. But to Smeal it sounded exactly like a Japanese trench mortar going off.

"Mortar attack" flashed in his military crippled mind. His heart jumped to his throat. Although it was many years old, a conditioned response from the war controlled his body. He dropped to the ground and covered the back of his head with his hands. Before he had become a prisoner of war, he had had many close calls with mortars. These portable muzzle-loading cannons fired shells at low velocities, and they sounded like heavy tin being hit with a hammer. Although the mortars had short ranges, their high trajectories would rain down without warning. Then the Japanese soldiers would come. They were small, lean, and fast. Their endurance and stamina seemed to have no end. If a combatant wanted to live, he had to act fast, because the efficient Japanese would ferret out a solider like a terrier hot on a rat's nest. Smeal knew what mortars and the Japanese could do. He still awoke in the middle of the night with the stench of burning flesh in his nostrils, listening for the shouts, the sobs, and the screams.

In the yellow dirt of the parking lot, he rolled to one side and surveyed the area for Japanese soldiers. Too late, he realized the sound wasn't a mortar.

"Son-of-a-bitch," he cussed, "I never got out of the war." He remembered that surviving torture wasn't physical strength. It was about how mentally tough a person was, and for a moment, he had lost his POW toughness.

He struggled to his feet. Before he could bush himself off, he doubled over in a coughing seizure. With snot running over his lips and down his chin, he stumbled and managed to lean against the fender of the Oldsmobile. Although it was a prolonged, echoing, rattling cough, no one came near him. They knew he would rebuff any assistance. If he let them help him, it would be a sign of weakness, the sign of a dying man. After his coughing finally stopped, he wiped the snot from his face and regained his tough edge. Straightening his suit coat, he walked around the Oldsmobile and smiled. But Blondie had rolled up the driver's side window. With the barrel of his PPK, Smeal tapped on of the window.

Blondie rolled down the window and held up his hands. "Okay, you got our attention. What do you want?"

"Don't get smart with me." Smeal snarled. "You never delivered that vault. If you think I'm going to let you get away with that, you're crazy."

Blondie let out a mirthless chuckle. "If you wouldn't have given me a truck you stole from the junk yard to haul it in, we wouldn't be here today."

Smeal glowered at him with blameful hatred. "That truck was good enough for the short distance you had to haul that vault." He threw his hand into the air. "What did you want me to do? Rent a truck from the truckers?"

"You should have stolen something better. That junk you got me wasn't good enough to haul the air around it."

"It must've been good enough to haul that vault to wherever you took it." He looked toward door of the bar. "The man inside just called. He said you were looking to sell gold. What did you do with the vault?"

"I thought you took it."

Smeal felt his eyebrows shoot up in disbelief. "If I took it, would I be here?"

"I figured you gave me a junk truck and knew it would break down. That way, when I went to get help, you could come and get the vault."

"I had no such plan," Smeal said with a thick infuriated voice. "You seem to forget that I was to get a percentage of the money."

Without taking his eyes off the PPK, Smeal had pointed at him, Blondie pounded his fist on the steering wheel. "For crying out loud, Smeal, the truck was overloaded, both back tires blew out. I couldn't fix two flats. So I went to get help. When I came back, the truck was gone."

Keeping the PPK pointed at Blondie, Smeal waved the barrel in a small circle. "If that's true, then why are you looking for someone to buy gold?"

Blondie's response came out slow and deliberate. "The bartender knew about the vault. I figured he might have been in on the scheme to take the truck. If he thought I had more gold, he might lead me to the guy who took the truck and the vault."

Smeal wondered if there was some truth in Blondie's statement, but his words came out before he could stop them. "That's so stupid it might be true."

Blondie expelled his breath in an explosive whoosh. "If you didn't take the vault, then somebody else did."

"So what do you want me to do about it?" Smeal asked with a superior air.

"I don't care what you do." Blondie snorted and looked straight ahead. "I'm still going to look for that vault. If you want to follow us, that's all right with me."

"You don't have to care what I do," Smeal shot back. "I'll follow you whether you like it or not."

Blondie glanced down at Smeal's PPK. "Put that pea shooter away and follow us." He held up his hands up in surrender. "We'll show you where we think the vault is. But you won't like it, and it might take a while to get used to the atmosphere."

"If I knew where the vault was, I'd shoot you right here."

Blondie dropped his hands and dismissed Smeal's threat with a wave. "Once we get there, you'll know just as much as we know."

Smeal held Blondie's gaze but said nothing. Giving him a lecherous look, Smeal lowered his PPK and gestured to the man standing behind Greenie. "Carlo, get in."

Radiating supreme arrogance, Carlo ran his hand along the side of his greasy black hair. His well-manicured nails seemed out of place with the rest of his body, and his skin was white except for the deep amber strains on his fingers, where he held his cigarette. As his snake-like eyes glared at Smeal, Carlo's face seemed to broadcast suspicion and distrust.

Smeal figured Carlo was in his thirties. Scars on his neck and face showed he was old beyond his age, and ugly. He had told Smeal he didn't care how his face looked. It was only the price of doing business, but his exercised-hewed body showed he could still take anything someone could dish out.

Carlo hopped into the '58 Chevy and started the three hundred forty-eight cubic-inch engine. It roared with definite power.

Smeal nodded and walked toward the '57 Ford. Greenie sat behind the steering wheel, pumped the accelerator, and ran the starter. The electrical system crackled and died. The engine would not start.

Carlo leaned over and opened the passenger side door of the Chevy. Smeal thrust his index finger at Greenie. "When you get that piece of shit started, follow us." He walked over and slid into the front seat of the Chevy.

The Ford backfired with a loud bang. War reflexes cautioned Smeal that it could be a gunshot. He cringed but he didn't hit the dirt like the last time. The engine of the Ford smoothed to a rough idle and died. Smoke rolled out from under the hood.

Smeal nodded to Greenie. Greenie jumped out of the disabled Ford and slid into the back seat of the Chevy.

With a smug expression on his face, Blondie slammed the transmission into gear and slowly pulled away from the Green Parrot Tavern.

And Smeal followed.

Chapter 29

With Blondie's grip on the Oldsmobile's steering wheel loose and relaxed, Freddy watched out the side window. The sun dropped behind a stretch of dark clouds, and a light rain began to fall. As they drove on, the rain dropped from the sky in great drops. Familiar buses and mill traffic swished up and down the road, splashing in puddles. Alongside the road, construction workers, getting paid overtime for waiting for the rain to stop, sat under the cover of road crew trucks and peered out of steamed windows, waiting to go home. But Freddy and his friends couldn't go home. Smeal and his two goons were following them.

Freddy hunched over the front seat and turned toward Blondie. "Are you going to the mausoleum?"

Without turning his head, Blondie shouted into the windshield, "No way. That vault's ours." He swung his fist down. Smack! He hit the seat. "Smeal has no right to it."

Feeling embarrassed for asking a stupid question, Freddy eased back off the seat. "Are we really going to the dump?"

"I haven't decided yet." Blondie looked to Neal. "You got any ideas?"

Neal lifted his hand and pointed out the windshield. "The dump's right down the road."

Rolling his hand, Blondie made an encouraging gesture. "And?"

"And, there's so much garbage in that place, something will pass for a vault."

"I still don't think Smeal will fall for something

like that," Freddy said and paused. "Hey wait a minute. The last time we were there, right at the edge of the garbage there was a huge block of cement. They might think that's the vault."

"The bulldozer guy moves that garbage every day," Neal said, making a pushing movement with his hand. "That block might be buried."

"So what?" Freddy said. "We'll tell them the vault's there anyway. If they want to find it, they'll just have to root around in the garbage."

Blondie shrugged and cut the steering wheel to the right. "Well, here goes."

He drove down a garbage-flecked yellow dirt road and stopped in front of a Cyclone fence gate. Rain continued to fall on the Oldsmobile, but it formed a curtain of falling water that didn't go beyond the gate.

Freddy gestured to the "No Trespassing" sign clamped on the gate. "It looks like the rain is afraid to go into the dump."

With a look of wonder on his freckled face, Rafferty looked through the shimmering curtain of rain and stared at the dry road beyond the fence. He flashed Freddy a dazzling missing-tooth smile. "What do you expect? The gate's closed and there's a No Trespassing sign."

"I can fix that." Freddy jumped out of the Oldsmobile and opened the gate.

Shaking his head, Blondie drove a ways past the open gate and stopped.

While Freddy jumped back into the Oldsmobile, Rafferty looked at the dirt road ahead. "Are you going to drive all the way back?" he asked with pleading concern. "That way if some rats come after us we can jump in the car."

"We can get close," Blondie said and continued to drive. "But we can't drive all the way back there. It's pretty dry now, but if it rains back there, we'll get stuck in the mud."

Blondie drove down the road and stopped. In the distance, a sign, too far away to read, hung on a chest-high steel cable stretched across a makeshift road. Smeal pulled the '58 Chevy up behind the Oldsmobile. Smeal, Greenie, and Carlo got out and walked to Blondie's window. Smeal placed his hands on his hips and peered down at Blondie. "What are you trying to pull?"

"I don't know if it's true," Blondie said in his most convincing tone. "But a guy at the Blue Danube said that somebody had a big cement box he wanted to get rid of. No one would take it because it looked like a coffin. So he said he tricked some guy into hauling it to the dump this morning."

"Yeah," Neal added. "The guy said he got some half-wit to haul the cement thing away. He laughed and said the dumb ass thought he could get big money from the brass covering. He gave him twenty bucks for it and hauled it to the dump, said he knew the man at the dump and he could get him to break the cement away from the brass with his bulldozer."

In fake haste, Neal eagerly jumped out of the car. "They bury the garbage every day. I hope we're not too late."

Smeal cast a suspicious look toward Neal. "That sounds like a bullshit story if I ever heard one."

Neal held his palms up and hunched. "We don't know if the guy's story's true. "We're only here to check it out. It will be a shame to have somebody break the cement away and find the gold, and if they don't, the bulldozer can bury the vault under tons of garbage."

Smeal looked hard at Neal. Then he jerked his head toward the road. "It's getting dark." He gestured to Greenie. "Get the flashlights out of the car and let's go."

Walking toward the dump in the gray evening light, Freddy looked toward a little building at the edge of the road. Built with weathered boards, the building looked like an outhouse without the crescent moon cut in the door. A ways from the building, fat iridescent flies rose in humming clouds from the rotting piles of sun-activated, rapidly decaying garbage. The odor hit him first. It rose into his nostrils, and his throat closed against the bilious surge in his stomach. He pulled the front of his T-shirt up over his mouth and continued walking.

A horde of flies buzzed around Freddy's head. He swatted at them with his open hand until they were gone. Rafferty walked next to him, but not a single fly buzzed around his head. The flies returned to buzz around Freddy's head. He shook his head and looked to Rafferty. "We're not even there yet, and the flies are so thick here you can't breathe without getting one in your mouth."

With a faint glimmer of mischief, Rafferty pitched his voice as high as he could, "Bitch, bitch, bitch." Before he could utter another word, a fly buzzed right under his nose. He looked at Freddy.

Freddy shrugged and they took off at a trot.

Smeal and the others followed suit. As they neared the scattered remnants of restaurant garbage, hundreds of seagulls ceased feeding and turned their wary eyes toward Rafferty. Rafferty clapped his hands. The sound echoed across the dump, sending the seagulls into startled flight.

Still trotting, Freddy turned and watched the seagulls climb and darkened the sky. "We're hundreds of miles from the ocean and this place has seagulls."

"They're not seagulls," Rafferty said. "They're garbage gulls."

Beneath the gray and white wings of the seagulls, the black cloud of flies, hovering above the little building, dispersed for a moment, but immediately returned and buzzed in the summer air.

The temperature climbed and the humidity from the recent warm rain caused Freddy's clothes to stick to his skin. But when he looked back at the others, they acted as if they were in no hurry to get to where they were going. Freddy slowed to a leisurely walk.

When they stopped, Smeal mopped his sweating forehead with a white handkerchief. In front of them, chicken wire fenced in the bottom of a narrow plank shed that squatted on the tops of wooden four-by-fours, three feet off the ground. Two steps up,, a padlock secured a filthy white door. The facade of the building was spattered with yellow dirt, and bits of butcher paper, speckled with dead flies, lay all around. Some kind of dark fabric hung behind a lone filthy window. Pasted at random places on the walls, "No Trespassing" signs warned people to stay away. A weak slice of sunshine shimmered on another yellow sign with red letters. It read,

HOURS OF OPERATION
Open 8 AM until 4 PM
Open Saturdays 9 to Noon
Closed Sundays

As they walked closer, the humid summer heat of the falling night, enhanced sour smells of decaying garbage, mixed with skinny wisps of smoke, and like ghost snakes, they swirled around and crawled into Freddy's nose.

Amidst the stench, the last rays of the setting sun cast a brassy glare over the enormous conglomeration of garbage. Although little light came from the setting sun, Freddy could read a red "Danger, Do Not Enter" sign hanging from the sagging center of the chest-high steel cable stretched across a makeshift road.

Neal reached over, ripped the sign off the cable, and threw it onto the ground. "We don't need signs telling us what to do."

"I'll keep that in mind," Blondie said and ducked down to go under the rope.

Neal held up his hand. "Wait!"

So no one would have to bend over to go under the neck-high cable, he used his forearm and lifted the cable. The others ducked under and stopped momentarily on the spot.

Sweating in the humidity of the steamy evening, Freddy reached up, wiped his forehead with the sleeve of his shirt, and looked ahead. A huge, pointed pile of cans and bottles, clustered around greasy paper, reached up as if it were trying to touch the darkening sky.

Smeal looked to Blondie. "Okay, where is it?"

"How should I know," Blondie said and shrugged. "It might not even be here?"

Blondie clicked on his flashlight and pointed in the direction of the dump. Although there was weak light from the sky, the flashlight beam leveled out and illuminated the dark area. Amidst the sounds of rats scurrying to hide, smoldering wet garbage sent plumes of sour smoke into the air. What little orange and blue flames managed to survive caused shiny tin cans to twinkle in various colors. Deep drifts of garbage spread everywhere. Paper cartons and piles of unidentifiable rotten matter humped up in irregular tiny mounds. Here, rats tunneling beneath the surface caused the tiny mounds to look like moving dead bodies.

Sweeping his hand toward Greenie and Carlo, Smeal nodded. "Okay, get these boys to work."

Greenie smiled a rotten-toothed smile. Without warning, he slapped his flat-handed palm into Freddy's back. "You heard him. Start looking."

Unprepared for the sudden slap in the back, Freddy stumbled forward. He managed to catch his balance, but ended up knee deep in filth. He stood in one spot and scanned the dump.

Carlo flipped his Italian head back. His greasy black hair fell into place. Then with extreme reluctance and a look of undisguised revulsion, he bent over and pulled a rusty pipe from a lump of rotting cabbage. With the end, he gave Freddy a warning jab in the back. "Get moving."

Remembering how Terry had been killed with a pipe, Freddy kept a wary eye on the pipe.

Rafferty picked up a dented alarm clock. "Yeah, we better get moving." He threw the alarm clock. As it sailed into the air, his merriment swelled. "Time's a flyin'. I just saw a Dago by."

Greenie started to laugh at the ethnic joke but held it in.

Rafferty's jab about Carlo's Italian heritage didn't seem to enter Carlo's limited mind. Carlo grunted and viciously prodded Freddy in the lower back with the pipe. Freddy slowly plowed through the knee-deep garbage. Carlo jabbed the pipe into Freddy's back again. He moved faster. When he was far enough away from the pipe that Carlo couldn't poke him, Freddy slowed.

Walking into the conglomeration of garbage, Freddy, Blondie, Neal, and Rafferty spread out. When Freddy stopped at a huge pile of garbage, it hunched over as if it were going to tip over. Occasional boards, sticks, and two long rusty pipes jutted awkwardly from the back of the pile. Stringy strands of something white, hung from various sections of rotting lettuce that was interlaced with rags. And the sharp, pointed edges of broken bottles seemed to be eating the side of the pile. Anything and everything sat below, over, and inside the pile.

Combinations of noxious odors, constantly crawling into Freddy's face, required most of his concentration not to throw up. At one end of the pile, the flies were so thick, it was impossible to dodge out of their buzzing path. Freddy whipped his hands around in the air and managed to flee from the flies, but he stopped just short of falling down a steeply slanted drop off of yellow clay that led to a deep pit. Thinking Smeal wasn't buying the vault in the dump story, Freddy figured he might have to run to a place safe from blazing bullets. He made a mental note of were the drop off was.

In the distance, the powerful diesel engine of a bulldozer with a broken exhaust pipe thumped near.

Rafferty lifted his arm and pointed toward the sound. "Somebody's coming. Maybe they're coming after the vault." He pointed to a huge pile of garbage. "It looks like it's under there."

All heads snapped sideways and zeroed in on the huge pile of garbage. As if it were camouflaged, the end of a huge block of cement stuck out the pile of garbage.

The bulldozer crawled close.

All heads turned toward the sound. When the bulldozer was ten feet away, its engine slowed and the tin flap over the rusted exhaust pipe jangled to an idle. The operator placed the palms of his hands on control lever knobs as big as pool eight-balls and shifted the transmission out of gear. He looked to be on the young side of thirty with a bronze face and sun-bleached blond hair that looked as if it hadn't been combed in years. Black grime coated his coveralls. Dirt filled the creases on his neck and arms. Although filthy, his clenched fists gave the impression he was ready to fight. Before he could do or say anything, he sneezed thunderously six times. He wiped his nose with a clean spot on the back of his sturdy wrist, climbed down off the dozer, walked over to Blondie, and began sneezing again. This time he staggered sideways on rubbery legs. He raised his elbows to fend off each seizure but it didn't work. When he finally stopped sneezing, he stared at Blondie through watery, puffy, and inflamed eyes. "What are you doing here at night?" he asked with a voice entangled in phlegm. "Can't you read?" Sniffing spasmodically, he reached down and rested his hand on the handle of the 22-caliber pistol in his holster. The muscles in his rocklike jaw bunched up into quivering knots. "We're closed."

Blondie tensed and snaked his hand toward the Colt under his arm.

Neal stepped forward. The man recognized him, took his hand off the 22, and smiled. "Neal, you old flim-flam man. You're not coming late to steal some scrap metal, are you?"

Blondie relaxed and looked to Neal.

Neal opened his arms and smiled big. "Nothing like that, Router. We're looking for something somebody threw away and wants back."

Freddy knew Router from before. The house Router had tried to grow up in looked like a black-and-white picture from the 1930's: a ramshackle shack in a coal town in Appalachia. Having nothing all his life, Router had gotten the name Router from his ability to rout around in the town's old dump. Like a pig with a snout, he could sniff out and uncover valuable things no one else could. Loud-mouthed and always eager to agitate someone "just for the hell of it" Router could be a very obnoxious person. He let people he knew call him Router, but others were immediately made the object of his disrespect. He stared at Blondie's suit coat and then glanced at Smeal and Carlo. "You must be looking for something pretty important to drag a bunch of assholes in suit coats into a dump."

As if going along with Router, so he wouldn't chase them out of the dump with the bulldozer blade, Neal grinned at Carlo and Smeal with scornful satisfaction. "Sometimes they want to see how the real world is." He gestured to Router's 22. "You still shooting rats?"

Router's bronze face lit up. "Before I ran out of bullets, I got three. But I wish you'd tell me when you're coming." He jerked his head to the bulldozer's blade. "That blade's so big that when it's dark and I push garbage into the pit, I can't see if anybody's in front of it."

Carlo tilted his head back and looked down his nose at Router. "Hey, Router, are you going to start pushing now?"

Router stiffened with mock resentment and hostility. "Who are you calling, Router?" He defiantly stared right into Carol's face.

Freddy figured Router was going to start something with Carlo just for laughs. But it didn't happen.

Carlo reached out to grab him by the front of his shirt, but Router stepped away. Carlo flashed Router a look of hurt. "Hey, pal, do you know a good doctor?"

A look of concern filled Router's face. "Yes, I do." As if looking for an injury, his eyes scanned Carlo's body. "Did you get hurt?"

Greenie slid his hand under his suit jacket and came back out with a chrome-plated 38 Colt. He swung his hand around and let loose with a single shot. The bullet hissed past the top of Freddy's head, close enough for him to feel the concussion and make his ears ring. Images of the flame from the muzzle of the gun caused waves of unexpected color to swirl in Freddy's vision, but he could clearly see that the bullet had hit Router right between the eyes. With the sky in its last vestiges of twilight, the back of Router's head exploded into a pink mist and showered the air with a cloud of bloody brain tissue and splinters of bone. Router stood for a second and tilted forward. As a flood of crimson washed down the front of his shirt, one of his knees buckled. He fell to his side. His shoulder thumped on the ground. As if it were a delayed reaction, he rolled over and faced the sky. And his face flopped next to a pile of greasy smoldering rags.

Greenie slipped the toe of his shoe under Router's body and flipped it over. The back of Router's raw hamburger-like head flopped into the pile of smoldering rags. Pointing to what was left of Router's head, Greenie let out a big horselaugh. "See if your doctor can fix that."

As Freddy's ears rang from the gunshot, Neal ran to Router and dropped to one knee. Router's feet kicked. His now bluish-gray body trembled and he went limp. Neal turned Router's head to the side and looked into his lifeless eyes. Then he looked up at Greenie. "He's dead."

Carlo pressed his thumb and forefinger together and flashed Greenie an okay sign.

Greenie nodded. "Now that we've gotten rid of that lever-pushing pig, we can pick up that vault."

Looking at Router's brain tissue and splinters of bone laying on the ground, Freddy wanted to throw up. He checked back his building rage and turned away. It only took a moment, but his self-survival mechanism that shut down his feelings kicked in. Then he wasn't sick anymore.

Rafferty glanced at Greenie. Greenie pointed his Colt at him. Rafferty held up his hands. His small, intimate smile showed a hint of mischief. "I hope you brought your army and three men and a dog to lift that vault."

Greenie seemed intrigued. "What are you talking about?"

"Simple," Rafferty said and lifted his head with a significant air. "If you'd put down your comic books once in a while, you'd realize that if you shoot us, you won't be able to pick up that vault."

Greenie's voice became low and guttural. "Think again, sonny. What do you think that bulldozer's for?"

Rafferty started to say something, but only smiled his usual smile.

Freddy looked to Smeal. Obviously Rafferty didn't see Smeal's hand tighten on his pistol grip. Freddy jerked his head toward Smeal's hand. Smeal's knuckles turned white and his wrist shook. He closed his eyes. A small tremble formed on his lower lip. In one smooth motion, he snatched his PPK pistol from his shoulder holster, along with a spare clip, and racked a round into the chamber. Then he pointed the weapon at Rafferty's mouth. "I'll shoot that grin right off your smiley face."

Blondie held up his hand. "Wait. Without the boss's express approval, you can't paint his house outside your territory."

"I don't need the boss's approval," Smeal said and paused. "I'm acting as an independent. I'll shoot who I damn please."

Rafferty's face tensed with fear. Trying to slough it off, he turned to Blondie. "I don't think we're wanted here."

Freddy spoke up. "If you kill any one of us, you'll never find the vault." He pointed to the huge block of cement. "That's not it!"

Smeal began to squeeze the trigger, but for some reason, his face filled with confusion. His finger backed off the trigger.

The tension in Rafferty's face fell, but Freddy knew his casual demeanor hid vigilant tension. Even though the PPK was aimed at his face and he could die at any moment, he bravely managed to calmly say, "You should've shot me by now. What are you going to do, kiss me first?"

Smeal's brow furrowed with confusion and the PPK shook.

Blondie reached up and gently grabbed Smeal's hand. Watching the expression on Smeal's face fade, he slowly pulled the PPK away from Rafferty's face. "Come on, Smeal," he pleaded. "We had a deal before. Why can't we share the vault?"

"I shouldn't even answer that," Smeal snapped back. "After you've been around as long as I have, you find out that no matter how much you get used to the idea of having money, you'll never know how long it's going to last. And when it is all gone, someone will blame you for losing it."

Blondie turned his head skyward. "You're getting near the time when you'll meet your maker. Don't you have a sense of right or wrong?"

Smeal gave Blondie a hard stare. "I decided a long time ago that life is not about right or wrong.

It's about winning and losing. And today, you're losing."

In an almost begging tone, Blondie pleaded, "You have to trust someone in your life."

"Actually," Smeal said and smiled a weird mischievous smile. "Now that we've found the vault, I think it would be prudent to kill all of you right now?"

Blondie lifted his hand and inched it toward his shoulder holster.

Greenie jerked the barrel of his Colt in front of Blondie's face. "Take it out, slow and easy."

Blondie reached into his shoulder holster and took out his Colt.

Greenie grabbed it with one hand. With his other hand, he slipped his chrome-plated Colt into the shoulder holster under his arm. He turned Blondie's Colt to the side and admired it. "One can never have too many 38s."

"Okay, boys and girls," Neal said without looking at his audience. "We're going to get serious here."

The gruesome fact that Greenie had shot a likable man like Router without the slightest hesitation, and for no good reason, caused anger to keep swelling up in Freddy's chest, but he refused to get angry. Don't get mad at the situation, he told himself. Use it. He wrinkled his nose and looked to Neal. Neal nodded. Freddy knew he knew what he meant. If they were going to be allowed to live, they were going to have to show Smeal and his friends that the huge chunk of cement under the garbage wasn't the vault. While they were distracted it just might give them a chance to flee.

Neal gestured to the chunk of cement. "Before you waste your bullets, why don't you make sure that's the vault?"

As if he were saying something brilliant, Carlo tapped his finger on his forehead. "We're in no hurry."

Freddy figured it was true. Carlo seemed to be the type of a person who didn't want to get impatient and make mistakes.

Neal placed his hands on his hips and assumed a superior posture. "It's not our fault you guys are morons."

Smeal turned toward Neal with a sudden start. Glaring at Neal, his eyes narrowed. "What?"

Neal jerked his thumb toward the block of cement. "That's not the vault. You kill us, you'll never find the damn thing."

Greenie waved the Colt at a spot beneath a stack of broken glass. The side of some sort of a box with green coloring protruded from a mix of rotting lettuce, dirty meat paper, flies and one dead rat.

"You kids never learn," he said and pointed to the block of cement. "I know that thing's just a hunk of concrete." He turned and pointed to the green box. "The real vault's right there."

Freddy stared at the green box. At first, he thought it could actually be another vault, but upon further examination he concluded that the green coloring was too light to be oxidized brass. He shrugged and looked to Greenie. "Are you sure that's it?"

"You're damn right I'm sure."

As if he had already been shot, Blondie

stiffened. "If it wasn't for us, you would never have found it. The vault's half ours."

"That's right," Neal added. "Let's be fair about this thing."

Carlo's mouth spread into a hideously diabolical grin. "It *is* fair. You find it, we take it."

With his head lowered like a little kid who didn't get anything for Christmas, Rafferty stepped forward. "You mean you're not going to share?"

Greenie grinned wolfishly and placed his hand on Rafferty's back. "You know, you're such a wise ass, I might just let you live." He turned, and rammed the barrel of Blondie's Colt into Smeal's gut. "The only things I'm going to share with you, old buddy, are the bullets in this gun."

As Smeal let out a painful grunt, a look of surprise filled Carlo's face. He backed away from Smeal as if he were radioactive.

Again, Greenie jabbed Smeal's stomach with the barrel of the Colt. "Okay, Smeal, get your ass over there with those kids."

Bent over, holding his stomach, Smeal backed away from the barrel of the gun and stood stunned. "Greenie, why are you doing this to me?"

"Hey, you old fool. You didn't think I was going to let someone who belongs in the old folks home take the vault, now did you?" He looked directly into Rafferty's face, smiled an exaggerated full tooth smile, and held it. "See, I can be a wise ass, too."

With a half-smile on his face, Rafferty cautiously nodded.

Perplexed, Smeal looked to Carlo. "Carlo, I helped you when you were down. What's the deal?"

Carlo tilted his head back and looked down his nose at Smeal. "Not only are you an old man, you're an idiot."

Smeal placed his hand on his PPK and talked through clenched teeth. "I should have shot both you bastards when I had the chance."

Neal elbowed Rafferty and tilted his head toward Freddy. Freddy knew Neal wanted them to cause a ruckus. It was a life and death chance, but he figured if they didn't do something they would be shot and buried in the dump. Any chance was better than no chance. Smeal's beat-up POW body was too fragile for a physical fight, so he would rely on his gun. If they could start a fight with Greenie and Carlo, Smeal might try to shoot them. While Greenie and Carlo were ducking or stopping Smeal's bullets, they might be able to zigzag through the piles of garbage, leap down the drop-off, land in the pit, and make a dash toward the river.

Rafferty formed his hand into a gun and waved it toward Smeal. "If you want to conclude the entertainment part of the program, shoot him right now." He brushed his hands together. "We can bury him with the rest of the garbage."

The wisecrack broke the tension for a moment. Greenie tried not to laugh, but let out a giggle.

Carlo walked right up to Rafferty and yelled into his face. "Do you think you're some kind of a comedian?"

Rafferty shrugged. "Well," he said and tipped an imaginary top hat. "You did seem rather hard up for entertainment. And I know you won't shoot us

410

until you really know if the vault is here."

A hint of uncertainty filled Carlo's face. Freddy knew Carlo, wouldn't shoot until he was absolutely sure the vault was in the dump. Freddy figured he wouldn't be ducking bullets but would have to fight. He wasn't ready for a fight, but if he wanted a chance to live, he knew someone had to start one, and Rafferty could do it.

Carlo lifted his fist to strike. "I'll give you some entertainment."

Rafferty bowed his head. With doe eyes, he looked toward Carlo. "Before you do anything, could you do me a little favor?"

Carlo's forehead wrinkled with curious confusion. Freddy held up his hand. Rubbing his eyes, he signaled Neal to get ready.

"Do anything you want," Rafferty said. "But, Carlo, please don't talk to me when you have penis breath."

Carlo's jaw dropped and his face flushed with complete bewilderment.

Greenie broke into a huge horselaugh.

Although Rafferty was trying his best to be a sociable sort who could fit into Greenie's sick world and not be bothered by the threat of death, Freddy knew people like Carlo didn't like to be made fun of. He tensed for the onslaught.

Carlo turned his back to Rafferty, but suddenly wheeled around and pointed an Army issue, 45-caliber, semi-automatic right at Rafferty.

Carlo's face exploded into a full rage. "I don't care what you know or don't know about that vault." He viciously jerked his hand into the air. "We've had enough of your smart mouth."

Rafferty glanced at Router's body. Freddy did, too. For a moment, the smoke from the smoldering rag, floating around Router's head, made it look like his ghostly spirit was coming from his body. Imitating Router, Rafferty let out a thunderous sneeze. Carlo jerked his head toward the wisp of smoke coming from Router's head. As if seeing a ghost, his eyes flew wide open. But he kept the 45 pointed at Rafferty and fired once. His jittery hand and the buck of the 45 sent the round high over Rafferty's head. Instead of firing again, he tucked the 45 into his belt. Cussing under his breath, he reached into the bulldozer's toolbox, picked up a wrecking bar, and raised it over Rafferty's head. "You think that's funny? A bullet's not good enough for you."

As if he had just been injected with some kind of Jekyll and Hyde serum, Greenie's jovial demeanor instantly changed. In a rage, he threw Blondie's Colt at Rafferty. Rafferty ducked. The Colt flew under the bulldozer.

With his eyes glowing red, Greenie growled like a wild animal fighting for meat from a fresh kill. He reached out with his large left hand and grabbed the front of Rafferty's shirt. Then he drew his right arm back and made a fist.

Displaying his extraordinary cockiness, Rafferty defiantly looked into Greenie's face. "If you had any sense of decency you'd quit blowing your penis breath into my face."

With the wrecking bar clinched in his hand, Carlo stepped next to Greenie and stared at Rafferty. Carlo's eyes grew cold, ice-like, and distant. "Let me beat that smart mouth right off his face."

Greenie glanced at Carlo. "No way, he's—" His voice trailed off. Staring menacingly at Rafferty, he raised his clinched fist. "He's mine." He started his vicious swing, but he never landed the punch.

In a flash, Blondie stepped forward. Using the momentum of his step, he whipped his arm around and whapped the side of the Greenie's face with the back of his fist.

The force of the unexpected blow caused Greenie to let loose of Rafferty's shirt and rock backward. Holding his hand to the side of his face, his cheeks reddened with pain and humiliation. He reached into his shoulder holster, pulled out his chrome-plated Colt 38 and aimed it at Smeal. "Okay, hand it over. Now! Or you're all going to die."

Smeal pulled out his PPK and held it by the barrel with the handle facing Greenie. Just before Greenie touched it, Smeal did the old cowboy road agent spin. With his finger in the trigger guard, he let the PPK fall. In one quick motion, he rolled the PPK around, caught the handle in his palm, and pointed the barrel at Greenie. "Okay, you, drop it."

In a rare moment of surprised terror, Greenie let his Colt fall to the ground. Smeal pulled the trigger. The PPK didn't fire.

Rafferty looked at Carlo and let out a mocking laugh.

Carlo snapped his head around in Rafferty's direction. "You don't laugh at me."

Swinging the wrecking bar like a scythe, Carlo charged Rafferty. At the instant he lunged at him,

Rafferty dropped to his hands and knees. Unable to check his momentum, Carlo stumbled over him. The bar flew from Carlo's hands, and he went crashing, hands first into a pile of broken glass. Before he could get to his feet and use his bleeding hands to grab the bar, Freddy leaped on his back.

Like a bull rider on a mad bull, Freddy held the back of Carlo's shirt with one hand and clutched Carlo's sides of with the heels of his feet. With his other hand, he reached around and pulled the 45 from Carlo's belt. Before he could get his finger on the trigger, Greenie jumped up, grabbed the wrecking bar, and slung it at Freddy. Freddy saw it coming. He hung onto Carlo's back and dodged to the side. The wrecking bar hissed through empty air and whapped the 45 from Freddy's hand. Then Neal and Blondie were on Greenie.

Thwack! Thwack! Thwack! Smeal slammed his PPK on his thigh and jacked a shell into the chamber. Now he was ready to fire.

He aimed at Carlo.

Freddy pushed away from Carlo's back and landed on his feet. Smeal pulled the trigger, but, again, the gun failed. Seeing no threat from Smeal, Carlo turned back toward Freddy. With blood dripping from the cuts on his hands, he made a fist, wound up, and took a vicious swing. Freddy rolled under the speeding fist and stepped in close. With all his might, he smashed his fist up into Carlo's kidneys. Carlo let out a painful cry. Freddy knew he had caught him good. He stepped away, stood still, and watched.

Carlo grabbed his ribs and bent to one side. His deep-set dark eyes shone slimy and repellant, but the blood loss from his cut knees and cut hands seemed to be weakening him. He picked up a huge board with a nail in the end, charged, and swung, but missed. After a dozen fruitless swings, Carlo's tactics became futile. He panted and staggered. The violent exertions and the adrenaline overload seemed to have spent him, but Freddy wasn't taking any chances. He was going to finish him off.

Before he could deliver the final blows, the light from the bulldozer suddenly came on. A beam spilled over the ground preventing Freddy from seeing if friend or foe was operating it. He eyed Carlo for a weak spot. And there it was. Carlo was grasping his side. His midsection was wide open.

While training for boxing, Freddy had been hit with a heavy blow to his stomach. It had shut his whole midsection down. Great pain and a diaphragm spasm had caused him to fall to the ground and struggle to breathe. Later he had found out why. In the abdominal cavity, just behind the stomach's midsection, is the largest autonomic nerve center. A good hit in this celiac plexus, more commonly called the solar plexus, upsets the whole nervous system. Freddy needed to hit Carlo there. He loaded up. With all the strength he could muster, he let his fist fly right into Carlo's solar plexus. A painful huff of air escaped from Carlo's lungs. One of his knees buckled. Gasping for air, he clawed at his chest. Falling to the ground, he hit, face-first, into a foot-wide puddle of black greasy water.

With his hands on his knees, and sucking in much-needed breaths of air, Freddy looked up. Somehow Greenie had fought off Blondie, Neal, and Rafferty. Greenie now had his chrome-plated 38 Colt pointed at Neal. Before Greenie could pull the trigger, Freddy, prayed he could get another solar plexus shot. He screamed and rammed his head into Greenie's stomach. A painful whoosh flew out of Greenie's mouth. Greenie grabbed his stomach with his left hand. The Colt in his right hand swung down, hung from his finger for a second, and fell. It landed in a loose pile of cans, where it rattled down and out of sight.

Freddy jerked his head to the right. Neal took off running headlong around the bulldozer and through a lone patch of uprooted underbrush. In a flash, Freddy was right behind him glancing up to see who was on the bulldozer. It was Smeal, but he didn't seem to have any idea how to operate it. All he managed to do was turn on the lights.

Crossing the dump, like the others were doing, Freddy sprinted and zigzagged around mounds of garbage and broken glass piles. With the stench of sulfur in the air, his breath tore in and out of his lungs. As he ran, the dark grew thicker and the humid night air heavier. When his feet jangled across a stretch of lose cans, he scared out a few rats. They went running for cover in all directions.

At the edge of a steep embankment, a half-buried rag snagged his foot. He stopped his fall with his hands, but they splatted into a patch of yellow mud. While the mud oozed around his fingers, he held his body in a prone push-up position and looked down. Directly in front of him, the ground dropped off into a steep embankment and stopped at the bottom of the huge pit he had seen before. He pulled his hands out of the mud, jumped up, and began leaping down the side of the pit. After three painful thumps of his feet striking the side of the embankment, he was at the bottom. On almost level ground, he ran right next to Rafferty. "They're trying to kill us."

Huffing for a good breath of good air, Rafferty managed to blurt out, "You just noticed?" He sprinted away and out of Freddy's sight.

Above the embankment, a huge floodlight came on and illuminated the area. Freddy figured Smeal had finally figured out how to operate the bulldozer. He glanced up toward the light. Around the rim of the pit, huge piles of garbage perched thirty feet above his head. The bright lights coming from the bulldozer blinded his dark adjusted eyes, but he saw movement. Underneath the revealing blanket of white light, Greenie grabbed the seat of Smeal's pants, tossed him over the embankment, let out a huge mocking horselaugh, and yelled, "Get down there with the rest of the garbage."

Smeal tumbled over and over until he stopped twelve paces away from Freddy. As a small avalanche of loose garbage rolled down the hill, Smeal tried to dodge an old ringer-type washing machine, but his aging movements were too slow. The machine raced right for him. In a feeble defense, he held up his arms. Just as the heavy machine was about to crash into his body, it took a weird bounce and plopped into the yellow mud next to his left foot.

Covered with garbage, Smeal breathed a sigh of relief. And then, as if it were on a spring, the machine flopped over and whapped his foot, sending it into a slosh of soft gray clay. He turned to pull out his foot, but the suction held it firm. Up above, the bulldozer's diesel engine powered up, and black exhaust fumes spread over the air. Freddy realized Greenie was on the bulldozer. He was going to push the teetering mountain of garbage over the edge and burry them alive. He felt like a hopelessly trapped rat.

Looking up at the impending doom, Smeal yanked on his foot. Either he was too weak to pull it out, or it was wedged in something. He shook his fist and roared something at the bulldozer, but the sound of the racing diesel engine with a broken exhaust pipe drowned out his pleas for help. He aimed his PPK at Grennie and let loose with three shots. They harmlessly pinged off the bulldozer's huge steel blade. As a cloud of diesel fumes crawled down into the pit, Smeal looked to Freddy and pleadingly stretched out his hand.

Freddy took a step to run away, but stopped. If he let Smeal be covered with tons of garbage, that would be the end of him. He stared at Smeal's outstretched hand.

Neal called out from the darkness. "Blondie and Rafferty are already at the river. Leave him there."

Freddy broke into a trot. At the other side of the pit, he looked up. At the rim of the pit, silhouetted against the sky, Neal waved his arm in a hurry-up gesture.

Freddy clawed his way toward Neal's dark figure. When he made it to the top, Neal's dark figure vanished near a thicket of bushes. Freddy turned back and looked down into the pit. Sitting in a soup of filth, Smeal frantically pulled on his trapped leg.

Freddy couldn't bring himself to just let Smeal be buried alive. He looked toward the bulldozer. It was sitting in one place. Greenie wrestled with the control levers. Freddy figured they had jammed, giving him enough time to pull Smeal out. He leaped back into the pit and ran to Smeal.

Freddy had always thought of Smeal as an absolute idiot. But when looked into Smeal's eyes, pain from despair seemed to drop into infinity. As if he'd seen horrors no person should ever see, his eyes emanated the pleading eyes of refugee children Freddy had seen on posters, begging money for CARE Packages and posters showing pitiful eyes of starving kids filled with suffering and swollen stomachs from malnutrition, crying out for help. Whatever Smeal had experienced, it looked as if he had never come back to a normal life.

Above the pit, Greenie jammed the levers on the bulldozer back and forth. Looking toward the heavens, Freddy was thankful the bulldozer didn't move. When it did, Greenie would plow more garbage into a growing heap and push it into the pit.

The primitive part of Freddy's brain told him to forget about Smeal. Let him be covered by the growing mountain of garbage. No one would ever find him. Then the number of people trying to take the vault would be reduced by one. But he fought the temptation. Keeping an eye on the impending threat from above, he reached for Smeal's leg and pulled. It remained solid.

Above, a few bundles of bound newspapers rolled down the hill. Greenie had gotten the bulldozer to move again. One good push and the mountain of garbage would break free of its balancing point and tumble down on their heads. Freddy tipped the washing machine away from Smeal's foot and grabbed a broken board. Using it as a shovel, he dug the gray clay away from Smeal's foot. The shoe was pinched between a rock and an odd piece of rusted metal. He dug more clay away. Looking up at the bulldozer and holding his PPK at the ready, Smeal pulled on his own leg, but it stayed solid. Freddy dropped the board and looked around for something to use as a pry bar. Ten feet away, a bent pipe stood slanted in the ground. He went to it and pulled with both hands. It didn't move. With all his weight, he wiggled it from side to side. It slowly loosened. He squatted down. With both hands, he grabbed the pipe, pushed with his knees, and pulled. The pipe slid out of the mud. He rushed over to Smeal and jammed the pipe between the rock and the rusted metal. A bundle of bound newspapers flew past his head. He ignored it and pulled the pipe sideways. Smeal's foot still wouldn't budge. He tried again. The metal moved slightly but not enough to free the foot.

As dark flicking shadows of falling garbage jumped along both sides of them, Freddy reached down and untied Smeal's shoe. Above, the garbage mountain began to lose traction on its precipice. As pieces of garbage nipped at his heels and the back of his legs, the mountain's looming shadow tilted ominously above their heads.

Freddy bent over and yelled in Smeal's ear. "Okay, when I pull, pull your foot out. You'll lose your shoe, but we got to get out of here."

Chapter 30

At the bottom of the garbage pit, Smeal felt his foot being crushed solid. Searching for something he could use to free his foot, he looked up. The mountain of garbage was about to avalanche down and smoother him and Freddy. If he were younger, he would have the stamina to fight and get free, but booze and cigars had shortened his wind. There was no chance of escape. In a frantic dismissive gesture, he waved his hand in front of Freddy's face. "Leave me here. You'll get killed for helpin' people. Wise up. Get tough like me, or you'll get hurt."

A confused look filled Freddy's face.

Remembering how he had been treated every time he had tried to help his fellow POWs, Smeal continued. "Don't be a dummy. Look out for yourself, and nothin' will touch you."

Freddy didn't answer. He kept on trying to free Smeal's leg. Even though Smeal had conceded that he was about to die, watching Freddy try to save him had a calm and soothing effect on his mind, and he felt ashamed that he couldn't help. In the old days, simply by plunking down one hundred and seventy-five dollars, he would have bought a Thompson machine gun. It was considered a rifle and didn't require a permit. He would have slammed the one hundred round drum magazine into the gun. Right now, it would be in his hands. He wouldn't be holding a twenty-two caliber PPK. He'd be spitting forty-five caliber bullets at an incredible rate of eight hundred rounds per minute. Thriving on danger, his adrenaline and endorphins would be surging through his body. He would be on a high that only those who had been there, done that, understood. Greenie would be nowhere near the bulldozer, and Freddy and he wouldn't have to die.

Freddy took both hands and pushed on the pipe. The metal moved. As a gamey odor of meat, on the verge of rotting, filled the air, a rat ran alongside Smeal's body and across his ear that a rat had eaten half off at the POW camp. His old prisoner of war feelings jumped up from deep inside and took over his very soul. The calm soothing effect of watching Freddy trying to save him immediately vanished. The will to live renewed with a vengeance. Feeling his eyes grow wide with fright, he dropped his PPK, grabbed his leg with both hands, and pulled. Tremendous pain caused him to make a face and yell into the night. His piercing shriek and the bulldozer's laboring motor added to the confusion.

Freddy let out a long exasperated breath of air and stepped back. "Thanks a lot."

Smeal wondered why Freddy had jumped back. Then he looked down. In the sudden adrenalin rush, he had pulled his leg free, shoe and all.

Freddy bent over and scooped up the PPK.

Now that Smeal's leg was free and he knew Freddy had a gun to defend them, he felt the odds had evened a little.

Freddy stepped back toward Smeal. "If you want to get out of here, you got get up."

Still adrenalized, Smeal looked up and flashed Freddy a lopsided smile. But right above their heads the shadow of impending death from the threatening tons of garbage loomed large. As the bulldozer continued to plow more and more garbage toward the edge of the pit, tuffs of old carpet and dirty cotton-fluff, filled the air. The threatening mound teetered on the edge and began to fall.

Smeal tried to get to his feet and run, but his leg wouldn't move. He looked up and to his left. Neal, who could help, stood at the top of the other side of the pit, momentarily confused by what Freddy was trying to do. Freddy was the only person helping. Smeal had never seen such compassion in anyone. Confused, he looked up at Freddy. "Why are you doing this?"

"I don't really know," Freddy said. "I guess I care about people who live and breathe."

Smeal let what Freddy said sink in for a moment. For the first time since he had escaped from the POW camp, he realized that it was his own fear of getting hurt, cheated, or killed that made him shun friendships and kill anything that bothered him. He had never shared any memories from his POW life with anyone. All these years, he had been protecting himself. It had been all for himself. This Freddy kid had no fear or thought for his own safety. He was showing his kindest attention. From deep inside a hidden place, Smeal felt the need to stay sitting down and cry.

But he didn't have time to cry. The garbage should have buried them by now. To see why it hadn't, he looked skyward. Lights from the bulldozer illuminated wavering curtains of a heat mirage from the day's stored heat in the garbage. But he could see that the mountain of garbage was halfway down the hill. It seemed to be stuck, but was slowly moving. For a moment, he wondered if

Freddy was physically and mentally able to lay his life on the line for him.

As if it were a delayed reaction to his past experiences in the POW camp, Smeal's life of crime flashed before him. He didn't deserve to live, but Freddy did. He tried to move his leg. There was no feeling. He struggled to his feet and took one step. There was no control in his leg. He fell, face-first, into the garbage. Freddy reached down to help. Smeal rolled over and whipped his arm around in a threatening swat. "Get away. Save yourself."

Freddy hunkered down, took a handful of the front of Smeal's suit coat, and pulled him upright. "I *am* saving myself. But you're coming with me."

In one smooth motion, Freddy grabbed Smeal's elbow and picked him up in a fireman's carry. Smeal looked downward. Freddy's knees were sagging. With his chest on Freddy's shoulder, he could hear Freddy's heart pounding, and he felt Freddy's lungs heaving for air. Smeal figured Freddy would stop and drop him. But Freddy staggered on.

Above, Greenie cussed at the controls, and the bulldozer plowed into the moist yellow earth of the side of the cliff-like hill. Again and again, the bulldozer instantly responded to Greenie's commands. Without a trace of hesitation, it chewed the earth fighting to push the stuck pile onto Smeal and Freddy.

Neal yelled to Freddy from a thicket on the rim of the pit. "Get out of there."

Just as it seemed that one more push would topple the mountain of garbage, the bulldozer's blade hit something and stopped.

Smeal knew Freddy should drop him. Then he could easily flee the danger. If Freddy continue to hold him on his shoulder, Freddy could make no misjudgment. He had to make the right move. If he moved left, he could get stuck in the thick yellow mud. If he moved right, the pile would surely get them both. One more push, and the mountain of garbage would let loose and hurl toward them faster than Freddy could run.

Greenie backed up the bulldozer until he was at the top of the hill and stopped. With the engine idling, he yelled down at Smeal and Freddy, "Get ready to be buried in hell."

With a precisely measured jerk, he grabbed its control levers and slammed them forward. With the throttle wide open and black smoke streaming out of the exhaust stack, the bulldozer rushed down the steep embankment. The speed at impact would have been enough to jolt the mountain of garbage and send it down. But one side of the blade on the bulldozer struck something solid. The bulldozer swung around and tipped up. For a moment, it teetered on the edge of one of its treads, and its pounding engine slowed to a muffled throb.

Neal leaped down into the pit and ran to Freddy and Smeal. "Give me that gun."

With his free hand, Freddy pulled the PPK from his pocket and handed it to Neal. Neal aimed the PPK at Greenie and fired a succession of shots until it was empty.

Trying to dodge bullets, Greenie jumped off the bulldozer, but landed right in its path. Without a driver, and one tread getting traction and the other tread slipping, the heavy bulldozer made a sharp left turn. It appeared Greenie would not be hit. The heavy bulldozer tilted on one side, balanced for a moment. Then as if someone were directing one of the lights, it turned and beamed right on Greenie. With a dull flash of yellow, the bulldozer rolled onto him. The sound of ribs breaking cracked in the air. Blood and guts erupted from his side and slithered down the side of the pit into a soggy pile. Freddy's face paled, but Smeal, who had performed many brutal killings, stared grimly without displaying emotion, and the bloody head flopped off Greenie's shoulders and landed in the mud with a sickening plop. For a moment, an eerie plume of blue smoke danced in the bulldozer's lights. The lights slammed shut, and the bulldozer continued to roll down the steep cliff-like face. With garbage and the bulldozer avalanching right behind them, Freddy and Neal dragged Smeal up out of the pit.

Chapter 31

With Neal making a path and leading the way, Freddy carried Smeal on his back and walked along the thick brush boarding the Shanango River. At a small break in the vegetation and away from the dangers of the dump, he stopped and stood next to the flowing water. Here, Neal held up his hand and pointed to the inky path alongside the river.

With his body sagging under Smeal's weight, Freddy stopped for a moment, and felt the strength from the adrenal aftershock of having narrowly escaped death wearing off. He staggered a good twenty feet down the path. To catch his breath, he stopped next to a river willow. With Smeal still on his back, he leaned forward and braced his tired arms on a low-hanging tree limb. Thick vegetation and trees captured any breeze that would clear the night's warm muggy air.

As if he had just awakened out of a deep sleep, Smeal muttered, "Let me down."

Freddy let him slide down off his shoulder. Smeal stood but it was with effort like an old man whose legs did not work as well as they once did, especially after a great deal of excitement. Freddy watched the low midst on the river. Like spirit fingers, the midst's fringes crawled over the water and rolled up onto the shore. It would be difficult to see anyone who might be chasing them.

Blondie shouldered his way through a tangle of low lying tree branches, came up to Freddy, and stopped. He violently jerked his finger at Smeal. "He's nothing but a cheap thug trying to use other people for his own gains. Why didn't you let him get buried?"

Standing off to the side, Rafferty made obscene gestures with his right hand for the benefit of Smeal, who could not see him.

For a moment, the moonlight illuminated Smeal's haggard face. A look of realization seemed to fill it, but he didn't say a word. He doubled over, coughing, tears flowing from his eyes, and snot running over his mouth and down the front of his chin.

As Freddy watched the coughing seizure, he didn't know why he hadn't let Smeal get buried. Maybe it was because Smeal looked like he was dying. But he didn't know what to tell the others about his sudden affection for Smeal's well-being. When Smeal quit coughing, Freddy figured that if he used some of Rafferty's humor it might smooth out the situation.

Before he could say anything, Neal stepped out of the fog. "We don't really know why we saved him," he said and smiled. "We figured it would be okay just as long as we didn't make a nightly ritual out of it."

Blondie's forehead wrinkled with confusion. "I don't get your drift."

"Let me explain," Neal said and pointed to Smeal. "Greenie and Carlo double-crossed him. As I see it, now he has to be on our side."

As if thinking about it, Blondie nodded. "You might be right." He jerked his head in the direction of the dump. "With Carlo and Greenie still up there, we'll need all the help we can get."

Freddy stared at the trees and brush that concealed the dump. "We don't have to worry about Greenie. When he was trying to burry us, he got in a big hurry. The bulldozer tipped over and smashed him."

Blondie's eyes swiveled left then right. Just beyond the fog, a wall of trees and underbrush loomed dark and threatening. "What about Carlo?"

"I don't know. The last time I saw him, he was bent over holding his stomach."

"Don't let that fool you," Blondie said with defiant mistrust. "He's still got a gun, maybe even a couple of them. And he won't hesitate to use them."

Freddy reached into his pocket. "We got one too." He pulled out Smeal's PPK."

Smeal reached for it.

Blondie knocked his hand away and took the PPK. "Don't get that thing near him. He'll shoot us all."

Freddy stared into Smeal's eyes trying to figure out if he could trust him.

Chapter 32

Cloaked in the mist of the Shenango River, Smeal turned his back to Freddy. Feeling a few arthritic joints pop, he gritted his teeth, and held in a moan. Like a streak of fire, knife-like pain shot up his leg that had been trapped in the mud. But pain was nothing new. Injuries from his POW days ached every minute of every day. Sometimes it took all his self-control not to show the effects of his agony, but he never once allowed others to see the pain he constantly suffered.

As the pain subsided, he hunched his shoulders, and tried to figure out the best way to stay alive. Now that Greenie was dead, Carlo surely feared he would be next. But regardless of how scared he was, Carlo was like the people he hung around with: He feared what he hated, and what he hated, he killed. For a moment, Smeal felt a hint of compassion for Carlo and hoped that he would just go away. But he knew if he let his feelings control his thoughts and actions, Carlo could kill them all at any moment.

Fighting overseas had forced Smeal to learn how to control his feelings when there was a job to be done. Back then, if he started feeling too much, it didn't matter how much nerve he had, the nervous tension would build up and confuse him. When he had seen the enemy use little boys and girls as shields, a man standing next to him, had let his feelings cause a split second of hesitation. The man's hesitation had been a very stupid thing to do, and it caused him to be shot. After that, Smeal learned not care about anything or anybody.

The atrocities of the war, the scent, and the stench of the POW camp were forever tattooed in his mind. Since his discharge from the military, his dreams had been mixed with things he had done during and after the war, but he still controlled his feelings. He never got close or became friends with anyone. If he would have made a single friend or started to care about others, he wouldn't be able to shoot his targets in the back of the head, right behind the ear, and at a decent range so the blood wouldn't splatter back on him.

Carlo was out there in the dark and would shoot without the slightest bit of hesitation, and Blondie's remark, "He's nothing but a cheap thug trying to use other people for his own gains," played on Smeal's mind. Even though he did use other people, his business had made no allowances for friends. In combat he had suppressed the empty feelings he had suffered when his friends had been killed. This had caused him to have very little feelings for others. People around him weren't really real. They were only objects. Whatever happened to them was not important, but it caused his empty feeling to grow. If he wanted his empty feelings to end, he would have to start to care about someone, but that could be dangerous. And to make matters worse, a place inside his heart, nobody had touched since his POW days, yearned to be touched. He didn't know if it was because of Freddy and Neal's kindness of saving his miserable life, or if it was because he was nearing judgment day. But he did know if he were finally going to be able to put the inner demons and the raging psychosis from the past behind him and start a new path, he would need a least one friend. Helping Freddy would at least start him on the long road to healing.

As Blondie's penetrating blue eyes seemed to be searching Smeal's very soul, he reached up and pushed on his shoulder. Waving the PPK around, he said, "I'll bet you would like to get your hands on this thing and blow us away."

Feeling a strange pain welling in his chest, Smeal didn't answer. For some reason, unknown to him, his hands began to tremble. His body shook and sweat rolled down his face.

Freddy crossed his arms and looked Blondie in the eye. "I don't think he would do that."

Blondie looked at him as if he were off his rocker or turning soft, but Freddy's defense of Smeal caused him to have something he hadn't had in years: True feelings for another human being. It wasn't so much the words but the compassion in Freddy's eyes. As if jarring him out of a fitful sleep, the ever-occurring sounds of his nightmares erupted from someplace place deep in his mind. But this time, the sounds of armed Japanese prison personnel, on noisy motorbikes, continually driving past his narrow feces-filled cage, melding with the screaming of complex languages, he could not understand, and the never-ending static erupting sporadically from the metal speakers on wooden poles, stopped.

Suddenly, a flood of pent-up compassion swept over him. Trying to give Blondie an answer, he opened his mouth. But he couldn't talk. Instead, he sobbed, quietly at first, but it grew until his body quit shaking and his hands stopped trembling. He didn't like to be seen crying in front of anyone, but

432

he couldn't help it. And to make it worse, Blondie, Neal, and Rafferty were staring at him. He turned his tear-filled face and looked to Freddy.

Freddy placed his hand on Smeal's back. "It'll be all right. Take a deep breath."

Smeal felt confused. What did a kid like Freddy know about anything? He wanted to tell Freddy to get his crummy hand off his back, and that he wasn't some kind of a baby that needed comforting, but his voice wouldn't work. He shook more.

"When my father died," Freddy softly said, I didn't cry or even shed a single tear." He stepped close and whispered. "I didn't want to show I was weak, so I kept all my feelings inside."

Smeal felt something he hadn't felt since he was a little kid. Tears forming in his eyes. Not wanting anyone to see, he turned his head down.

"Take a deep breath," Freddy said again and waited for Smeal to do it.

Smeal took a deep breath. His trembling slowed.

Freddy continued. "If you're like me, you kept your emotions bottled up for a long time, but that doesn't mean you don't have any." He waved his hand in the air and raised his voice. "Hell, everybody has emotions. Yours just came out in a rush in the end, just like mine did. It's no big deal."

Looking down at the dark ground, Smeal whispered in h harsh voice, "I couldn't just turn the killing off." He paused. "During the war, we would talk about the things we were going to do when we came home. Hank was going to open an ice cream stand. Ice cream was one thing we could

433

never get. Hank said we would be able to come and eat all the ice cream we wanted. But he got his head blown off. Frankie planned to live by the sea, charter fishing boats. We could fish for free anytime. Frankie stepped on a mine, blew himself into a thousand pieces."

The empty feeling he had suppressed for years crept into Smeal's chest. He lifted his head. "All I wanted was a friend that wouldn't get killed, but I lost too many friends to count. So I didn't want any friends."

Rafferty attempted to shatter the glum mood with merriment. "What are we going to do? Stand here all night and cry?"

Smeal stopped trembling and realized that even though Freddy was a kid, he may have something here. Freddy may actually be the friend he had been looking for since he had gotten out of the army. His mind cleared. The harshness left his voice. A slight smile formed on his lips. He nodded to Rafferty.

"You're right. We have things to do."

Again Blondie waved Smeal's PPK in front of Smeal. "You want this, don't you?"

Smeal looked to Blondie. "I'm not going to shoot anyone," he said, his voice cracking from being on the verge of crying. "I couldn't if I wanted to." He swallowed to stop the tears and looked to Neal. "You shot all the bullets at Greenie. I had an extra magazine, but it must've fallen out when I rolled down the hill."

Blondie turned the PPK over and looked in the bottom of the pistol's grip. "He's right. The magazine's gone, and there's no bullet in the chamber." He patted the pocket of his suit coat. "I have a few 38's, but they won't fit. This thing takes 22 long rifles." He looked to Smeal. "You sure you don't have some loose bullets somewhere?"

Smeal felt his pockets. "Nothing." Searching for Carlo, he peered into the darkness. "We better get out of here."

"Carlo's only one man," Neal said. "We should be able to outmaneuver him."

Smeal knew better. He shook his head. "Carlo's not your usual thug. He's a sleazy weasel. He'll sneak around. If he can't get us himself, he'll go get help."

Pacing and gesturing with his hands, Neal looked toward the dump. "If somebody makes enough noise, Carlo will come down here."

"What do we want him down here for?" Rafferty asked with alarm. "Are we going to put on a vaudeville act for him?"

Neal flashed Rafferty a dazzling smile. "Yeah, you're going to star in it. Maybe you can make him laugh to death."

Ignoring Neal and Rafferty's attempted humor, Smeal searched his mind for a way to eliminate Carlo. He knew if he were alone, he could remain silent until Carlo couldn't stand it any longer. Then Carlo would expose himself and make an easy target. But neither Neal nor Rafferty could sit still long enough to do that, and besides, they didn't have any bullets. Then he thought about how he had created a ruckus and escaped from the POW camp. "Why don't we create a diversion?"

"Good idea," Neal said. "One guy could sneak around and get the car."

"Good idea?" Rafferty questioned and fretfully

looked around. "Who's going to stay here and make noise?"

As if a great strain had been lifted from Smeal's head, he no longer felt he could solve every problem by killing it. "You saved my life," he said and bowed his head. "The least I can do is save yours."

Blondie tilted his head back, lowered his eyes, and studied Smeal. "I don't know if we can trust you. It smells like a double cross."

Smeal lifted his head. "I can't blame you for not trusting me. But what do you have to lose? I have no gun and Carlo does. You'll be out of here by the time he gets down here."

Blondie tilted his head to the side. "What about the vault? You still looking for a percentage?"

"I don't know what happened the last time, but if I live through this, I'll give you a better deal than before."

"Why would you do that now?"

For the first time since Smeal had been captured and became a POW, he felt embarrassed. He looked to Freddy and Neal. "Since I got out of the Prisoner of War Camp, you two guys are the only ones who ever helped me." His embarrassment was quickly replaced with anger. He rubbed his forehead and continued. "And besides, I didn't know the vault weighed over two thousand pounds."

"Hey, wait a minute," Rafferty said. "How do you know how much it weighs?"

Smeal let a small smile form on his lips. "You don't get to live as long as I have without covering all your bases. I know you were going to

436

Radkowski's bar to try and cash it in for less than what it's worth."

Freddy stared dazedly at Smeal. "You have a long reach. Is there anything you don't know?"

Smeal offered his right hand. "There are a lot of things I don't know, but right now, I'd like to shake your hand for saving my life."

Freddy reached and grasp his hand. Smeal immediately felt the hidden strength of Freddy's youth. Wanting Freddy to live a long life, he let go of his hand and looked toward the dump. "You know, if you don't get out of here, and fast, Carlo will be down here and use us for target practice."

Neal held up his hand. "Nobody gets left behind. We know the area. He doesn't."

Neal's act of kindness and concern caused a tear to well up in Smeal's chest. For years he had used people as if they were tools. After they were of no value to him, he had thrown them away. Until this moment, he pitied people that had morals and principles. As far as he was concerned, those poor misguided suckers believed in a perfect world and chased dreams that would never be. But the big problem was that years of loneliness had been his reward for his lifestyle. He had never breached the chasm that separated revenge and a trusting friendship. But now, these kids had shown him that even in an imperfect world, dreams could come true. They deserved a chance to chase their dream, but he wasn't sure they had enough deep down desire to do it.

Freddy was strong, but he didn't have an overly muscular body. He emanated an inner strength and a no-quit attitude. If he lived long enough, some day he would become an old smart bull. He was a person anyone could trust, the type of person who wouldn't have a second thought about jumping on an unexploded grenade to save others.

Smeal took a deep breath and exhaled. "I've stared at the Devil and spit in his eye once too often. My time to die is approaching fast. It wouldn't matter much if I stayed here and let Carlo shoot me, but too many people know about the vault. You need me to cash it in, and we have to do it fast."

"We don't need you," Blondie said. "We can take the vault to Radkowski's bar all by ourselves."

"Sure you can. But the guy that's buying it is a gyp. He may not give you a dime." He held up a finger. "And... if he does, he won't give you a fourth of what it's worth."

"So how much can you get for it?"

"I know a guy that will give us a million for it."

Rafferty cupped his hand to ear and stepped close to Smeal. "How much?"

"One million dollars," Semal said hoarsely. "I'm only looking for enough money to last me until I kick the bucket. After the vault's cashed in, there'll be more than enough money to do that."

Neal hooked his thumbs in the sides of his pants pockets and cocked his head with suspicion. "The vault's only worth eight-hundred-forty-thousand. Why would anybody give you more for gold that's illegal to own?"

"The guy that's putting up the money is some kind of a kook. He claims he's a descendant of Egyptian royalty and wants to be buried in a gold vault."

Blondie slowly nodded. "If that guy's a kook,

he better be a rich one."

"No problem," Smeal said and grinned with satisfaction. "He's giving cash with no questions asked."

Neal peered into the darkness. "That all sounds just swell, but we got to get out of here first."

"We're faster and smarter that Carlo," Freddy said with confidence. "We can throw sticks and rocks, and make all kinds of noise. We'll make him look like a dog chasing its own tail. It'll be easy to get away. And besides, he can't see us in this fog."

"We'll get away, if we run," Neal said and placed his hand on Smeal's shoulder. "No offence, old timer, but you're too old to run." He looked at Smeal's foot. Even though it had come out of the mud with a shoe on it, now the shoe was gone. "And even if you could run, you only have one shoe." He turned and faced Blondie and Rafferty. "You guys take Smeal, cut around the dump, and come back up by the bridge and wait. After we get Carlo out of the way, me and Freddy will get the Oldsmobile and pick you up."

"I don't know," Smeal said shaking his head. "Carlo's a good shot. You sure you'll be all right?"

Neal waved his hand down. "Nothing to it. While Carlo's chasing his tail, we'll circle back and get the car."

A mosquito with a high-pitched whine flitted next to Smeal's face. He waved it away. "Carlo's used to vertical targets," he said with concern. "He'll be looking for somebody standing upright. Stay low and he probably won't see you."

Rafferty held up one finger. "Can I make a suggestion?"

439

Irritation filled Neal's face. "What?"

"Before you circle back and get the car, why don't you look for Smeal's shoe?"

Shaking his head in disbelief, Blondie smiled and held up the keys to his Oldsmobile. "You think you'll need these?"

"Well, ahem," Neal said. "It would save a little trouble."

Blondie flipped him the keys. He caught them. With Freddy right behind him, Neal vanished into the dark.

Rafferty took a hold of Smeal's arm and gestured toward the riverbank. Flanked by Blondie and Rafferty, Smeal started down the hazy path. After a few steps, Rafferty turned back. "My hair's wet," he said. "Why don't we wait until Carlo is close enough to breath down my neck and dry my hair?"

Smiling, Neal shook his head and pointed to the path. "Get moving."

Smeal's shoeless foot hurt, but his legs and whole body ached, too. He wanted to lie down in a warm bed or sit on his front porch in the sun. But in the POW camp he had survived worst. He had lived like a sewer rat, fighting and clawing, outwitting those stronger than himself, and his sheer will to live had enabled him to survive where others had quit. With Blondie and Rafferty supporting him, and with the knowledge that what worked once would work again, he trudged into the cover of the dark fog.

Chapter 33

Standing on the dark path, at the riverbank below the dump, Freddy watched Smeal and the others. With their heads and bodies bowed, they dashed along and wove their way through brush. Freddy could see that the recent near death and life experiences must have taken a toll on the old gangster. Like a person with numerous broken bones, Smeal's ancient stooped-over body seemed to be racked with pain. As Smeal and the others attained the sanctuary of the thick trees along the river, they blended into the darkness.

Freddy looked to Neal. "You want to wait here for Carlo?"

Neal held up his hands in a halting gesture. "No way, man. Guys like Carlo don't know that distances look shorter than they really are in the dark, and they take so much dope, it makes them afraid of the dark. He'll be waiting by the car."

Freddy nodded in agreement. "It's a smart move, but why didn't you tell Smeal?"

"I still don't trust him."

Freddy remembered the pleading helpless look in Smeal's eyes just before he carried him away from the avalanching garbage. "I think we can."

"Why?"

"Just a gut feeling," Freddy said and thought about it. "Actually, more than that. It's like when you see a dog, and right away you can tell if it's going to bite you."

"I know the feeling."

"Something really bad must've happened to Smeal, and it made him hate everybody. But he might be okay now."

"You may have something there," Neal said with a crafty gleam in his eye. "If he was in the War, maybe he got battle fatigue or some kind of delayed reaction."

"I hope we don't have to put him in the nut house before we cash in the vault."

Neal pushed a low tree branch out of his path. "Me too. But first, we have to get past Carlo."

After they slipped around the fringes of the shadows of the dump, they stopped behind a ten-foot high pile of broken glass. While they surveyed the area to their right, the never-ending, stinking vapors swirled up from the bacteria-generated heat of the rancid steaming dump and clinking and tinny sounds of rats scampering over cans and bottles, seemed to be a prelude to some kind of sick symphony. In the distance, one of the spotlights on the tall post had died, spilling gloom over half the dump and Router's body.

Carlo stood in the fringes of the dim light. The long orange glow of the ash on his cigarette moved to his mouth. Holding the cigarette between his thick lips, he reached into his back pocket and took out a pint bottle of Four Roses whiskey. He took a deep pull and wiped his mouth with the back of his hand. After taking a deep-in-the-lung drag from his cigarette and making the long orange ash even longer, he blew smoke into the night. In his other hand, he waved his pistol around, pointing it at every sound. The running feet of a rat tinkled across a pile of tin cans. With both arms outstretched and looking straight ahead, Carlo held his gun in both hands and moved his body from right to left. With streaming strings of his cigarette smoke curling before his eyes, he lifted his ruddy, sweltering intoxicated face and stared ponderously at the pile of cans sitting atop of old newspapers, abandoned clothing, and a splash of maggot-ridden, uneaten food.

Freddy couldn't believe how heartless Carlo was. He didn't even try to see if, Greenie, his so-called buddy, was all right.

Like leapfrogging soldiers, Freddy and Neal separately advanced to forward positions and took turns watching Carlo's actions until they were in front of Blondie's Oldsmobile.

Freddy opened the passenger door and slid into the front seat. Neal opened the driver's side door, started to get behind the wheel, but stopped and held up his hand. "Watch for Carlo. If he comes, turn the headlights on. It should blind him just long enough for us to get away."

Neal guardedly stepped to Carlo's blue '58 Chevy and silently lifted the hood. With sparks showering around his hand, he ripped out a fistful of wires in the motor compartment.

The crack of a pistol cut the still night.

Freddy looked toward Carlo.

From a hundred yards away, Carlo began running toward Neal.

Neal sprinted back to the Oldsmobile. Freddy reached around the steering wheel and felt for the headlights. Before he could find them, Neal jumped behind the wheel. His grin blossomed into a big confident smile. "He can't follow us now."

Wide eyed, Freddy stared at Carlo rushing toward them. "Yeah but he can shoot us."

Neal turned the ignition key. The engine caught and exploded with a loud roar. He let off the gas. "I didn't know this thing had this much power." He hooked first gear. Thirty yards away, Carlo tripped over a dark mass. He jumped back up. Waving his pistol, he came running down the path the bulldozer had cut. An orange muzzle flash followed a zinging sound of a bullet from his gun.

Freddy gasped. "This thing can't outrun a bullet."

Neal grimaced. "I think he's going to shoot us."

Without warning — Awwck! Carlo cried out and grabbed his throat. His feet flew out in front of him. Thump! He fell onto his back. A great gush of air whooshed out his open twisted mouth.

Freddy rubbed his eyes to make sure he saw what he saw. "What happened?"

Neal flashed Freddy a glowing grin of self-satisfaction. "It's a good thing I ripped that no trespassing sign off when we first came in." He giggled with nervous joy. "Carlo just ran into the cable."

Freddy looked toward the dark sky. "Somebody must be on our side."

Rubbing his throat, Carlo stood up. With his face filled with befuddlement and disillusion and pieces of wet garbage clinging to his pants and the front of his shirt, he took careful aim. Freddy braced for the bullet of death to come through the windshield and end his quest for the vault.

Neal hit the high beam headlights. Strong light shot though the darkness. Carlo held up his arm to shield his eyes from the harshness of the unexpected burning brightness. His back pocket, where he had placed the glass pint of Four Roses whisky, was wet and speckled with shards of glass. Around him, loose rubble, strewn on the bulldozer's path, cast threatening shadows, but the pile of broken glass glinted like tiny diamonds. Neal cut the wheel to the left and tromped on the accelerator. With the back wheels shooting dirt and stones in Carlo's direction, the Oldsmobile spun into a one hundred eighty degree turn and raced down the dump's yellow dirt road. When the car hit the state highway, Freddy watched in the rearview mirror.

Looming in a cloud of yellow dust, the rusted out '57 Ford that had been at the Green Parrot Tavern blinked its headlights. Its tires smoked and screamed across the asphalt.

Wham! Freddy was slammed back against the seat. As breath whooshed from his mouth, his head jerked back as if his neck were about to snap off. The Ford had rammed right into the back bumper of the Oldsmobile.

Freddy shook his head, turned, and squinted at the man behind the windshield of the Ford. The man tried to clinch his teeth, but his front teeth were gone. Neal had kicked them out. It was the square-jawed man from the fight on the road. Panic rose inside Freddy. He tugged on Neal's elbow. "Don't let that toothless troll in that piece of junk catch us."

Neal depressed the clutch and downshifted into second gear. "Let's see what we can do."

He stepped down on the accelerator. The big block engine screamed in protest. The two four-barrel carburetors kicked in and let out an ear-shattering moan. A surge of raw power transferred to the wheels and the positive traction rear-end commanded both back tires to grip the pavement. Rolling in a haze of blue smoke, they squealed like a gigantic river rat escaping sudden death. The Oldsmobile effortlessly climbed the steep hill, headed away from the dump, and dropped down the other side. The Ford hopped over the top of the hill and smashed down. Snaking from side to side, its underside grated against the asphalt, sending sparks behind it.

Although the Oldsmobile's accelerator was already flat to the floor, Neal stomped on it. As the wind whipped through the open window of the Oldsmobile, the Ford wallowed behind until its headlights paled in the distance.

Under the beams of the zooming headlights, tall grass at the side of the road whooshed to a blur. As the speed odometer climbed past the one hundred mark, Freddy felt exhilaration and then fear. When Neal hit overdrive, the duel throaty exhaust pipes of the Oldsmobile roared with contentment. Although the speed odometer needle pegged at the one hundred twenty mark, the Oldsmobile's powerful engine had plenty more to give. But up ahead, the road split into five directions.

When Freddy realized where they were, he leaned sideways and to Neal. "God Almighty!" he said with disbelief. "We're almost at Five Points."

Neal eased on the brakes. But the car was traveling so fast the brakes seemed to have no effect. He downshifted but didn't let out the clutch until the speed odometer crawled down to thirty-five. The powerful engine protested, slowed, and the Oldsmobile rolled through the five point

Intersection. Neal turned out the lights, spun the steering wheel to the left, and killed the engine. The Oldsmobile silently coasted into a parking lot and came to a stop in the pitch-black driveway behind the Five Points Café.

Trying to calm his nerves, Freddy leaned back in the seat and put his hands behind his head. Watching out the side window, he and Neal waited.

Out on the road, the brake lights on the Ford blazed red. It stopped at the intersection. As if the square-jawed man inside were trying to figure out which way to go, he hesitated. Then he took the road to the right.

Neal stared at the Ford's taillights until they vanished into the dark. Then he turned to Freddy and nodded. "I knew he would do that."

Freddy took his hands from behind his head and sat upright. "What are you a mind reader?"

"Not really, but when two equally attractive bales of hay are put in front of a jackass, he'll always picks the one on the right."

"What's that got to do with it?"

"In case the jackass can't decide which one to eat, it's nature's way of keeping it from standing in one spot and starving to death." He motioned toward the road. "There was a jackass in the Ford. I knew he would turn right."

Neal pulled out of the parking lot and pointed the Oldsmobile back toward the way they had come.

At the bridge, below the dump, he slowed. Rafferty, Blondie, and Smeal came hustling up from the side of the cement bridgehead.

Neal stopped and opened the doors. The trio piled in. The Oldsmobile's big engine carried them

447

away.

Tomorrow they would cash in the vault.

Chapter 34

The next morning, at ten minutes to six, Freddy sat in the back seat of Blondie's Oldsmobile in the dirt parking lot of Radkowski's Bar. As if it were an omen, a burst of golden sunlight broke through the clouds.

Although the golden sunlight gave him hope, Freddy scanned the area for possible hidden thugs intent on stealing the vault. Seeing none, he focused on the electric sign in the front window of the clapboard sided building. Neon purple and white glass letters spelled out Beer and Liquor. But the black and white cardboard sign behind the green wood screen door read,

CLOSED

"Check around the back of this place," Smeal said businesslike.

With his hand on the door handle of the Oldsmobile, and poised to get out, Neal shaded his eyes against the brightness of the new day and looked toward the bar. "Do you expect trouble?"

Smeal craned his neck to look around the side of the building. "We're trying to pick up a million dollars selling illegal gold for more than it's worth. We'd be stupid not to expect trouble."

Blondie followed his gaze. "Any sign of trouble and we're outta here."

Two minutes later, Neal had circled the building and was back in the car.

"Anybody around back?" Smeal asked.

"Didn't see a soul."

"Okay," Smeal said and turned to look out the back window.

Across the street, three cars pulled into the dirt parking lot and stopped. The men inside didn't get out, but one raised his arm and looked at his wristwatch.

Freddy hunched over the front seat. "How are we going to make a deal to sell the vault when the place is closed, and there are three cars with guys in them watching us?"

"No problem," Smeal said. "Radkowski's bar always opens at six. Those guys are probably working day turn in the mill. They'll go in for breakfast. Later on, midnight turn fellows will come in for a few beers and a baloney sandwich."

Leaning toward Smeal, Neal impatiently rolled his opened hand. "Come on. Let's get this show on the road. We didn't come here to eat baloney sandwiches."

"That's true," Smeal said with undaunted calmness. "But there are too many people looking for a ticket out of their dead end lives. We have to make sure someone isn't trying to horn in on our deal. The owner knows everybody that comes in. If a stranger comes in, he'll let us know. This place is a good front to seal the deal.

Across the street, the three men in the cars opened their doors and walked to the front door of the bar. They stopped on the stoop. A muscular man with arms like railroad ties reached into his pocket and handed out cigarettes. They all lit up off one match. Then making gestures with their hands and laughing, they blew smoke into each other's faces and talked.

Freddy didn't like the way they looked. He turned toward Smeal. "Three on a match is bad luck. You sure those guys are all right?"

Smeal let out a discouraged breath of air. "Those guys walk like they want to get things done. They probably work on a production line where they have to work fast. By habit they have little wasted movements. Those guys are like trained monkeys. They think they work for a living, but they're only wasting their lives away."

At exactly six a.m., the owner opened the front door to the bar, reached up, and flipped the closed sign over. Now it read,

OPEN

The muscular man placed his hand on the worn handle of the green screen door and pulled. As the door opened, the skinny spring that kept the door closed, stretched and let out a screech. The three men entered the bar. Behind them, the screen door slapped shut.

Anxious to get out, Neal placed his hand on the door handle of the Oldsmobile. "We going in?"

Smeal lowered his head and looked down. "Don't be so eager to get the vault that you become irrational."

As if agitated by having to wait, Neal's face grimaced with discomfort. "What's that got to do with anything?"

Smeal answered without looking up. "An irrational man can turn into a panicked man. When he does, it's easy to take him out." He lifted his head and turned toward Neal. "Let's wait for a few minutes, make sure no one's snooping around."

Neal nervously tapped his foot on the floor of the Oldsmobile and looked to Smeal. "That vault's worth a lot of money. I hope you know what you're doing."

Blondie glanced at Smeal and then looked at Neal. "He better know what he's doing. I don't need another trip into the river."

Smeal gave Blondie a reassuring nod. "We should have all the bases covered this time." Keeping his hand on his thigh, he lifted one finger. "But in this business, you never know."

As if getting impatient, Blondie leaned back in the seat and exhaled a stream of air. "That's why we're not going after the vault until we have at least half the money in our hands."

Smeal nodded in understanding.

Neal opened the door and scanned the area. No other cars were in the parking lots. He rubbed his hands together and gestured toward the bar. "Let's get this thing done."

"Wait a minute," Blondie said. "Don't forget to make the buyer uneasy."

Neal opened his door, placed his foot on the parking lot ground to get out but stopped. He turned toward Blondie. "What do you want us to do? Grab him by the throat?"

Smeal's face grimaced with discomfort. "No! It's better if you make him think you're going to do it. The threat always last longer than the act."

"I get it," Neal said and placed his hand on the door to stand up. "Even though we'll be in there alone, if we act like we have people outside or in the bar, it'll make the buyer think we have back up."

Blondie's manner took on a shrewd and significant air. "Even if you don't know someone in the bar, act like you do. Nod or signal them with your hand."

Neal's forehead wrinkled with apprehension. "What if they come over and want to talk?"

"Don't worry about it," Blondie said and opened his door. "People are usually too busy trying to figure out if they know you. They don't want the embarrassment of not knowing your name. They will stay where they are or act like they are too busy to talk to you."

They all got out of the car and started toward the screen door. Freddy followed and was the last to enter. On the right, the bar stretched to the other side of the room. Directly across from his elbow, a wire rack, filled with Wise potato chips with a little blue owl on the snack size bags offered a tasty treat. Next to that, a slanted shelf not only offered Hostess Snowballs and Twinkies that mill workers would buy, place in their metal lunchboxes and take to work, it also created a little privacy area for a black rotary phone.

On the left, men's work jackets hung on brass coat hooks that had been screwed into posts on the sides of the wooden booths with high backs. Square tables with various colors of tablecloths and wooden chairs, dotted the open area. A cloth curtain hung across the door to the kitchen and back room. At the center of the bar, the three workingmen from the parking lot huddled with soft mill worker hats on their heads eating the special of the morning: eggs and peppers.

The muscular man with arms like railroad ties swiveled on his bar stool and smiled at Smeal. "How's it goin'?"

Freddy cringed. He knew what Smeal was

453

going to say before he said it. And he hated it.

"Oh, just great," Smeal said, slipping into the vernacular of the mill environment. "What turn ya' workin'?"

"Just started day turn," the man replied as if it were the most important thing in the world. "Was sure glad to get off that graveyard shift."

Freddy thought it was a waste of time repeating week after week the insignificant information of what turn a person was working. More than ever he wanted to cash in the vault and never have to work in any mill.

Smeal's face took on a look of shared sorrow. "Yeah, I wouldn't wish midnight turn on anybody."

"It's a living," the man said, swiveled on the stool, and went back to eating his peppers and eggs.

Smeal turned toward the bartender. The bartender gestured to the curtain that led to the back room. A man with pure black hair swept back in a high pompadour walked out from out behind the bar and flapped his hand at the curtains. They swept aside. He stepped through the doorway. The curtains closed behind him.

Smeal walked to the curtain. With his hand on his shoulder holster, he whooshed the curtain aside and stood in the doorway.

Freddy looked over Smeal's shoulder and into the room. Off to the left and out of earshot, the man with the pompadour sat at a single table. His dark umber eyes glared out from his round face. No tablecloth that could conceal a man's hand on a gun hung from the sides of the table.

Smeal looked right, then left, then walked to the table and sat next to the man. Freddy, Rafferty, and Blondie piled into the room and pulled chairs up to the table. Neal closed the curtain. As if he were guarding the entrance, he crossed his arms, and leaned against the wall.

As the man looked around the room, his mouth flashed white perfect teeth. "Hey," he said and playfully pointed to Smeal. "You're a popular guy."

Keeping a stone face, Blondie shifted his eyes toward Smeal. "His reputation precedes him."

"Yeah, but he's not as popular as the man who used to sit in this chair." The man bent his head downward, lifted his hand, and pointed to the chair he was sitting on. "Yep, John Dillinger sat right here." He lifted his head and smiled. "That old jackrabbit taught the owner of this place how to play cards right at this table."

Nodding reluctantly, Blondie looked at the man. "Sorry, pal, but we didn't come here for a history lesson."

The man's jovial demeanor turned cold. "No need to make this unpleasant. You got the merchandise?"

Smeal directed an angry stare at the man. "If we didn't, we wouldn't be here. Where do you want it?"

"Take it to the old celery farm on Route 846. There will be a tow truck. It will unload it. After you leave, we'll take it from there."

Neal held out his hand. "What about the money?"

"We'll pay you after the vault's delivered."

Blondie stiffened his spine and sat upright. "We didn't come here to see you act like an idiot."

455

The man stared blankly at him. "I didn't mean anything by it."

Blondie cleared his throat. The man turned toward him. As if someone were standing behind the curtain, Blondie silently signaled with one hand. "It's about time you find out what this game's really like."

The man glanced toward the curtain then back at Blondie.

As if someone were standing behind the man, Blondie nodded in the direction behind him and said, "It's half now and half when delivered."

A look of panic flashed from the man's face. He swung his head around and looked behind himself. Seeing nothing, his look faded. He laced his fingers together and carefully set them on the table. "This is business, gentleman," he said with an air of dominance. "You'll get your money."

Smeal calmly smiled at the man. "You know me. You know what happens to people who try to cross me."

Blondie stood up, huddled close to the man, and whispered in his ear. "Like I said, 'half now and half when delivered.'"

The man's air of dominance came to an abrupt halt. Holding up his hand up in a defensive manner, he bent away from Blondie. "Don't get excited," he said lamely with a crooked smile. "I'll have to make a call first." Flushing with embarrassment, he squeezed out of the chair, got up, and took a step toward the curtain. Blocking his exit, Neal stepped in front of him.

The man stopped.

Neal looked to Blondie for approval.

Blondie nodded.

Neal stepped aside.

The man swished the curtain aside, and walked to the end of the bar.

Freddy got up and held the curtain open just enough to peek through. Hunching down behind the Wise potato chips and the Hostess Twinkie shelf, the man picked up the phone receiver.

With fire in his eyes, Blondie stood next to Freddy. "That bastard better not try anything." He looked to Smeal. "I'm not dying over this thing for him or anybody else."

Expecting Smeal to say something to Blondie, Freddy looked toward Smeal.

Smeal gave Blondie a reassuring look. "I wouldn't worry about it."

Freddy directed his gaze back at the man. Nodding, the man talked on the phone. Then he hung up, came back to the room, and sat down. A sense of relief emanated from his body. "The buyer says, okay."

Smeal persisted. "What about the money?"

Turning toward Smeal, the man looked immensely pleased with himself. "I won't be here this afternoon, but half the money will be."

Blondie interrupted. "Afternoon is a long time. Have the money here by nine o'clock or the deal's off."

The man looked taken aback. "I don't know if I can do that."

Smeal and Blondie stood up, looked at each other, and shrugged.

Smeal turned to go. "Then the deal's off."

Freddy and Rafferty stood up and looked down

at the seated man.

Neal threw his hand into the air and grabbed the end of the curtain but didn't pull it back. "Are we outta here?"

The man jerked his face toward the curtain so fast it seemed as if his head was going to snap off. With excitement in his voice, he jumped up out of his chair. To stop Neal from opening the curtain, he held his hand on it. "No need to call it off," he hastily said. "I'll make another call. The money will be here."

Neal held his hand on the curtain and braced himself to rip it from the man's hand and fling it open. "Are you sure?"

The man took his hand off the curtain. "Just come back in an hour and ask the bartender if George left him a package. He'll give you the money. You drop off the vault and you'll get the rest."

Smeal nodded but didn't speak. His unreadable gaze fixed on the man. As if deciding whether to run or stay, the man's eyes flicked to one side. He placed his hand on the curtain to leave, but Neal stood in front of him.

Smeal's face twisted in anger. He cleared his throat, leaned back, and folded his arms across his chest.

With his hand still on the curtain and Neal blocking his path, the man turned back toward Smeal and frowned. "Is there a problem?"

Smeal inclined his head and stared at the man for a long moment.

The man's hand on the curtain moved with a slight tremor, but his body slowly tensed. The curtain's movement stopped. He stood as if terrified.

"No problem," Smeal said and waved his hand in a dismissive gesture. "Just don't be an idiot."

For the briefest moment, the man's eyes flicked toward the chair where John Dillinger had sat.

Neal stepped aside.

The man exhaled a breath of relief, opened the curtain, and walked out.

Freddy turned to Neal. Freddy tried not to show it, but his voice came out in an awed whisper. "We're going to pick up a half a million dollars, get the vault, drop it off, and get the other half."

Blondie stared at him with a faint smile. "In this business, you don't count your money until it's in your hands, and the other man is dead."

"I don't know what the big deal is," Neal said. "All we have to do is get the money, deliver the vault, and get the other half of the money."

Smeal grunted with disapproval. "We're not going to get the money and then pick up the vault."

Surprised, Neal flashed him a puzzled look. "Why not?"

"It'll take too long. The longer we stretch this thing out, the more chance there is that someone will attack our plan. And most of those guys run whore and gambling houses. They stay up all night playing cards and drinking until the crack of dawn." He let out a wistful sigh. "They're lucky if they get up before eleven in the morning."

Neal impatiently asked, "So what do we do next?"

"We'll rent a truck. While we're picking up the vault," he looked at Blondie, "you'll drive your car back here and pick up the money. Then go to the shooting gallery at the bottom of Myers Hill and wait. After we go past in the truck, if no one is following us, we'll take the vault to the celery farm and collect the other half of the money."

Shaking his head, Blondie looked to Smeal. "I don't want to let you out of my sight. You'll ride with me."

"I don't blame you, "Smeal tapped his head with cryptic insight. "But do you trust these boys with the vault?"

"They're not boys," Blondie snapped back.

Smeal gave Blondie a penetrating gaze. "At my age, you're all boys."

"Well," Blondie said. "These young men haven't crossed me yet. And it'll look fishy if I show up to collect the money and you're not with me."

Freddy placed his elbow on the table and held his hand under his chin. "What if you two take off with the money?"

Rafferty, who was balancing his chair on the rear legs cut in. "It doesn't really matter. We'll still have the vault." He let his toothless exaggerated smile spread across his face. "If you take the money and run, we can still collect the other half of the million."

Slowly turning his head, Neal stood at the curtain and smiled at them all. "Gentleman, it looks like our troubles are over."

Chapter 35

Fifteen minutes after Freddy, Neal, Rafferty, Smeal, and Blondie left Radkowski's bar, Blondie brought the Oldsmobile to a stop in the cracked blacktop parking lot of a whitewashed cement block building. On the left side, four closed garage doors concealed what was behind them. On the other end of the building, a lattice of square, grime-coated windows laced the front of the building and created a huge window. Behind the windows, sun-faded posters hung, announcing outdated events. On the left side of the window, a green door with a painted-over window and a worn doorknob provided a backdrop for a black and white tin sign that read,

OFFICE

Light from a lemon sun beamed down from a blue sky and sliced through the half open door, highlighting a grease-stained concrete floor that led to chrome-legged bar stools in front of a tall counter with a cracked Formica top.

Blondie flashed a troubled look in Smeal's direction. "Are you sure these guys aren't with the truckers?"

Smeal reached up and rubbed his chin. "When Hudson tried to get higher wages and better working conditions from the money machines of big business...." His voice trailed away in icy silence. As if he were holding back tears, he swallowed and stared straight down. He took a deep breath and continued. "Until Hudson got help from the mob, big business had the police on their side. Most truckers are okay, but when there's money to be had, you can never be sure of anybody." He pointed to the double garage doors on the left side of the building. "This is supposed to be a mom and pop place, too small to unionize."

Freddy looked to the parking lot on the left side of the building. Haphazardly slotted, side by side, a 1949 Ford with a broken windshield and two Chevy trucks with dented fenders, waited to be repaired.

"There's a lot truck drivers in the truckers," Freddy said. "But it looks like mostly mechanics work here."

As if he were bored, Rafferty leaned back in the seat. "They can't all be gangsters." A crafty expression formed on his face. Then his lips parted into his missing tooth smile. "Besides," he said. "This place looks like they could have a staff meeting in a phone booth."

"I hope you guys are right," Smeal said and tightened his lips. "But if they are on the take, we should still be okay. Like I said before, 'Those guys don't get up until the afternoon.' By that time, we'll have the money for the vault."

Smeal looked to Blondie. "If you or me go in and there's guys on the take, they'll recognize us." He turned to Neal. "You go in and rent a truck."

"Good idea," Neal said and held out his hand. "But what will I do for money?"

Smeal flipped his wallet open and fished out a wad of bills. "This should take care of it." He placed the money in Neal's outstretched hand. "When you go in, act like you're not in a hurry."

"What for?"

"You got to kill the guy's curiosity. Try to talk him down on the price. Tell him something boring, like you're moving furniture for a sick aunt or something. That way he won't get interested in what we're doing."

Nodding in understanding, Neal placed his hand on the door handle of the Oldsmobile. Blondie grabbed him by the shoulder. "And get a truck big enough to haul that thing. I don't want to be going into the river again."

Neal opened the door. "No problem."

As if he had all the time in the world, Neal ambled into the office.

Five minutes later, one of the overhead garage doors opened. With the transmission in first gear, Neal slowly drove a white GMC pickup truck out of the garage. The truck crawled to the Oldsmobile and stopped next to Blondie. Neal stuck his head out the window of the truck. "How do you like it?"

Blondie let out an anguished moan. "Go back and get a truck that can haul something."

"This truck will work," Neal said and jerked his head back toward the rear of the truck. "Check under the fenders. This thing has beefed up springs." He opened the door and placed his hand on the floor shift. "It's practically new. It's a 1961. It's got a three-o-five V-8 engine and a four speed transmission."

Blondie stared at the back of the truck. "You sure those springs will hold the weight of the load?"

Neal opened the door, turned, and let his feet hang over the outer edge of the seat. "I should know about springs. I fixed enough of them on our dump truck."

"You better get something to chain the vault down," Blondie said uneasily. "I don't want it to shift and knock you off the road."

Neal jerked his thumb toward the back window of the truck. "We got chains and ratchet load binders that'll tie that thing so tight it'll scream for air."

Blondie nodded in approval. "You ready to pick up the vault?"

Neal swung his feet back into the truck and sat behind the steering wheel. "I'm ready anytime you are."

"Now, remember," Blondie said and held up his hand. "After we get the money, we'll park at the shooting gallery. If no one is following you, I'll flash my headlights three times and keep on watching. Then in fifteen minutes, we'll meet you at the road to the celery farm."

"That's nice," Neal said and adjusted the rearview mirror. "But what if someone's waiting for us?"

"Then I'll pull out, I'll be right behind you." Blondie put the Oldsmobile in gear and jerked his head toward the road. "Let's get going before the bad guys get out of bed."

As Freddy and Rafferty headed toward the truck, Freddy glanced into the bed of the truck. The chains and the ratchet load binders lay in a two neat rows, but the binders didn't have handles to ratchet the chains tight. He walked up Neal's door. "Those load binders don't have handles."

"Well," Rafferty said and let his hands despairingly fall to his sides. "What good are they?"

"Don't get excited," Neal said, waving his hands around his head. "The guy inside said they had too much stuff stolen off trucks. So they took the handles off and replaced them with bolts. That way, if a thief doesn't bring a wrench, he isn't going to get the chains off what he wants to steal."

"So?" Rafferty said. "Do you have a wrench?"

"No problem." Neal lifted a wrench off the front seat. "The man inside said this will work fine."

Rafferty stared at the wrench. "Good luck with that. It's metric."

Neal examined the wrench. "Damn, it is." He jumped out of the truck, stretched his body over the truck's back fender, and tried the wrench on one of the binders. It didn't fit. He threw the wrench into the bed of the truck. Before it clunked on the metal bed, he was on his way back into the garage.

Three minutes later, he came back with another wrench. This time it was a standard size that fit.

Rafferty and Freddy hopped into the truck. Before the doors were fully closed, Blondie and Smeal took off in the Oldsmobile and headed toward Radkowski's bar to pick up the money.

Traveling toward Oakwood Cemetery to get the vault, Neal powered through the gears. As the strong motor pulled the truck and effortlessly responded to the slightest push on the accelerator, Freddy felt his body being pushed back into the seat. "This thing's got a lot of power."

"You noticed that?" Neal said, leaning into a turn and hanging onto the steering wheel with both hands.

Rafferty looked to Neal. "Why did you get a white truck?"

Neal smiled big. "It's the only one they had, and besides, good guys wear white."

At the Oakwood Cemetery, under a sky that glowed unworldly and hellish, Neal and Rafferty talked while Freddy warily looked around for signs of movement and hugged the side of the mausoleum.

On the outside of the iron picket fence that surrounded the cemetery, a man approached from the west. All conversation dropped to a hushed tone. Freddy squatted next to the back tire of the truck and out of the approaching man's line of sight. Neal and Rafferty pressed themselves against the sides of the truck and waited. For five minutes unspoken hostility filled the air.

When the man didn't show up, Freddy stiffly stood up and whispered, "I think he's gone."

"Don't kid yourself," Neal said. "Three people can keep a secret if three of them are dead. Greenie's the only one dead. Somebody has to be watching."

"So, what do we do?"

Neal took one step toward the tombstone next to the mausoleum and pointed off in the distance. "Let's go visit the gypsy queen."

Rafferty squinted off into the direction Neal was pointing. "What are you talking about?"

Motioning for the others to follow, Neal took off walking. "Follow me. You'll see."

Neal stopped at a tall tombstone with a cross perched on top. Strings of cheap beads, of various colors, hung from the cross. The name Lena Miller had been carved in the stone with a burial date of May thirteenth, 1921.

As if he were praying, Rafferty stood next to Neal with his hands crossed. "This lady died years ago. The favorite question of the day is, what are we doing here?"

A slight smile formed of Neal's lips. "If I told you, I'd spoil the surprise." Getting serious, he bowed his head. "They say thousands of people pay their respects to this gypsy." He gestured to the beads hanging from the cross. "They leave junk and beads like those all the time."

"What for?" Rafferty asked.

Neal shrugged. "I guess they put them here for good luck. When she was buried, gypsies threw gold coins into her grave and sealed it with a big fat flagstone. Then a gypsy guard stood here for six months."

Freddy took a moment to visualize gypsies tossing valuable coins into the open grave. "I guess they think it's some sort of wishing well."

Rafferty peered into the distance looking for the man. "That's all well and dandy. But the favorite question of the day still is, what are we doing here?"

Neal kept his head bowed and whispered, "Don't look at that guy."

Rafferty turned toward Neal and whispered back, "Who do you think we're trying to fool, all of the people all of the time?"

Holding back a grin, Neal continued, "Pretend you've just finished praying. Make the sign of the cross. That guy will think we only stopped to visit the gypsy's grave. Then just get into the truck and don't stop to look where he is."

Freddy bowed his head and crossed himself. "What's the plan?"

"That guy doesn't know we have a rented truck. If he sees us drive away and keep on going, he'll

467

think we're not coming back."

"Yeah," Rafferty said. "He'll probably forget about us. And then he won't see us coming back because he won't be watching anymore."

Disbelief crept into Freddy's voice. "That's the dumbest thing I ever heard."

Neal waved an encouraging finger at him. "Sometimes dumb things work."

After Neal had driven the truck down Clark Street, he slowed to a walking speed. As he weaved the truck through the side streets of the flats of Sharon, he glanced from side to side and constantly checked the rear view mirror. When he turned onto Vine Street, a blue Cadillac with its power steering squealing went around a corner, followed.

Whipping his head around to look at the Cadillac, Freddy let out a startled gasp. "Now what?"

"Let's find out," Neal said and slowly threaded the truck through the congested stretch of parked cars that lined the street. The Cadillac pulled over and parked at the first open space. Rafferty turned toward Neal. "Why are there so many cars here?"

Neal pointed toward his right. "That's why."

Behind the diamond wire of a backstop, an early game of fast-pitch softball was in action.

Freddy watched the beer-bellied pitcher. His underhanded pitch zipped past the batter so fast, all Freddy saw was a black blur. "That old guy's good."

Rafferty's brow began to knit. "What are we going to do? Watch softball all day?"

"Not really," Neal said and leaned back in the seat. "But it's a good time to see if anyone's following us."

Whap! The batter hit the ball. It sailed into center field. The center fielder caught it. A smattering of applause came from the spectators sitting on the four-tier bleachers.

Neal looked into the rearview mirror, put the truck in gear, K-turned, and drove on. Around the bend, a slow moving freight train blocked the road. Neal stopped at the railroad crossing and waited. Off to the right, a medium sized billboard stood between a stand of maple trees. A leather suitcase spattered with various colors of paint, sat at the feet of man painting red letters on the sign.

"Who's that guy?" Rafferty asked. "I never saw a man painting a billboard before."

"That's Cecil Myers," Neal said watching the man slowly drag his paintbrush around the curve of the letter R. "He can paint anything, but people don't pay him enough. So he has to work in the General American Tank Car factory."

"If this deal pans out," Freddy said. "We'll never have to work in a factory or a stinkin' steel mill."

As the railroad cars laboriously clacked past, Neal watched in the rearview mirror. "Nobody followed us," he said with relief. "It looks like that guy at the cemetery wasn't after us after all."

Watching a noisy wheel of a railroad car clack past, Rafferty's head moved from left to right. "That guy at the cemetery was probably the caretaker."

"You're probably right," Neal said and studied the cars in the rearview mirror. "But with the amount of money we could lose, we can't be too careful."

Freddy twisted in the seat and looked out the back window. Three cars waited behind them, but the drivers all wore the soft cloth caps of mill workers. "Yeah, no suit and ties back there."

Rafferty held up his hands and briskly rubbed them in front of his face. "Blondie and Smeal probably got the money by now. Let's go get that vault and cash it in."

***

Back at the cemetery, Neal backed the truck up to the mausoleum, and they all jumped out. Rafferty clandestinely picked up the metric wrench from the bed of the truck and laid it on the floor of the truck. With excitement and expectation surging through their veins, it took less than a minute to push the vault onto the bed of the truck. Neal stood in the bed, draped the chains over the vault, hooked up the ratchet load binders, and held out his hand. "Hey, Rafferty, reach into the truck and get me that wrench."

Rafferty reached into the truck, picked up the metric wrench off the floor, and handed it to Neal.

Neal bent over to tighten the ratchet load binders. The wrench didn't fit. He cussed and looked down at Rafferty. "All right, dip shit, give me the right wrench."

Rafferty giggled but pulled the standard wrench from behind his back. Neal shook his head, took the wrench, ratcheted the load tight, and jumped back into the truck. He threw the wrench on the floor. After it collided with the metric wrench at Freddy's feet, Neal put the truck in gear and pulled away.

Now they were on their way to the celery farm.

At the bottom of Myers Hill, they slowed to a crawl. Freddy scanned the road to the shooting gallery for Blondie's Oldsmobile. Three flashes from Blondie's headlights filtered through the foliage.

Neal slowed the truck and looked toward the shooting gallery. "I hope he's there."

Trying to keep the truck's speed up, Freddy leaned forward. "He's there. I just saw the signal."

"Damn," Neal said and tromped on the gas. "Your eyes are better than mine. I didn't see anything."

Freddy twisted around and looked out the back window. "No one's following us either."

At the top of Myers Hill, Neal hit the brakes. The heavy vault slammed against the back of the truck, but the chains held. The blanket that had been under the seat slid under Freddy's feet. His shoulder painfully slammed into the dashboard. He grabbed his shoulder, whipped his body around, and faced Neal. "What are you trying to do?"

Looking out the windshield, Neal stared straight ahead. "Just trying to stay alive."

Then Freddy saw it. An orange full-ton flatbed truck with duel back wheels had come right at Neal. His quick reflexes had saved them from a head-on collision, but the driver in the orange truck jumped out with a Thompson machine gun in his hands. Under a bad gray toupee, his lopsided head looked like it sat on a two hundred forty pound six-foot frame. The sides of his hair were cut short and almost matched the toupee. Under a long wispy mustache, a cigarette with a long ash hung from his

471

mouth.

Apparently not seeing the machine-gun, Neal flung the door open and jumped out, shaking his fist. "What the hell's the matter with you, buddy? Can't you drive on your side of the—"

Neal cut his remark short and looked at the machine gun. He held up his hands in a surrendering gesture. His demeanor changed from rage to kindness and forgiveness. "Say, buddy." He smiled. "What seems to be the problem? You having a little trouble with the steering?"

Blowing smoke from his mouth while he talked, the toupee man waved the machine gun at Neal. "The little problem is that I need some boys to load a vault onto my truck."

Rafferty looked at the vault and then at the toupee man. "If you need help, hire yourself a partner."

Toupee jerked the barrel of the machine gun in Rafferty's direction. "You tryin' to be funny?"

"I'm not trying to be funny," Rafferty said and pointed to the vault. "That's only a brass box. We're taking it to the junk man for scrap."

Toupee pointed to the end of the vault. Where the brass and concrete had been knocked off when it had slid through the back window of the green truck when Blondie had crashed into the river, gold gleamed.

A big smile spread across Toupee's face. "Yeah, right."

From around the back of the orange flatbed truck, another man came with his hand on his shoulder holster. It was Carlo. As his eyes widened, he drew a deep breath. "These kids gave me a hard time at the dump." He pointed to his neck. "Look what they did to me." A red burn mark with the pattern of a steel cable curled around his Adams apple. "They almost made me cut my head off." He reached under his arm and pulled out his 45. "I'm gonna shoot the sneaky bastards right now."

Toupee held up his hand. "Wait a few minutes." He looked at the vault. "I'm not bustin' my ass unloadin' that heavy vault. We'll shoot them after they unload it."

Knowing that after they loaded the vault they would be shot, Freddy racked his mind for a way to stay alive. Past experiences had shown him the three greatest assets in a situation like this were, numbers, surprise, and confusion. They had Toupee and Carlo outnumbered, but they didn't have Thompson machine guns. If Blondie and Smeal showed up, they may be able to create a diversion and escape in the resulting confusion. Freddy glanced down the road. No cars were in sight. He would have to find ways to stall for time.

Waving his hand toward the vault, Freddy looked toward Toupee. "Why should we load the thing? You're going to shoot us no matter what we do or what we don't do?"

Toupee smiled big. "Just think of it as a stay of execution." He let out a weird chuckle. "Hell, while you're unloading the vault, the governor might call and grant you clemency."

Neal took Freddy's lead and put on a slowdown. "We'd like to help," he said. "But that thing's too heavy to lift."

Rafferty flashed Freddy a knowing grin and put

his hand on the small of his back. "I'd be glad to help, but I might break my bad back, and we don't have a wrench for the ratchet load binders."

For a moment, Toupee coldly stared at Rafferty. Then he motioned to Carlo. "Let's get this thing loaded."

Carlo jumped in the orange truck, put it in gear, pulled around the white truck, and then backed the flat-bed of the orange truck right even with the bed of the white truck.

Toupee gestured with the barrel of the Thompson toward the bed of the white truck. "Okay, boys, get up and there and push that thing onto our truck."

From around the bend, the motor of a car roared.

Hoping it was Blondie, Freddy looked toward the sound. The car neared. It was the '57 Ford that had chased them to Five Points.

It pulled off to the side of the road. Carlo ran over to it and started talking to the driver.

With a look of sarcasm, Rafferty looked to Neal. "It's a good thing Blondie's watching out for us."

Neal shook his head, once. "I think we've been had again."

Toupee grabbed his stomach and hunched over as if he were laughing. "You didn't think Smeal was going to cut you in on this, did you?"

Neal gave the man a sincere look. "Sometimes a man's word is good enough."

Toupee straightened up. "Oh," he said through tight lips. "You have my word that if you don't get up on that truck and start sliding that vault, you're gonna to have an ass full of lead." He poked Neal in the ribs with the barrel of the machine gun.

Neal arched back from the pain of the barrel and jumped up onto the truck. Rafferty and Freddy held on to the back bumper but didn't get into the bed of the truck.

Toupee waved the barrel of the Thomson toward them. "If you want to live, you *will* get your asses up on that truck."

As if he were going to pull himself up, Rafferty placed his hand on the side of the bed. "I'll get up," he said. "But I already told you. We can't undo the binders."

Freddy shrugged. "He's right."

"Don't feed me that crapola," Toupee growled. "You tightened them, so you have to have a wrench to loosen them."

As if he had just remembered something, Rafferty put his hand on his head. "Oh that's right. We have the wrench in the truck."

Toupee jabbed him in the rear end with the barrel of the machine gun. "Get that wrench and get your smart ass up on that truck."

Holding his rear end, Rafferty reached into the truck and felt under the blanket on the floor. He found and grabbed the metric wrench that wouldn't fit the bolt to release the ratchet load binders.

Freddy knew he was doing this to delay the inevitable. He hoped it would give Blondie time to get there.

With the wrong wrench in his hand and acting like he was in pain, Rafferty pulled himself up into the bed of the truck and looked back at Toupee. "I don't know if this will fit."

Staring at Rafferty, Toupee slowly nodded. "I don't know if that wrench will fit up your ass. But if you keep up your bullshit, I'm going to make sure it does."

Rafferty shrugged. "Oh well. You get a little gold and the whole world hates you." He attempted to place the wrench on the binder's bolt and looked down at Toupee. "See, it doesn't fit."

Carlo quit talking to the driver of the '57 Ford and stepped to the Truck. "What's the hold up?"

Holding the wrench, Rafferty tapped the ratchet binder. "Anybody that thinks this wrench will fit needs to see a proctologist for a brain exam."

Rafferty's attempted humor was too much for Carlo's limited mind. He didn't even crack a smile. He jumped up on the truck and held out his hand. "Give me that wrench."

Rafferty gave him the wrench.

Trying to fit the wrench over the bolt, Carlo looked down at Toupee. "He's right. This thing's metric."

Toupee snarled. "They just loaded the thing. They have to have a wrench that fits. I'll look in the truck." He reached into the truck and shouted, "What's this flea rag doing in here?"

He grabbed the blanket off the floor and threw it onto the ground. Then he grabbed the standard wrench off the floor. Shaking the wrench at Rafferty, he said, "After that vault's loaded, I'm shoving this thing up your ass until it comes out of that smart mouth."

As Rafferty bent over and strained to push the heavy vault, he whispered to Freddy, "After we push this thing, we'll be going to the hospital for hernias. While we're there, I'll have them take that wrench out of my ass."

Freddy couldn't believe Rafferty's ability to keep a sense of humor when they were about to be shot. He shook his head in disbelief.

Toupee waved the gun at Rafferty and growled. "What did you say?"

Rafferty flashed Toupee an exaggerated ear-to-ear smile. "I was only telling my friend here," he gestured to Freddy, "how common the world would be if you weren't here."

Toupee stared at Rafferty for a long moment but didn't say anything.

Try as they may, Freddy, Neal, and Rafferty could not stop the process of transferring the vault to the orange truck.

When they slid the heavy vault onto the orange truck, a bigger section of the thin brass that covered the gold vault peeled back. As sunrays beamed down on it, Rafferty's eyes fixed on the gold in front of him. For a moment, the gleaming reflections, from its surface, illuminated his face like golden fire. In a few minutes, chains were thrown over the vault and clinched tight.

Carlo stepped next to Neal and held out his hand. "Okay, bright boy, give me the keys."

Neal shrugged and handed him the keys to the white truck.

As if he were using a prod to herd cattle, Toupee nudged Freddy and his friends into the cab of the white truck and closed the door.

Rafferty stuck his head out the window and looked down at Toupee. With exaggerated doe eyes, he said, "Are you going to let us go?"

Carlo stepped up to the window. "Don't listen to that jackass." He pointed at Rafferty. "Shoot that half-wit and push the truck down the hill. The river will take care of the rest."

Toupee reached up on the bed of the truck, placed his hand on the wrench, and looked at Rafferty. "Before I do anything, I'm going to shove this thing—" He stopped talking and looked to his right.

Freddy heard the familiar throaty roar of the engine in Blondie's Oldsmobile. Not wanting a passing car to see their weapons, Carlo holstered his 45.

Looking toward the sound, Toupee took his hand off the wrench, faced the road, and hid the Thompson behind his back. He turned his head. Directing his voice at Neal, he talked over his shoulder. "Don't make us turn around and shoot your asses."

While they were distracted, Neal slid down under the dash of the white truck, pulled out three wires, and hot-wired the motor. Freddy quietly unlatched the passenger door and got ready. Neal sat up behind the steering wheel and held his foot on the accelerator.

To block Toupee's view of Freddy, Rafferty turned sideways, waved his hand and yelled out the window, "Hey, toupee man! You forgot to stick that wrench up my ass."

Toupee looked back over his shoulder and let out an angry snarl. Then he turned back and focused his attention to the sound of the coming car.

Freddy quietly stepped out of the truck, bent over and picked up the blanket. He looked to

Rafferty. Rafferty nodded to Neal. Keeping his foot on the accelerator, Neal started the motor. It rushed to a full fast roar. Keeping low, Freddy ran around the truck. Toupee spun around and whipped the machine gun from around his back so fast his gray toupee slipped down the side of his face. Before he could fire, Freddy threw the blanket over Toupee's and Carlo's heads. Then he dropped down and grabbed one of each man's ankles. At the same time, he rammed his shoulders into their knees and pulled their ankles forward. Windmilling their arms, they both tumbled to the ground.

While Toupee and Carlo struggled to clear the blanket off their heads and get to their feet, Neal let out the truck's clutch. The truck lurched forward. Freddy jumped back into the moving truck and slammed the door. Toupee got to his feet. He lifted the Thompson. Just as he was about to fire, the truck's back tires shot a huge spray of gravel and dirt into his face.

With his toupee stuck to the side of his face, and one hand covering his other eye from the spraying gravel, he let out a stream of bullets. Being in a hurry and having his vision blocked by his bad toupee, the barrel of the machine gun traveled upward, spitting the bullets high and zinging over the roof of the truck.

A bullet from Carlo's 45 slammed into the back window of the truck, whizzed past Freddy's head, and exited thought the windshield. Freddy crouched down and looked into the rearview mirror. In the distance, Blondie's Oldsmobile came screaming around the curve and right at Carlo and Toupee. Carlo and Toupee jumped out of the way and ran toward the '57 Ford.

On down the road, Neal shifted into high gear and tromped the accelerator of the white truck to the floor. The force from the powerful engine threw Rafferty and Freddy back into their seats. Blondie was right behind him, and the Ford was behind Blondie.

The barrel of the Thompson poked out the side window of the Ford. Fire spit from its end. Blondie swerved to the left. Bullets chunked through the roof of the steel skin of the white truck. Freddy's heart slammed desperately inside his chest. He turned and looked out the back window. As heavy clunks came from the roof of the white truck, he watched bullet holes appear in the windshield of Blondie's Oldsmobile.

"Get out of the way!" Freddy found himself yelling.

As Neal kept the accelerator jammed to the floor, the tires on the white truck squealed around a tight S-curve.

The Ford behind Blondie disappeared in the sweeping curve.

With his knuckles tightening around the steering wheel, Neal looked to Freddy. "We got to get away from that machine gun."

From a protective fetal position on the floor of the truck, Rafferty mumbled, "Throw something out the window. Maybe it'll give him a flat tire."

Neal leaned into another sharp bend. "I would, but Blondie's right behind us."

Chapter 36

Driving behind the white truck, Blondie sat behind the wheel of the Oldsmobile and looked over to Smeal. "Throw something out the window."

Smeal shook his head. "There's nothing to throw. If that idiot at Radkowski's bar would have given us the money I could throw some of it out. They'd stop for that."

Smeal started one of his coughing spells. His face reddened. The veins in his neck and forehead turned blue and distended. He looked like he was going to die, right there in the front seat. But his coughing subsided and he seemed to regain his composure.

Without moving his head, Blondie shifted his eyes to the right. Although Smeal has his back turned toward him, he looked like he'd returned from a trip to hell. His aging body portrayed an image of defeat. When he looked back over his shoulder, huge black circles ringed his eyes. Concerned that old age was beginning to take a toll on Smeal, Blondie hoped it wasn't a fast start of a bad time.

Up ahead, a dump truck hogged the center of the road, blocking Neal and the white truck. Blondie checked the rearview mirror. The distance between the back bumper of the Oldsmobile and the '57 Ford was narrowing. Just like Smeal, the slow-moving truck was old, slow, and a hindrance. Blondie had come too far to have a lethargic dump truck stop him now. He laid on the horn for Neal to get moving.

Black smoke blasted out of the tailpipe of the

white truck. Neal steered alongside the road and zoomed around the sluggish truck. Blondie accelerated. Kicking up gravel from the side of the road, he followed the white truck. Looking in the rearview mirror and hoping it wouldn't follow, he watched the '57 Ford. It veered to the side of the road. For a moment, it fishtailed in the gravel, but cut back onto the road. To Blondie's dismay, it passed the dump truck. When it pulled close behind them, Toupee held the Thompson out the passenger side window and fired. But only two bullets clunked into the trunk of the Oldsmobile.

"Good," Blondie said. "They're out of bullets."

Displaying a cold disregard for the danger they were in, Smeal sighed. "As long as they're behind us, they're not driving away with the vault."

Blondie clinched his fist and swung it down. "Damn, there was another man in that Ford. He might be taking the vault." He lifted his foot from the accelerator. "We go to get back there." The heavy Oldsmobile slowed. The Ford came up fast and just nicked the back bumper. If Blondie could get the Ford to hit the heavy bumper of the Oldsmobile at a decent speed, there was a good chance the Ford's flimsy chrome grill would be pushed into the radiator.

"Oh," Blondie said. "So, you want to play?"

He increased the speed. The Ford came at the back bumper again. But this time Blondie mashed on the brake. The front of the Ford plowed into the heavy bumper of the Oldsmobile. It was a pretty good hit and dented the grill, but it didn't push it back far enough to pierce the radiator. Blondie hit the gas. The Ford fell behind but continued to follow. Blondie mashed the brake again. The Ford slowed, but this time, it didn't hit the bumper.

"So, you're wise to that," Blondie said with taunting laughter. "Let's see how smart you really are."

Right before the bridge that crossed over the Shenango River and led to the little town of Sharpsville, Blondie accelerated again. Instead of hitting the brake pedal and sending a warning through the brake lights, he pulled the emergency brake. This time, when the Oldsmobile slowed, the Ford didn't slow. Going full speed, it slammed right into the solid back bumper of the Oldsmobile. The impact was enough. It sent the Ford's grill into the fragile radiator. A stream of white steam hissed out it and blocked Carlo's vision. With the front end of the Ford smashed into the back bumper, Blondie let the Oldsmobile slow to a stop. Carlo reached out the window and fired three shots from his 45. The bullets harmlessly cut through the growing cloud of steam and ricocheted off the steel beams of the bridge. Blondie hit reverse and stomped on the gas. The Ford moved backwards a few feet. Its engine's rpm's rose. Trying to fight back, the back tires on the Ford uselessly spun in a whirl of blue smoke. The wimpy 272 cubic-inch V-8 engine under the hood of the Ford was no match for Blondie's 427 cubic-inch V-8 engine that had been pulled from a police car and rebuilt from top to bottom and provided more than enough power for its heavy-duty transmission. Carlo and Toupee were being driven back faster and faster. At the end of the bridge, the back of the Ford rammed into the steel abutment. Blondie kept the gas on, but the

Ford was stopped solid.

Machine gun bullets erupted.

"Damn," Blondie said and hunched low to make a smaller target. "He's reloaded."

Hunching over, Smeal looked up. "Now what?"

Blondie hooked the transmission into low. "Now we get out of here."

Before he could move forward, Neal's face appeared behind the windshield of the white truck. He was heading right for the Ford. The machine gun bullets stopped. With his face filled with fright, Toupee whipped the machine gun back into the Ford. Neal rammed the front bumper of the white truck into the side of the door of the Ford, pinning Carlo behind the steering wheel. Blondie shifted out of low, hit reverse, and mashed the gas. The tires on the Oldsmobile spun in a haze of blue smoke.

Pushing on the Ford, the engine in the white truck moaned deep and powerful. Like a cry for mercy, the engine in the Ford screamed as if was in terrible pain. But Blondie and Neal kept right on pushing. The engine in the Ford slowed to a burble. In a cloud of purple smoke — clunk! It stopped dead. The end of its broken crankshaft dropped to the asphalt.

With the engine blown, the tires on the Ford ground to a halt. Slowly but steady, the white truck and the Oldsmobile pushed, more. The Ford unwillingly inched its way toward the edge of the bridge. With his face filled with fear, Toupee tried to open the passenger side door, but it was jammed up against the bridge railing.

Trapped behind the steering wheel, Carlo shouted, pointed, and gestured wildly at the front of the truck. Next to him, Toupee tried to fire the machine gun, but it seemed to be jammed.

Neal kept right on pushing. The railing broke free. The Ford slid sideways and the hanging crankshaft tore a strip of pavement off the bridge. A shower of gravel pattered down to the water below. The Ford balanced on the edge of the bridge for a moment. Carlo's frantic movements were replaced with a horror-filled face. Then the Ford free fell straight into the river below.

If the police came, Blondie would be taken to jail. Without stopping to see where the Ford went or if anyone had survived, Blondie backed the Oldsmobile up and signaled for Neal to take off.

Neal turned the truck around. Before Blondie could wrestle the Oldsmobile off the bridge and turn around, Neal, Freddy, and Rafferty were on their way back to Myers Hill.

Blondie hoped the vault was still there.

Chapter 37

Back at Myers Hill, Freddy jumped out of the white truck before it had rolled to a stop. Seeing that the orange truck still had the vault in its bed, he hopped into it. But he thought it was strange that Carlo and Toupee had taken off after them and left a million dollar vault where anyone could take it. He was glad the side of the vault that had gold showing was not facing the road. And he was glad the eyes of people driving past could not penetrate the vault's thin brass covering and see the gold below.

Neal stepped out of the white truck and tugged on Rafferty's arm. "Are you ready to load that thing back into our truck?"

Rafferty climbed up onto the bed of the orange truck and held his hand on one of the load binders. "Get the wrench and I'll loosen these things."

Neal reached up and handed Rafferty the standard wrench, but before Rafferty could grasp it, Blondie pulled up in his Oldsmobile and got out. "Hey, what are you doing?"

Neal lowered the wrench. "We're putting our vault back on our truck."

As if he were looking for someone, Blondie quickly scanned the area. "What for?"

"So, we can haul it to the celery farm and collect the money."

Blondie gestured to Freddy. "Are the keys in the orange truck?"

Freddy nodded. "They're still in the ignition."

Rafferty jumped down off the orange truck and opened its door. Blondie stopped and studied the front of the truck. "They left the keys in the truck, and the driver of the Ford stayed here for a reason. Did you check under the hood for a bomb?"

The threat of a bomb stopped Freddy in his tracks. He reached up and slapped the side of his own head. "Damn! Where did the other man in the Ford go?" To make matters worse, he knew checking for bombs should have been a common practice. He couldn't believe he had forgotten the fact the so many car bombs had been planted and exploded in Youngstown that it was referred to as "Bomb Town."

Rafferty opened the door of the orange truck, jumped into the front seat, slammed the door, and slide to the center of the seat.

As if he were in extreme pain, Neal cringed. He looked to Rafferty. "Don't move."

Ready to jump, Rafferty reached for the door handle. But being in the center of the seat, he couldn't reach it. Sitting perfectly still, he froze in fright.

Neal cautiously stepped to the front of the truck, bent over, and peered through its grill. "I don't see any wires, but it doesn't mean they didn't give this thing a Youngstown tune up."

Standing next to the truck, Blondie looked up at Freddy. "They like to put a detonating switch under the seat. But since Rafferty's still in one piece, it might be someplace else." He jerked his thumb toward the ground under the truck. "Sometimes they wire them from the bottom off the starter."

Neal dropped to his knees, rolled onto his back, and crawled under the front of the truck.

Blondie bent over and looked toward Neal. "See anything?"

On the floor, under Rafferty's feet, Freddy heard Neal's fingers scratching.

Then Neal's muffled voice came from beneath the truck. "Somebody took a wire off the starter so the truck wouldn't start, but I don't see any dynamite or detonating wires."

Tilting his head to the side, Blondie nervously listened and scanned the road. "They probably went for reinforcements and took the wire off so nobody could take the truck."

Freddy figured if Neal put the wire back on the starter, it might trigger a switch and set a bomb off. He jumped down off the bed of the truck and bent over. "Hey, Neal, don't put that wire back on."

But Neal had already put the wire back on the starter, secured the tiny bolt with his fingertips, and wiggled out from under the truck. Brushing his hands together, he said, "It should start now." He opened the door of truck and gestured to Freddy. "Hop in."

Freddy got in the truck, but Rafferty still sat, solid as a statue, blocking Neal.

"It's okay, Neal said with a wave of his hand. "Go ahead move over."

Rafferty leaned to the side but didn't move. "Are you sure it won't blow me sky high?"

"I checked it," Neal assured him. "Quit wasting time. I need room to shift the gears. Slide your scared ass over."

"Okay," Rafferty said. "But if I get blown up into the sky catch me on my way down." He moved over.

Blondie motioned to Neal. "Haul our vault to the celery farm. I'll follow."

Neal's forehead wrinkled with confusion. "What about our rented truck?"

"No problem," Blondie said and placed his hand on the bed of the orange truck. "We'll give whoever's at the celery farm the vault and this truck, too. Then we'll drive you back here and take the white truck back." He paused and smiled. "You know, if we want too, we'll be able to buy ten of these trucks."

Blondie jumped back into the Oldsmobile, but before he could pull away, the blue '58 Chevy that had been at the dump approached so silently Freddy never heard it coming. It pulled right up to Blondie's front bumper and started to push the Oldsmobile toward the hill. Carlo's Chevy was doing the pushing, but Carlo had just been pushed off the Sharpsville Bridge and into the Shenango River. Someone else was behind the wheel.

Rafferty wiggled around in the seat of the orange truck and looked out the back window. "Now what?"

"Now we know where the Ford driver went," Neal said and pointed to the Chevy. "He's in Carlo's Chevy trying to push Blondie into the river. Next, he'll come after us."

"No way," Freddy said. "That Chevy's no match for Blondie's Olds. He got a police transmission and a big 427 engine in that thing."

As the Chevy pushed, the tires on the Oldsmobile slipped in the loose gravel.

Freddy gasped. "If Blondie gets pushed onto the green grass, he'll have no traction at all."

"We'll fix that," Neal said and started the engine. He pushed the floor shift into creeper gear and let out the clutch. The powerful truck crawled until it made contact with the back bumper of Blondie's Oldsmobile.

Neal smiled a fiendish grin. "Okay, Carlo's friend, let's see what your little 348 engine can do."

With Blondie's powerful Oldsmobile and the orange flatbed truck with the heavy gold vault pushing the Chevy sideways and its back tires spinning in protest, the driver tried to aim his gun and fire. But it was in vain. Every time he took a hand from the steering wheel, he lost control. As the Chevy lost ground, its wheels spun onto the slippery green grass. It started down the steep hill toward the deep water above the raging rapids. Neal gunned the engine of the orange truck. The driver in the Chevy hit the brakes, but the slow steady strength of the creeper gear was unbeatable. Neal gave Blondie's Oldsmobile one final push. It sent the Chevy down the hill and away from the Oldsmobile. Picking up speed, the Chevy hit something and jerked forward. Its right front tire flapped. Steam billowed in front of the windshield. The driver could hardly be seen. He opened the door, but didn't jump.

Gathering more speed for the inevitable plunge, one of the wheels on the Chevy hit a rock. It splayed outward and the door thunked shut. As the deep water waited below, the steep hill yawned in front of the Chevy. Its underside took the brunt of an impact with a rock, causing the rusted front suspension to tear away. Increasing speed, the two-wheeled body of the Chevy slid down the grassy hill. As the cry of a few crows faintly traveled across the river, the Chevy flew right over the muddy riverbank. Its momentum caused it to ski across the surface of the water and slow to a stop. It bobbed once, hung for an instant, and sank into the green water of the Shenango River.

Neal looked to Freddy. "If we don't get that rental truck out of here, and the police come, they might trace it back to us."

Rafferty put his hand on the door handle to get out. "I've had enough excitement for today. I'll hide it at the tower road. When you guys come back, we'll have enough money to keep the people's mouths shut at the rental place."

Freddy held up his hand. "Why should we give them extra money?"

"Do you need glasses," Rafferty asked. "When they see the bullet holes, they're going to want to know what happened."

Feeling ignorant, Freddy glanced at the white truck. "Oh, I forgot about that."

Neal gave Rafferty a quick stare. "You sure you want to trust us with the vault?"

Rafferty shrugged. "What good's the money for the vault if we're sittin' in jail?"

Neal nodded an exaggerated nod. "Good thinking."

Blondie walked up to Neal's window. "You ready to get out of here?"

Neal's lips curled into a canny smile. "Let's cash this thing in before somebody else comes."

As if expecting more trouble, Blondie looked right then left.

Smeal walked up to him and stopped. "Is everything all right?"

"The people at the celery farm will be

expecting people in an orange truck, so we should be okay." He looked back at his Oldsmobile. "But we have to be on the lookout for another round? Are you up to it?"

Smeal held up his hand in approval. "I'm always ready for anything. Let's get this deal over with."

"That's the best advice I've heard all day," Rafferty said, and climbed into the white rental truck. Before he started the truck, he leaned out the window. "Hey, if you guys don't make it, I'll put my tooth under Blondie's pillow. The tooth fairy might give us enough money for gas so we can drive to the poor house."

Smiling his missing-tooth smile, Rafferty bobbed his orange-haired head and drove away.

Chapter 38

Following Blondie's Oldsmobile, Neal drove the vault-loaded, orange truck along River Road. On Route 846, he took a left on an unpaved road. Neal slowed the heavy truck and followed. The road ran along for about a half a mile then curved to the right. Freddy looked out the back window. Heavy foliage and yellow dust obscured River Road. Another right and they were traveling down the long drive that led to the old, abandoned celery farm. Blondie pulled off the drive and parked in a little turnaround that had been freshly brush-hogged.

Neal pulled next to him and stopped. Leaning out the window, he asked, "Now what?"

Smeal leaned over Blondie and talked through the driver's side window. "We wait exactly ten minutes. If nobody shows up, we toot the horn two longs and one short."

As Freddy and Neal waited impatiently, in the truck, the ten minutes seemed like ten hours. Then Blondie's horn sounded two longs and one short.

For a couple of minutes, no one spoke about what they were going to do with the money from the vault. Then Neal started to say something about living on the wide-open road. But in the excitement of the moment, Freddy didn't pay any attention to him. He looked back and focused on the vault. Now that they were finally going to cash it in, it seemed as if he were losing an old friend. But his grief was interrupted. Brandishing browning automatic rifles, called BARs, three men wearing brown suits whished through the bushes and stood in front of Blondie.

A trapped feeling of terror invaded Freddy's body. He knew the BARs could hold 600 rounds of thirty-ought-six armor piercing cartridges that could zip right through the steel doors of the truck. These men were serious, and there was no place to hide. Freddy looked to Neal and threw up his hands in exasperation. "Does this ever end?"

Two black Cadillac's flew out of nowhere, nosed together into a V, and blocked the exit.

Neal looked to Freddy. "I guess not." He reached down to start the truck.

One of the men kept his BAR lowered. With a crowbar in his hand, he motioned to Neal. "Come on down. We got business to do."

Freddy couldn't keep his eyes off the BARs. For some reason, he remembered the date of July 18, 1933. On that day, Browning Automatic Rifles were the type of machine guns that had blasted through Bonnie and Clyde's steel car and made Swiss cheese out of them. Freddy knew the doors on the orange truck would not stop bullets from these BARs. The longer he stared at the BARs, the more terrified he became. And the thought of having his head caved in with a crowbar didn't help either. He gave a resigned shrug and turned toward Neal. "Maybe this is the end."

Neal blinked and opened the driver's side door. "Let's find out."

Freddy opened the passenger door, slid off the seat, and stepped down from the cab of the truck. When he walked around the other side, Smeal, Blondie, and Neal were shaking hands with the three men.

The man with the crowbar leaned his BAR against the tire of the truck and jumped up onto the bed. He looked at the front end of the vault. Where the brass and cement had been knocked off, gold glimmered. He smiled and nodded to the others.

Freddy figured he was just making sure it was the real gold vault. But then, the man stepped to the other end of the vault, bent over, and used the crowbar to pry back a foot long piece of the thin brass covering. He tapped on the thin layer of concrete until it cracked. As he brushed the pieces away with the back of his hand, the newly exposed gold gleamed into the bright blue sky day.

Now Freddy knew the man wasn't taking any chances that only one end of the vault was gold. But the man kept on pealing back brass and breaking cement. After he had exposed a long line of gold with strange symbols, he smiled and gave his entourage a thumbs-up. "This is it."

His entourage nodded all around.

The man threw the crowbar down, jumped down off the truck, walked up to Freddy, and offered his hand in friendship. "Nice little job there, young fellow."

Freddy nodded and shook the man's clammy hand. The man wheeled around and faced the others. "Let's get this thing done."

One man with a BAR, who looked to be Japanese, reached into the brush, pulled out a brown paper bag, and offered it to Smeal. "You guys didn't waste time getting rid of Greenie and his friends like we told you to."

Smeal shrugged and went along with the misinformation. "Anything for an extra buck."

"Yeah," the man said and gestured toward the vault. "And that kook that's buying that thing has a lot of extra bucks. He says he wants to use it for a coffin. The dumb ass thinks he's a descendant of Egyptian royalty and needs to be buried in a gold vault." Shaking his head, the man smiled. "Just because it's illegal to own gold, he's forking over two million dollars for an eight hundred forty thousand dollar vault."

Freddy figured the three men would have to have a cut, but he didn't know how much. Evidently, the men hadn't figured out that the wrong people had delivered the vault. He wondered how Smeal was going to talk his way out of that.

Smeal took the brown paper bag and held it up. "You got your share out of this, didn't you?"

"If we didn't, we wouldn't be here."

Another man with a BAR stepped toward Smeal and nervously scanned the forest behind him. "We know your pal with the orange hair is out there somewhere," he said referring to Rafferty. "He probably has a high powered hunting rifle aimed at us."

Smeal lowered his head and went along with the man's fears that Rafferty was out there. "You can never be too careful."

The man gestured toward the bag. "You want to count it?"

"It's not necessary," Smeal said. "If anything's missing, I know where to find you."

"So, we have a deal?"

Smeal gestured to Neal.

Neal held out his hand and offered the man the keys to the orange truck. "You might need these."

496

The man grabbed the keys. With subdued jubilation, he threw his hand in the air. "This is the easiest five hundred thousand I ever made." As he headed toward the truck, he looked back over his shoulder. "Tell Hank I said thanks."

While Freddy wondered who Hank could be, the two Cadillacs vanished as mysteriously as they had appeared. The three men piled into the flatbed truck and hauled the vault away in a cloud of yellow dust.

Neal reached for the paper bag. "Let's count it."

Smeal stared down the dust filled road. "I have a bad feeling about this place. Let's get out of here."

Without saying a word, they all jumped into the Oldsmobile.

Kicking up another cloud of yellow dust, they raced down the unpaved road. At Route 846 they stopped.

An eighteen-wheeled semi-truck coming from the left blew its horn. The red-haired driver wound down his window, flicked out a cigarette butt, and waved.

Neal waved back. "That's Tommy."

As a backwash of diesel fumes filled the air, the orange truck came into view. It was about the length of a football field away, parked at the side of the road and the vault was gone.

As if he had been hit full force with the back of a long-handled shovel blade, an enormous thump, like the beat of a gigantic base drum, hit Freddy's chest. Grabbing his chest as if he had been shot, he looked up. The sky was filled with black pieces of something flying upward. Then shards of metal and glass, mixed with unidentifiable fragments, rained down over the highway. Flames roared from the orange truck and shot up to meet the falling rubble. Thick smoke billowed upward and ragged pieces of upholstery and matted clumps of wadding from the seat of the truck floated and danced downward.

Neal caught his breath and looked to Smeal. "Was that dynamite in the truck all the time we were in it?"

Smeal took on a look of innocence. "Maybe. This is a rough business."

Trying to get rid of the feeling that the shock wave had punched him, Freddy rubbed his chest. "Why did they blow it up?"

"Youngstown tune ups leave no lose ends," Smeal said. "One hand never knows what the other hand does. Now, there is no way to tie the orange truck to us or them."

Thinking about what Rafferty would have said, Freddy flashed Smeal a crooked smile. "Maybe Tommy finally got that job driving a dynamite truck."

"Either that," Neal said, "or they got mad cause they tried to use the metric wrench."

Shaking his head, Blondie hit low gear and sped away from the scene of the burning remains of the orange truck. On down the road, as purple smoke of the fire filled the sky behind them, Smeal opened the bag and dumped the money onto the seat between him and Neal.

" Staring at the money, Smeal spoke. "It's a battle from the cradle to the grave. In the end you lose. But this time we won."

Neal ran his hand through the money. It rustled like leaves.

The vision of the dry money that had fallen from the railroad trestle flashed in Freddy's mind. He gasped, "That's not going to blow away, is it?"

Neal turned toward Freddy and smiled. "No. It's only the sound of freedom." He quickly counted the money and looked up in amazement. "They're all big bills. There's a million and a half here."

Leaning over the seat, Freddy stared in rapt fascination at the money that would bring him and his mother a life of leisure.

Neal turned toward Freddy. "Now you'll be able to take Julie out in style."

Although he had dreamed of taking Julie out, now that he had the means to do it, his mother's words burned in his brain: "When you get around those uppity people, just remember, if you're a rotten person before you become rich, you'll still be one after you're rich."

Then it dawned on him: Before he had become rich, he was just as good as anyone in the stinking mill town. If Julie didn't care for him when he was poor, she surely wouldn't care about him now. Sure, she would go out with him now, but she would only be a parasitic girlfriend who really didn't love him. He didn't want to go with her to parties where unimportant people told one another how important they were. After what he had been through, compared to him, she was just a naïve girl, definitely unaware of the world's cruelty. She wouldn't change and he wouldn't either. Now that her social stratum was within his reach, she didn't seem important anymore. His plans to buy 1932 five-window coup hot rod and have it professionally painted a pagan gold color to impress her, vanished.

He felt free.

Neal glanced down at the money. "I thought you said the man was going to give you a million."

"He was, but we cut Greenie and his middlemen out."

To make sure he wasn't dreaming, Freddy leaned over the seat and placed his hands on the money. "Why didn't they just take the vault when we first got it?"

Smeal glanced sharply at Freddy. "Those guys work for the big man. He knew what we were up to, and he loved it."

"What do you mean he loved it?" Neal asked. "He only got part of the money."

"The big man has been in this game a long time. He knew he could sit back and wait until one of us became smart enough to bring him the real vault."

Freddy felt his voice crackle with disbelief. "You mean there is more than one?"

Smeal thoughtfully nodded. "There are fakes out there. No one has been smart enough to find the real one until now."

Neal held up a finger. "Will the big man come after the money we got?"

"Not likely. It's just like wars. People who start them never fight in them. They only collect the profits."

Freddy had never thought of wars as moneymaking schemes. It wasn't what he'd read in the history books. But now it all seemed to make sense. He looked to Smeal. "But what if he thinks the war's not over?"

"If there's another real vault, the war will start all over. But this deal's done. The big man got what he wanted, and I got my retirement money."

Freddy wondered who the big man was. He looked to Smeal. "Is the big man someone like Al Capone or John Dillinger?"

Smeal let out a giggle. "Don't believe what the ignorant public is led to believe. Capone and Dillinger were only little soldiers. The big man has always been in charge, and he always will be."

Neal reached over and waved his hand over the money. "This is a lot of money, but what about Capone's skeleton and the five hundred thousand dollars in his pocket?"

"I thought that money would be there, too." Smeal tapped the side of his head. "If you think about it, the big man in charge who arranged Dillinger's fake death owed him that money. After the public believed Dillinger was dead, Dillinger went back into the mine, took the other half of the million out of Capone's pocket, changed his name to Ralph Alsman, got married, and moved to Oregon."

Freddy shook his head with amazement. "I'll bet you'll never see that in the history books."

Smeal chuckled. "Some day, if the man in charge wants it in there, it'll be there."

Although Freddy was overjoyed with the money, he figured a million and a half was a lot for a vault only worth eight hundred forty thousand dollars. And the big man had gotten his cut, which would have been more than he paid them to get the vault. The vault had been covered with a layer of thin brass. Beneath that, a thin layer of cement concealed the gold vault, but the man on the truck had exposed a line of gold with weird symbols and said, "This is it."

Suddenly, Freddy wondered if there were another layer. He turned toward Smeal. "They gave us a lot of money when they really didn't have to." He paused. "And blowing up that orange truck seemed to be overkill. Do you think the vault has another layer of something worth more than the gold?"

As if suddenly shocked, Smeal's eyes lit up for a second, but he regained his self-control and shook his head. "If you guys are smart, you won't worry about that."

"Why not?"

"Because you'll end up something that's already been." He paused and held up a finger. "And you won't have to live a life like I had to."

As if a great weight had been lifted from his shoulders, Neal let out an easy laugh. "What if we find another vault or something worth more money?"

Smeal turned and gazed impassively at Neal. "Do whatever you want." As if he had just finished running a twenty mile marathon, he wagged his weary head. "Just don't tell me about it."

502